Praise for *Driven*

'A great read … a great plot … I couldn't put it down'
Murray Walker

'Toby Vintcent has captured the atmosphere of F1'
Max Mosley, former President of the FIA

'The real stars of Vintcent's novel are the incredible machines, the people behind them, and the steel-nerved drivers who race them. You don't have to be a racing fan to relish this exciting thriller'
Publishers Weekly, USA

'Author Toby Vintcent takes inspiration from F1's on-track action and off-track paddock politics in weaving together a page-turning conspiracy thriller. His attention to detail captures the spirit of current F1'
F1 Racing **Magazine**

'*Driven* – it howls along like Lewis Hamilton round the streets of Monaco!'
Boris Johnson

'Fiction in motor racing? I wasn't convinced … And written by Toby who? … But I gave *Driven* a try … and, you know what? – I was hooked! It's authentic, the plot's great and boy is it a page turner! The moment I finished it, I started his next one, *Crash*. A thriller series in Formula 1 is something new and very different … and it really works'
Tiff Needell, *Top Gear*, *Fifth Gear*, Racing Driver

'A fast-paced read for ~~~~ speed ~~~'emon'

Praise for *Crash*

'Reminiscent of the best Robert Ludlum-like thrillers'
The International New York Times

A Recommended Summer Holiday Read 2016
Marie Claire

'A really exciting and gripping read. I genuinely found
it hard to put down (and it's not often I say that)'
TripFiction.com

'What a fantastic book! I started reading it on the train and it was
literally unputdownable. The fact that someone like me – who
hates all cars, but particularly fast ones – can get so quickly hooked
says a lot about Toby's skill as an author. He is a consummate
professional who knows how to make a reader turn the pages
– and he has made me aware of and respectful of the human
drama in F1 … The tension leading up to the crash is superbly
managed – a master class in leaving the reader breathless'
Edward Wilson, Author: *A Very British Ending*

'Reading this book will cause you sleeplessness, irregular heartbeat
and spikes in your blood pressure. I read it just before and during
the journey to Russia for the recent Grand Prix, and while I
was out there, but the plot resonated so much that even on the
nights I told myself I really had to sleep, I could never get more
than four hours because I literally didn't want to put it down'
David Tremayne, *GrandPrix+*

'Like the sport it describes, *Crash* is fast-paced and thrilling,
deftly capturing how sport can be manipulated by politics.
Whether you're a fan of F1 or not, you'll keep reading'
Jonathan Legard, F1 TV and BBC Sports Commentator

THE RINGMASTER

About the Author

Toby Vintcent served as an officer in the British Army with the 16th/5th The Queen's Royal Lancers during the Cold War as part of NATO's Rapid Deployment Force. He then had a successful career with Merrill Lynch in the City of London. As a volunteer, he was Director of International Affairs at the British Equestrian Federation. Toby Vintcent's lifelong passion for Formula 1 resulted in his first book, *Driven* (2014), which was followed by *Crash* (2016). He lives in Oxfordshire, the heart of F1 country, with his wife and son.

THE RINGMASTER

TOBY VINTCENT

A

Arcadia Books Ltd
139 Highlever Road
London W10 6PH

www.arcadiabooks.co.uk

First published in the United Kingdom 2018
Copyright © Toby Vintcent 2018

ISBN 978-1-911350-13-2

Typeset in Garamond by MacGuru Ltd
Printed and bound by TJ International, Padstow PL28 8RW

ARCADIA BOOKS DISTRIBUTORS ARE AS FOLLOWS:

in the UK and elsewhere in Europe:
BookSource
50 Cambuslang Road
Cambuslang
Glasgow G32 8NB

in Australia/New Zealand:
NewSouth Books
University of New South Wales
Sydney NSW 2052

To the Spirit of Formula 1

About the Formula

The Formula referred to at any point in this story is a fictional composite: while it may include authentic elements used by the FIA over the years, no similarity with any given year's Formula should be looked for or expected.

Aide Memoire

Recurring People

Suleiman Al-Megrahi	Tunisian. Team boss: Calabria Formula 1 Team
Gabriel Barrus III	American. Founder and CEO: Salt Lake Media
Tex Brubaker	American. Investment banker: the London-based Klyman-Messner
Colin Chapman	British. Founder and team boss: Team Lotus Formula 1 Team
Dr Chen	Chinese. CEO: Mandarin Telecom, sponsor of the Ptarmigan Formula 1 Team
Il Commendatore	Italian. Ancient form of honorary chivalric address: Used in Formula 1 to refer reverentially to Enzo Ferrari
Enzo Ferrari	Italian. Founder: Ferrari Formula 1 team; referred to reverentially as *Il Commendatore* or the godfather of Formula 1
Yoel Kahneman	American. Advertising executive: Benson Mathias, mainly acting for tobacco companies
The Earl of Lambourn	English. Founder and team boss: Lambourn Formula 1 Team
Salvador Makarios	Greek. President: the FIA, the governing body of Formula 1
JJ McKay	Scottish. Team boss: Ptarmigan Formula 1 Team

Tahm Nazar	Indian. Team boss: Ptarmigan Formula 1 Team
Dominic Quartano	Maltese. Founder and Chairman: Quartech International, a substantial defence contractor
Arno Ravilious/ The Ringmaster	Ulsterman. Founder and CEO: Motor Racing Promotions, the Formula 1 commercial rights holder
Remy Sabatino	Maltese. F1 driver: Ptarmigan Formula 1 Team
Marquis of San Marino	Sammarinese. President: the FIA, the governing body of Formula 1
Jake Stuyvesant	American. F1 driver: Massarella Formula 1 Team and reigning IndyCar Champion
Tifosi	Italian. Collective name for Italian motor racing fans, typically aligned with the Ferrari F1 Team
Benedict Wasserman	British. Investment banker: the London-based Ziebart Blauman
Hanfried Von Wittelsbach	German. Founder and CEO: Frankfurt Capital, a German bank
Naama Zellman	American. Investment banker: the New York-based Staten Nantucket

Acronymed Bodies and Other Organizations

ACEA	Association des Constructeurs Européens d'Automobile, a trade body of motor manufacturers
BRDC	British Racing Drivers' Club: owner of the Silverstone circuit

Calabria Hotels	Italian firm: owner of a Formula 1 team
FIA	Fédération Internationale de l'Automobile, the governing body of Formula 1
F1CA	Formula 1 Constructors' Association, forerunner of FOCA
FISA	Fédération Internationale du Sport Automobile, the former governing body of Formula 1; a division of the FIA
FOCA	Formula 1 Constructors' Association, a group of England-based Formula 1 teams
FOTA	Formula 1 Teams' Association, a consortium established to break away from Formula 1
Frankfurt Capital	A German bank
GPMA	Grand Prix Manufacturers' Association, a consortium established to break away from Formula 1
GPWC	Grand Prix World Championship, a consortium established to break away from Formula 1
Klyman-Messner	British investment bank, based in Canary Wharf, London
MRP/Motor Racing Promotions	The commercial rights holder – the business arm – of Formula 1
The Whittlebury Group	A consortium of teams and historic circuits, established to break away from Formula 1
WCR	World Championship Racing, a consortium established to break away from Formula 1
Ziebart Blauman (Ziebarts)	British investment bank, based in the City of London

BOOK ONE

CONTROL

ONE

Silverstone was buzzing. Several days before the British Grand Prix, and the transformation from bleak Northamptonshire wartime aerodrome to small city was almost complete. Flags, glass-sided double-decker tents, vast motor homes, expanses of temporary grandstands and an abundance of noise – all signalled the might of the invasion. Something strange, though, was going on.

With no warning, thousands of cars and caravans were queuing up outside Silverstone Woodlands, the circuit's official fifty-acre campsite. In a matter of hours it was full; by mid-morning on Thursday it had to be closed to new arrivals. Those turned away were lured to unofficial campsites popping up nearby: local farmers hurrying to cash in on this unexpected influx, offering little more than hastily topped fields, with nothing in the way of amenities.

Anticipation was amped up two days later, as Qualifying loomed. From early Saturday morning, people streamed out of the campsites into the circuit. The A43 approaches to Silverstone from both north and south were nose to tail. Day visitors drew up in their droves. Queues formed at every gate. No one wanted to miss a moment of this year's British Grand Prix. It seemed that one colour, turquoise, was everywhere – as was one name: Remy Sabatino.

Within the circuit complex, an elderly figure jogged down the steps from one of the biggest motor homes and into the early morning sun. His bearing was taut, some might have said athletic – his presence eye-catching, a result of being tall, slim and bald. As ever, he wore a Jermyn Street navy blue silk shirt, white chinos and, handmade by Ducker & Son, his signature two-tone Oxford brogues. Striding out, Arno Ravilious pulled the wraparound shades, perched on the top of his head, down over his eyes – as if lowering a visor. He was self-contained, remote, his demeanour and body language projecting detatchment. Ravilious's focus, anyway, was on the screen of his phone as he thumbed out a reply to an email:

'*Sir TJ: The Yacht Club's application is most welcome,*' he typed. '*You have met MRP's criteria. A Hong Kong Grand Prix could be added to the calendar in two years' time for the stated fee of $50 million (US) per race: I'll look forward to hearing your decision.*'

As Ravilious pressed Send his phone beeped with an SMS:

'*Boeing yet to fix Papa Delta's flight deck. Latest assessment: little chance before Singapore.*'

He tapped Reply: '*And finding a replacement?*'

By return, came: '*They've said: no chance – this deep into the holidays.*'

'*Okay, Jim – I've got this*' and he hit an icon on his phone.

Ravilious was approaching the strictest cordon at any grand prix circuit: the entrance to the pit lane. Those already queuing started to move out of the way as he strode through the checkpoint without stopping, without being asked for any accreditation – or being challenged. Without even breaking his stride.

Ravilious could soon hear the drawling ringtone for the United States. He didn't care what time of day it was over there, or even that it was the weekend; Seattle happened to be in the graveyard hours of the morning.

'Arno?' breathed the just-awoken CEO.

'Jumbo Four *still* grounded,' he stated, his voice sounding edgy, sharpened by the softness of his Ulster patois. 'I'm now told yous can't find us a replacement. I've to get three teams to Singapore by Tuesday.'

'Arno…' he breathed, '… it's two … *a.m.*'

Ravilious paused.

The aircraft boss, though, volunteered nothing more.

'How about I put the teams sponsored by airlines on that plane's manifest?'

The American suddenly sounded a lot less groggy; inhaling audibly, he asked for a couple of hours' grace and signed off.

Arno Ravilious emerged into the pit lane.

Silverstone's progress seemed to parallel this man's time in Formula 1. Here was a circuit that had metamorphosed from little more than the perimeter road of a disused wartime airfield – with prefab concrete huts and its track edged by oil drums and straw bales – to today's state-of-the-art grand prix complex. Silverstone now boasted extensive grandstands, an iconic Wing hospitality centre, a permanent motorsport business hub and an economic impact of at least three-quarters of a billion pounds a year. And yet this was just one circuit in one country touched by the transformation of Formula 1.

Ravilious's phone wasn't quiet for long. The next caller's ID caused him to collect himself: the issue in question was giving him the most aggravation from the teams.

'Dr Hamasaki,' Ravilious said firmly, 'three sets of your tyres delaminated in Austin – at high speed. I want a guarantee and technical recommendations, on PSI and compound, before first free practice in Singapore. Any further failure and you'll leave me no choice but to bring Pirelli back in.'

Sounding agitated, the Japanese CEO pledged his immediate attention.

Ravilious wasn't convinced. He fired off a one-line email to Gerald Taylor, asking the motorsport director of Pirelli to call him, just in case.

He was back on the move.

Numerous myths had built up around the 'Ringmaster'. The one most often referred to by commentators, pundits and journalists was the 'Ravilious Effect'. No one could explain it fully. Something happened whenever he appeared. People could sense his approach; could sense a presence. Hundreds of people were in the pit lane that morning – team mechanics, marshals, officials, media teams, camera crews, VIPS, celebrities and guests – and now, suddenly, all of them seemed to be behaving slightly differently. Conversations sounded a little quieter, everyone appearing a little self-conscious.

Ravilious remained disinterested in his surroundings. He walked on and straight into another call, this one from Gianni Medici.

The president of the *Commissione Sportiva Automobilistica Italiana* sounded agitated: 'How can-a you even *think* of increasing Monza's fee to 15 million dollars?' he all but bellowed. 'This is the *Italian* Grand Prix for heaven's a-sake.'

'Which is why your fee's only 15 million dollars, Gianni.'

'We *can't* afford-a that.'

'No one's forcing you to host a race.'

'How can you *not-a* have the Italian Grand Prix?' blasted Medici, before the race promoter launched into a machine-gun tirade.

Thirty seconds went by.

'Gianni ... *Gianni* ... You've had my offer,' sighed Ravilious. 'It is, of course, entirely up to you. I'll look forward to hearing your decision,' and ended the call – before Medici could start up again.

Ravilious had no respite.

Within seconds, George Kovacs was on the line – from ATVN, the American TV Network in New York:

'Hey, Arno – just got your message. I think you mentioned something about the upcoming review.' Then, with an old-pal chuckle, he said: 'I take it you want to stiff us with your previous escalator?'

Still on the move, Ravilious extracted a notebook from his back pocket and flicked it open. As he thumbed over the pages, he said: 'Remind me, George, what your audience was for the Brazilian Grand Prix ... the season before last.'

'Sorry, man – wouldn't have those figures to hand—'

'Twenty-five million.'

'I'd have to check that.'

'And your number after Sabatino's showdown for the title in Brazil at the end of *last* year?'

'Again, I'd have—'

'*Eighty*-five million, George ... F1 gave you a threefold bump in audience, 10 million bigger than you got for the Indy 500, and yet you've just paid the Brickyard 200 million for the remaining two years of your contract with them...'

Kovacs seemed to pause for a moment. 'How the hell do you know *that*?'

Ignoring the reaction, Ravilious said: 'You can have a continuation on the remaining three years with us, George, for 500 million.'

'Come off it, Arno ... an *extra* 250 million dollars ... you're kidding me.'

'I never kid about value.'

'A quarter of a billion dollars ... for, what? ... the *Sabatino* effect?'

'The audience is what it is. I'm giving ATVN a hefty increase in numbers for no extra effort on your part – on the back of which, according to Nielsen, your ad rates are soaring. You're doing pretty well out of us, George.'

'But an *extra* 250 million dollars!'

'Of course it's entirely up to you. I'll look forward to hearing your decision.'

TWO

Qualifying could hardly have produced a tighter outcome. In the last moments of the top-ten shootout, the three drivers at the top of the rankings for the Championship were out on track, even crossing the line in sight of each other and the chequered flag: all clocking lap times within two-tenths of a second. Lambourn's Muammar Al Baradei, Formula 1's first driver from the Kingdom of Saudi Arabia, had made it onto the front row in P2. Jake Stuyvesant – the American driver, also the reigning IndyCar Champion – in the Massarella was a whisker behind in P3. While the crowd's favourite had prevailed:

Remy Sabatino in the Ptarmigan *had* clinched pole – by a thrilling three-one-thousandths of a second.

The build-up to this weekend had seen extraordinary anticipation, and Qualifying had not let the fans down: they had just experienced a spectacular overture to the British Grand Prix. They were about, though, to be taken completely by surprise – beginning with the soundscape.

Noise from the race cars' 750 horsepower engines began to fall silent.

Urban legend had it the skies over Silverstone, during the grand prix weekend, made for the busiest airspace in the world. True or not, a never-ending stream of helicopters had been flying the corporate big shots and super wealthy into the circuit, not just from London and the major airports but also from some of the most luxurious accommodation nearby. The background noise of helicopter traffic started to recede.

When it ceased altogether, the stands around the circuit, also, began to fall silent.

Then – over the quietness – a single engine could be heard…

…some distance away.

Getting louder.

An aircraft was closing in.

Before long, a sleek shape loomed into the centre of the cloudless sky. A maroon Sikorsky S-76C++. It stood out against the expanse of unbroken blue. The helicopter was soon hovering above the middle of the circuit; then, lowering its undercarriage, it started to descend.

People became aware of its distinctive markings, its registration – G-XXEB – and the emblazoned symbol on the gleaming fuselage. A logo of sorts, but not a corporate one.

It looked pretty grand.

Some started to recognize it…

A murmur rippled through the crowds.

As the helicopter touched down, a well-known television voice came up on the circuit's public address system:

'Ladies and gentlemen, we have for you now an unannounced – and very special – event. In the history of Formula 1, there have only ever been a few chances for non-F1 drivers to experience what it's like to be in a F1 car. The McLaren team built a two-seater in the 1990s, and gave a very select few that chance. They included the inspirational leader of the FIA during F1's safety overhaul, Max Mosley, and, famously, motor racing legend Murray Walker. Formula 1 has not had a two-seater for over a decade … Until now!

'This year Ptarmigan have revived the tradition.

'We are delighted to offer you, ladies and gentlemen, a double treat. Drivers' Championship leader and pole sitter for tomorrow's grand prix, Remy Sabatino, is about to drive a very special guest around our circuit. The BRDC is honoured to welcome His Royal Highness Prince William, the Duke of Cambridge.'

Applause erupted around the circuit. No one's politics were going to get in the way of this moment. What mattered was that two of the most famous people on the planet were about to appear on the track, right in front of them.

A live TV image flashed up on the large electronic screens around the circuit. It showed a close-up of the helicopter on the helipad, except it didn't show BRDC officials waiting to receive the royal guest; filling the shot was the unmistakable bald head and slim figure of Arno Ravilious.

The Prince, wearing his khaki flying suit, walked from under the slowing rotors. Ravilious smiled and shook hands. His body language was polite, but there was no neck bow – no signal of ingratiation or deference.

The image on the screens cut away from the helicopter to show the Ptarmigan team boss, Tahm Nazar. The distinguished-looking Indian was standing in front of the team's garage in the pit lane, next to the two-seater. Behind him was a semi-circle of Ptarmigan mechanics, all wearing the distinctive qing livery – the turquoise – of Mandarin Telecom.

Unexpectedly, this Mandarin sponsorship had been one of the stimuli to Formula 1's current surge in popularity: through their tie-up with the Chinese telecom giant, Ptarmigan had landed the largest sponsorship deal in F1 history – $750 million over three years. Such a statement of belief in Formula 1 had even crossed over, prompting mainstream interest in the sport.

On the other side of the two-seater, within a corral of aluminium barriers, was a mass of cameras and TV presenters, manned by a platoon's worth of orange boiler-suited marshals.

The jumbo screens switched images. Ravilious could be seen leading the royal party through the back of the Ptarmigan garage. Team mechanics, standing against the walls to either side, broke into applause. The royal visitor, followed by his entourage – which included his armed SO14 close protection officer – smiled broadly and raised a hand in reply.

Prince William was soon in the pit lane. Ravilious led His Royal Highness across to Tahm Nazar and, standing next to him, Remy Sabatino's race engineer, Andy Backhouse. Introductions were made.

The driver was in the car, ready to go.

The Prince looked relaxed as he pulled on his helmet. From behind the barriers, hundreds of camera shutters went off as the press determined to capture every second of this scene.

The royal visitor climbed into the Ptarmigan. He was strapped firmly in the rear seat and connected to the car's intercom and radio.

Through his helmet he could hear Sabatino's dismembered voice: 'Hope we're getting you comfortable, sir?'

Confirmation came back that he was.

Seconds later – from behind him – came an explosion of sound. The two-seater F1 car's 2.0 litre V8 was fired into life.

The press pack jostled again as they tried to capture the moment of the car moving off.

'Right, sir, here we go.'

Sabatino dropped the clutch and pulled away.

All eyes were on the turquoise Formula 1 car as it ran down the pit lane. Here was the world championship-leading driver taking the future king of England out onto the hallowed track of Silverstone.

Sabatino started powering up the car.

To prevent unwanted listening in, all radio communication – between the car and the pit lane – was to be encrypted. Such 'exclusion' infuriated the media. As a result, not all their interest was trained on the car: a large number of cameras were also pointed at Andy Backhouse, Sabatino's race engineer, now manning the team's command centre on the pit wall. Being in radio contact with the two-seater, the media were focusing on him, hoping to infer from his expression what might be going on around the track.

Steadily, the two-seater F1 car rounded Village – and then the Loop. Along the Wellington Straight, Sabatino opened up a little, to reach fifth gear. Spectators were glued to the large screens as they followed the Prince's progress round Luffield and through Woodcote.

A heliborne camera provided an overhead shot of the car's progress, the same image being shared with the 24-hour television news networks, most of which were broadcasting this live. The sight of the turquoise car, seen from directly above, streaking through the left-right-left-right of Maggots through Becketts to Chapel made for a stunning spectacle, all the more so knowing that two of the most iconic individuals on earth were riding on board.

Midway round the second lap the car started to slow.

As the car exited into the Hangar Straight, it came to a standstill … right in the middle of the track.

A buzz went around the crowds.

Commentators on the media channels almost started hyperventilating.

Everyone was wondering: What had happened?

Had something gone wrong?

The car stayed immobile – for nearly a minute.

Then everyone saw the two-seater Formula 1 suddenly launch forward – accelerating down the centreline of the track – throttling hard – straight up the gearbox. After a few seconds – the moment the Ptarmigan seemed to hit top speed – it threw off two plumes of blue smoke from the front tyres – and began dramatically decelerating.

Sabatino brought the car to a stop.

What was going on?

Wasn't this just Sabatino demonstrating the car's capability … its acceleration and stopping power? But who had initiated this? Was it the Prince asking to see what the car could do? No one was ever going to know the answers. Everyone's attention was about to be diverted.

The Ptarmigan two-seater started pulling slowly forwards, little more than trundling down the middle of the Hangar Straight.

Andy Backhouse, on the pit wall, was then seen talking animatedly over the radio. He leant sideways, lifting the right headphone and speaking directly into the ear of Tahm Nazar, the team principal.

The race engineer looked up at the command centre screens above him; he seemed to be studying a number of data points.

What was going on?

THREE

The turquoise Formula 1 car was little more than rolling down the remainder of the Hangar Straight.

Andy Backhouse reached for a button on the pit wall console and spoke into the radio, but only for a moment.

All of a sudden, the car started speeding up.

Heading down towards Stowe, the Ptarmigan continued to accelerate. As it did so, Sabatino began weaving aggressively – throwing a pronounced series of zigzags. The driver was now using more of the circuit, clipping the red-and-white kerbstones on the left of the track as the car was set up to turn into the right-hander.

The well-known TV voice was back on the loudspeaker:

'*Ladies and gentlemen, I may be jumping the gun here – but Remy Sabatino is very clearly warming up the tyres, building up the pace. Might we be in for a treat? Could this be the Ptarmigan two-seater about to put in a … hot lap? Could His Royal Highness be about to experience for himself exactly what it's like to travel at the full speed of a modern Formula 1 car?*'

'*In any event,*' the commentator went on, '*Remy Sabatino – Ptarmigan – could surely not commit to a hot lap without the Prince's consent. In which case, all credit to His Royal Highness for such a show of spirit.*'

Sabatino was still building up the pace: as the two-seater entered the International Pits Straight, the Ptarmigan hit top speed.

'*There they go – that's them crossing the start/finish line.*'

Even with the extra weight of a passenger, and the difference in height of its centre of gravity, the handling of the two-seater was not that different from Sabatino's grand prix car – capable of performing to within a second or two of this season's race pace.

Moving over to the left, to open up the corner into Abbey, the driver – with no lift or touch of the brakes – turned in hard, committing fully to the entry. At such speed, those on board were feeling the full effects of pulling 4.6 G through the turn.

Exiting Turn 1 – still at full commitment – Sabatino drifted the car towards the track limit to the left, staying on that side of the circuit. Village, the right-hand, hairpin-like turn, was coming up. Sabatino braked hard, and, flicking the left paddle behind the steering wheel five times, changed down to second, the engine management system pulsing the revs on each downshift.

Having turned into the right-hand corner, Sabatino was soon throttling hard, accelerating through the apex and the exit, already pulling across to the right – setting up for the upcoming Loop, the left-hander.

At the end of the Wellington Straight, the Ptarmigan pulled 4 G around Brooklands.

Through their helmets and over the scream of the engine, Sabatino and the Prince could hear the noise from the crowds. The packed stands were roaring – cheering the turquoise car on as it swept through the high-speed corners in front of them.

The Ptarmigan gave everything asked of it as Sabatino set it up for the National pit straight. To the spectators along there, the car loomed into view only to disappear a matter of moments later, heading away towards Copse.

On they ran.

Round the top of the circuit – through Maggots, Becketts and Chapel – the two-seater looked like it was running on rails: the driver showing total confidence in the balance, downforce and grip of the car, as they ran at full pelt through this unique succession of meandering turns.

They were back in the Hangar Straight.

The two people on board felt the acceleration as the car went up through the gears to 7th, the Ptarmigan running utterly true.

Sabatino could see the next turn, Stowe, in the distance at the bottom of the gentle slope. As the Ptarmigan shot the footbridge, a quick flick of the eyes down at data crammed into the display on the steering wheel confirmed everything was optimal.

'We're doing just over 210 miles an hour, sir,' Sabatino declared over the intercom, 'not much slower than I'd be doing in my race car.'

An enthusiastic acknowledgement came from the rear seat.

Turning in hard, the car clipped the right-hand apex of Stowe, the car's right-hand wheels riding up and over the red-and-white kerbstones. Despite banging the suspension – uncomfortable for the driver and passenger – Sabatino feathered the power and kept pushing.

The Ptarmigan was running down towards Vale.

One more corner complex to go.

A few moments later the Ptarmigan was slicing through Club, accelerating hard – and about to cross the line.

The crowd erupted all over again.

'Ladies and gentlemen, I can tell you … our temporary Royal Formula 1 car has been fast. Impressively fast. Remy Sabatino has just taken His Royal Highness round in a lap time of one minute thirty-one point two – would you believe it, barely two seconds off the time Remy achieved to secure pole less than an hour ago in Qualifying.'

The Ptarmigan started winding down on its in-lap.

Heading back down the pit lane, it pulled up in front of the Ptarmigan garage. Sabatino brought the two-seater to a stop and killed the engine.

The mood in the stands, among the commentators, media and among the TV audience at home was euphoric. All were glued to their screens to see how the second-in-line to the throne was going to look as he emerged from the car.

Arno Ravilious stood to one side, taking in the scene. He suddenly started striding towards the press and media enclosure. Holding up a hand to one of the marshals as if to say 'It's okay', he grabbed an aluminium barrier and hinged it outwards, breaching the corral. Seconds later, members of the press poured through the gap and were rushing towards the car.

Thousands more pictures were taken, untypically close to royalty, as the driver and the Prince emerged from the cockpit. Ravilious had no doubt this scene would dominate the next news cycle and be splashed across the front pages of the world's newspapers the next day.

Remy Sabatino pulled off her helmet and fire-retardant balaclava and rubbed her fingers through her short dark hair several times. She turned towards her passenger and smiled. The Prince had removed his helmet. He, too, was beaming as he leant forwards and shook Remy Sabatino's hand.

No one could fail to be enthralled by the moment.

If Formula 1 hadn't already drawn attention to itself ahead of the race on Sunday, it was certainly going to do so now.

That year's British Grand Prix attracted the largest crowd ever to watch a race in the United Kingdom – as well as the largest proportion of the TV audience since James Hunt's world title win in 1976.

The race had everything: Remy Sabatino as the first competitive female Formula 1 driver; the thrilling fight for the leadership of the Drivers' Championship – a three-way contest between the first woman, the first Arab and a reigning American IndyCar Champion; as well as the scale of the sponsorship that Formula 1 was now attracting.

Capping it all was the excitement sparked by Prince William's lap around the Silverstone grand prix track, its coverage by the media removing any possibility that the public at large could be unaware of this year's Formula 1 season.

There was an extraordinary buzz around the sport.

F1 seemed to be all-pervading that summer ... becoming an integral part of the cultural landscape ... a talking point, even a regular topic of current affairs.

Formula 1 had never ridden higher.

TWO YEARS LATER

FOUR

There would have been few situations in which Dominic Quartano might have felt apprehensive. Little fazed him at this stage in his career, being the CEO, chairman and founder – forty years before – of Quartech International, the now $50 billion defence contractor that partly incorporated his name. Ahead of this meeting, though, he was decidedly uncomfortable.

Just over three years earlier, Mandarin Telecom had become the largest sponsor – commercial partner – Formula 1 had ever seen. Handling the negotiations personally, Quartano had persuaded the Chinese telecom giant to sponsor the Ptarmigan F1 Team. Which had been no mean feat. At the time, he had been pitching little more than an act of faith. He had only just bought the marque from the receiver, its previous management forced into bankruptcy by the team's creditors three months before. All Quartano could offer was a promise that, with his firm's backing – its financial support, people, technological support and understanding of marketing – Ptarmigan would re-emerge as a competitive force on the track and provide a promotional platform from which Mandarin Telecom could introduce itself to the world.

Dr Chen and his directors had been sold on the proposal, committing to an unprecedented deal worth $750 million. Despite the risk and cost to Mandarin Telecom, it proved exceptional value: in their first year together Ptarmigan won the Constructors' Championship and their Quartano-appointed driver, Remy Sabatino, came within one point of winning the Drivers' title. Attention on the team was near universal – Sabatino, being the first properly competitive woman in F1, had fast become a media obsession. And by association, Mandarin Telecom had been able to reach a worldwide audience, establishing itself well enough to take on its market-leading competitors in all key territories.

As gratifying as that sponsorship arrangement had been within F1, its cash value to Dominic Quartano was of lesser importance. Western companies had always struggled to gain access to Chinese markets. As far as China's defence and armaments sector went, they had been completely barred. Through Formula 1 and Ptarmigan's new sponsors, Quartano had found himself a priceless key. Mandarin Telecom was a near-monopolistic supplier of telephony services to China's military-industrial complex, and Mandarin's directors were fanatical in using the cachet of hospitality at grands prix to entertain those clients. Via this sponsorship, Dominic Quartano had been able to strike up his own personal relationships with most of the significant figures in the Chinese defence sector and government. Within a year of the tie-up with Mandarin Telecom, Quartech was doing business on an ever-widening range of its products and know-how, generating millions of dollars' worth of revenue. Quartano was convinced he had barely begun to mine this seam. To keep that seam available to him, though, he needed – at all costs – Ptarmigan's relationship with Mandarin Telecom to continue.

The Mediterranean was calm. *The Melita*, at anchor offshore from Valencia harbour, had been lying there throughout the weekend for the reinstated European Grand Prix. Onshore, most of the Formula 1 circus was in the process of pulling out, heading to Silverstone for the next weekend's race.

In the dying light of the evening, a Riva Aquarama motor launch – the varnished mahogany glinting in the orange sunlight – headed away from the marina and closed in on the 1930s superyacht.

Dominic Quartano was informed of the approach. From the saloon, he and Tahm Nazar emerged onto the quarterdeck, ready to greet their guests.

The helm of the Riva deftly brought the launch in alongside, allowing his passengers to come aboard.

'Dr Chen,' said Quartano with a smile, 'you and your directors are most welcome.'

The middle-aged Chinese businessman bowed gracefully as he shook hands and reintroduced his colleagues.

A tray of drinks appeared, presented by a white-tunicked steward, as Quartano led his visitors into the yacht's stateroom.

Places were taken, with the tycoon sitting at the head of the table. Dominic Quartano's air of welcome should have put his guests at their ease. Energy, more like that of a teenager's than a septuagenarian's, radiated from his piercing blue eyes; the thick mane of gun-metal grey hair intimated further youthfulness. Only the lines etched in his Mediterranean face betrayed his 70 years, the weather-worn look adding significantly to his presence. Yet, for all Quartano's charisma, it was not going to carry this meeting. He sensed, all too soon, what he had feared.

There was a tone of reservation among the visitors.

Pre-empting immediately, Quartano broke with Chinese protocol and cut straight to the topic in hand, saying: 'I think it is fair to state, Dr Chen – gentlemen – that our relationship has exceeded both our expectations, but we are all aware that, as of today, Formula 1 is in some trouble.'

The Chinese looked relieved to hear Quartano's unprompted admission.

Dr Chen responded: 'We are sad as much as concerned. We do not know how, in such a short time, an organization could go from such self-confidence to where it is now.'

Quartano's expression was already reflecting his agreement and concern.

'Its high point,' added Dr Chen, 'was two years ago, at British Grand Prix – when the future king of England was driven round Silverstone. It is confusing to us how the number of spectators have decreased so quickly since then.'

Quartano nodded, there being no advantage in denying what was unarguably true.

'We have our own opinions,' continued Dr Chen, 'but would like to hear your understanding.'

Quartano, turning to Tahm Nazar, invited the Ptarmigan boss to reply.

The professorial-looking Indian smiled sympathetically – apologetically – as a beam of low sun washed through the stateroom, highlighting his white hair, white moustache and the deep mahogany tone of his skin. 'There seems to have been a conspiracy of small reasons,' he said. 'An obvious one must be Formula 1's concerted push away from free-to-air television coverage to pay-per-view and subscription TV.'

Dr Chen showed no disagreement but hardly looked sated.

Reading the man's expression for himself, Nazar went on: 'That's only a factor of the medium, though, and not the message. The drop-off in audience is more to do with the *content* of the broadcasts. Grands prix have lost their excitement. They've become far too predictable ... virtually processional.'

At this admission, the Chinese directors offered a bigger set of nods.

'Predictability of races,' Nazar went on, 'stems from a move made by the governing body some time ago, prompted by the financial crisis. The FIA was desperate to limit the costs of competing in F1. They hoped that by capping team spending, specifically banning the teams from the almost unlimited costs of testing between races, they could avoid losing the Formula 1 teams owned by mass car makers in the recession that everyone feared. Unfortunately, though, this policy decision had other consequences.

'Before the ban on testing, a team result in Melbourne – right at the beginning of the season – might have been team A, then B, then C. But three races later, because of innovation and testing, the team order might then have been B, C, A; three more after that and it might even have been D, F, A.

'But, now – with the ban on testing – the A, B, C in Melbourne has every chance of being A, B, C in Abu Dhabi, right at the end of the season. After any major rule change, the teams that don't get the new technology right for the first race never have the opportunity to catch up – because they are denied the subsequent opportunity to test and revise their set-up. The result is that the drama … the spectacle … the excitement … has gone.'

Quartano was pleased to see that Dr Chen was not resisting Nazar's analysis; in fact far from it. 'One needs to remember,' interjected Quartano, with the first hint of a counter view, 'that whatever the issues arising from such restrictions – on testing, et cetera – they are all man-made; they are nothing to do with the natural physics of the cars. What I mean to say is that these rules can be quickly reversed.'

'Indeed,' said Dr Chen, 'there have been many such opportunities to do that, except the governing body has always seemed to go the wrong way. Refuelling the cars, mid-race, was no longer allowed. All cars carrying a full fuel load, right from the start, seems to make it harder to overtake. Before, cars were able to run at different weights – to give themselves a short-term advantage.'

'Indeed they could,' replied Nazar, 'and the advantage of that rule was that, over the course of a race, it was a level playing field: equal for all competitors. We would pay a price for any such short-term advantage – the lighter cars having to make more pit stops, costing us more time. But at least the trade-off was the teams' decision.'

'Except, Mr Nazar, that our concern goes deeper than refuelling. When the sport withdrew variable fuel loads, and reduced the scope for overtaking, it made questionable rule changes to try and rectify. It brought in tyres *designed to deteriorate*. We don't understand the governing body on this. What elite brand has ever purposely intro-duced obsolescence into its product?'

All Quartano could do was nod passively.

Dr Chen added: 'Now, sirs, we are not experts,' he said, without self-deprecation, 'but to us the sport is giving with one hand and taking with the other. Degrading tyres also puts debris on the surface of track…'

'…marbles…'

'…thank you, yes … marbles … which cover nearly all of track except for the fastest path?'

'The racing line,' agreed Nazar.

'Thank you, yes. So,' continued Dr Chen, 'as we understand it, a driver going off the … racing line … close to a corner is risky? The driver can lose control on all that debris – and so affect, badly, braking and turning?'

There were nods from the Ptarmigan side of the table.

'We do not see how a driver *can* attempt overtake into corner, if he's scared to leave the racing line? In addition, it would seem the cars have become too reliant on aerodynamics. We do understand that they make the cars more stable, but not when they are behind another car; then, the 'dirty air' – is it? – hurts the aerodynamics. Chasing cars cannot get up close behind, for fear of losing stability … losing grip. We have heard commentators say that cars cannot get within one-and-a-half seconds of a car in front? How can a chasing car overtake from that far back? Formula 1's aerodynamics seem to have been badly thought out.'

Quartano was nodding once again. 'And that's before we get on to the idiotic Drag Reduction System, a half-baked attempt to enhance overtaking, although that does only apply on the straights.'

Dr Chen nodded something of a concession. 'DRS does seem to allow the car behind to take over, but again, we don't see logic. When Drag Reduction System is working, the cars are no longer same. The physics of each car becomes different. To us, it is like a high-speed walking race at Olympics, where athletes must keep one foot on ground at all times…'

'…but then allowing the man behind to break into a run to help him get past,' finished Quartano. 'We *do* understand, Dr Chen … truly … but again I feel it is worth pointing out that all these matters *are* reversible decisions.'

'They may be, Mr Quartano, yes, sir. But our concern then relates to the effectiveness of such decision-making. We are troubled by the introduction of the Strategy Group. This body, as we understand it, was agreement between Mr Arno Ravilious, Jehangir Banyan – the President of the FIA – and six of the teams to try and improve decisions.'

Nazar's face looked like it was already making Dr Chen's point for him: 'The Strategy Group has produced almost the opposite effect.'

'Indeed it has,' said Dr Chen. 'Why would a team – succeeding in Championship – ever vote to change a rule that could take away its advantage? People might not have liked intensity of the Ravilious dictatorship, but everyone did know who was in charge. The moment something did not work, he made sure the governing body put it right. Because the Strategy Group has so obviously failed, decision-making in the sport has all but collapsed. So I disagree, sir … we have no expectation that any of these disastrous policies are to be reversed soon.'

To the frustration of the Ptarmigan officials, neither felt they could take against this analysis.

'And the sport has political corrosiveness,' Dr Chen added. 'It has got worse since bribery scandal with European Union.'

A hint of exasperation showed in Quartano's voice: 'That was, indeed, an unedifying episode.'

'And what about this man Al-Megrahi?' added Dr Chen. 'What on earth is *he* doing? The damage he does to Formula 1 is most unwelcome. He is always undermining the sport, its leaders … so critical. These "politics",' continued Dr Chen, 'suggest that Formula 1 can no longer be controlled…'

'And yet, despite all this,' said Quartano, with a suggestion of disbelief, 'the television audience remains enormous, far bigger than it was when we started out together. It still represents an unparalleled marketing opportunity for sponsors.'

For the first time Dr Chen seemed to show an air of resignation. 'For how much longer? What about latest attack – by Grand Prix Drivers' Association? These GPDA people are threatening to undermine public support. Their public letter, also criticizing F1 and its leadership, was insolent. Too much. When champagne-spraying millionaires start complaining, we fear the ordinary spectator loses sympathy and interest.'

Nazar's nod of confirmation carried a hint of disapproval and regret.

'So, to us, Mr Quartano, sir,' said Dr Chen, turning to tacitly consult his colleagues for the first time, 'we are troubled. We are being asked to pay a lot of sponsorship money for what is there *now*. Formula 1 is not what it was – when we started sponsoring Ptarmigan three years ago. It is not as reliable – not as valuable.'

Quartano sighed inwardly, acknowledging that this was why he had felt so uneasy ahead of this meeting.

'Mr Quartano,' Dr Chen said, adopting the tone of a summation, 'we have benefited, truly, from our relationship with the Ptarmigan F1 team – and with you, sir. We have nothing but pride in our involvement with Quartech International. But ... we feel Formula 1, as a marketing vehicle, has become tarnished. We could still reach large numbers of consumers, even with the drop in TV audience and spectators. But, sir, I am no apologist for Mandarin Telecom; we *are* old-fashioned: we set great store by face. We feel there is a risk to Mandarin Telecom – of loss of face – if we partner with a sport now so chaotic and occupied by in-fighting. Formula 1 has lost all sense of direction ... seems bedevilled, is that right word, by its key elements – who keep on criticizing its leaders and management.

'As a result, Mr Quartano, I'm afraid we are unable to see the renewal of our sponsorship, sir, in the same way we saw your proposition three years ago.'

FIVE

After Valencia, the next race in the Formula 1 calendar was to be seven days later, at Silverstone – for the 73rd running of the British Grand Prix.

This year, though, the atmosphere was completely different.

Silverstone Woodlands, the circuit's official campsite, was less than half full. There were no other campsites near the circuit, as demand didn't warrant them. Advance tickets for the weekend had sold barely a third of the number of two years before.

After the Italian Grand Prix, the British GP was the second oldest continuous fixture in Formula 1 history. The British may not have had such an exotic word as the Italians had for their motor racing fans, the fabled *Tifosi*, but the Brits were every bit their match in passion and commitment. Silverstone's numbers may have been down, but the atmosphere was not. Hardcore followers were just as ready to worship at the altar of their sport's cathedral. For the devout, being at Silverstone for the Thursday evening – the start of the British Grand Prix weekend – still held all its magic.

At eight o'clock that same Thursday evening, having left the Silverstone paddock forty minutes before, the car carrying Arno Ravilious reached Woodstock in Oxfordshire. As it reached the village, it turned off the Oxford Road to pass through the magnificent gates of Blenheim Palace. A moment or two later it emerged from under the trees to be hit by a blaze of summer evening sun. The full majesty of the landscaped gardens opened out. None of these surroundings were of interest to Ravilious; he was on his phone, looking down, drafting an email to one of the Formula 1 team bosses:

I need you to reconsider Musa bin Osman before rehiring Paddy Aston. Aramco say Osman would be significant for audience and

*sponsorship in Malaysia. Of course it's your choice … I'll look forward
to hearing your decision.'*

Ravilious's car swept round in front of the Vanbrugh façade and
into the Great Court. The lowering sun bathed the palace in a honey-
tinted light, almost matching the colour of the stone. The car pulled
up at the foot of the North Steps.

A patrician-looking man in a handmade dinner jacket appeared
through the huge doors of the building. The 7th Marquis of San
Marino walked down the wide flight to the edge of the gravel. Reaching out as the car drew to a halt, he opened the rear door.

Ravilious climbed out to be greeted by the former President of the
International Automobile Federation, the FIA. Despite the lateness
of Ravilious's arrival, San Marino showed no discontent, welcoming
his guest and engaging him in conversation as he escorted him up
the steps towards the main entrance. Ravilious was about to switch
his phone to Vibrate when it started to ring. Looking down, he saw
who was calling. Using only his eyes, Ravilious indicated that he
needed to take this call.

The former FIA president did not show his displeasure.

Talking into the phone, Ravilious said: 'Your Royal Highness…'
and then fell silent. He listened to the caller on the other end for
nearly a minute before saying: 'Of course I recognize 110 million
dollars per grand prix – for ten years – as a substantial offer, sir.'

Then, sounding like he was interrupting, Ravilious said: 'Your
Royal Highness, sir … *sir* … All you've done is raise the price. You've
not withdrawn your conditions. It is admirable that Saudi Arabia is
trying to reform, and Formula 1 would be delighted to contribute to
that process – but, with the conditions you've set, sir, I cannot help
you.'

San Marino's expression showed disappointment, but not with
Ravilious – more with himself for failing to heed the lesson he had
taught himself long ago: of never letting himself be surprised by
anything Arno Ravilious said or did.

Once the phone call came to an end, the only apology the former president received was a curt nod of the head and a show that Ravilious was silencing his phone.

San Marino was finally able to walk his guest in through the main doors of the palace.

The Great Hall was quite a sight. Two lines of tables ran away from them down either side of the room. A top table was set laterally between them at the far end. With a near fifty-minute delay in Ravilious's arrival, the gala's other guests were already seated, chatting, and well into their second or third drink. There was quite a hubbub, the noise bouncing off the columns and baroque flourishes, filling the room, right up to the ornate ceiling several storeys above them.

This noise soon subsided, replaced by a chorus of chair legs moving on the marble floor as two hundred people rose to their feet. Applause broke out as San Marino escorted his guest of honour across the space between the tables.

Ravilious's expression seemed to be one of discomfort. He looked into some of the faces around the room. Everyone seemed to be here. It was a near-complete *Who's Who* of the last fifty years of motor racing. Ravilious knew them all … liked a handful of them…

…didn't like a number of the others…

The ovation continued as Ravilious was walked around the end of the top table to his place at its centre. San Marino held the chair for his guest as he sat down, before moving to his own chair one place along. A tabletop lectern had been set up, as well as a microphone.

'Honoured friends,' said San Marino over the continuing applause, his deep voice and cosmopolitan accent gently catching everyone's attention.

The clapping started to fade.

Seats were retaken.

The room fell silent.

San Marino, with his voice echoing around the huge room, began: 'Blenheim Palace is a fitting backdrop against which to celebrate the anniversary of a spectacular forty-year career…'

Someone interrupted, shouting: '…why … has Arno gone and bought it?'

The heckle caused a snigger from different parts of the room, some sharing the jibe; others appearing discomforted by it.

San Marino's 1950s film star looks hardened for a moment, projecting a this-is-neither-the-time-nor-the-place indication of disapproval. The heckler and the sniggering were silenced.

Without referring to notes, San Marino continued: 'The first Duke of Marlborough was pre-eminent in the history of his time. Arno's pre-eminence in *our* world has been just as influential. Anyone who can read a newspaper knows that forty years ago he took a gentleman's hobby – pursued by a handful of playboys – and transformed it into a global business. Today, Formula 1 turns over in excess of 10 billion dollars a year and is one of the most prominent sports on the planet. Arno Ravilious should be hailed as an extraordinary entrepreneur; it should not be unreasonable for us to declare him the sporting world's equivalent of a Rockefeller, a Carnegie or a Vanderbilt.

'In whatever way history comes to record you, Arno,' San Marino added, 'to us in motor racing you will always be our founding father. We are delighted you have joined us this evening, allowing us to express our appreciation for your years of commitment and commercial leadership. At the same time you have made a large number of our brethren, here tonight, exceptionally wealthy.'

San Marino reached for his champagne. 'I am keen to thank you. Motorsport is keen to thank you. Friends,' he said, raising his glass in salute, 'I give you … Arno Ravilious.'

Another rumble of sound came as everyone re-stood to join in the toast.

Ravilious remained seated, continuing to look uneasy.

There was an effusive round of applause.

Ravilious stayed seated, making no sign of moving – until San Marino's expression suggested he might respond.

Just as Ravilious made to stand, he felt his phone vibrate. As everyone retook their seats, Ravilious used the distraction to look at his messages. Two emails had come in:

'Hartstein still being a cunt I'm afraid. No chance of compromise. Threatening to file first thing on Monday. So sorry. DFK.'

Ravilious became aware there was now silence all around him.

He looked up and across the Great Hall, realizing he was the focal point of two hundred pairs of eyes; he still took the time to look down to read the second email.

'Rumour about Dramma Sportivo TV *seems to be true.'*

Ravilious was thinking hard.

He scrolled down to the email he had received the day before and asked himself if he was still ready:

'MOU is a go, Arno. Yes to cash element. Yes to split between trusts. Yes to valuation of $7 billion. Yes to management arrangement, GB III.'

He breathed deeply and realized he was.

It said something of San Marino's status that, after his tacit admonition of the heckler, no one was now brave enough to indicate impatience, even though their guest of honour's attention was very clearly somewhere else. All the room could see was the top of Ravilious's bald head as he looked down and started replying. Using only a small number of cues from his thumbs on the screen, he CC-ed it to one other person and typed in a single-word response:

'Done'.

Ravilious shut down his phone.

Had anyone been paying close attention they might have spotted the tiniest smirk on the Ringmaster's face.

Putting the device back in his hip pocket, Ravilious looked up at the room and rose to his feet. 'Thank you, Lord San Marino, for your generosity,' he said, his Northern Irish accent making his voice sound no less edgy. 'Except, for the comparisons you made with those commercial legends – Rockefeller, Vanderbilt that is. Such talk can only endear me more to some of the people here…'

A murmur came from the room, agreeing, disagreeing – a number smiling at the self-deprecation.

Ravilious added with a humourless smile: 'No one in the middle of an ecosystem as complex as a global sport can *ever* please everyone. In the forty years you referenced, Bo, I have been criticized at some time or another by every interest, probably every person in this room. Circuit owners, race promoters, F1 teams, the FIA, national authorities, drivers, engine manufacturers, tyre manufacturers, sponsors, spectators, fans, media and politicians – have all had their beefs with me. I'm blamed when rule changes don't work out … which have, in any case, never been anything to do with me. And, of course, all those criticisms come at me for very different reasons. Had I listened to each of them, let alone at the same time, I could only have become a stark raving schizophrenic.'

A more empathetic response came from the guests, some acknowledging the observation with a hint of amused sympathy.

Ravilious continued: 'Formula 1 is now far better rewarded for the spectacle it provides, even though it could always earn more,' he said, without any suggestion of levity. 'Sharing the spoils of that reward has always been an issue between the stakeholders. I rest easy, though … no one in this room is the poorer because of me.'

This time, instead of a murmur, there was a smattering of hand-claps – finally tripping the room into a full round of applause; even the begrudging seemed to join in.

The reaction died down.

Blenheim Palace's magnificent Great Hall fell silent once more.

Arno Ravilious, never one to stand on ceremony or show feelings one way or another, was getting ready to drop his bombshell. Part of him relished the theatrics and consequences of what he was about to do.

'For those of yous who have had your issues with what I've done,' he said, lowering his Ulster voice, which some could have heard as adding a hint of menace, 'I might finally be able to offer some long-awaited relief. As of a few minutes ago, I have indicated a readiness to sell my entire interest in Motor Racing Promotions Ltd … lock, stock and barrel. I am also considering plans to step down as the company's chief executive at the end of this season.'

Ravilious stopped talking.

His expression acted like a full stop.

Ravilious had clearly finished.

The room was silent. And stayed so, for what seemed like an age.

The news was extraordinary.

No one seemed to know what to say ... *how* to react.

Everywhere else, the news of Arno Ravilious's retirement was explosive.

In a matter of seconds, Tweets, texts and a couple of snatched mobile phone pictures – taken from inside the dinner at Blenheim Palace – had been uploaded before Ravilious had even sat down.

Within ten minutes of his speech, before any kind of official announcement or confirmation, Ravilious's sale of Motor Racing Promotions, and his relinquishing control of Formula 1, was 'breaking news' across mainstream broadcast media. Editors of television stations went into hyper-drive, splashing the story as the lead item in their subsequent bulletins.

Most broadcasters had partly-produced packages on the forty-year Arno Ravilious story backed up, just in case; after all the man was getting on and he had to go sometime – one way ... or another. The films were rapidly updated to include this latest development and put on air. The programmes that went out had a peculiar feel to them, seeming more like obituaries than a news item.

Perhaps because no one had *ever* expected Ravilious to retire.

No one thought the man would do anything but die in the job.

Formula 1 was about to go into deep shock, particularly at Silverstone where the inner core of the F1 community was gathered in conclave. In the paddock, down the pit lane, in the grandstands and among the caravans and tents in the dew-covered campsite, this was all anyone could talk about.

Around the globe, those with financial interests at stake – team owners, team bosses, circuit operators, TV companies and sponsors

– were concerned about the ramifications of Arno Ravilious stepping down. What could it all mean?

Arno Ravilious was all they had ever known.

He was the Ringmaster.

He *was* Formula 1.

SIX

It was cold, making the place smell even more metallic. There was plenty of metal around: the solid doors, the framework of the bed, the bucket under it, not to mention the bars across the windows. The rest of the Nieuwe Wandeling cell was just as harsh. Unadorned concrete.

Yoel Kahneman was doing what he always did at this time of night – all he could do, all he was permitted to do. Just lying in the dark. Long ago he had realized that thinking was a bad – and frustrating – idea.

Noises of a prison block echoed up and down the landing. Shouting, moaning, farting, self-pleasuring, Tourette-like outbursts, yells of animal rage, frustration.

Then came a more deliberate sound.

Metal caps could be heard clacking on the concrete landing: the sharpness of the sound echoed through the walls. Kahneman heard the footsteps getting louder.

There was a sound like a gunshot. The cigarette packet-sized hatch in his cell door was flicked open. The prisoner flinched, starting to sweat.

'Kahneman,' growled the guard in English with a heavy Dutch accent. 'Your friend Ravilious has just announced he's giving up. About time, eh?'

Kahneman sat up, although sitting up or lying down made no difference to his interaction with the guard: he couldn't see or be seen in the darkness. 'What's happened?'

'It's all over the news. He's selling out and stepping down.'

Kahneman jumped to his feet. Approaching the door, he tried to look through the aperture at his only contact with the outside world. 'Did they name any companies? Say who he's selling to?'

Nothing came back in return.

Kahneman's head was spinning; his heart rate soaring. He now felt warm, despite the cold. He peered through the gloom at the pupil staring back at him through the hole. 'I need a phone, Mr Van Der Bijl. I *will* be grateful.'

'*How* grateful?'

'Twice the usual?'

There was no response from the other side. 'This is bigger news than that, don't you think? It would have to be ... *at least* ... four times.'

'Extortion!' was all Kahneman could reply.

The whole cell – the whole corridor – echoed with the second gunshot-like sound as the hatch was slammed shut. Footsteps indicated the prison officer was already walking away.

Kahneman slammed the door with his fist. 'Bastard!' he yelled. 'Fuck it, alright ... *alright!* ... Four times!' he shouted.

But there was no reply from the retreating warden.

Hanfried Von Wittelsbach was trying to wind down. He drove up the narrow lane, a single-track road traversing the cliff face of the Odenwald Mountains. For months he had promised himself a break ... a long weekend. Finally, this Thursday evening was when it was meant to start.

Reaching the end of the lane, he manoeuvred his i8 easily round the last few twists and turns, then under the stone archway, before hearing the wheels clatter over the wooden slats of the drawbridge. Entering the tunnel through the fortified wall of Heidelberg Castle the BMW passed beneath the portcullis and over the ancient cobbles under what was the gatehouse. He emerged into the courtyard at the heart of the medieval fortress. Staff from his home in Frankfurt had come on ahead; his butler was there, waiting to receive him.

Hanfried Von Wittelsbach stemmed from a cadet branch of the *Uradel* Counts Palatine of Lotharingia and, so, the Dukedom of Bavaria. He may not have had seniority, genealogically, but his success with Frankfurt Capital, the bank he started 30 years before, made him the senior man of the family, financially – even when the Duke's estates, holdings and extensive art treasures were taken into account.

Heidelberg Castle had been owned by the House of Bavaria from the 13th Century. Since 1720 it had been a ruin, when the-then Elector Palatine moved his court to Mannheim.

As Hanfried Von Wittelsbach's business succeeded, he wanted to make a statement. Signing a peppercorn lease on the castle for 100 years with his cousin, the current Duke, he commissioned renovation work and, after spending untold millions, a Wittelsbach was back in the ancient family seat once again.

The current tenant walked through the house – the spectacular hallway and sitting room – out through the tall French windows and onto the terrace. From halfway up the steep-sided hills of the valley, Hanfried Von Wittelsbach looked down through the evening haze. Three hundred metres below, the Neckar – a tributary of the Rhine – meandered down its gorge from right to left. For a setting, let alone the siting of a military stronghold, there were few places on earth to match the splendour of Heidelberg Castle. For a moment he stood there, drinking in the warm evening air, soaking up the view – savouring the realization that he was at last getting away from business for a few days.

Mid-sixties and six foot five, Count Wittelsbach's white hair, swept back off his forehead, white eyebrows, wide face and sky-clear eyes created a formidable impression in any setting. The double-breasted dark blue suit, which he'd worn from the office, added to his air of command.

A marble table was laid up for dinner. The Countess, tending some of the place settings, broke away and greeted him with an affectionate peck on the cheek. Similar in age and height, she was slim and tanned; born a Nassau-Weilburg, making her a relative of the Grand Duke of Luxembourg, she, too, conveyed effortless confidence and bearing.

Their guests would be arriving in half an hour, she explained, before gliding back inside the castle to check on the chef's *sauerbraten*. Wittelsbach crossed to another item of marble furniture, a sideboard, to check on the half dozen bottles in the coolers, and called for the butler to open the Dornfelder, allowing it time to breathe.

Once he had been poured a glass of Riesling, he walked back to the ornate balustrade at the front of the terrace.

And that's when his phone rang.

He cursed.

His office had been told not to disturb him unless it was business-critical.

He couldn't not answer it.

His treasured weekend of relaxation was about to come to an end.

Answering the call, Wittelsbach listened for a few moments, then said: 'He's done *what*?'

There was a pause.

'Oh, for fuck's sake.'

Countess Wittelsbach emerged from inside the castle, her expression changing in response.

Into the phone, Wittelsbach said: 'Christ, I've *had* it with that man. Email him – get him on the phone – either way tell him – whatever he's doing – cease and desist. Immediately. If he doesn't respond, send him a formal letter.'

Wittelsbach ended the call.

His wife, seeing the colour in her husband's face, tentatively asked: 'Freddy, what's wrong?'

The patrician figure turned and shrugged.

'...Oh, God, no ... not again?' she said. 'What's Ravilious gone and done this time?'

'Only announced a sale of Motor Racing Promotions.'

'Without having discussed it with you ... I'm guessing?'

Someone else was given the news later that night, although the person delivering it was sure it never got through – that it never registered … at the time.

In the dark, he hadn't been easy to find.

With the warm night air, there were naked bodies all over the villa – around the house, on the terraces, throughout the extensive hillside gardens and all around the pool.

Corsica was cloudless and under a crystal-clear sky. There was no moon, barely any ambient light. The promontory was remote: the glow of Porto-Vecchio, some way below, was too distant to have any effect. What little lighting there was came from moody blue LEDs at floor level, the attractive but ineffectual glow from the pinpoint white lights woven through a number of overhanging branches, and the underwater lights of the swimming pool.

The host finally found him.

Leaning over one of the sun loungers, Aigle Lavarese looked down through the gloom – only just able to recognize the Tunisian's profile. The man he sought was immobile, lying half on, half off the pale slim form of a naked girl: Suleiman Al-Megrahi was naked too, sweating profusely. The air may have been humid and balmy, but it didn't look like Al-Megrahi was sweating because of exertion.

The girl flinched at the appearance of the figure looming over them. Ignoring her, Lavarese said: 'Sulei?'

There was no reply from Al-Megrahi.

'*Sul*eiman?' he said sharply. 'For fuck's sake, the bastard Ravilious's selling up *and* stepping down.'

The host continued to look for a reaction from the naked man, but there was none. Lavarese switched his attention to the girl: 'Okay, puss, you're done here.'

There was no response from her either, until he beckoned her away with a flick of his fingers. Only then did she seem to understand.

Wriggling awkwardly, the girl struggled to extricate herself, it being an effort to slide her body from under the dead weight of the man half lying on top of her. As she got to her feet, Lavarese saw for the first time how stunning she was. How young she was. Five feet eleven, bean-pole thin, a tiny chest, and, apparent even in the villa's low-level lighting, flawless skin. She met the host's eye.

Concern crossed her face.

Adding to her discomfort, Lavarese was now staring at her – taking in her short blond hair, beautiful petite face, huge eyes and full, exquisitely shaped mouth. She must be one of the Russians. Trying to ingratiate himself, possibly for later, he picked up a robe lying over a neighbouring sun lounger and offered it to the girl. She grabbed it suspiciously, clutching it to herself, and quickly shuffled away.

Above the noise of the pulsating music from inside the villa, and the piercing screech from crickets all around, Lavarese heard a groan from the prostrate man on the lounger. Bending down, he caught an overpowering whiff of cognac. Lavarese lifted the man's chin with his fingers, trying to attract Al-Megrahi's attention. Attempts to communicate were clearly going to be futile. Al-Megrahi's face was drawn downwards, as if reacting to getting water in his eyes, both of which were floating anyway. Drool ran from the corner of his mouth. White dust caked his nose and top lip; a trail of the same led from his face across the cushion of the sun lounger to an adjacent knee-high glass-top table. On there, among a range of bottles and glasses, were three disturbed lines of cocaine.

'Oh, for fuck's sake, Sulei. This is it, you arsehole. It's *what* we've been waiting for.'

SEVEN

Instead of accepting their invitations to the Blenheim Palace gala dinner, Dominic Quartano and Tahm Nazar were entertaining the directors of Mandarin Telecom at Le Manoir aux Quat'Saisons. Great Milton was a convenient base for Silverstone. Quartano was putting the Chinese up in the Orchid, Passion Flower, Botticelli and Rouge et Noir suites. He was not giving up on the sponsorship renewal.

Sensing the mood during their meeting aboard *The Melita* the previous Sunday, Quartano had deliberately backed off – preventing Dr Chen from drawing their discussion to a conclusion. To buy Quartech some time, he proposed a follow-up meeting over the next weekend, during the British Grand Prix. He suggested both parties present their evidence, then, on the viability or otherwise of continuing Mandarin's involvement with the Ptarmigan Formula 1 team.

During the sixth course of dinner and their third wine from as many vineyards, just as Quartano felt he had made some progress in stabilizing the situation, Tahm Nazar was distracted. Despite his phone's Do Not Disturb mode, the thing was vibrating in his pocket.

Whoever was calling had been granted the highest precedence.

Discreetly, the team principal looked down at his screen.

An email caught his eye. There was a message from Lord Lambourn, owner and boss of a Formula 1 team. Nazar tapped it open...

Mindful of the ceremony and the dignity Quartano was investing in the evening, Nazar interrupted, as tactfully as possible: 'Dom, there's a message here I think you should see.'

Quartano looked at him with a hint of impatience.

Nazar nodded in reply; the importance of the message was written across his face.

'Would you forgive me, a moment?' said Quartano to Dr Chen as he took the device, turned it round and read the note.

Nazar stared at the tycoon, alert for any reaction.

Quartano's expression never altered.

'Dr Chen,' he said as he looked up. 'Dr Nazar has just been informed that Arno Ravilious has announced his decision to sell up and step down as CEO of Motor Racing Promotions.'

In sharp contrast, Dr Chen's face creased into a frown. 'What disquieting news,' he said.

Quartano, all too aware of the threat this development posed to the confidence the Chinese had in Formula 1 and therefore in Ptarmigan, looked Dr Chen in the eye. 'I will put together a report on the consequences of this development and submit it to you as soon as I can. Clearly, I would not hold you, Dr Chen, to any part of our relationship – or even our existing agreement, for that matter – if you, or I, are not assured of the future of F1 and the commercial risk this represents to both of us.'

Having drawn the evening to an early close, the Mandarin directors retired to consult colleagues in Shanghai and their government in Beijing. Quartano walked with Nazar out onto the sweep in front of the hotel. Their cars had been called. A late sun was still illuminating the summer evening.

'Christ, Tahm, what the hell's Ravilious doing?'

From the moment it had come through, the tycoon had been feeling this news viscerally. Countless journalists, feature writers and even documentary film-makers had tried to chart, understand and explain Quartano's success. None had come close to understanding how he had achieved what he had. Few if any could relate to a man who had built a business with a GDP now bigger than the 68th largest country, as listed by the UN. From early on, journalists resorted to a small lexicon of glib phrases to describe him: 'golden touch', 'business acumen', even the word 'genius' was bandied about. To Quartano's surprise, such pabulum had led to the media and commentators revering and romanticizing his success, creating some sort of myth. The illusion had served his purposes well; soon allowing him to be a bigger presence – in meetings, in negotiations, in deals – than he felt he warranted at the time.

What the media didn't know, because Quartano had never discussed it, was the degree to which he attributed his success to instinct. There was always the rational weighing up probabilities between risk and reward, but Quartano had never seen the world as wholly rational; he had never acted solely on an intellectual argument. For him to take a view on any situation, Quartano also had to *feel* it. These convictions, or whatever they were, didn't only spark positive possibilities: more often than not they enabled him to mitigate disasters or avoid them altogether.

At that moment, Quartano was doubly engaged by the Ravilious announcement, vexed for one simple reason. He couldn't resolve whether he felt Ravilious's announcement as good or bad news. The 'bad', he suspected, had the upper hand, not least because there was one thing Quartano *was* sure about: the world of Formula 1 – without Arno Ravilious – was going to be hugely uncertain.

'This could be a disaster or a salvation,' Nazar suggested.

Quartano nodded. 'Let's make sure we do what we can to prompt a favourable outcome. Talk to people about why this is happening now, will you? Let me know the moment you hear anything credible.'

Quartano's Ptarmigan Mirage drew up in front of him. His chauffeur, getting out from behind the wheel, walked round and opened the rear door. The tycoon lowered himself into the back.

Before the the car was even drawing away, Quartano was drafting a text:

'Ben: have just heard – Ravilious announcing the sale of F1 and intention to step down at the end of this year. Sorry for the hour – call me at EARLIEST convenience. DQ.'

Quartano then made a phone call, fully expecting it not to be answered. Recording a voicemail, he said: 'Arno? Dom Quartano. I assume congratulations are in order on your exit. Be pleased to discuss matters over the weekend, if you've the time.'

As he ended that call his phone rang.

'Ben,' he said, 'thanks for coming back to me. Sorry it's after ten.'

Benedict Wasserman replied: 'I was watching the news. The Ravilious story's *everywhere*. We had no warning; heard nothing beforehand. By the way, there's no mention of a buyer in any of the coverage – I'm assuming it means he didn't say who?'

'Exactly why I'm on to you now. Put out some feelers straight away, would you? I've got to know who the hell he's selling to. The Chinese were this close to the door anyway. I've got to reassure them with something fast, or I'm going to lose them.'

'Wall Street will still be going, and Tokyo opens in just over an hour: I'll give both offices a call. I'll get onto the other key centres first thing in the morning.'

Quartano added: 'Arno'd never get this away as a public flotation, after what happened last time. One thing we can be sure of, though – he won't be giving it away. Whoever's buying, Ben, has got to be one of the big players. Call me the moment you hear anything … whatever the time.'

EIGHT

Gabriel Barrus stood by the floor-to-ceiling window, a habitual stance he considered appropriate when something big was going down. For spiritual comfort and support he took solace from the view. Twenty-two floors up, this office – particularly its windowed corner – empowered him. He could look out over the roofs of the city towards the Salt Lake Temple, then raise his eyes to the snow-capped mountains down either side of the valley. Even the tallest buildings of this isolated community were dwarfed by the Wasatch and Oquirrh ranges. Spectacularly at that moment, the midday sun was catching several of the eastern peaks.

The Lord is truly around us.

Such a dramatic landscape would induce a sense of the numinous in most people; for Gabriel Barrus it went a whole lot further. The isolation of this high-altitude settlement, and Utah's remoteness in the middle of the North American landmass, offered him a deeper comfort. Sixty-two per cent of this state's population were his co-religionists, while the city below him was the de facto capital of the Church of Jesus Christ of Latter-day Saints. For Gabriel Barrus, third-generation Mormon, right here – Salt Lake City – was his spiritual home.

His communing with the view had been prompted by some momentous news, not least because it had been long in the coming. There had never been any certainty it would come at all or that, even if it did, it would fall in his favour. But Gabriel Barrus had never been short of faith.

Except the news *had* just come in over the phone's loudspeaker on his desk.

'We've, this minute, received the electronically signed Memorandum of Understanding,' stated a dismembered female voice from the other end.

'And the documents we asked for?'

'Some, but nowhere near all.'

'How do they look?'

Naama Zellman said flatly: 'It's just as well I trained as a lawyer.'

'Why's that?'

'Lord ... er, whoever ... knows how many contracts there are.'

Something caught Barrus's eye across the flat valley floor. An Alaska Airlines 777 had been static for a while having taxied around a part of Salt Lake City International airport. It was starting to accelerate down the runway. Barrus watched the aircraft – the afternoon shuttle to Anchorage – build up speed, rotate and lift into the air. As ever, it took some time for the aircraft to climb to an altitude that cleared the mountains all around.

Barrus refocused: 'Why wouldn't there be a lot of contracts? There'd be a lot of stakeholders.'

'Forgive me, Mr Barrus – I am not expressing myself well. What I mean is ... all the contracts are with different entities ... within the group ... barely if ever are they with the same entity twice. There seems to be no central hub. No hierarchy. It's the most extraordinary case of parallelism and multilateralism I've ever seen.'

'But the contracts *are* enforceable?'

'Appear to be, at first glance.'

'And assignable?'

'Those I've seen, bearing in mind they only arrived first thing Eastern Daylight Time, do have relevant clauses in them.'

Barrus withdrew from the window and crossed his spacious office to stand behind his desk. Glancing at his electronic schedule, he said: 'I'll come to New York tonight. Have the plans we discussed to re-organize the group ready for eight o'clock tomorrow morning.'

Dominic Quartano was changing all of his plans as well. The Ravilious situation demanded that he be back in London, at least until he had a clearer understanding of what was going on. As the summer sun lowered behind him, the Ptarmigan limousine pulled effortlessly up through the cutting in the Chiltern escarpment, a rich orange hue falling on the chalk cliffs to either side.

His phone rang.

'Ben?'

'I've been on to our offices in both New York and Tokyo; I've even woken the head of the Zurich office, who looks after our Lichtenstein business.'

'And?'

'They've heard nothing.'

'*Nothing?*'

'No one's heard anything – at all.'

'A 5 to 7 billion-dollar deal getting done without *anyone* giving something away? There have to be rumours, particularly now it's all been made public – speculative chatter, at the very least?'

'Oh there's plenty of gratuitous market chatter,' agreed Wasserman, 'but what's noticeably strange is the lack of any word from the buyer.'

Quartano was quiet, trying to mull these circumstances. This was not normal. It was not impossible for a high-profile transaction of this magnitude to be put together with none of the prominent market players knowing anything about it, but it was almost unheard of. Why was this being kept so quiet? Particularly after the deal had been announced?

Quartano's attention was now fully engaged.

He shuffled his thoughts like a pack of cards before saying: 'I told the Chinese I would produce an immediate report on the consequences of Ravilious's sale of Motor Racing Promotions and his retirement. I even said I would not hold Dr Chen to the remainder of the existing Ptarmigan contract if he or I were not confident in MRP's future.'

'Good God.'

'I need to tell them something, Ben – as soon as possible.'

Wasserman grunted acknowledgement.

'I want you to brief one of my directors first thing in the morning.'

'On what, specifically?'

'A plan of action.'

'With a view to doing what?'

'Let's say Matt Straker has a flair for a particular kind of research.'

'Sounds intriguing … I'll be here … and ready when he is.'

Signing off from the investment banker, Quartano was oblivious to the countryside either side of the M40.

He started drafting another text:

'Matt. Join me for breakfast – tomorrow – Queen Anne's Gate, would you? If you get this in time, make it 7:30. DQ.'

As his car glided down through the High Wycombe valley, Quartano's feelings about the Formula 1 situation were well and truly amplified. Weighing up his bullish/bearish instincts over the deal, now though, was no abstract or academic exercise. He was facing the collapse of his world-beating coup: using the access the Ptarmigan Grand Prix team had gained him to the Chinese defence market. This news about Ravilious was calamitous.

As his Mirage crossed the M25 heading into London, Dominic Quartano was at least sure of one thing.

The fate of Formula 1 was now fully occupying his attention.

NINE

A Tedworth House bedroom always seemed to take Matt Straker back in time. Unadorned magnolia walls. Hard-wearing floor tiles. Fluorescent lighting. Utilitarian furniture. All were strong reminders of basic training.

To his annoyance, the National Association of American Veterans had caused his session to be delayed, until as late as after dinner. Straker left his room and made his way down through the grander communal parts of the former garrison mess – including the cavernous hall – and out through the main façade. Outside, he savoured the warmth in the lowering sun and its apricot wash of the gardens, polo grounds and the landscape beyond.

Turning left, he walked across to the Palm House at the end of the East Wing and knocked on the door of a small consulting room.

'Come in, Colonel,' offered Dr Carson. 'I'm sorry we had to push this back so much; we've only just said goodbye to the Americans.'

Straker barely hummed in reply.

'I appreciate you might not have been so accommodating … sorry. Please come and take a seat. Tell me how you think you are doing?'

Straker sat in the shapeless chair. In here, too, the furniture was frugal. Lessening the spartan effect of the consulting room was a window; although small, it did give out onto the Wiltshire country-side, allowing the room to be bathed in the same wash of evening light.

'Not as well as I want,' he said.

'Go on…'

Dr Carson looked at her patient and listened. She was involved in the lives of some extraordinary people, most of whom were trying to come to terms with some extraordinary experiences. Matt Straker was one of her notable cases.

She had only known him since his ordeal, so she didn't know whether he had always been this intense. Straker's dark eyes, the skin above them which fell away diagonally downwards, the straight – nearly vertical – line of his nose from his forehead to its tip and his dark hair and eyebrows would have always created an air of severity. She could see how his appearance, along with his six-two frame and unruffled demeanour, could inspire others to follow him. It came as no surprise to Dr Carson that this man had been one of the youngest half colonels in the British Army. But she also knew Matt Straker was a deeply wounded individual.

Externally, though, there was nothing to show for it; he was, very obviously, in the peak of physical condition and fitness. Dr Carson, in preparation for their sessions, always reread his file and her notes. Doing so affected her every time. Royal Marines, a tour with 14 Int Company, Selection, SBS, two active tours – in Afghanistan and Iraq: Colonel Straker was quite a soldier, hence her disquiet at seeing such a stellar career brought to an end. And all because of the Americans. His file offered only an outline of the incident, but there was enough to haunt the psychiatrist with the needlessness of what had happened.

An infiltration, deep into Taliban territory, had gone incalculably wrong. Operation Mountain Thunder, a throwback to Mountain Blizzard, had been set up to disrupt the supply of opium-funded arms and, specifically, the lethal IED scourge into Helmand from Pakistan. The Pashtu-fluent Straker spent three gruelling weeks in the mountains before coming across the smugglers' staging camp, in a rocky pass. Acting as a Forward Air Controller, he directed four RAF Tornado fighter ground attack aircraft onto target. The Taliban caravan was strafed off the mountainside and completely taken out.

Unexpectedly, the narrow valley had then been overrun.

Elements of the US 506th Infantry Regiment – part of the 101st Airborne Division – swarmed in aboard four double-rotored Chinook helicopters.

It didn't take long for the Screaming Eagles to realize they were too late. As they stood down, Straker decided to break cover from his observation post and declare his presence – at the very least, they could get him back to base quicker than his prospective 200-mile yomp down through the foothills. For cover, Straker was dressed in Afghan peasant garb; given his colouring, and with three weeks' dirt and beard, he looked pretty convincing. The Americans, though, misconstrued his fieldcraft; they suspected him of being an enemy combatant. Major Matt Straker of the Royal Marines suffered capture, extraordinary rendition to Djibouti and sustained bouts of waterboarding on behalf of the CIA in a camp somewhere in Morocco. It took the British more than four weeks to find him.

Dr Carson considered Colonel Straker's wounds to be clinically severe. Torture was an ordeal to survive under any circumstances, but to suffer its infliction by an ally could only create a different level of psychological pathology. Because of this, Straker had lost faith in almost everything. For a soldier vested in a distilled code of values, betrayal of this kind would be felt all the greater.

Dr Carson could not help studying her patient with admiring sympathy. 'Injustice is a heavy burden to bear,' she said gently, 'no less of a burden than a physical one. How have the episodes been?'

'Better than the time I was in Buhran.'

'After you left the Marines?'

'With my new employer, Quartech International. After that I was deployed on an assignment with their Formula 1 team.'

'Sounds a bit lighter?'

Straker shook his head.

Dr Carson looked surprised.

'Several bouts of anxiety and a couple of episodes,' he said. 'Then came an active assignment in French Guyana; that *was* a strong distraction, although I had a couple of occasions. The best distraction was the *Help for Heroes* trek across the Arctic … I was episode-free for a full three months.'

'Well done on that – and for getting everyone home safely. Quite an achievement.'

'Before it ended I was called to Russia on another assignment. That, too, was intense – as well as immersive, but I came close to an episode midway through.'

Dr Carson was taking notes as Straker spoke, noting the facts but focusing more on aspects of his disposition as he recalled his activities. 'So the frequency does seem to be lessening?'

Straker shrugged a restrained 'Yes'.

'And sleep – how have you been coping?'

'Not well.'

'Has the heavy blanket helped?'

Straker nodded. 'It does seem to work, surprisingly well for such an apparently unsophisticated idea. Except, at 40 pounds, it's not something I can lug around – and I've been travelling a lot.'

Dr Carson put the file and the pen down on the small table between them. Looking up into his dark eyes, she said: 'I know I'm repeating myself, but to suffer the intelligence equivalent of "friendly fire" is a psychological trauma of a major degree. My professional opinion, let alone any personal one, is that your recovery – for all the discomfort of your episodes – is astonishingly strong.'

'When it's cost me my marriage?'

Dr Carson nodded gently. 'PTSD is as much a burden to those around us. Is there any chance of a reconciliation, now that you're coming to terms with your illness?'

Straker slowly shook his head.

'I am truly sorry,' replied Carson. 'Sadly, that too is not uncommon in pronounced cases.'

Straker's eyes froze in a stare.

The psychiatrist was slightly taken aback. 'From the way you speak of it, Colonel, your new role for Quartech is doing you a significant amount of good.'

Straker's attention still seemed to be elsewhere.

'An occupation that inspires, stimulates and immerses,' Dr Carson went on, looking at him closely to gauge his engagement, 'can be one of the best aids to recovery.'

Straker continued to stare – looking forwards, unfocused – into space.

After an awkward pause, he *was* distracted, but not by the psychiatrist.

His phone was vibrating in his pocket.

'Sorry, doc – this is highly filtered. Only *one* person could get through.'

Dr Carson looked resigned. 'Go ahead.'

Straker took out his phone. The caller ID confirmed it was the one person. Opening the message, he was genuinely surprised.

Dr Carson was studying him; trying to read his reaction. She asked: 'What's up? Why are you ... smirking?'

Straker looked up. 'I've been asked to breakfast.'

'When for?'

'Tomorrow morning.'

'What ... in nine, ten hours' time?'

Straker nodded.

'Who asks you – *this* late the evening before?'

'My boss.'

'Talk about the call of duty. Does this happen often?'

Straker shook his head.

'It must be something urgent then?'

He repocketed his phone.

For all Dr Carson's patience and attention, Straker was now some-where else entirely, focusing on whatever might be significant enough to prompt a breakfast meeting with less than ten hours' notice.

His pulse was quickened because of it.

Dr Carson could see he was now lost to their session. Trying to salvage something from it by keeping the conversation going, she asked: 'Did he say what the breakfast meeting was about?'

Straker shook his head with a smile. 'No,' he replied gently, 'but if it's that urgent, I'm pretty sure it'll provide me with the best possible kind of therapy.'

At six o'clock that evening, Mountain Daylight Time, Gabriel Barrus's Bentley Continental GT pulled into Salt Lake City International airport. Gliding its way through the complex, it pulled up outside the VIP lounge. His PA had already come on ahead to facilitate his passage; Barrus did not have to waste any time on the bureaucracy of his departure: he was soon being driven on, out to the steps of his jet.

Within a further ten minutes, having settled into the luxurious cabin, the Learjet 60XR was on the move.

Six minutes later Gabriel Barrus III was being accelerated down the runway, lifting off and climbing steeply into the chilled evening air of the Utah Mountains. Once the corporate aircraft had cleared the surrounding peaks it banked onto its east-bound flightpath, heading across the continent for Teterboro airport, New Jersey – five miles to the west of Manhattan.

TEN

Within minutes of receiving the summons, Straker was making plans to leave. He packed hurriedly and checked out of Tedworth House, striding towards his car. Securing his case on the luggage rack over the boot, he climbed into his Morgan Roadster. He barely noticed the drive to London.

At home in Putney he hardly slept.

Waking just after five – unable to settle – Straker slipped into his running kit and let himself out through his front door. Emerging onto the waterfront, he found it was light even though the sun had yet to rise. By twenty past five he was running westwards under the trees along the towpath of the Thames towards Mortlake. From the sights, smells and sounds, the heatwave felt set to continue. A number of boats from the rowing clubs were already out on the river, trying to make the most of the cool air before the unrelenting heat of the day to come.

Because of the breakfast appointment, Straker cut the run short. Returning home, he showered, shaved, and dressed inside twenty minutes.

Emerging from his Georgian villa, Matt Straker walked along the bank of the Thames in the other direction, crossing Putney Bridge towards the underground station. He breathed in the views up and down the river. Everything felt unexpectedly spacious here – tranquil and even detached – despite being so close to the centre of London.

There was a news stand inside the station. He couldn't miss the Formula 1 story. Headlines about it and pictures of Arno Ravilious were splashed across the front pages of all the morning's papers. Straker had a strong hunch. He bought a copy of the *Daily Telegraph*, *The Times* and an *FT* to read on the tube.

Above ground in Westminster, he walked the short distance to Queen Anne's Gate. The sun was haloed by the early morning mist. The air was still; temperatures were rising fast.

Quartano's front door opened within seconds of his knock. A butler led Straker into the house and up the oak-panelled stairs to the first floor. A pair of double doors were opened, allowing him to be shown into a large dining room. Facing him were two floor-to-ceiling windows looking out over St James's Park. With the room facing north, the crystal chandelier above the middle of the table needed to be lit. He was distracted by the smells of coffee, freshly baked croissants and bacon, all of which were laid out on a white linen tablecloth in front of him.

From his seat at the left-hand end of the breakfast table, Dominic Quartano rose as he appeared. The tycoon looked immaculate – wearing a pale blue houndstooth shirt and the waistcoat and trousers of a three-piece suit. His tie showed the simple and elegant colours – and famous zigzag – of the Fleet Air Arm. Quartano's blue eyes flashed as he smiled a welcome to his guest. 'Sorry everything had to be arranged at short notice,' indicating that Straker might take the laid place facing the windows as he retook his own chair.

The butler held it for the visitor. A crisp linen napkin was laid across Straker's lap.

'You can't have missed the news about Arno Ravilious and Formula 1?'

Straker smiled, disrupting his intense expression; his hunch had been right. 'It's hard to imagine the full consequences of him stepping down.'

'They can only be enormous and unpredictable,' replied Quartano. 'Any organization dominated by a single individual for that long is inherently unstable. His departure can only create a vacuum.'

As the butler poured him a cup of coffee, Straker said: 'The articles about his departure were strange: some of the *Telegraph*'s coverage took me back to Kosovo – to thoughts of Yugoslavia after Tito?'

Quartano smiled disconsolately.

'Any idea who Ravilious's successor is likely to be?'

'That'll be in the gift of the buyer,' said the tycoon. 'The challenge is that no one within Motor Racing Promotions seems to have been groomed to succeed. Whoever takes it on will find themselves on an extraordinarily steep learning curve. God knows how Ravilious has managed to hold the divergent, conflicting and mutually exclusive interests in Formula 1 together – or at bay – for so long. And yet he's done it, in an atmosphere of tolerated opposition, for over forty years.'

'A player within F1? Someone with credibility in the sport?'

'They could, but it would be far from plain sailing. Anyone with enough weight would bring pre-existing associations with them, inevitably making the other stakeholders suspicious.'

'Wouldn't an *out*sider struggle to control some of the F1 people?'

Quartano shrugged resignedly.

'So without the right leadership, then, Formula 1 *could* be looking at its own Yugoslavia?'

Quartano's response to Straker's further reference to the Balkans was more intense. 'Christ, I hope not. Formula 1's appeal would be savaged if it fought among itself, imploded, fragmented, let alone broke up. In the wrong hands, the prospective value of the Ptarmigan F1 team would be crippled. But, for us, Matt, none of this is an abstract concern. Tahm and I had dinner with Dr Chen last night. With the way F1's been going, Mandarin Telecom was already iffy at best about renewing their sponsorship. Now, in light of the Ravilious news, our chances have all but disappeared.'

'Costing Ptarmigan 750 million dollars?'

Quartano nodded solemnly. 'Losing out on that would be disastrous to Ptarmigan. But for us, the threat would be catastrophic. If Mandarin pulls its sponsorship, Quartech would see *billions* of dollars at risk: our access – through the Ptarmigan relationship – to the Chinese government would be lost. Formula 1 has created a priceless key to those markets for us, a degree of access not achieved by any other Western company. We've generated sales of at least 500 million dollars so far. No Western company has ever got close to the vast military-controlled space/satellite market in China – worth tens of billions. And yet *we have*. Ptarmigan has been critical to Quartech in creating that access. As a consequence, Formula 1 has become critical to that sizeable business opportunity for Quartech International as a whole.'

Straker had never heard Quartano put this relationship into such strategic context before; he had never seen the defence tycoon adopt this tone and demeanour. It was quite unsettling.

'Matt, your immediate task is clear. I want you to get out in front of this. I want to be able to reassure Mandarin Telecom about the future of F1, but can't do that without knowing who is going to be running MRP. The biggest indication of that will come from who's buying it. I've *got* to know who it is. I want you briefed by Benedict Wasserman, the moment we've finished here.'

'And who's he in all this?'

'Quartech's investment banker – runs the corporate division for Ziebart Blauman. Ben handles all our takeovers and divestments.'

Straker was now surprised. 'Why would you involve Competition Intelligence – my department? Why not leave it all up to the specialists at this bank?'

Quartano dabbed his mouth with his napkin. Looking Straker in the eye, he said: 'The moment I heard Ravilious's news last night, I spoke to Wasserman. For all the monitoring his firm does, he hadn't heard anything about the sale of Motor Racing Promotions, let alone anything about a buyer ... even *after* the news broke. He contacted other Ziebart firms, in New York, Switzerland and the Far East. None of them had heard anything about it either ... not even rumours of who it could be.'

'And that's strange?'

'Motor Racing Promotions is worth comfortably north of 5 billion dollars. Few trade buyers would have that sort of cash just lying around to fund an acquisition on this scale. Raising that amount of capital would have to involve a raft of things: arranging credit lines, setting up securities issuance, syndication, underwriting, not to mention pre-placing of big blocks of shares – or corporate paper – with institutions.'

'And you would have expected Wasserman's firm to hear of that sort of activity?'

'Ziebart Blauman is one of the most powerful investment banks in the world, with one of the sector's largest balance sheets. Ziebarts would have the clout to take this entire deal onto its own books, if it wanted to. In relation to any corporate acquisition, it, undoubtedly, has the biggest placing power – a huge client base to buy lines of stock. Even if Ziebarts wasn't appointed as the lead manager, a company would have to have a damn good reason not to approach them to part-fund this sort of deal. In any case, their information sources, market intelligence and networks should enable them to hear about most market activities around the world, well in advance of any announcements.'

Straker was struggling with many of these terms and practices, but the unusual expression on Quartano's face indicated their significance: 'And yet, I take it, they've heard nothing about any of this?'

The tycoon shook his head in agreement. 'Go and talk to Ben. I want you to help him find out what the hell's going on.'

ELEVEN

Hanfried Von Wittelsbach was getting increasingly annoyed. He had managed to shut out the Ravilious news for the duration of dinner, but after his guests had retired for the evening he could no longer do so. Just before midnight he rang and left a message on Frankfurt Capital's chief investment officer's phone, insisting they speak first thing in the morning.

By the time Wittelsbach awoke, just after six thirty, Amelie Hesse had already texted him an update:

'Still no response from Ravilious … no return of any emails, SMS messages or voicemails.'

From his breakfast table on the terrace of the castle, Wittelsbach looked out at the haze hanging over the river in the valley below.

Inwardly he swore.

Ringing Hesse, he said: 'I had better come back in. Ten o'clock – my office?'

Matt Straker left Quartano's house in Queen Anne's Gate and climbed into the back of the Ptarmigan Mirage waiting for him outside. The car found its way round Parliament Square, dropped down onto the Victoria Embankment and ran north beside the Thames towards the City of London.

Even after fifteen years in the Royal Marines, having operated and fought in a range of hostile terrains from jungle to desert, London was still the most alien environment he had ever known. Straker's lack of familiarity with urban life was about to be challenged further. The ancient City of London, the financial district, was to reveal another distinction altogether.

Entering the Square Mile, Straker immediately sensed a different atmosphere, obvious from watching the people on the pavement. Their clothes were drab. Formal. Conservative. Everyone – men and women – scurried along, seemingly on autopilot. There was none of the dawdling of tourists or shoppers, which so often frustrated him around Quartech's headquarters in the West End. At this hour of the morning, just before nine, he imagined the people on the streets were commuters heading for their offices. Around St Paul's and down Cheapside they were in a hurry; from the expressions Straker read on their faces, though, few of them were doing this with any apparent enthusiasm or sense of anticipation. Straker was curious. This couldn't be the attitude that had built the City into the pre-eminent financial centre on the planet. He reasoned the leaders – the entrepreneurs, the innovators – must be already at their desks, creating the next opportunity. From what he had seen at street level, Straker was interested to know what a City of London thought-leader might look and sound like.

Turning off Cheapside, Straker's car ducked down King Street, heading towards Guildhall. At the next T-junction it turned left again – into Gresham Street. The car drew in beside the pavement outside Ziebart Blauman's global headquarters.

Seven storeys up, Straker emerged from the lifts onto the investment bank's reception floor, its decor a subtle manifestation of the firm's brand, conveying solidity, tradition and modernity.

Straker was shown into one of the meeting rooms. A long window offered an elevated view of Guildhall, home of the Corporation – the governing institution responsible for the City of London having thrived as a business centre for the last 600 years.

Inside the room a figure was sitting at a small leather-topped table, scrolling through what looked like a stream of company news announcements and share prices on an iPad. As Straker was announced by the receptionist, Benedict Wasserman looked up, rose to his feet and stepped forward to introduce himself.

'Delighted to meet you,' said the banker in a tenor-pitched voice.

Straker heard the door shutting behind him. 'Mr Quartano is grateful you could see me at such short notice.'

Wasserman offered him coffee and the chair opposite. 'I'm

delighted to make the time,' he replied as they sat down. 'We are aware of Mr Quartano's concerns. Ptarmigan's sponsorship relationship with Mandarin Telecom is significant; the access it gives Quartech to China is business-critical for the entire group.'

Straker found himself settling in a lot quicker than he might have expected – feeling he was in the company of someone unthreateningly confident. Dark curly hair, dark eyebrows and the blackest – obsidian – eyes projected seriousness from Wasserman, but the expressiveness of his round face and ready smile softened any potential harshness. There was a clear invitation to engage. For the calming authority he exuded, Straker would not have been surprised if he had been told the fortysomething was the maître d' of a top hotel, a conductor of an orchestra or even a mathematics professor. Declaring his status as a City banker, though, were the large pair of black-rimmed glasses, the Turnbull & Asser shirt, its double cuffs, the gold cufflinks, heavily pin-striped suit and the John Carpenter Club tie.

'I should pre-empt with a warning,' said Straker. 'I'm afraid I know nothing of investment banking.'

Wasserman nodded and smiled, which again put the visitor at his ease. 'Before we get on to Formula 1 and Motor Racing Promotions, then, perhaps I might explain a little of what we do?'

Straker indicated his thanks with a nod.

'We are what the British used to call a merchant bank, a term we've since Americanized to "investment" bank. Ziebarts, though, only looks after companies. We offer expertise to help firms be more efficient financially. One way of doing that is to help them raise money as cheaply as possible: we design and issue "investment products" in our clients' companies – shares, IOUs or bonds, or a range of hybrids in between – which we then bring to market and sell to investors. The proceeds from those sales go back to our clients for them to invest in their businesses.'

Straker nodded.

'Corporate efficiency also comes from a company having a clear business strategy,' said Wasserman. 'We specialize in helping clients develop theirs, particularly through finding, buying or selling companies to help them achieve their objectives. Getting the right price or paying the right price only comes when we have a full understanding of a company's value; and to do that, we analyze what we call its fundamentals – its sales, costs, profits, debt levels, et cetera – which determine a business's overall strengths and weaknesses.'

Straker nodded again, partly out of relief; so far, he felt he was keeping up. 'Mr Quartano said something about you having unequalled sources, intelligence and networks across world markets.'

Wasserman smiled self-effacingly. '"Sources", "intelligence" and "networks" are probably a little dramatic for what we do, but in the course of our activities we do tend to hear what's going on: who's in the market to buy, which companies are for sale, and what they might be worth.'

'And yet,' said Straker, 'I don't believe you *have* heard anything about the sale of Motor Racing Promotions?'

Wasserman's demeanour never changed. 'Our not knowing anything about this transaction or the prospective buyer does make this a strange development.'

Straker studied the banker intently. He was enthralled. Wasserman hadn't sounded the slightest bit arrogant making such a categorical statement, nor was he giving off any defensiveness or culpability either.

'The reason I can say it's strange,' added Wasserman, 'is that I have a team of three analysts monitoring MRP 24/7.'

Straker's eyes widened. 'You commit *how* much resource?'

Wasserman nodded.

'Exclusively for Quartech?'

Wasserman leant across the leather-topped table and put his hand on a weighty, office-bound booklet that was easily two inches thick. The investment banker slid it across the top of the table towards him. Even though it was upside down, Straker caught sight of its title and was amazed to read:

'FORMULA 1 – POST ARNO RAVILIOUS'

Something else about it was striking.

The document was dated three years earlier.

Straker was seriously intrigued.

Wasserman said: 'Mr Quartano has one of the shrewdest business minds Ziebarts has ever known. He takes any relationship Quartech might enter into extremely seriously, wanting to understand a potential partner long before he ever does business with them. The fate of a counterparty, of course, can seriously affect a company's brand, its commercial performance and its market standing. His mantra, now almost a myth in the City, is that he "won't do business with anyone he wouldn't be prepared to lend money to".'

Straker was listening but struggling to concentrate; he was trying to process the scale of the research and surveillance Quartano had been investing in Formula 1.

'Before making a bid to buy Ptarmigan,' said the banker, 'Mr Quartano asked us to produce a report on the commercial aspects of the sport. He wanted to understand the risks of F1. He didn't want to be embarrassed, should anything go wrong.'

'What does it tell you, then, that Ravilious has been able to sell MRP without Ziebarts hearing about it?'

Again without appearing defensive, Wasserman declared: 'I have full confidence in our methodology. The question becomes: what does Ravilious doing a deal – *on the quiet* – tell us?'

Straker shrugged, indicating that he saw the question as rhetorical.

'The immediate answer,' said Wasserman, 'is nothing … not for certain, anyway. We can hazard *some* cautious deductions. Ravilious is known for his secrecy, so a clandestinely arranged deal would not be out of character. Discretion, on its own, implies nothing untoward – it's actually a valuable business attribute. Silence around the deal, though, could indicate different things.'

'Such as?'

'Companies with a listing – those with their shares publicly traded on a stock exchange – must, by law, make official declarations whenever they do something that materially affects their structure or value.'

'And that would include selling itself, or being taken over?'

'Most certainly. *Private* companies, though, don't have to announce anything at the time. Motor Racing Promotions is made up of numerous companies, many held in different ways – some through family trusts – but, overall, MRP would be classified as a private vehicle. If the buyer was *also* a private company, neither party would be under any obligation to make an immediate public announcement; they'd not be compelled to tell anyone anything.'

'So would MRP being private be one of your cautious deductions for the market's lack of awareness of this deal?'

'It's a key possibility. Another common reason for silence is when the party being sold is distressed, as action might be required urgently to retain confidence in the business. Formula 1 is in the doldrums, but we're confident enough to say that MRP is in reasonable financial health, so I think we can rule that out.'

Straker studied the banker's face and found himself saying: 'Or?'

'There might be a "technical" possibility for the silence,' replied Wasserman.

'Which is what?'

'The tense Ravilious used.'

'The *tense?*'

Wasserman nodded. 'We've seen no transcript of the announcement he made during the dinner last night. If we did, would it show Arno Ravilious saying that he had "sold" the business – in other words, was he talking about a done deal … would it show that he had used the present tense – "am selling" … or would it show he used the subjunctive – suggesting that he "would sell"?'

'And that kind of phrasing makes a difference?'

'Most definitely – and a big one. Deals between companies are rarely straightforward or quick. Buyer and seller have to go through numerous stages, marked out by different levels of commitment to each other: the first would be the Non-Disclosure phase; this enables a conversation – about a deal – to be had between the two parties in confidence. After that would come a Memorandum of

Understanding, which sets out a period of exclusivity, preventing other parties from bidding on the same transaction, as well as defining the timetable for due diligence.'

'Sorry ... what does that mean?'

'Forgive me ... the process during which the buyer is given detailed and highly confidential access to the business to be bought. This means that every asset, liability, outstanding contract can be examined and fully understood. Due diligence essentially allows the buyer to know exactly what he's buying.'

'Thank you.'

'And then, towards the end of all this, there is the negotiation of the contract itself. Signing the contract is the only point at which technically the transaction occurs: the point of commitment – the point after which neither party can walk away.'

'So are you saying that the silence around Motor Racing Promotions could be because the deal might not have been completed yet?'

Wasserman smiled in confirmation.

'Whatever state this deal might be in, though,' Straker replied, 'Mr Quartano is anxious that I get out in front of it. He wants me to find out who the buyer might be, so that he gets an idea of who will be running MRP going forward. But if you've been monitoring this company round the clock for years and haven't learned anything about the sale or the buyer, how *do* I find out who's involved?'

Wasserman's face indicated a degree of resignation: 'The answer to that is, I'm afraid, not without a significant amount of difficulty.'

TWELVE

Hanfried Wittelsbach drove himself back to Frankfurt. Approaching the city, he watched the high-rise skyline of Germany's key financial centre – 'Mainhattan' – appear through the mist. Coming in after the peak of rush hour, his journey was relatively smooth. He crossed the Friedens Bridge and navigated the one-way systems and pedestrianized zones to Kaiserstrasse, before reaching Gallusanlage and the park. There, he turned left and drove his i8 into the firm's basement garage, leaving the keys with security.

Gaining the top floor, Wittelsbach strode into his light and airy office. As he walked round behind his desk, he caught sight of the opera house below his window and, in the distance, the River Main disappearing off into the haze to the east.

Amelie Hesse was asked to join him. 'We've still no response from Ravilious.'

Wittelsbach's face clouded over. 'What the hell's he up to, Amelie? Why's he selling Motor Racing Promotions *now*? Formula 1's in the shit; he could only get a crap price for it. Are we sure MRP isn't in trouble?'

The chief investment officer's expression mirrored her boss's concern. 'We reassured ourselves, only two months ago, the company was okay.'

'But not via a formal valuation?'

'No, sir, we'd all accepted our bond might have fallen by about 15 to 20 per cent. It might have fallen a little further since then, but not dramatically.'

Wittelsbach turned to look down at the Opernplatz, now being bathed in sunshine as the morning mist was burning off. Still facing the window, he said: 'Let's damn well hope MRP can meet its interest payments. If Ravilious *can't* service that loan, we're facing a 1.8

billion-euro hole in our balance sheet and a breach of our ratios. It could even put us under.'

Amelie Hesse took the assessment badly; she had never seen her boss like this before.

Turning to face his chief investment officer, he said: 'I need you, Amelie, to reassure us that Motor Racing Promotions *is* solvent. Most importantly, do whatever you can to understand why Ravilious has decided to sell now. We've got to know what the fuck he's up to.'

Wasserman broke the short silence in the room. 'Stringent rules govern the access to corporate information,' he said to Straker, 'and that goes for any business, whether public or private. Some news can substantially affect the value of a business – an oil company striking oil, a large product recall, a profits warning or a takeover bid. We call that kind of information price-sensitive and it is always highly confidential. No knowledge of that kind can be acted upon if it's been gained through a privilege position – by dint of someone being a director of the company, a professional agent acting for the business, such as its bank, lawyer, accountant or PR firm. Professionals like that are specifically trusted: they have what's called a fiduciary duty to keep any such privileged information they've been given confidential.'

'I don't understand something, then,' said Straker. 'If Ziebarts aren't involved in a particular deal directly, how does your market intelligence work? How do you come by your information … a bit of cloak and dagger?'

Wasserman shook his head perfunctorily, but the denial carried conviction. 'We only get our information by talking to as many owners and managers of businesses in different countries and sectors as we can. We then piece snippets together, like a huge detective game.'

'But doesn't that mean that the information *we* need isn't "out there" – it's not obtainable?'

'Oh, I wouldn't say that. Share prices often move in advance of a big announcement, before anything about it is announced officially. Human beings are not very good keepers of secrets, particularly when money might be made.'

Straker was the one now shaking his head. 'Are you saying we *would* have to solicit the information we're after? Mr Quartano would never encourage professionals to breach their trust.'

'Absolutely not.'

The meeting went quiet for a moment.

Straker felt he was running out of ways to understand how he could do what Quartano had asked him.

Bells from the Saint Lawrence Jewry clock, heavily muffled through the double glazing, could be heard sounding the quarter hour.

'So there's no way we can find out what we need to know?'

Wasserman paused. 'Let me give you something of an example,' said the banker with a slight tone of conspiracy. 'Imagine you're a company director ... your industrial relations are becoming increasingly strained, and there's a strong likelihood of your workforce walking out ... possibly on strike. Were you to act on that knowledge – perhaps by selling the story to a newspaper, because you expected this to be newsworthy, or by selling your shares in the company, because you thought the company's share price would fall when news of a strike became known – you would be in breach of trust and guilty of insider dealing. You would have used privileged information for personal gain.'

Straker's face remained neutral.

'There are, though, certain grey areas,' Wasserman said. 'Imagine, in the same scenario, you had nothing to do with that company – but, instead, you just happened to be walking on a hill overlooking the factory when you noticed that the workforce, en masse, was heading for the gates. You might reasonably deduce that this was the beginning of a strike. You *would* be able to act upon *that* knowledge, because it would not be considered to be privileged.'

'So, the "greyness" comes from gathering information at a distance?'

'You could put it like that, yes.'

'Applying that approach to Motor Racing Promotions, are you suggesting that if I happened to see Ravilious, say, at the theatre or in a restaurant with a third party, I might conclude that the person he was with might be the potential buyer?'

Wasserman gave him a slow shallow nod. 'Provided you didn't act on information given to you by a member of staff at the theatre or restaurant, then, no, that information would not be privileged. You *could* use it. Of course, you might have drawn entirely the wrong conclusion, but you would have come by your information legitimately.'

Straker's face clearly showed he was processing this.

'The same conclusions would also apply,' Wasserman went on, 'to the personnel of professional agencies involved in MRP's affairs, which might include its lawyers, accountants, investment bank, and such like. You could legitimately observe them in public and legitimately infer things from whom they met, which companies they visited, et cetera…'

' …so long as it was done at a distance…'

'Precisely.'

'So finding the identity of the buyer would not be impossible, but it might require a fair amount of arm's-length surveillance?'

'And considerable luck, of course: you'd have to be able to catch sight of any such meeting or encounter – when it happens – in public.'

'How do we find out the identities of such agencies acting for Motor Racing Promotions?'

Wasserman paused for a moment before he pushed the two-inch document across the leather-topped table towards him. 'What we know of MRP is in there,' said the banker. 'Mr Quartano suggested I give you a copy of this document, as a briefing on Motor Racing Promotions.'

Straker picked it up. Opening the front cover and flipping over the first few leaves he saw how thorough it was; its contents section alone ran to six pages. His face broke into a smile. 'But won't all these considerations be academic anyway, the moment Ravilious announces his buyer? How long have we got before he makes that announcement as a matter of course?'

'Impossible to answer ... without being on the inside,' replied Wasserman. 'Even if it *is* a private transaction, meaning the parties involved are not legally bound to the timetable of *The City Code on Takeovers*, they're still highly likely to follow the same stages I mentioned. Should every aspect of the MRP deal have already been agreed, and the negotiations over the contracts finalized, the announcement could be any time. It could be immediately ... today ... tomorrow ... now.'

'But if the deal is that advanced, I'd have very little chance of getting out in front of it in any case.'

Wasserman nodded and shrugged. 'And there'd probably not be much to be gained from it either, even if you did.'

THIRTEEN

Mid-morning sun, already high in the sky, bathed the terrace in a bright, almost-white light. A gentle Mediterranean breeze took the edge off the humidity; it also carried the intoxicating scent of the maquis from the dense scrubland all around the villa.

Outside by the pool, breakfast for twenty had been laid since seven o'clock. A handful of guests had emerged from their indulgences of the night before; those that had were finding the morning something of a challenge. The worst for wear appeared around eleven.

Suleiman Al-Megrahi walked out through the large open sliding doors. The fine features of the Tunisian's burnished ebony face looked strained as it scrunched up in the glare. His eyes were reduced to slits. Light was reflecting brightly off everything: the white marble around the pool, the gleaming white walls, the brilliance of the bougainvillea draped over them and the bright turquoise of the sea stretching off towards the horizon.

Al-Megrahi's head was causing him considerable pain. Trying to lessen it, he pulled on a pair of Ray-Ban dark glasses. They didn't seem to do much to ease the discomfort.

Al-Megrahi was tall, trim and muscular with a full head of lively black hair. Middle age hadn't detracted from his body shape or carriage, both of which were matador-like. Not today, but his face normally looked a decade younger than his fifty-five years. Even feeling as rough as he did that morning, Al-Megrahi was still able to pull off a look of rugged chic: an expensive pale blue shirt was open to his navel, its sleeves rolled up his forearms, while the tails of the shirt fell outside the waistband of his dark blue Bermuda shorts. Even on a bad day, he would have what it took to blend effortlessly into the most glamourous settings and company.

Their host sat at the far end of the breakfast table, shaded by a large wooden-sparred umbrella. The Buddha-shaped Aigle Lavarese was as removed in physique from Al-Megrahi as was possible; mid-sixties, overweight and balding with a fleshy, wide face that looked like it had been compressed, top to bottom. A harshness in his expression suggested the Italian survived more on his wits than his looks, something not inconsistent with the moral complications of running the Mediterranean's largest chain of casinos.

Lavarese nudged a chair out from under the table with his foot, indicating that Al-Megrahi should join him. The Tunisian winced at the scraping noise its legs made on the marble.

'This Ravilious news is a real fucker,' said Lavarese.

Al-Megrahi lowered himself into his chair. A steward dressed in white offered him a cup of coffee. Even the smell from the cafetiere was enough to repulse him. Al-Megrahi waved the steward away. 'What news?' he asked, grimacing at the sound of his own voice.

'Man, you were in a state last night.'

'*What* news?'

Lavarese looked at him judgementally. 'That arsehole Ravilious is selling MRP ... going at the end of the season ... said so last night, at some fancy kiss-arse dinner laid on by San Marino. Ravilious is selling up.'

Al-Megrahi looked distracted from his discomfort for the first time that morning. He pushed a thumb in hard against the muscles down the back of his neck.

Lavarese's expression switched to disdain. 'Christ, Suleiman, you're in a fucking state ... you can't even think. Hey ... *HEY!* ... don't you understand – Ravilious has fucked *everything*?'

The Tunisian was jolted by the other man's tone. Al-Megrahi fought to concentrate, shaking his head to try and clear his thoughts. 'Who's the buyer?'

'Doesn't matter, does it,' snapped Lavarese. 'If he goes liquid ... you've missed our chance.'

Al-Megrahi groaned. Heaving himself to his feet he staggered back inside the villa, desperate to find a fistful of painkillers, the largest Bloody Mary and the coldest shower he could bear.

Straker thought for a moment before saying to Wasserman: 'Can we just go back to your point about "tenses" again? The subjunctive one, to use your word ... Starting from the very beginning of a transaction, if a deal has only just been agreed in principle, how long could it take to complete?'

'Quite literally any time, but six months would not be uncommon – unless, as I said, the vendor company's in distress.'

'So, in theory, we're looking at a formal declaration of this takeover happening anywhere between any-second-now and six months' time?'

'Pretty much.'

Straker looked pensive.

'But even if Ravilious did use the *past* tense last night,' Wasserman said quietly, 'meaning that it is a done deal, they may still not announce it today.'

'And why's that?'

'I can't be certain, of course, but there's normally one factor in a takeover that plays a pretty big part.'

'Which is?'

'Human beings can't resist a ceremony,' said Wasserman. 'For some bizarre reason, corporate executives see mergers and acquisitions as something between a wedding and an armistice. Businessmen love signing ceremonies: maybe ceremonies make things feel more official for them ... permanent ... enshrined ... more important? I say this because when deals *are* signed, particularly one of this size and profile, it's invariably looked upon as an event – typically marked by the popping of champagne corks and a press junket.'

'A bit of an occasion?'

'Exactly.'

'So if Ravilious wanted to ram home his fait accompli, he would want to announce it all – and, presumably, introduce the buyer – on a big occasion?'

'And, unquestionably, the next big occasion in the Formula 1 calendar is Silverstone this weekend, one of the highest-profile grands prix of the season.'

'Coming that soon after his announcement to sell up and retire, it would certainly keep Ravilious in charge of the news flow,' acknowledged Straker. 'But if the announcement *is* made over the weekend, sometime in the next 24 to 48 hours, we couldn't reasonably hope to discover the name of the buyer within that timeframe anyway, could we?'

'I fear not.'

'If the announcement *isn't* made at Silverstone, then, would it be fair to conclude that the deal might not yet be completed?'

'I would say so. The negotiations could well have further to go.'

'Any delay of Ravilious's announcement of the buyer, though, could give us the time to try and get ahead of him.'

The banker was nodding.

'Meaning then, for us,' said Straker, 'it's Silverstone – do or die?'

'Pretty much.'

'Benedict, thank you – you've given me a lot to mull over.'

But as Straker stood up, he was given a whole lot more to think about.

'It's not my place to second-guess Mr Quartano,' said Wasserman, 'but seeing your degree of engagement in this matter, I might volunteer this. The amount of research we were asked to do on MRP three years ago,' said the investment banker pointing at the two-inch report on Formula 1 on the table in front of Straker, 'was far more akin to something we would prepare on a takeover target, than it was to offer reassurance for buying a Formula 1 team from the receiver…'

FOURTEEN

Eleven o'clock in the morning was heavily anticipated. Inmates of the prison were granted their hour in the exercise yard. Any relief from the claustrophobic, dank, Victorian-style Nieuwe Wandeling building was desperately prized.

A barked order prompted Kahneman to stand back from the prison cell door. Only when the warder, peering through the hatch, could see the prisoner had placed both hands on his head, did the bolts of the door clang back. Two prison guards entered the cell. The prisoner was ordered to strip. Once naked, one guard went through his clothes; the other ordered Kahneman to rub his hands back and forth through his hair while watching closely for anything that might be dislodged. The prisoner was ordered to dress. One guard slapped a handcuff on each wrist while the other fixed manacles around his ankles. Chains were attached down the back of the orange fatigues, connecting all four restraints.

Kahneman was manhandled out of the cell, along the landing and down the clanking metal stairs. On the ground floor he was escorted through a set of metal doors into a room no bigger than a large lift. When the three-man party was inside it, the doors were shut behind them. A ding came from a sensor and another set of metal doors in front of them opened, giving out into the exercise yard. As Kahneman shuffled forwards, he inhaled, savouring the outdoor humid air. It carried smells that always got to him; everyday smells from the streets of Ghent outside the prison walls: urban living, exhaust fumes, earth from the park opposite, even rank odours from unemptied waste bins. The sounds, too, were intoxicating. Everyday things – a car driving by, children playing in the park, birdsong. Prosaic sounds and odours offered him a glimpse of freedom.

Twenty other inmates were already outside, shuffling anticlockwise round the ancient prison courtyard.

Kahneman joined in, the chains restricting the movement of his arms and legs.

After three circuits of the yard, he caught the attention of a guard standing at the edge of the ring. 'Sir, I need the toilet.'

His addressee didn't acknowledge him for thirty seconds. The guard eventually ambled over. Without speaking or warning he patted the prisoner down.

Two minutes later Kahneman was waiting in front of a closed single door set in the tall red-brick wall of the prison block, otherwise only punctuated higher up by two rows of small but heavily barred windows.

The guard bellowed at Kahneman, pushing him through the door and into the small cubicle. But as he did so, he slipped something unseen into the inmate's hand. The door was slammed shut and locked behind him. Another aggressive instruction, which echoed round the yard, was yelled at his back.

Inside the cubicle, Kahneman strained to pull his left hand round his hip to his front. Breathing excitedly, he fumbled with the phone, his movement severely limited by the chains. From memory, he tried to punch in a number.

Raising the handset to his ear, the chains rattling as he did so, he willed the call to be answered.

It started to pulse out.

Finally the line clicked and he heard a voice answer the call.

Kahneman said: 'It's me.'

'Shit, you've heard, then?'

Kahneman grunted. 'That bastard *can't* be allowed to cash in. It's time the cunt got his comeuppance – I'm ready … I'm ready, now, to give you all of it … I'm ready to spill…'

Straker emerged from the Ziebart Blauman offices in Gresham Street. Thoughts were as heavy on his mind as the two-inch document on

Motor Racing Promotions he now carried. Leaving the comfort of the air conditioning, he felt the heat of the day, thankful he wouldn't have to suffer it for long. Waiting alongside the pavement was the Ptarmigan Mirage. Straker climbed in and asked Quartano's driver to make for the company's headquarters in Cavendish Square. Straker tried to order his thoughts.

The urgency involved – of being summoned, after midnight, to a breakfast meeting for that same morning – had to be a clear indication of how seismic Quartano saw this development in Formula 1. Straker could see that the tycoon would be agitated over the possibility of losing Mandarin Telecom's $750 million sponsorship of Ptarmigan, but what he didn't understand was how learning the name of Ravilious's buyer marginally in advance of an inevitable announcement could be of any help in managing that relationship? Straker struggled to see this as the incentive for him to 'get out in front of this deal'.

Quartano's principal concern, of risking billions of dollars of prospective business – should his access to the Chinese government be threatened by any collapse of Formula 1 – was a much weightier point. To put their minds at rest, advance warning of Ravilious's buyer might well enable some speedy approaches to be made to Chinese firms and government departments. But Straker couldn't see how 'getting out in front of this deal' could be anything more than managing a few expectations. Again, how could having slightly advanced knowledge of the buyer benefit those relationships either?

A couple of things Wasserman had said kept coming back to Straker:

The declaration that three Ziebarts people had been monitoring Motor Racing Promotions 24/7. Such a level of commitment might be consistent with maintaining Quartano's relationship with the Chinese, but wasn't that significantly over-engineered, even for attentive management?

And then there was that last remark the banker had made:

Wasserman's comment that the report Quartano had commissioned on MRP was more in tune with the kind of research that Ziebarts would do on a takeover target...

Straker picked up the document from the seat beside him and thumbed through its pages. The leaves cascaded from right to left. It looked extraordinarily detailed. As the car crossed over the Holborn Viaduct, snippets of Wasserman's initial description of an investment bank's role echoed round his head ... *business strategy ... help clients develop theirs ... find, buy or sell companies to achieve their objectives ... understand a company's value ... how it works ... its strengths and weaknesses ...*

Holy shit.

Did this mean what he thought it did?

FIFTEEN

Aigle Lavarese was reading the *Financial Times* when Al-Megrahi reappeared on the terrace. By now the villa's staff had re-laid the table for lunch.

The Tunisian was moving a little more steadily. He walked past the pool to sit next to his host at the table.

'What's *your* take on this Ravilious thing then?' asked Al-Megrahi.

'The old bastard had to go some time, but it looks like he's completely outmanoeuvred you.'

'You think he knew?'

'Just asking that question shows you how much you've underestimated him, or that you've shoved that much shit up your nose. How could you possibly think Ravilious wouldn't get to know what you were doing – and have a response ready?'

Lavarese folded his *FT* and dropped it onto the table beside him. 'You scored with a succession of punches. You attacked Formula 1 for its ridiculous rules, its poor televisual appeal, its falling audiences, its drop-off in advertising. All of that *must* have had an effect and contributed to Ravilious's decision to step down. Sniping from the outside is the easy bit. You've got to recognize who – and what – you're dealing with. Overnight, Ravilious has left you behind … he's moved the story on.'

Al-Megrahi sneered dismissively. 'You don't know for sure.'

'Not completely,' nodded the other with a hint of concession. Lavarese leant in. 'But he has taken action, leaving you to react. The window he's left you is only *this* big,' he said, indicating aggressively with finger and thumb.

The younger man looked like he might at last be regrouping. 'This isn't over … or a done deal,' said Al-Megrahi, trying to sound dismissive. 'With Ravilious gone, there will be a power vacuum within F1, whoever takes over.'

Lavarese was shrugging, although seeming fractionally reassured. 'Get back in there, then, and stake our claim. Formula 1 can't ignore you. For fuck's sake, though … Suleiman … at least *appear* to be sober.'

Naama Zellman had her colleagues baffled. She contradicted their usual terms of reference. She did not look like she was there for the normal trappings of a career on Wall Street. Mid-thirties with the rank of Senior Vice-President of Staten Nantucket – in mergers and acquisitions, to boot – Zellman would have been substantially well paid. None of this super wealth, though, was reflected in her appearance. She conspicuously shunned the Gucci-Hermès-Hublot trifecta. Her off-the-peg clothes were barely a level up from functional. Those around her were unnerved by someone who was in investment banking if they weren't an alpha – a peacock – in it for the strut factor. Male colleagues were baffled on another level: constantly questioning her 'deal'. Was it men? Women? The company of cats?

Naama Zellman was physically striking – unconventionally attractive – with short dark hair, brown eyes, a pale complexion and a slim face with fine features. Nothing about her made any kind of statement: even her posture and bearing understated her tall, slim figure, and projected little in the way of social confidence. Zellman didn't care. Her mind and energies were invested in deeper things. The buzz she sought came in a different form; her deal – her form of strutting – was taking people by surprise, particularly those who underestimated her. For the early meeting that morning, she felt ready to deliver one of her biggest surprises yet. Everything for it was ready, set up in the Staten Nantucket boardroom.

As the negotiation had been edged closer to the line, Zellman had been agonizing to keep a part of her brain under control, but towards the end she knew she had been on the verge of failing. She couldn't believe what she'd uncovered. And now, having been granted access to some of the key files, contracts and financial statements, she had no reason not to. Even so, she couldn't convince herself that she hadn't misinterpreted something. After numerous re-runs of her thinking, including several reconstructions of her model, she couldn't find fault with it.

To make triply sure, Zellman had gone back and started the analysis again from scratch – rebuilding her evaluation: coming at everything from as opposite an angle as possible.

Naama Zellman felt a sense of anticipation – believing that she *had* discovered something substantial. Having lived with her now-incontrovertible confirmation overnight, she was fearful this discovery might cause her to become excited.

As a calming mechanism, Zellman looked out of the window while she waited for her client. Her expression still showed a tense energy. She studied the view, trying to contain her impatience. Stretching out below her was the southern tip of Manhattan and the Hudson River. Fog hung in large patches above the water. Ellis Island was completely obscured. The Statue of Liberty looked as if she was standing on her own cloud, creating an even more majestic sight than usual.

Zellman flinched as the door at the end of the boardroom flew open.

Without a knock – without warning – without a greeting, Gabriel Barrus barged in. 'What have you got?'

At such a lack of grace, Naama Zellman found it easier to bring her excitement under control. She replied flatly and slowly: 'Motor Racing Promotions is far more of a byzantine mishmash of companies and relationships than any of us thought.'

Barrus dropped his briefcase onto the table and yanked out a chair.

Zellman said: 'MRP has virtually no structure. I have, though, attempted to visualize the company in roughly three blocks of revenue.'

'Which are?' said Barrus, as he opened his briefcase, extracted some papers, closed the lid and clicked the catches.

'One stream of income,' said Zellman, trying not to react, 'is paid by circuits to hold the grands prix. The second is income from MRP's on-track hospitality and advertising. The third comes from the proceeds of the global television rights.'

Barrus looked up at her but without any sign of engagement or response.

'The total net profit across those three areas last year,' Zellman continued, 'was circa 1 billion dollars. In Staten Nantucket's initial consultation, we suggested that a business of this kind would typically be valued on a multiple of earnings; our view was that a 7 times multiple would be fair, which would put a price tag on the whole of Motor Racing Promotions, therefore, of 7 billion dollars.'

Barrus's expression and body language remained detached.

'Going through the Black Books, and some of the correspondence Ravilious sent over yesterday,' said Zellman, 'I've discovered areas of headroom which could offer substantial lifts to current levels of income.'

'Such as?'

'Fees from circuits, for one. Ravilious has a haphazard range of fees from different races. To hold their grands prix, China, Bahrain and Abu Dhabi are each charged 40 million dollars a race. One of the latest to appear on the calendar, Hong Kong, was granted its race at a rate of 50 million per grand prix. And at the very same time,' Zellman went on, 'for the Italian Grand Prix ... held at a place called Monza ... Ravilious only charges 15 million. For the grand prix held in Monaco, he makes no charge – at all.'

Zellman looked at Barrus and still didn't read any change in his expression.

'But that's not the only observation to make on race fees,' she went on. 'Ravilious has been in negotiation with the Kingdom of Saudi Arabia.'

Barrus's eyes suddenly locked onto Zellman's face.

'Crown Prince Fahd approached MRP some time ago, bidding to hold a grand prix in Riyadh.'

'What are *they* prepared to pay?'

'A lot more than was first offered.'

The businessman's demeanour changed in an instant.

'Prince Fahd's *first* application,' Zellman replied, 'was on the basis they would be guaranteed their race for ten years. Ravilious quoted them 80 million dollars per race, rising by 5 per cent a year.'

'Where does 80 million rank in size of fees per race?'

'Right at the top, by some margin.'

'But you said what they *first* offered?'

Zellman nodded. 'From the correspondence he's just sent over, it looks like Ravilious has rejected the Saudis three times. And yet Prince Fahd has kept coming back, increasing his offer *each* time – the last one being made only last week.'

'How much is he offering *now*?'

'One hundred and twenty million with a 7 per cent escalator.'

Barrus just stared. 'And?'

'Ravilious still hasn't accepted it.'

'Why ever not? Why on earth wouldn't he?'

'I've not got enough to go on here … maybe it's a negotiating tactic … maybe he's holding out for more?'

'That is interesting research,' Barrus said in a voice that showed the first hint of generosity. 'We've got to find out more about this.'

Zellman nodded but said: 'The Saudi race is of interest, but my reason for raising Monaco, Monza, Hong Kong and Saudi is to illustrate that Ravilious's race fees are all different … some wildly so. If, instead, all the grands prix were put on a standardized fee, say of 50 million,' Zellman said as she lifted a sheet of paper and handed it across to him, 'MRP could increase its revenues by 200 million dollars a year.'

'And that includes the Saudi deal?'

'No, sir. A grand prix in Riyadh would add a further 70 million to that 200 million.'

'And if the price per race were hiked like that, I wouldn't lose any of the existing grand prixes?'

'Oh you would, sir, undoubtedly – except there's no shortage of other countries queueing up to offer themselves, as well as their cash, to host *new* races. You would easily fill the gaps from any withdrawals.'

Barrus looked down at the breakdown of the $200 million.

The Lord in his wisdom.

'But that's not all, Mr Barrus,' said Zellman.

The client looked up.

'Motor Racing Promotions gets involved in providing freight services.'

'We know that,' replied Barrus. 'He flies all the Formula 1 teams to the overseas races.'

'We did know that ... but *not* that he does it free of charge.'

'Free? ... For all of the teams?'

'To what they call the flyaway races, yes, sir.'

'How much does that cost?'

'Too much, is the answer. MRP operates a fleet of four 747 Jumbo Jets. He sells some freight space to third parties, but, from what I can tell, Ravilious's transport service endures a net loss of 70 million dollars a year.'

'As much as that?'

Zellman nodded. 'If one of the restructurings of the group was to shut this down, even outsource it – perhaps pushing the travel costs onto the teams – Motor Racing Promotions' profit and loss account could be improved by 70 million per annum.'

Barrus inhaled.

'But again, sir – that's not all,' said Zellman wondering whether her client might finally be starting to see things the way she was now inferring them. 'One piece of correspondence, which came to light in the partial disclosure, is a series of emails between Arno Ravilious and George Kovacs, of American TV Network. It's of interest because the ATVN contract is out of sync with Ravilious's other TV deals. In one email, he pointed out that Kovacs's F1 audience had quadrupled since the relationship started. As a result, Ravilious declared his right to exercise the review clause and demanded a significant bump in TV rights fees for the remaining three years of the contract.'

'From what to what?'

'From 250 million to 500 million.'

Barrus smiled briefly.

'And that's only the first such review, because it's out of step with the normal cycle. All the others come up for renewal at the end of this season. I've sampled their contracts. That review clause is one of Ravilious's boiler plates: he always builds in an escalator, calculated on ratings points. If he's invoked it with the American TV Network, it would be feasible to push through a similar increase across all territories when they come up for renewal. Some of Formula 1's audience figures may have softened recently, but they're still significantly higher today than when Kovacs renewed. There would be considerable scope to push through higher rates. If you only did that in the top ten markets, the profits from MRP's TV rights fees would all but double.'

'But what about making bigger share payouts to the teams, to the governing body?'

Zellman shook her head. 'As far as I can tell from the Concorde Agreement, any such increase in revenues would create no additional costs or liabilities – as those have already been met or capped. Any increases of this kind would, therefore, be clean – and drop straight through to the bottom line.'

A strange expression seemed to pass across Barrus's face.

Zellman paused, allowing her analysis to sink in for a moment.

Barrus, now fully engaged, said: 'What could the increase in P and L be, then – with the adjustments you've mentioned?'

'Conservatively,' replied Zellman, 'I would estimate that the standardization of the race fees, the rationalization of the freight costs and a revaluation of the TV rights would add an extra 770 million dollars in profit per year … clean.'

The Lord be praised.

'But that's not including the Saudi deal,' Zellman added with a little more force. 'If *that* proposal were agreed as well, the total increase could be lifted to 840 million. If we applied a 7 times multiple to that, it would add 5 billion dollars to the value of the business.'

Barrus was now smiling properly.

Zellman nodded in response. 'If the Saudi deal *did* come to fruition, though, something else would happen: Prince Fahd seems insistent on a 10-year contract. If a 10-year time horizon could become the norm with *each* grand prix venue, that scale of timeframe would add significantly to the predictability – to the quality – of MRP's earnings.'

'Making a multiple of seven seem rather conservative?'

'A multiple of 10 times earnings, or maybe even higher, would have to be feasible. Not only would that make the new revenue levels I've described more valuable, but, of course, it would also prompt a revaluation of MRP's *existing* earnings.'

Barrus stared at the investment banker.

Zellman went on: 'If we were to add this prospective 840 million-dollar increase to the 1 billion of current profitability and applied, say, a 10 times multiple, the new combined valuation of MRP would be 18 billion.'

'My paying a total of 7 billion.'

'Even this modest set of rationalization measures, including the Saudi deal, would induce an 11 billion-dollar increase in the value of your investment. If a rationalization of the business was clearly demonstrated, it ought to induce enough investor confidence to achieve more than a 10 times rating. Maybe it could warrant a 12 times earnings multiple? On that basis, your capital gain, net net, could be as high as 14 billion dollars.'

Blessed be the name of the Lord.

The American sports mogul was already extrapolating what this could mean – not only for the immediate cash rewards, but for the effect such a huge turnaround would have on his own standing with the Street – in the country, for heaven's sake.

Barrus said: 'I want your written proposals in full – for my lawyers to assess – by Wednesday at the latest.'

Naama Zellman lifted a modestly bound A4 document lying on the boardroom table and offered it to her client. 'It's all in there, Mr Barrus,' she said. 'I've set it all out – supported by samples of the key contracts and a full copy of the Concorde Agreement. A significant capital gain seems to be right there for the taking, sir.'

SIXTEEN

Straker's car ran on down High Holborn. Since leaving the City he had been thinking through what he had – and hadn't – been told. He realized he needed to prioritize his response. Trying to work out what was really going on would have to come later.

After Wasserman's briefing, though, how on earth was he going to set about uncovering Ravilious's buyer?

He needed a way to rationalize his thinking. To be logical.

He decided to focus on timing. If an announcement about the deal and the buyer were going to be made, at the most logical time and at the most logical place, it would have to take place at Silverstone this weekend. If that happened, this phase of the game was all but over already – not only would trying to identify the buyer in such a short timeframe be far-fetched, but the benefit of achieving such limited advance notice could also only be minimal. Straker was soon resigned: an announcement of the buyer at Silverstone would tell them everything anyway.

What, though, if that didn't happen, maybe because Ravilious wasn't ready to announce or because the deal wasn't complete and further negotiation was needed? Straker tried to think through the dynamics of that, again in respect of timing. Under those circumstances, when would Motor Racing Promotions engage with the buyer to finalize their negotiations? It could be up at Silverstone, couldn't it? Wouldn't the grand prix be the perfect pretext for them to get together? But if Ravilious *did* conduct his negotiation there, though, wouldn't that inevitably reveal the identity of the buyer? And yet secrecy was clearly very important here, otherwise why wouldn't Ravilious have named the buyer already? Logically, an eagerness to conclude the deal in secret ought to mean the buyer *wouldn't* be at the grand prix. In all likelihood, conducting negotiations at

Silverstone might even be a challenge; the focus for MRP and its staff would have to be on the race for the next three days, wouldn't it?

Didn't that, therefore, put Silverstone *in the way* of concluding the deal?

Straker shifted in the back seat as he reanalyzed his assumption. But he couldn't dismiss it. He was inclined to think that any keenness to close the deal would be expressed by the two parties resuming their negotiation – once the temporary distraction of Silverstone was out of the way. In other words, this weekend might still be significant, but as the trigger for the negotiations to restart rather than being the time or the place to conduct them?

If so, what then?

If MRP was impatient to get the deal finalized, the Ringmaster would prioritize re-engaging with the buyer as an early priority. If this were a valid supposition, how soon – and where – would any such resumption of the negotiations take place?

Two organizations are expected to meet. One of the parties Straker knew about, the other he did not. So what?

Don't think institutions, he said to himself – think people!

Who, then, might Straker observe for clues as to the identity of the buyer?

Without doubt, the controlling mind behind MRP was Arno Ravilious – he would have to be pivotal to the sale of Motor Racing Promotions, wouldn't he? As the myths surrounding Ravilious's business style had it, no crucial decision was ever likely to be made without him. An awareness of the people Ravilious met from now on, therefore, could reveal what Straker needed. How could he gain that awareness? How could he ever get to know where Ravilious was going to be in advance, let alone get that close to him? For all Quartech's size and importance, the company had no powers of surveillance or intercept. And having been warned by Wasserman about breaching fiduciary duty and against the use of inside information, Straker knew he couldn't go after the information he wanted from professionals working for MRP either. As the car crossed Kingsway,

Straker found himself asking: *How would I ever get into Ravilious's diary?*

He sighed and then started smiling.

Straker realized, as of that moment, he *did* have an 'in' to Ravilious's future commitments. He only need think again of Silverstone, and the grand prix this weekend. Ravilious had been up there for the dinner the night before – and he would have to be there for the race. As a consequence, Straker did have a clear idea where Ravilious was likely to be, at least over the coming weekend. If the man could be spotted at Silverstone during the grand prix, there was – in theory – the possibility of being able to track Ravilious from there on.

How, though, without official powers, could Straker track him in practice without drawing Ravilious's attention to any kind of surveillance?

And how could that be done without implicating Quartech?

Just before eleven, the intercom sounded on Wittelsbach's desk. Leaning over to answer it he heard his PA announce that Amelie Hesse was asking to see him.

As Frankfurt Capital's investment officer walked in, Wittelsbach asked: 'What have you found?'

'I took the plunge with a couple of journalists who follow Formula 1,' she said.

'Without letting on who you are?'

Hesse ignored the comment. 'From what I can gather, MRP *is* still okay.'

'Just *okay?*'

'At least solvent, then – for now,' she replied. 'They acknowledge the decline in the watchability of grands prix, causing a loss of audience appeal – and therefore the drop-off in TV audience numbers – but explained this shouldn't be hitting MRP's top line ... at least for the moment. Race fees are strong and rising fast enough to compensate for any softness in trackside hospitality and advertising, while all the current TV rights were contracted a couple of years ago. On renewal, there should still be improvement as the TV audience is a long way ahead of what it was when those deals were struck. In equity valuation terms, Motor Racing Promotions' future value will have been diminished to a small degree, so the conversion value of our bond will have fallen too, but if we don't convert it and just hold the loan, we should be okay. My sources were sure that MRP is cash-flow positive; the estimates they gave me would more than cover the interest on our bond. To that extent, therefore, MRP does seem to be solvent.'

Wittelsbach appeared to be comforted. 'It doesn't sound like insolvency, then, is the reason Ravilious has taken this dramatic step to sell now?'

'No, sir. Another source – one who covers the business side of F1 and writes for the *Wall Street Journal* – did talk about something else though.'

'What's that?'

'He told me there are rumours circulating in Italy about *Dramma Sportivo TV* … that *it* might have gone down. Seventy per cent of its staff have been on strike for a number of weeks and their advertisers have been deserting them. People could be thinking, therefore, if *Dramma Sportivo* collapses, what happens to its stake in Motor Racing Promotions?'

Wittelsbach could see the validity of that interpretation: '*Dramma Sportivo* owns, what, 31 per cent?'

Amelie Hesse nodded. 'Some think Ravilious could have acted because that sizeable holding of Motor Racing Promotions could be about to change hands.'

'But even if that happens,' said Wittelsbach, 'it would be less than a third of the voting stock. How is that enough to prompt Ravilious to take such drastic action?'

SEVENTEEN

Straker looked out of the window as his car passed along Oxford Street. Thousands of tourists were shuffling through the heat.

His eyes glanced idly along the shopfronts.

Images flashed in and out of view.

Had he subliminally made a connection between the photograph of a world-famous model in one of the window displays and her frequent appearances with Ravilious at Monaco?

Whatever the trigger, Straker was suddenly thinking of the images taken of Arno Ravilious at grands prix – the countless shots of him walking up and down the grid and the pit lane.

Wherever the man went, he was surrounded by dignitaries and … celebrities and…

Of course!

And that was when Straker got it.

First Free Practice at Silverstone began later than usual, just after eleven o'clock. The circuit, though, had a strange atmosphere. Spectator numbers were even poorer than expected. Diehard motor racing fans were still happy, soaking up the sights, sounds and smells of the cars they idolized – particularly the thrill of seeing their heroes flying past in such proximity. To the vast majority of fans, though – mostly following Formula 1 on television – motor racing should be about the racing, about the raw competitiveness, about hard-fought wheel-to-wheel battles in a grand prix on Sunday. For them to be re-engaged, the pace of all the cars – one team to the other – needed to be much closer together.

Most in the stands that morning were resigned to the order on the leader board being utterly predictable. The Lambourns would be a second faster than the rest, giving that team a front row lock-out for the race, which had been the case at the last four races. Massarella would occupy the second row, P3 and P4. And the Ptarmigans, struggling this season to control heavy tyre degradation with the tighter aero-surface restrictions, were going to be P5 and P6.

Friday practice had barely been going for twenty minutes when the fans' prediction came true.

The order of the cars was exactly as expected.

The grid positions looked like they would end up being the same.

Sunday's running of the British Grand Prix was set to be a foregone conclusion … yet another procession.

Unaware of the team's schedule up at Silverstone, Straker called the boss of the Ptarmigan Formula 1 team, and caught him before the practice session had finished.

'Matt, how are you?' said Nazar, his Indian accent sounding more pronounced as he raised his voice above the scream of a high-pitched engine passing in the background.

'Am I calling at a bad time; is that the cars out on the track?'

'It is, but don't worry. We're nearly at the end of FP1. If this call means you're back with Ptarmigan, we must be in serious trouble.'

Straker chuckled. 'DQ's got me looking into the sale of Motor Racing Promotions.'

'I'm glad – the Chinese are *seriously* concerned.'

'Precisely why Mr Q wants to know who the new owner's going to be.'

'Arno might announce something up here, at the race on Sunday.'

Straker smiled at the similarity of thinking. 'That would clear things up if he does, but I am preparing a contingency plan. If nothing further *is* said, it would mean I would have to try and find out who the buyer is myself.'

'I'm afraid I can only caution you, then, to prepare for disappointment, Matt. If Arno doesn't want us to know, it won't be easy. He's a master at secrecy – a genius, one might say.'

'I have some ideas about how I might do this.'

'Like what?'

Straker explained.

Nazar inhaled and sucked his teeth. 'Are you sure that's a good idea?'

'It's worth a shot, Tahm. But to give it a go, I'm going to need some Ptarmigan-sponsored passes for Silverstone.'

'How many?'

'Ten-ish?'

'Good God … *how* many?'

Straker was beginning to feel he wasn't winning Nazar's support. 'Would any accreditations you *could* provide, though, allow the holders anywhere near Ravilious's motor home?'

'Paddock passes would, but I'd struggle to give you ten of those.'

'I'll take whatever you can manage. I'm going to get on to Bernie Callom. Karen will be in touch with you shortly to give you the names.'

'Are you sure this idea is wise?'

Straker continued to head west across London. He rang the office and was put through to the group's PR director, Bernie Callom.

'Matt, what can I do for you?'

'Are you going to be around in ten minutes?'

'I can be.'

'I'm coming to see you.'

Straker's car pulled into Cavendish Square. Circling the municipal gardens he found himself looking up. Quartech International's mirror glass-sided headquarters soared twenty-seven floors above him. On the top of the imposing structure was an array of microwave aerials and satellite dishes, there to communicate with Quartech's subsidiaries, suppliers and clients around the world. The building's presence dominated the West End: a fitting aura for the nerve centre of one of the world's largest defence contractors.

Straker's car disappeared down the ramp into the subterranean car park. Not long after, he reached the ninth floor, with the Ziebart report in his hand. He made his way into Competition Intelligence's area in the corner of the building; from his department's light and airy space he could see panoramic views out over London taking in Cavendish Square Gardens below, Regent Street and across the rooftops to the Houses of Parliament.

'Karen, we've got a new assignment.'

His quiet, highly efficient assistant drew a pad of paper towards her, ready to take notes. While he spoke, Straker poured two cups of coffee, placing one of them on Karen's desk in front of her.

As he finished the briefing, Karen declared: 'I'll get on to Tahm and start sorting out the passes you want for Silverstone straight away.'

'I'll be back the moment I've been to see Bernie.'

Up on the sixteenth floor Straker walked into the Media Department. Around the walls were images from Quartech's previous promotional campaigns, highlighting some of the group's products – aeroplanes, ships, tanks, orbital launch vehicles, satellites, Ptarmigan cars from their luxury range and, of course, the Formula 1 team. Straker made his way to the only enclosed office at the far end of the room. In an art deco style, 'Bernie Callom, Director' was frosted into the glass of his door. Straker knocked and went in.

Callom, at his desk, stood to greet Straker warmly. Quartech International's PR director was mid-fifties, five feet six with a closely shaved head; wearing pastel-coloured clothes, he had a pair of amethyst-coloured glasses pushed up onto his forehead. There was a hard but vulnerable look to him.

Straker explained what he was planning to do. 'While we're observing Ravilious, I don't want our watchers to be conspicuous.'

It was now Callom's turn to sound unconvinced. 'What if these guys get spotted? The people you want to use, Matt, are not spies. They won't know what to do. They could easily give you away.'

'They won't give anything away. I'm not asking them to be spies. They already know what to do.'

'But they're photographers.'

'Precisely – and they'll be up there *as* photographers – all they've got to do is take photographs. Silverstone will be awash with photographers. It'll be the perfect cover. They'll completely blend in.'

'What about recognition of the people … they won't be able to identify anyone Arno's likely to talk to?'

'That's the beauty of this idea,' said Straker, '*they* won't need to. All they've got to do is to take digital photographs of everyone Ravilious meets, then upload their pictures to a Dropbox. It'll be up to me, with help from others, to identify any of the people they photograph.'

'And you want them to follow Ravilious, *after* Silverstone?'

'Particularly then – as that's when I'm hoping he'll lead us to his buyer.'

'And what about their "cover" at that stage? How do they not give themselves away when they're out in Civvy Street? They'll stick out like sore thumbs. I say again, Matt … these people are *not* spies.'

Straker smiled. 'Bernie, the sale of Motor Racing Promotions is the biggest news story going. Every media outlet will be shadowing Arno Ravilious around the clock. More to the point, he gets this kind of attention all the time … it's an occupational hazard. Ravilious wouldn't think anything of being trailed by paps.'

EIGHTEEN

Straker returned to his office in Competition Intelligence.

'Bernie's going to recruit a number of freelance photographers, who'll need to be accredited up at Silverstone. He's going to send you some names.'

'Will you be going too?' Karen asked. 'Do you want me to add you to the list for passes?'

'I'll go up there as soon as we've arranged the first batch of photographers at the circuit.'

Straker retrieved his laptop from a drawer in his desk, picked up the Ziebart report on Formula 1, and took both into the quiet room over by the plate-glass windows. He wanted to put some detail on his plan.

Before starting, he took a quick flick through Wasserman's document. There was a huge section at the front describing the background and history of MRP. Straker dipped in for a paragraph here and there and was immediately fascinated, but fought himself from being drawn in; going through any of that would have to wait until another time. Straker's priority was to get an idea of the overall structure and extent of Motor Racing Promotions. How big was it? How many divisions did it have? How dispersed was it? How many employees were involved?

He found a series of charts indicating some of MRP's complexity. One thing became obvious. Ravilious's name cropped up in each division of the business. He was clearly the man in charge. Straker was more convinced than ever his initial hunch was valid: Ravilious had to be the person to focus on for this investigation.

What Straker needed now was a sure way of 'acquiring' the man, after which he would then attempt to shadow him.

He rang Nazar again at Silverstone: 'Where's Ravilious likely to be while he's at the grand prix?'

'You're not still thinking about putting him under surveillance?'

'I am, Tahm. You, the team, Formula 1 are not coming up with any useful information, so I'm going to have to try and find it out for myself.'

Straker thought he heard Nazar sigh. 'He's most likely to base himself in his motor home.'

'Thank you, and do you know where, at Silverstone, he normally eats?'

'In the MRP facility, within the paddock.'

'How often does he walk around – at a circuit like that?'

'Not much. He might go into the MRP hospitality suite in the Wing – he's seen on the balcony up there from time to time. He'd certainly be in the pit lane during Qualifying, and then on the grid before the race on Sunday.'

Straker jotted some notes. 'And where does he normally sleep?'

'No idea, for sure, I'm afraid. The motor home is pretty much self-contained. He's occasionally seen in a nearby hotel, Whittlebury Hall, but he's not there as a matter of course.'

'Thank you, Tahm. One more question? How does he get in and out of the circuit? How does that work?'

'He's got a reserved access road through the back of the industrial estate. There's a tunnel under the track, which gets him into the paddock.'

'Very helpful, thank you. You wouldn't have a map with these places marked out, by any chance?'

Count Wittelsbach was no less concerned. At the time of setting up the loan to Motor Racing Promotions, Frankfurt Capital declared – to their auditors and regulators – that they had an exposure of €1.8 billion to Formula 1 via MRP. On its own, that wouldn't have been of too much consequence, given the overall size of Frankfurt Capital's loan book. But since then, other parts of Wittelsbach's bank had become troubled.

Frankfurt Capital had a huge exposure to Greece: the Greek

government was fast approaching its third moratorium on debt interest in a year, pushing Frankfurt's repayment schedule back by possibly a decade.

Sector-wise, the bank had taken a bullish view on energy prices, building a significant exposure to the oil sector – lending to exploration and upstream service companies, the likes of drill bits, pumps, rigs and oilfield equipment. Except those had all been extended before President Obama made America's peace with Iran. His diplomacy partly ended the 40-year embargo, allowing Iran to sell oil to the world once more. Within a few weeks, the country was pumping 2.6 million barrels a day, which rapidly softened the price of crude. The profitability of upstream oil companies collapsed: a number of Frankfurt Capital's borrowers were now in danger of defaulting.

With its injudicious lending to Greece and the oil sector, the quality of Wittelsbach's loan book was deteriorating rapidly.

'Remind me of our next capital adequacy declaration to BaFin?' he asked his two senior executives.

Frankfurt's legal counsel, Markus Lüneburg, replied: 'At the end of next quarter.'

'September, yes,' Amelie Hesse confirmed.

'Let's all hope, then,' said Wittelsbach, 'at the point of Ravilious's sale of MRP, we can invoke our drag and tag rights – and invite the acquirer to buy us out at the same time.'

'How do we indicate our interest in being bought out,' replied Lüneburg, 'when Ravilious won't talk to us – and when we've no idea who's buying?'

Straker was looking at a map of Silverstone sent to him by Nazar. He was pleased. It had some useful pointers.

Straker's next consideration was how to use this to 'acquire' Ravilious while he was there. He contemplated the locations where he might deploy his photographers. He reckoned on several key places: the MRP motor home, the paddock, the pit lane, the MRP balcony in the Wing and, most importantly, Ravilious's VVIP exit from the circuit. Covering the latter would have to offer him the best indication that the Ringmaster was about to leave the complex.

But what would happen when Ravilious *did* leave the racetrack? How could Straker have any comfort in keeping up with him once he was away from there? His immediate thought was his photographers should be mobile. Ringing Bernie Callom, he asked: 'Do freelancers come with their own transport?'

'Paparazzi do; some, on motorcycles – but not all.'

'What if owning a motorcycle is a requirement for the photographers you're hiring?'

'We can do that, sure – but it'll reduce your pool of recruits.'

'I don't think that can be helped.'

Straker went back to mulling the challenge of trailing Ravilious on the open road. He soon had serious doubts. Even on motorbikes, would his proposed followers be able to keep track of Ravilious's car? Speed and traffic could easily baulk them. There was a very real chance his photographers would end up 'losing' Ravilious. And, then, what if his photographer/watchers were spotted as they tried to keep up? What if they were then discovered to have been commissioned by Quartech? How embarrassing would that be?

Straker found his mind returning to one of the pages in the Ziebart report: it identified the man's homes – in Belgravia and Oxfordshire. If the photographers *did* lose the man, Ravilious was surely going to head for one house or other. That assumption offered Straker some comfort that he should be able to 're-acquire' his quarry at one of those other locations. But that could be of scant consolation: who might Ravilious meet during any time he might be 'lost'. Such blind spots would render this entire exercise ineffectual.

Straker saw the scenario of the open road as a huge challenge.

He had to come up with something else.

But what?

With no answers coming to him, Straker pushed on with other possibilities of shadowing Ravilious.

He had to believe this renowned workaholic would be back at work in one of the offices within Motor Racing Promotions before long.

In which case, where were those offices?

Straker reverted to the Ziebart report.

For the second section of his plan, Straker compiled a list of all MRP's places of business. The main centre was in central London, being the company's headquarters in Berkeley Square. How might Straker conduct any form of surveillance in such a built-up area? Invented 'covers', such as posing outside as road maintenance engineers or water board workers, was a possibility, but he was far from comfortable. Such guises could be unconvincing and, worse, had a high chance of being uncovered.

He had to think again.

In view of the media explosion around this story, how conspicuous would a photographer be in central London loitering outside MRP's headquarters? Who, at the moment, would question a paparazzo hovering around Ravilious?

Straker then discovered that most of the remaining MRP offices were in non-metropolitan locations; masquerading his photographer/watchers as paparazzi outside them could be incongruous. But as he plotted the last of the Motor Racing Promotions office locations, he found something surprising.

There was an unexpected concentration ... somewhere completely different. The bulk of Motor Racing Promotions' companies were not where he might have thought they'd be at all.

They seemed to be clumped together around a small airfield in Kent.

NINETEEN

Amelie Hesse's unease about this call was written across her face.

Hanfried Wittelsbach tried to comfort his chief investment officer with a smile as they waited for the man to ring back.

The phone finally sounded on his desk.

Answering the call, Wittelsbach switched it to loudspeaker. Amelie Hesse and Markus Lüneburg were standing in front of him, to hear what the caller had to say.

'This is Wittelsbach.'

The caller spoke: 'I already told your colleague. I represent an organization that is ready to buy your loan to Motor Racing Promotions.'

Hesse nodded, as if to confirm the voice was familiar.

'I'm sorry, and you are?'

'Prepared to pay you 750 million euros in cash.'

Wittelsbach replied: 'That's not remotely close to the current valuation. In any case, who are you, please? And which organization do you represent?'

The line was quiet.

Wittelsbach broke the silence. 'I will not contemplate any transaction further, without knowing your identity.'

There was still no response.

The voice came back flatly: 'You don't have long to consider this offer. As I told your servant ... we are going to send you a message ... to help you decide...'

Wittelsbach's eyes narrowed. 'What kind of message?'

But the line was already dead.

The banker clicked the button to end the call and looked up at his two senior directors. Whatever his thoughts on the tone and implication of the call, they were fully reflected on Hesse's face.

Realizing the situation needed leadership, Wittelsbach stated: 'I've had it with Ravilious and his blasted company. He's got to get us out of this mess, and,' he said, gesticulating dismissively at the loudspeaker, 'to keep us away from people like that. He's not had the courtesy to speak to us, so it's time we forced him.

'Markus,' he said to his head of legal counsel, 'get on to Jago-Meyerson in London and instruct them to launch an injunction against Ravilious's sale of MRP … immediately.'

As Straker wrote up the sections of his surveillance plan, something gnawed at his confidence. Was he at risk of putting all his chips on Ravilious and the MRP end of the deal? Should he not be trying to identify the person on the other side, the buyer? When, though, might they appear, and from where? How would he recognize them if they did?

Straker sat back in his chair as these questions ricocheted around his head.

Looking out of the window, he realized what a scorching summer's day he was missing. Below him in Cavendish Square Gardens, a mass of carefree people had collected and were sprawled out on the grass. Most had shed some of their brightly coloured clothes and were soaking up the sun as they escaped their nearby offices, shops and consulting rooms.

Straker forced himself to refocus.

If the two sides in the MRP deal were still just talking, they could meet anywhere. With the nature of Formula 1, MRP and, presumably the buyer – given the size they would have to be financially to fund the deal – they were all likely to be global entities. Ravilious could easily fly off and negotiate in another country. If that happened, Straker would have no chance of keeping any track of him.

But Ravilious had already announced the deal. The two sides must, therefore, have got beyond the talking stage. Wasserman had mentioned the practice of due diligence. If the deal had progressed that far, might the buyer now want access to MRP's books? Having no idea how this process worked, Straker picked up the phone to the investment banker.

'You remembered correctly,' confirmed Wasserman. 'Due diligence does give the buyer the right to study everything in the target company.'

'And where, physically, would that be done?'

'For convenience, and to ensure every document and record is available for the buyer's inspection, it can only be done properly in the offices and buildings of the company being sold.'

'And, presumably, that means *any* of MRP's businesses could be visited?'

'Very much so. It's not uncommon for those inspectors to be shepherded by the vendor's professionals.'

'So your point about observing the lawyers, accountants, and other agencies could be relevant during this due diligence phase?'

'I'd say *particularly* then,' said the banker. 'There might even be an advantage in doing so...'

'Why's that?'

'Because third-party professionals acting for Motor Racing Promotions, or the buyer for that matter, might not be so guarded as Ravilious. They'd be conscious of professional confidentiality, of course – but they're unlikely to be as secrecy-obsessed as he is. I mean, I would not expect them to adopt "cloak and dagger", to use your expression; I would not expect them to attempt to conceal their movements into and out of the MRP offices, or shield who they met. Inadvertently, the professional advisers are actually more likely to be the ones to give something away.'

'Yes, yes.'

'That report I gave you shows all the professional agencies that MRP uses. If any of them showed up at an MRP office accompanied by strangers, it would not be impossible for those strangers to be acting for the buyer.'

'And so could, theoretically, be traced back?'

'Exactly.'

'I'll work them into my plan.'

'Anything else?'

Straker's mind went back to thoughts about the buyer. 'This will be a ridiculous question, as I'm sure there's no standard answer…'

'Try me.'

'*If* the deal is not yet finalized, and they're still working through the takeover timeline – doing this due diligence stuff – at what point would a buyer personally, him or herself, enter the fray?'

'You're right, I'm afraid; there is no standard. There might be a couple of triggers: one would be if a deal-braker point comes up, and that prompts an emergency summit to thrash out any difficulties. The second, more likely occasion, would be right at the end, when the key issues have pretty much been haggled over.'

'Neither of those being predictable from a timing point of view, I take it?'

'Afraid not.'

'And if they did get together to discuss any due diligence issues, would they do that at an MRP office?'

'Again, there's no hard and fast rule about that either. If conclusions needed to be clarified or refuted, access to documents could still be useful – and that would have to be easier if they are nearby. Why are you focusing on this, in particular?'

'I'm trying to understand the likelihood of the buyer coming here to MRP and our being able to spot them.'

'The buyer could be British, of course, in which case the first time you might get wind of him would be when he met Ravilious somewhere. If the buyer is based abroad, you couldn't hope to spot him before his or her rendezvous with Ravilious. Only certain government departments would have the legal right and clout to watch every airport, railway station and sea port.'

Straker exhaled.

'And even then,' Wasserman went on, 'if the buyer is high-profile, this could be made all the harder for you.'

'Why so?'

'Because if the buyer *is* well-known, there'd be a high chance of them being spotted and identified at one of the major commercial airports, even accidentally. With the publicity surrounding this deal, Ravilious could well think an arrival of that sort risked blowing the deal's cover.'

'He might want to get the buyer here under the radar, you mean?'

'Pretty much. And if he *does* come into Britain, I'd think he's more likely to come in on a private jet to a regional airfield. Don't forget: money will be no object to these people. If Arno Ravilious doesn't want something known, he has the budget and determination to keep it secret.'

TWENTY

Straker ended his conversation with Wasserman feeling mostly sunk. It looked all but impossible to identify the buyer before they physically appeared near Ravilious or one of his companies. Wasserman's suggestion of shadowing the professional agencies, though, offered him some consolation.

Returning to the Ziebart report, Straker looked up the section devoted to Professional Advisers. All the external specialist firms were listed with their contact details. Sampling some of their websites, he found the majority of them had personal biographies and photographs of their key personnel, which might make recognizing them easier. The more Straker thought about this, the more he liked the idea of spreading his net wider.

He set about making notes for this as a third section of his plan.

As it took shape, he gave some thought to timings. When should his wider surveillance of professional agencies be up and running? Soon, obviously. But how soon? It was Friday morning now: were any of these professionals likely to be active over the weekend? With Ravilious driving everything with his usual zeal, Straker felt the answer to that was very probably: yes.

The German bank's patience was running out. Ravilious had still not returned any attempt to communicate with them. Frankfurt Capital was looking into serving an injunction: hoping that, by seeking to block Arno Ravilious's sale of Motor Racing Promotions, it would force him to talk to them.

Following the earlier meeting with Wittelsbach and Hesse, and the unnerving call from the anonymous buyer, Markus Lüneburg had been on the phone to the litigation partner of Jago-Meyerson, Frankfurt Capital's solicitors in London.

A barrister had been instructed.

Frankfurt Capital's legal counsel and Amelie Hesse, the bank's chief investment officer, were back in Wittelsbach's office.

'Here's a draft of our application,' said Lüneburg. 'The London silk has prepared a claim for Unfair Prejudice under Section 994 of the United Kingdom's Companies Act 2006.'

'How strong are these grounds for making an application?' Wittelsbach asked.

Lüneburg nodded. 'I double-checked. The barrister is content that the Solitary Share you negotiated is enough to grant us full rights to make the application.'

Wittelsbach nodded. 'And how compelling an argument for an injunction is this?'

'We've cited our rights under the stipulations of the Side Letter, specifically the clause obliging prior notification of any activity materially affecting the value of Motor Racing Promotions; we've also declared Ravilious to be in breach of numerous clauses relating to the treatment of minority shareholders.'

'Does our advocate think this would be enough to block Ravilious before he signs any deal to sell MRP?'

'He's really not sure,' replied Lüneburg. 'Our filing at this stage, before a deal has been presented to us – before the buyer is known – before we know what price the deal puts on MRP – can't carry much of a punch.'

'Because, so far,' Hesse offered, 'Ravilious hasn't actually done anything specific, he's only announced an intention.'

Wittelsbach shook his head before saying: 'I don't care. *File* it. The act of launching an injunction will be part of the message we want to send him. Make sure you motivate the PR department: they're to blitz every media outlet with news of this. Given the media response to the Motor Racing Promotions story so far, it ought to attract significant coverage. Hopefully, that on its own will be loud enough to prompt Ravilious to respond.'

Wittelsbach noticed his chief investment officer was pulling a face.

'What's wrong, Amelie?'

'I'm concerned, Hanfried – not about giving Ravilious cause for reflection, but about the brand damage this could do to MRP – and the value of our loan?'

Wittelsbach's expression was confident but not stern. 'We know we're already looking at a sizeable hit to our 1.8 billion euro holding,' he said. 'Ravilious must engage with us. And we've got to deal with the odious individual who called us this morning, haven't we? If Ravilious doesn't protect us, or goes and sells to the wrong person, we'll end up realizing even less. I share your concern, I do – but if Ravilious won't respond to any of our communications, we have no way of reassuring ourselves about Motor Racing Promotions in any other grown-up way. We have to resort to some form of leverage.'

Wittelsbach, turning to his legal counsel, said to Lüneburg: 'Go ahead and serve it, Markus. Let's give Ravilious some cause for thought…'

TWENTY-ONE

Straker finished the three prongs of his surveillance plan. These now involved watching Ravilious, 'acquiring' him up at Silverstone and watching his houses; the second involved watching Motor Racing Promotions' various offices in London and Kent; and the third prong focused on looking out for the appearance of any personnel from MRP's professional agencies. Using Google Street View, he scoped out the lie of the land around each location and estimated how many photographers he would need to create each observation screen. It was going to take a sizeable number.

Straker rang Bernie Callom in the PR Department, to check the recruitment process for his Silverstone contingent. Having added the condition of owning a motorbike, Callom had lost a number of potential recruits. Another agency, though, had been able to source substitutes without delay.

'Even so, I'm struggling to get the right number of passes up at Silverstone, Matt.'

Straker rang the Ptarmigan team boss at the circuit.

'Karen's been feeding me the new names,' said the Indian voice. 'This is too much. I haven't got anywhere near this number of spare passes.'

'Has Ptarmigan got any connections we could tap up? Any suppliers? A hospitality company?'

Nazar didn't sound particularly motivated. 'I'll see what I can do.'

Straker went on to explain his proposed surveillance approach; he expected another push back from the team boss.

'You're going to cover *all* those places – his houses, offices *and* look out for people from his professional agencies?' asked Nazar.

'I might have to cut some of them back, depending on the wider recruitment process. One of the outliers I wanted to talk to you about, though, was the cluster of MRP offices at an airfield in Kent.'

'Biggin Hill, you mean?'

'You know about that?'

'Arno's got a number of businesses down there. Biggin Hill, to all intents and purposes, is his operational hub. Motor Racing Promotions is pretty well administered from that airfield, a lot of which is air-freight related.'

'Like what?'

'MRP's obligations under the Concorde Agreement.'

'Meaning?'

'To the flyaway races, he ships all the teams' equipment, free of charge.'

'Wow. And flies all that from Biggin Hill?'

'Oh, no, he's got a fleet of 747s to do that – and they'd be far too big for that airport; but all the admin for it is handled down there. Also, Biggin Hill is where Ravilious bases Motor Racing TV Production, including the studio, editing facilities and depot. All his TV production equipment has to be flown to each race, and he *does* fly that out from there. Biggin Hill's also where he stations his private jets.'

'Tahm…' said Straker, as a thought came to him, 'do you know the kind of air traffic Biggin Hill normally takes?'

'No, but it's quite small. I don't think it handles scheduled airline services – it's used more by small-aircraft charter companies. Ptarmigan have often flown out of there. Most users would probably be private and corporate jets. Quite apart from any motor racing connection, of course, it's probably best known as the most convenient way for the über rich to get into and out of London.'

'So there aren't likely to be any crowds in the airport buildings?'

'Not the general public, no – at least not like a commercial airport.'

'And press?'

'At a private airfield? – I wouldn't think so – I'd imagine they could only be there by invitation.'

Straker's face broke into a broad smile. 'You won't be able to answer this, but my brain's just gone off on one … what if we thought Arno might try and get someone into the UK, under the radar so to speak. Would it be a stupid idea to think he might do it through Biggin Hill?'

'I'm not sure that would be a stupid idea at all. It *is* the airfield Ravilious would know best, the one that would know *him* best. Who knows what favours he might be able to pull in from the operator down there?'

Straker had had little to go on at the start of this investigation, but was now feeling a rush. Boosting his confidence was the fact that the Ptarmigan team boss had even sounded a little less sceptical.

Straker started to think about the brief he would give his photographer/watchers. What he told them – how he tasked them – the way he motivated them to contribute to his plan – would be crucial.

He set about compiling the presentation he would give members of his screen around Arno Ravilious at Silverstone, Ravilious's Oxfordshire house and MRP's headquarters in Berkeley Square. He drafted the core of it and then used it as the basis of a further brief for those watching out for MRP's accountants, solicitors and investment bank.

As he finished the last set of slides, Straker was beginning to feel that each of his target venues could be observed reasonably well.

There was, though, one element of his planning which still fell weak: the viability of shadowing the Ringmaster when he left the grand prix or the circuit and was out on the open road. How realistic was it to rely on motorcyclists to stay in visual contact, and to do so without alerting Ravilious to the surveillance he was under?

Standing up and walking to the plate-glass window of the quiet room for a leg stretch, Straker's attention was caught. He found himself looking up. An airliner was flying east over London, starting to bank to starboard – heading south over the skyscrapers of the City – setting itself up to land at Heathrow. In another part of the sky a police helicopter was hovering, pinpoint still, just to the north of the 50-year-old-but-still-futuristic-looking BT tower.

Straker froze before spinning round.

He dived back to the table and picked up his phone.

A minute later he was talking to Sam Bailey, a contact of his in Quartech's Aerospace Division.

TWENTY-TWO

Just before lunchtime on the Friday, Arno Ravilious broke cover for the first time since his shock announcement at the dinner in Blenheim Palace the night before. He had returned to the paddock immediately afterwards, and locked himself away in his superyacht-like motor home.

Seconds after leaving his sanctuary he regretted his decision.

The Ringmaster was descended upon by TV presenters, TV cameras, photographers, journalists and accredited visitors. Completely surrounded. People were baying at him, yelling over the top of each other.

'Who are you selling to, Arno?'

'Why are you selling now?'

'Who's going to take over from you?'

'Why didn't you involve the teams in the decision?'

Arno Ravilious said nothing.

It drove the media into a frenzy.

Saying nothing seemed to spark more media noise than if he had said anything at all.

Markus Lüneburg reviewed the documents from Frankfurt Capital's barrister in London one last time. These now included the petition for the Unfair Prejudice claim, the application notice for the injunction and an accompanying witness statement; the bundle also included copies of the Side Letter signed with Motor Racing Promotions Limited and the MRP shareholders' agreement. All these items looked to be in good shape. The legal papers were sent back to the Queen's Counsel in London. Via the covering email, Lüneburg instructed their solicitors to file them immediately with the Chancery Division of the High Court.

Lüneburg also reviewed the press release prepared by Frankfurt's PR director. He instructed the 14th floor to dispatch it as soon as word came through from London that the injunction had been filed.

Straker reviewed what he was doing. He was beginning to feel that through mounting this operation, he would have instituted some sort of attempt at gathering intelligence.

Except Biggin Hill was needling him.

It was clearly a major location for MRP.

Straker ended up saying to himself: 'What the hell,' and punted half an hour of his time googling the airport. Looking at the place from Ravilious's perspective, he could see, even with a superficial search online, how the airport would suit the Ringmaster's purposes almost perfectly. It was out of the way. And private. Straker even learned that MRP had Fixed-Base Operator – FBO – status there, meaning Ravilious's connection with the place was even closer than he thought.

Straker read a handful of articles, printed off several photographs and accumulated sheets of a large-scale map. He wanted a fuller understanding of the airfield and its layout. An airport, even a small one, could extend over a considerable area. He was sure that any opportunity at Biggin Hill would depend on how the operation was executed on the ground. To be surer of all this, Straker's mind chimed with a military favourite: *'Time spent in reconnaissance is seldom wasted.'*

Straker called Bernie Callom: 'How are we doing with recruiting the photographers for Silverstone?'

'All done,' said the PR director. 'Tahm's processing their passes as we speak.'

'That's great news. How many have we got up there now?'

'Seven snappers with motorbikes. What time do you want them on site, and who's going to brief them?'

'Let's go for five o'clock this evening – and I'll do it. I need to give them an easy meeting point at the circuit, somewhere discreet. I don't think all of them will have paddock passes, otherwise we could do it in the Ptarmigan motor home.'

'I'll chat it through with Tahm.'

'I've got some more requests for you.'

'Not *more* photographic spies?'

'I want to deploy photographer/watchers around Ravilious's houses – in London and his place in the country – as well as MRP's key offices.'

'Bloody hell. How many people will you need?'

'Fifteen on duty at any one time, split between the venues – three shifts per day.'

'The freelance press community will think Christmas has come early. When do you want them all up and running?'

'As soon as possible.'

'I'll get on to the agencies … we're likely to clean them out.'

'No doubt,' replied Straker. 'This operation has strategic significance. Ptarmigan's 750 million-dollar sponsorship is at stake, not to mention our access to China's military institutions – so pretty much hang the expense. Given the limited time and limited ethical affordances, this is the best approach I can come up with.'

Callom grunted his acquiescence.

'But that's not all, Bernie.'

'Oh, no … what else?'

'I want a similar reconnaissance screen around Biggin Hill airfield in Kent.'

'Good God … Why?'

Straker explained.

'Wow, and when do you want that to start?'

'As soon as…'

'…as possible … how many bodies do you want down there?'

'I don't know yet, but let's plan for four at any one time, with three shifts per day. I'm about to go down and take a look around for myself. If you can find a couple of photographers quickly, I'll call you with a suitable rendezvous while I'm still down near Biggin Hill itself.'

TWENTY-THREE

Straker asked Karen to join him in the quiet room. He ran through the PowerPoint slides he'd put together on his laptop. It served the purpose of briefing her fully on the assignment, as well as giving him the opportunity to stress test his presentation.

She looked up afterwards and smiled. 'Very sneaky.'

Straker asked her to send a copy up to the Ptarmigan motor home at Silverstone. 'Bernie will be calling you shortly,' he added. 'He's just started recruiting the photographers for London and Kent. I need you to set up a Dropbox. All the pictures the photographers take, at any of the venues, are to be uploaded to it as soon as possible. I will carry this laptop with me and be able to access them all. I'll then forward pictures received to various people on an "identification committee".'

'And who will that be?'

'Tahm Nazar at Ptarmigan, to cover F1 personnel; Benedict Wasserman at Ziebart Blauman, to spot any business-related people; Bernie Callom in PR; Sam Bailey at Quartech Aerospace; and Mr Quartano, for anyone he might know.'

'Okay.'

'Right now, I'm going down to Biggin Hill. I'll go via Putney, pack some things, pick up my car, and drive straight there. After that, I'll head for Silverstone. Can you keep me up to date on progress?'

'I'll liaise with Bernie and let you know if we have any problems we can't solve.'

The drive through South London gave Straker the chance to think. After his brief web research of Biggin Hill airport, his priority was to reconnoitre its VIP terminal. It had been a surprise to see an airport that small offer such stylish facilities; the pictures on the operating company's website – of the sumptuous lounge – gave him further comfort this hunch might not be so ridiculous after all.

Heading out through the suburbs of London, Straker revelled in the car in such weather: even in the inevitable congestion, it seemed there could be no better day to enjoy the luxury of his open-top Morgan Roadster in Connaught Green ... bonnet louvres ... wire wheels ... leather seats. Keeping him calm was a CD recording of the great Smokey Joe Picker playing saxophone live in New Orleans in 1967.

Reaching the outer edge of London, the landscape became more sparsely populated. Stretches of open fields and woodland took over from the Victorian and Edwardian pebble-dashed villas. Then, as he approached the village of Leaves Green, he heard an incongruous noise.

The sound of a jet aircraft.

It was rising above the trees from left to right in front of him: a gleaming white Gulfstream G650 climbed steeply into the sky.

Straker was obviously getting close.

Turning right onto the A233, he was soon being borne round to the left, hugging the southern perimeter of the airport. He tried to look through the wire mesh fence to get a sense of the layout. Straker could see a smattering of buildings and several aircraft parked out on various aprons; then, across that end of the runway, he spotted a conspicuously different building. It had to be the one he was looking for.

Straker turned left into Churchill Way and trundled along the feeder road towards his goal. Closing in, he turned right directly opposite it, into Wireless Road. Swinging the car round, and heading back towards the VIP terminal, he pulled over to the kerbside and stopped. Straker took in the topography around him. Verges ran down either side of the road; trees were frequent and full leaved; there were industrial unit-type buildings with small patches of car parking in between.

Walking forwards, Straker soon had a clear view of the VIP terminal and the small area in the front of it in which cars were dropping off and picking up their passengers. He was able to get within 75 yards; with a bit of guile, a photographer could easily find a spot along this road from where to get clear enough photographs of anyone using the facility.

Straker returned to his car and rejoined the A233, this time turning left – and kept turning left towards Berry's Green, into Luxted Road – heading for Single Street. Sunshine between the trees dappled the road as he wound his way up the hill. Straker passed the house identified as Charles Darwin's, before turning left into West Hill. Driving through this countryside on a summer's day in an open-top car, he reckoned, was about as good as England could get. Straker ran beside a beautifully kept fairway of the West Kent Golf Club. Passing the clubhouse, he pushed on up the hill, as the ever-narrowing lane took him higher and deeper into the woods.

Finally he reached the very end of the road.

A metal gate and grille barred the way across it, declaring: 'Emergency Exit.'

Pulling up close, Straker could see an expanse of sky beyond. He had reached the perimeter of the airfield – on the far side of Biggin Hill.

Straker climbed out and walked up to the gate. He found, as he had seen on the web, a footpath running to either side along the outside of this fence. Looking all around him – and listening out for a moment – Straker confirmed he was alone.

Turning left, he ducked in under some low-hanging branches to follow the footpath along the outside of the airfield.

Two hundred yards on he found what he was looking for. In behind the foliage of the treeline, Straker could see through a gap and be granted, from its slightly raised ground, a clear side-on view of the Biggin Hill runway. From the same concealed spot, he could see through the haze – some way down to his left – the other side of the VIP terminal. A number of private and corporate jets were parked up on the apron. Straker was feeling that this vantage point might just about offer him a crack at monitoring the place.

Circling the rest of the airport anticlockwise, Straker completed his reconnaissance, before pulling into a pub car park in Leaves Green. As he stopped he saw Karen had emailed him details of the Dropbox and its password.

Straker rang Bernie Callom in Cavendish Square. The PR man was keen to update him:

'The photographers destined for Silverstone have had their accreditation arranged. I've also recruited fifteen more for your other venues. Two are already on their way to watch MRP's headquarters in Berkeley Square, and another two will shortly be outside Ravilious's house in Belgravia.'

'Great work, Bernie.'

'That's not all. Two freelance photographers, from nearby in Sussex, are on their way to you in Biggin Hill.'

'How soon do you think they'll be here?'

'Being freelancers, they're used to rapid deployment. I spoke to the second of them about 45 minutes ago; they should be there any minute?'

'Can you have them meet me at the Kings Arms?'

Within ten minutes two men had driven into the pub car park in separate cars. One was in his fifties, balding and bearded; the other was mid-to-late thirties and wearing a leather jacket. Straker introduced himself and, laying a map of the airfield over the bonnet of his car, explained the task he was setting them.

'I want you,' he said to the beard, 'to find yourself a position to observe the entrance to the VIP terminal, over here. I want photographs of anyone coming out of that building.

'And I'd like you,' said Straker, turning to the leather jacket, 'to be sited up here,' as he pointed to part of a large-scale map. 'I'll take you up there to show you where. From the location I've found, you'll be able to see the length of the Biggin Hill runway, side on. I want photographs of every plane that lands. Specifically, I want records of their registration numbers, shown on the fuselage – the body of a plane – and tail fin. I've noticed that when executive jets land, they tend to pull up close to the VIP terminal. If you've got a good enough lens, I'd like shots of any passengers as they disembark.'

To both men he said: 'I want all your photographs uploaded here,' and, asking them to email him, he replied by forwarding Karen's login details and password for the Dropbox.

The two hacks nodded.

'You'll be relieved in four hours. Please liaise with my assistant, whose number's also on there. Karen'll handle whatever you need.'

Half an hour later, Straker had driven his two photographers round Biggin Hill airport and positioned them in his selected vantage points.

As he left the one up in the woods, Bernie Callom rang. Seven photographers were confirmed to be on their way to meet Straker up at Silverstone for five o'clock that afternoon.

TWENTY-FOUR

Driving up the M40, even with the Morgan's top still down, Straker could hear a succession of beeps coming from his phone resting on the passenger seat. In a traffic hold-up, before the junction with the A34, he chanced a quick look. He was encouraged. 'Returns' were already coming in from his photographer/watchers. He grabbed his iPad from the passenger footwell, fired it up and accessed the Dropbox to see the first images that had come through. One sequence of shots had been taken in Berkeley Square. An expensive Mercedes could be seen pulling up outside Motor Racing Promotions' headquarters. Three suited men had exited the car and walked into the building. Straker's man on the ground had found himself an excellent position from which to shoot people coming and going.

Straker even saw some photographs from Biggin Hill. Two executive jets had landed. From up in the woods, the leather jacket had caught the registration numbers on their tail fins perfectly; and, with a particularly long lens, had shot clear pictures of a Bombardier 6000 and its passengers disembarking as they descended the steps onto the apron. The photographer Straker had positioned in the road on the *other* side of the VIP terminal had then photographed the same group of passengers as they left the building, picked up by cars there to meet them. Straker's dovetailed surveillance screen seemed to be working.

Before he could do anything with these pictures, the traffic on the M40 started moving again. Calling hands-free, Straker spoke to Karen in Cavendish Square.

'I saw the first photographs have been uploaded,' she said.

'Can we send the shots from Berkeley Square to Benedict Wasserman and Mr Quartano? And the ones showing the arrivals at Biggin Hill to both of them and Tahm Nazar? Could you send the shots showing the aircraft registration numbers to Sam Bailey at Quartech Aerospace, and ask him to run them through a CAA-related or industry database? Let's see if we can make any sort of connection between the people in those pictures and Formula 1 or the City.'

As Straker approached one of the entrances to the Silverstone complex, his phone rang.

Urgently, Bernie Callom asked: 'Have you heard the latest news?'

'No, what's happened?'

'An injunction's been taken out against Motor Racing Promotions.'

'Wow, for what?'

'It looks like an attempt to block the sale.'

'Do you know who's filed it?'

'A company called Frankfurt Capital?'

'Never heard of it – does that mean anything to you?'

'Afraid not.'

'How did you hear about this?'

'It's all over Twitter – and has just hit the E-edition of the *Evening Standard*.'

Streams of people were leaving the circuit, the day's track events having ended. Only when Straker could extricate himself from the crowd was he prepared to call Benedict Wasserman.

'I've just heard,' said the investment banker.

'Who are Frankfurt Capital?'

'They're discussed in our report: they're a German bank with a substantial loan out to Motor Racing Promotions.'

'What can you deduce from their filing an injunction?'

'Something about the chaos inside MRP. Resorting to legal action suggests there's not much agreement between the people involved. Relations must have broken down. I'm trying to find out more.'

'Good – and, Benedict, my assistant will have sent you an email about a Dropbox we've established. We're going to be uploading a series of photographs. I'd like help in trying to identify anyone relevant in them.'

'I'll keep everything under close review.'

Straker collected his pass and made it through to the paddock. He walked down one of the avenues between the vast and hyper-expensive motor homes, each dressed in the livery of its team. They gleamed in the sunshine, light glinting off their metallic paint and smoked-glass windows. Ptarmigan's was resplendent in its familiar turquoise.

Straker keyed in the entry code and the door hissed open. He climbed the steps into the Ptarmigan Formula 1 team's mini-control room. Inside, it was quite dazzling. All the surfaces were polished rosewood. There was an abundance of chrome, while all the leather-work – the seats, the cushions on the banquette running the length of the left-hand side – were turquoise with navy blue piping. Down the right-hand side a bank of HD screens arched over a row of computer workstations. Eight places were visible, although only three were occupied at that moment. The impact of this space never failed to impress him.

Tahm Nazar was standing in the middle of the mobile F1 command centre. The Ptarmigan team boss was talking to a group of seven assorted individuals, five men and two women, all looking slightly out of place in the sleekness of the motor home.

'Ah, Matt,' said Nazar, shaking hands. 'I've been welcoming our guests. Your briefing material's been loaded, which you can show on the screen at the end of the room. The radios you wanted are over there,' he said pointing at a portable carrying rack on the floor. 'I'll leave you to it?'

Nazar seemed surprisingly enthusiastic. Straker thanked him for arranging everything and stood back to let him exit the truck.

'Ladies and gentlemen,' said Straker, indicating the table and curved bench down the left-hand side of the room, 'please make yourselves comfortable. Thank you for coming and for agreeing to join this team. I have a very specific task for you all and hope you'll enjoy it as something of a challenge.' Wanting to assess the engagement of these strangers, he added: 'This is likely to exercise your resourcefulness.'

To some of the photographers, the whole set-up – being welcomed into motor racing's inner sanctum, receiving a specific brief and being told they were part of a team – was unusual. Some were not sure how to react. A few, including both women, seemed to respond enthusiastically. A couple of the others looked jaded, as if they had seen it all before.

'Quartech wants to photograph this man,' said Straker as he tapped the keyboard on the table in front of him.

A photograph appeared on the large wall-mounted HD screen at the end of the motor home. It was a shot of a tall, bald man. He was wearing a navy blue silk shirt. Unmistakeably, the picture had been taken in Monte Carlo: the harbour and the hillsides of Monaco were ranged across the background.

'This,' Straker announced, 'is Arno Ravilious.'

Some of the photographers reacted; there were mumblings of surprise. Several seemed to know who he was, even giving off a hint of intrigue.

'I want you to photograph everyone this man comes into contact with over the course of this weekend. Your passes give you access to most of the places you'll need to go around Silverstone. This map, here, shows how I plan to place you initially around the circuit.'

From the image now on the wall, it was clear how the team would intermesh – from multiple angles – to cover Ravilious's whereabouts at any point around the circuit.

'I am going to give you each a radio. As you can see beside your name on the screen, you will have a call sign relating to your location. Because we want to be discreet, we will refer to Mr Ravilious as the Subject. If the Subject moves out of your area, I want you to announce this immediately over the radio, so the member of the team in the adjoining sector can be alerted.'

There were a few nods as this unusual operation became clearer. Straker's delivery – clarity, presence and authority – held the attention of the strangers, even the jaded ones.

'What happens if he goes into a private or restricted area, where we can't go?' asked one of the men.

'You won't be able to follow him in, but you can still alert the team – in case another one of us is watching a different exit. The main reason I'm keen to keep track of the Subject,' Straker went on, 'is to ensure that we get as much warning as possible if he's about to leave Silverstone.'

The expressions on the faces of the photographers now seemed to show a sense of anticipation.

'You've all been asked to be mobile, preferably with motorcycles?'

The photographers nodded.

'This is where I'd like your vehicles parked, so that they're ready for a speedy getaway,' he said, and, calling up the next slide showing a map of the complex, added: 'The Subject has a private entrance and exit which is shown here. The moment he looks like he's leaving, I will call you over the radio, asking some of you to return to your bikes. I then want you to give chase.'

Straker was pleased as a few smiles broke around the table. 'I appreciate this is going to be a very different kind of assignment for most of you,' he said, 'but it could be exciting. You will, at least, be well paid.'

A common reaction came from the group.

'There will be bonuses if we manage to capture the Subject's key encounters, either here at the race track or wherever he goes afterwards. You don't have to be the one taking the winning photograph; what matters is the team succeeds as a whole.'

There was now something of a buzz among this ragbag of freelancers.

Reaching to the floor, Straker lifted the plastic crate holding the radios. 'I am going to ask you to sign for these,' he said, handing out a radio to each person and a piece of paper. Once they each had signed the form, Straker explained how the radios worked. He got each of them to practise sending and receiving messages – to ensure the voice procedure was kept simple and short.

'If we do end up leaving the circuit,' said Straker, 'the radios only have a short range, so we would then need to switch to our mobile phones.'

Straker summarized his briefing and asked for questions. There were some, but all from a positive standpoint.

A few minutes later he released his photographers from the motor home; they moved out, ready to take up their positions.

When Straker was alone, he went straight back to the Dropbox.

There was some follow-on from the earlier pictures:

The three suits from the Mercedes in Berkeley Square had reappeared. This time they were seen exiting the Motor Racing Promotions' headquarters, departing roughly an hour after they'd arrived. They left in the same car they had come in.

Five more planes had landed at Biggin Hill.

And the first consignment of photographs from Ravilious's house in Belgravia had come in. Included in these were shots of a van pulling up and several parcels being delivered.

It wasn't much of a crop. How much activity, though, should he realistically expect this close to six o'clock on a Friday evening?

Straker's biggest concern was where Arno Ravilious might have dinner and sleep that night. If either or both of these were off-campus, his team of photographers would face their first big test.

Seven o'clock came and went.

The last of the spectators in the stands had long since departed. Activity in the pit lane and paddock was still busy, the teams continuing to prep their cars after the day's practice sessions. Around the teams' hospitality facilities in the paddock, music, voices and laughter could be heard – guests revelling in the cachet of their location and wanting to absorb every drop of the British Grand Prix weekend.

Approaching eight o'clock, Straker became tense.

If Ravilious was going to leave the circuit for whatever reason, the most likely time was any moment now.

By radio, Straker repositioned his team. He pulled the photographers from the pit lane and the far end of the Wing into the paddock, where they were to provide extra cover should Ravilious be about to leave.

One of the photographers offered Straker some reassurance, confirming she had a clear view of Ravilious's motor home, having positioned herself directly across the avenue from it.

All around Silverstone, the mood and atmosphere was enhanced by a warm yellowing sun that began to cast longer and longer shadows.

Straker kept his eyes and ears out for new uploads to the Dropbox. Easily 200 images had now been uploaded. Being a Friday evening, the number of photographs from the offices had started to dwindle, the more recent ones only catching the occasional staff member leaving late or perhaps the arrival of a night watchman. Most of the new pictures were from outside Ravilious's houses in Belgravia and Oxfordshire, and from the airfield at Biggin Hill. Straker culled the poor quality shots. Then, putting the useable ones in batches, he fired them off by email to his identification committee, asking them to take a look and to feed back.

The light over Silverstone started to fade.

Artificial lights soon fired up, bathing the paddock in a whitish halogen light.

Another hour went by.

There was still no sign of movement from Ravilious.

Only when the clock on his laptop showed eleven o'clock did Straker call a close to the day's surveillance. The Ringmaster, he reckoned, must have eaten inside his motor home and planned to sleep on board.

At eleven fifteen Straker radioed his photographers and stood them down, asking them to be back in position first thing the following morning.

Straker was frustrated.

He had no answer for his chairman. He had learned absolutely nothing about who the buyer of Motor Racing Promotions might be. His only consolation was that, with the surveillance in place, he shouldn't miss anything from now on.

Straker turned in, dossing down on the curved bench in the Ptarmigan motor home. His mind, however, wouldn't let him sleep.

What if Ravilious upped and left Silverstone unexpectedly?

TWENTY-FIVE

Straker woke at five with his brain already whirring. All his photographers – bar one – turned up by six. Having clocked in at the motor home and collected their radios, they went straight back out to their designated locations, ready to record whatever they saw.

Nothing of note happened for several hours.

The morning wore on.

Silverstone started to fill up: spectators arrived. Parts of the complex became reasonably crowded. Straker was getting concerned. His team could be hampered if he needed them to move quickly around the circuit.

At ten o'clock that morning, Remy Sabatino pulled out of the Ptarmigan pit lane garage for Practice 3; her appearance in the hour-long session sparked excitement along the stands.

Turning right, she ran down to the end of the pit lane at the limiter speed of 80 kilometres per hour. Once across the line she released the car, accelerating towards Abbey. Sabatino felt the hybrid 1.6 litre Benbecular surge as it whined up the revs. Its delivery of power – of acceleration – was good and reliable, but still wasn't working as well for Ptarmigan as it was for the Lambourns or Massarellas. Sabatino glided through the right-hander into Farm. She was suddenly aware of the weather. The wind was definitely getting up.

Setting himself up in the Ptarmigan motor home to monitor his surveillance, Straker felt an urgency – Arno Ravilious had yet to appear.

Straker even missed Sabatino's emergence onto the track. His attention was consumed in reviewing another batch of uploads to the Dropbox.

Practice 3 ended. There were no surprises. The Lambourns were fastest by a margin, then came the Massarellas and then the Ptarmigans – all as everyone had feared. There was every likelihood that Qualifying, in two hours' time, would be exactly the same … reminiscent of the antediluvian Arc … cars at the front of the grid, predictably, being ranked there … two by two.

At twelve thirty Straker's radio crackled into life.

'Subject's leaving the motor home … Subject's leaving the motor home.'

Straker grabbed the radio: 'Good work. Which direction's he going in, over?'

'Towards the pits.'

'Good work, John, out to you – hello, all stations, all stations – attention, attention. Be ready to spot Subject and record activities, out.'

Straker decided he should be out on the ground for this.

Leaving the paddock, he made his way through the back of the Ptarmigan garage and entered the pit lane. With fewer than twenty minutes to Qualifying, there was energized activity among the teams as they made their final preparations.

Some distance along, Straker could see a small crowd forming. A cluster of large fur-covered microphones on poles and cameras was being held above people's heads; all that, he thought, must be the media homing in on Ravilious.

Straker walked towards the commotion. He soon spotted one of the women in his gang of photographers. Jill was taking pictures from a distance. She was mid-forties, wiry-looking with an outdoor complexion and greying hair which she did nothing to hide. She was dressed in black jeans and a black suede jacket; her only concession to colour was the bright green scarf around her neck. Straker had deployed her to cover the pit lane.

When she lowered her camera, he asked: 'How's it going?'

'A bit slow until a few minutes ago,' she replied in a Black Country accent. 'I hadn't seen Mr Rav … sorry … the Subject until then.'

'He's been rather elusive so far.'

'What did you think of my pictures of the altercation?'

'What altercation?'

'Outside the garage with the red cars?' she asked.

'You mean Ferrari?'

'Don't expect me to know their names – but that lot over there,' she said, pointing two bays down.

'Sorry, Jill – I haven't seen them yet – how long ago did you send them in?'

'About five minutes?'

'I must have just missed them. What kind of altercation?'

'The Subject was completely surrounded by people.'

'Okay.'

'There seemed to be two types around him. One lot were journalists, who were pretty aggressive – firing questions all the time. The second lot looked like a bunch of kiss-ups.'

Seeming eager to tell him more, she added: 'There was this one quite distinguished-looking bloke – who came up to the Subject – just walking straight into the middle of his little gaggle … and then had a go at him.'

'What sort of a go?'

'A real one … heated … loud … argumentative. I don't know your Mr Subject from a hole in the road, but when the journos were shouting at him, he seemed to stay aloof. When this guy started, it was the only time the Subject didn't look like he was in charge.'

'Thank you, Jill – I'll go straight back and take a look. How many shots did you upload?'

'Twenty odd.'

At that moment Straker and Jill, the photographer, were distracted.

Some distance away from Ravilious another commotion was forming. Dozens of other photographers were rushing over, crowding around.

Straker watched, then – without taking his eyes off this second melee – he said to Jill: 'I wonder who the popular one is over there?'

'Don't ask me, love … I'm not into this stuff.'

'Quick, photograph him, would you?'

'The Arab-looking guy?'

Jill raised her camera and fired off a rapid sequence. After several more clicks she nodded to Straker. 'That worked. I got some clear shots of him.'

'Can you upload them immediately?'

She lowered the Nikon, studied the back of it, pressed a series of buttons and, after a few seconds, reported: 'Done.'

Straker thanked her again, shook her hand and set off back to the motor home.

He all but ran up the steps into the Ptarmigan command centre a few minutes later. Tahm Nazar was present, briefing three of his turquoise-liveried team. Straker squeezed round them, dived for his laptop, booted it up, logged onto the Dropbox and pulled up Jill's first set of pictures. It was just as she had described:

Ravilious was shown approaching the 'red cars' of the Ferrari garage. A few shots later an elderly man, wearing the livery of the Scuderia, emerged from inside it to greet Ravilious. Then, as the Ferrari boss was about to address the press gathered around them, Jill's incident took place.

It began with a figure appearing in the right-hand margin of the photograph.

The man had his back to Jill's camera.

He wore a pale blue linen blazer-type jacket.

Six feet tall, broad – imposing – he had a head of almost white hair.

He seemed to stride into the garage, away from the camera.

The white-haired man closed in on Ravilious and stopped right in front of him.

The Ringmaster appeared momentarily thrown by the encroachment of his space, until he recognized who it was. No hands were shaken. There was no greeting or preamble: the new arrival leant in towards Ravilious and started talking. Heatedly. Even through the silent medium of Jill's sequence of pictures, his rant looked loud. The man's body language was agitated, his gesticulations emphatic.

Straker looked through subsequent pictures, hoping to see Ravilious's face. He found a couple. The Ringmaster seemed passive. Placid, even. Wasn't recoiling; his expression never changed; he made no attempt to curtail the awkward conversation or even to move it away to somewhere private.

In one of Jill's next pictures, the Ferrari boss could be seen looking towards the back of the garage, trying to catch the eye of someone out of shot. Several Ferrari-liveried team members soon came forwards from within and started trying to usher all the non-Ravilious entourage people out of the space. Ferrari, at least, was showing some embarrassment at the altercation happening around Ravilious, and was trying to keep it private.

Straker reached the end of the sequence with the white-haired man.

He was now seriously intrigued.

Directly behind him in the motor home, Nazar's meeting broke up. As the team boss was making to leave, Straker managed to catch him: 'Tahm, there have been a couple of incidents in the pit lane,' he said. 'Could you bear to take a look?'

'Qualifying starts in ten minutes.'

'It'd only take a second,' said Straker, as he turned the laptop round. 'Do you know this guy?' he asked and presented Jill's best picture of the agitated white-haired man.

Nazar looked at the photograph. And immediately shook his head. 'Sorry, no.'

Straker was puzzled. How could this be? How could one of Formula 1's leading team bosses not know someone with the status to argue with Arno Ravilious and apparently come out on top?

Straker pulled up the shots of the Arab-looking man, who had also been attracting the attention of the press in the pit lane. 'Okay, what about this guy?'

Nazar's reaction to this was extraordinary. The team boss suddenly seemed no longer in a hurry.

'Tahm, what's wrong?'

'Oh, fuck no.'

'Why? Who is he?'

'Suleiman Al-Megrahi, that's who…'

'So?'

'…*he's* trouble … serious trouble.'

'In what way?'

'A totally rotten apple. Tunisian – a former team boss. Was F1's golden boy 10 years ago. Everything he touched came up roses – "won" three Constructors' Championships and three consecutive Drivers' titles.'

'For which team?'

'A backmarker outfit he renamed Calabria.'

'And now?'

'Effectively in exile. He was banned from F1 in 1992, having been found out for cheating. Al-Megrahi was hauled in front of the FIA. The man put up a fight but was found guilty of numerous infringements. He was officially barred from Formula 1 for five years.'

'But – 1992? … That's ancient history. The ban would have expired a long time ago?'

Nazar nodded.

'He's not been involved in F1 since?'

'No one'll have anything to do with him.'

'No forgiveness from F1, then?'

'It's more a matter of trust. He was dealt with severely because of his mouth. Al-Megrahi never stopped sniping at the FIA … at MRP … at Arno. The paddock was convinced he had an agenda – that he wanted to take over from Ravilious, even depose him. He's never stopped sniping. Been at it ever since.'

'Don't let me keep you from Qualifying.'

Surprisingly, the team boss held up his hand as if to say: 'No, that's fine.'

'Okay…' said Straker, making the most of this chance to ask questions, '…when was Al-Megrahi last at a grand prix?'

'Over a year ago … at least.'

'Can we read anything into his being here today then?'

'Oh, God, yes. Ravilious selling up would have triggered this appearance. He'd see Arno's departure as his long-awaited right to come back into Formula 1.'

'To do what?'

'That's the question, isn't it? There aren't any teams looking for a boss; the only vacancy big enough for Al-Megrahi's ego would be Ravilious's. Except he would be disastrous.'

'Does he have any allies?'

The distinguished Indian's tone sounded as if he was already apologizing for the gossipy nature of his next comment: 'Very few. Al-Megrahi's clout comes from the money behind him – which has always seemed unlimited. I wouldn't care to ask too many questions about where it comes from … a bunch of unsavoury backers from around the Mediterranean.'

'Money enough to take over MRP?'

'And some!'

Andy Backhouse appeared in the motor home, climbing quickly up the steps.

Nazar called him over: 'Andy, come over here … take a look at this.'

Backhouse's expression suggested he really didn't have time.

'Come and see who's back…'

The race engineer walked over and looked down at the face on the screen. 'Fuck, fuck, fuck … not Ali-fucking-Baba!'

Straker looked at the race engineer: 'That, too, is quite a reaction.'

'I thought we'd got shot of that shit. He can *only* be here because Ravilious is going. God help us all.'

'Would F1 *have* him back after those incidents?'

Nazar tried not to smile. 'I'm not sure moral rectitude was ever a pre-requisite for participation in Formula 1, but it would depend on how big a hole Ravilious leaves … and how desperate the sport gets to fill it. But with his financial backing, Suleiman Al-Megrahi's claim is probably as plausible as his ethics are unsavoury.'

Ptarmigan's team boss and race engineer soon headed off to the pit lane and Qualifying, leaving Straker in an energized quandary. As seasoned Formula 1 players, their reaction to Al-Megrahi had been revealing. Wasn't Al-Megrahi's reappearance on the F1 stage, then, the first major incident related to the sale of Motor Racing Promotions?

From what he had just heard, Straker would have to see Al-Megrahi as a prospective buyer of MRP, wouldn't he? But then he wondered: Al-Megrahi and Ravilious had both been in the pit lane at the same time that day; that would not have helped them keep a deal between them secret. Furthermore, they hadn't been standing close together. A deal between those two didn't seem to stack up.

Straker then thought about the incident in the Ferrari garage.

There was something about that interaction with Ravilious that didn't stack up either: the distinguished white-haired man and Ravilious obviously knew each other; there had been no warmth in their greeting; and their exchange seemed undignified.

For all the Ringmaster's imperiousness around the pit lane, Ravilious looked humbled by the other man. Who was he – and why was he so pissed off with Ravilious? Most intriguingly, how could *Nazar* have no idea who he was?

After a few clicks on his laptop keyboard, Straker emailed a picture of the white-haired man to members of his identification committee.

He was about to review the latest batch of uploads from his photographer/watchers, when his operation was forced into overdrive.

TWENTY-SIX

Qualifying was about to start. Anticipation was mounting. The pit lane was full to bursting. A series of whiny shrieks indicated the Formula 1 engines were being fired up, their sound reverberating along the canyon between the Wing and the grandstands opposite. Straker was calling up the broadcast TV feed to watch the start of Qualifying on his laptop, when a voice, sounding urgent, came from his radio:

'Hello, Matt, come in, Matt? Subject on the move – *Subject on the move*.'

Straker picked up his radio: 'From where to where, over?'

There was a loud crackle over the radio: interference. 'Climbing into his car. Looks like a posh black thing.'

'To leave the circuit?'

'The car's facing the exit … I'd say yes. There's no one else with him.'

'Good work, Barry – stay on him – can you get the car's registration, over?'

There was a pause. 'MRP1.'

'Excellent work – out to you; hello Carl – hello Jill, over?'

'Jill here.'

'How far are you from your bike, over?'

'Three hundred yards.'

'Can you make for it right now? Look to pick the Subject's car up as he exits the complex. Acknowledge the car registration, over?'

'Yep, got it.'

'Keep me posted, out.'

Straker stood up in the motor home.

The command centre was humming. With Qualifying about to start, all the consoles were now manned; all the HD screens were lit and showing a wealth of telemetry data on both Ptarmigan cars as well as a range of live and streamed pictures from around the circuit. Straker approached one of the team sitting at the bank of consoles and asked if he could use a radio link to the pit wall. He got through to the team principal.

'Sorry to interrupt, Tahm – it looks like Ravilious is leaving the race track; does he normally do that during Qualifying?'

'Not normally, no – not sure I've ever known him to miss Qually.'

Straker hurried back to his laptop. He pulled out his phone and rang his contact at Quartech Aerospace. 'Sam, we have a go for Ravilious – looks like he's about to leave the circuit.'

'Okay, Matt – hang on,' said Bailey after which his voice could be heard talking to someone in the background. 'Okay, Jane – take her up. Hold her steady at a thousand feet. For starters.'

Back on the line to Straker, Bailey said: 'We're getting airborne, Matt. Should be feeding through any second now … ready to acquire.'

Clicking on the relevant icon, Straker's screen changed. It displayed a new picture. In bright colours – in high definition – came a rising view of some countryside: lush green fields, full leaved hedgerows and a farm gate. The camera continued to gain height. A road came into view – a narrow country lane. Then, a little higher, a larger road – with traffic streaming in both directions. The vantage point then started to move forwards, flying over a dual carriageway. The A43. Into the shot came a field full of cars, a swathe of flags, tents and a mass of trucks – roofs of some of the Silverstone buildings.

The eight-rotor drone reached its initial operating height. From there, Straker could now see a wide-angle shot of the circuit, including an occasional flash of the cars in the far distance on the track during Qualifying.

The on-board camera showed it was zooming in, focusing on an area of tents.

Straker said into the phone: 'There, Sam, can Jane see that black Maybach?'

'Hang on, Matt,' said Bailey, who relayed ID of the vehicle to the drone pilot.

'Registration MRP1?' came the reply.

'That's him.'

A moment later Bailey said: 'Matt – we have contact … confirmed. We have acquired.'

'Excellent work. Now let's see where he takes us.'

Very quickly, though, something surprising became clear.

Ravilious's car moved slowly through the race complex. But it wasn't heading for the exit. It turned off in an unexpected direction, pulling into one of the car parks – and making off across the grass. The aerial picture from the drone was crystal clear. There was no mistaking Ravilious's car or the direction it was taking. Straker looked on ahead, trying to work it out. There was a tall belt of mature trees set in a hedge line. Why on earth would Ravilious be heading for that?

Grabbing his map of the circuit, Straker tried to extrapolate this direction of travel.

As the drone pilot followed on, the attitude of its picture changed, allowing Straker to see a gate in the hedge. Ravilious's car was making to go through it.

'Jane will take us up,' said Bailey over the phone.

The picture showed the drone rising. Gaining height, it was soon quickly level with the tops of the trees. Straker could see a stretch of Northamptonshire to the horizon and, in the foreground, part of a field directly below.

It seemed to be empty.

The drone edged forwards, skimming over the crown of an oak.

Those watching the screen suddenly saw something in the lee of this line of trees. A helicopter. A Bell Jet Ranger was on the ground, its rotors already turning.

'Shit, he's flying out of here,' Straker said to Bailey. 'Will the drone be fast enough to tail that?'

'Yes,' said Bailey, who could then be heard alerting the pilot in the background.

Straker picked up his radio and transmitted: 'Hello, all stations.

The pressure is off. Subject about to be flown out of here. Tailing by road will not be possible. New destination to be communicated once identified. All stations to stand down until further notice.'

Ravilious's car, now making its way slowly out into the middle of the field beyond the trees, came to a halt. Its right rear door opened. Straker could see the tall figure of the Ringmaster emerge from the car and walk across to the helicopter, ducking his bald head as he went in under the rotors. The drone kept its distance, hovering within touching distance of the treetops. Straker prayed the drone was aurally concealed, drowned out by the noise from the Qualifying session as well as the sound of the chopper's turbine.

The door of the Bell Jet Ranger was shut. The rotors increased their revolutions. No more than two minutes later the helicopter was lifting off into the air.

Bailey said over the phone: 'Here we go. Jane's ready to follow. She'll fly to its stern – below the tail rotor – concealing the drone's presence. We don't have to be too close. Now the drone's locked on to the chopper, as long as we get line of sight with it now and again, we shouldn't lose it.'

Suddenly the drone shot backwards, rapidly losing height; then it seemed to start tumbling. Was it falling? Straker thought it had been snagged in one of the trees.

'What's happening? Why's it crashing?'

Bailey replied: 'Jane's just taking evasive action, Matt. She'd spotted the helicopter was turning.'

'Were we quick enough?'

The drone was still spinning.

Then juddering.

Yawing.

'What's happening now?'

'It's probably getting caught in the downdraught from the heli-copter – I'd expect the chopper to be directly above us now.'

The camera stabilized. It swung round. Its lens panned upwards. The underside of the receding helicopter was soon in the centre of the screen. Overhead, the Bell Jet Ranger was dipping its nose forwards and rapidly gaining height. Moments later, the drone was gaining height too, accelerating off in pursuit of Ravilious's aircraft.

Bailey offered: 'That *was* reasonably close.'

Straker watched the camera picture on his screen but quickly reduced it to picture-in-picture; behind it, he called up a large-scale map of the Midlands. A small red dot appeared smack in the middle of this image, leaving a paler trace across the map showing its course so far. The helicopter was heading south-east towards London, at just under 120 knots. The military drone, comfortably keeping up, was concealed to its rear, a couple of hundred yards behind.

Nothing unusual happened with Ravilious's helicopter for 30 minutes. But then the size of the helicopter's image within the screen started growing larger, and its position relative to the horizon started to drop. The helicopter was slowing down and losing height. Almost immediately, the drone slowed too, to maintain its relative distance. It started to descend.

Straker clicked on the map, increasing the scale – trying to work out if anywhere ahead might reveal itself as a possible destination.

At a height of just under 1,000 feet, they were flying over Farnham Common.

'There's Stoke Park ahead,' suggested Bailey over the phone, as the iconic white mansion could be seen in the distance over to the left.

'I'd be surprised if he landed there,' Straker replied. 'Too many people around, and that crowd would be sure to recognize him.'

Straker googled the area. A number of other possibilities came up. Then, extrapolating their current flight path, he spotted something else.

'Sam,' he said, 'there's a largish house – a stately home directly in line – Stoke *Place*, it looks like. Aren't they heading towards that? Looks like there'd be more than enough space to land – and it's private.'

'Got it,' said Bailey, who was then heard speaking with the pilot.

'Doesn't look like there's a lot of cover,' added Straker.

'Jane will take precautions as we close in.'

Three minutes later the Bell Jet Ranger was making an approach.

'Stoke Place it is,' stated Straker. On the screen, he could see the helicopter decelerate to a hover.

Looking ahead – beneath the aircraft – Straker could see the setting of the mansion. Immediately below the drone was extensive woodland. In the middle distance was a sizeable lake. On the far bank of this was a belt of silver birch trees. Beyond that, an expansive and gently rising lawn led up to the front of a Georgian house with a façade like a doll's house.

Against this grand backdrop something in the landscape seemed out of place. And a little sinister. Contrasting with the oldness of the red brick house, and the large well-proportioned windows, two black limousines were parked on the gravel sweep. Even at this distance it was obvious that both had darkened windows.

Before Straker could study the view, his attention was caught.

The drone seemed to be dropping like a stone. Then, a matter of feet from the ground, it stabilized with a jerk before shooting forwards, across the surface of the lake – heading towards the clump of silver birch. Just before it reached there, the device came to another sudden stop. The camera's location was four feet off the ground. Its lens peered through a bank of bull rushes and the trunks of silver-barked trees – able to see across fifty to seventy yards of lawn towards the house.

The drone had got there just in time to see the helicopter kick up a flurry of sand and dust as the aircushion disturbed the gravel in front of the mansion.

Still in cover behind the reeds and birch trees, the pilot jockeyed the drone from side to side – trying to find the best view between the trunks – as the helicopter came in to land.

No more than seconds later, Straker could see the door of the helicopter being opened and Ravilious climbing out.

Why had the Ringmaster come here midway through Qualifying for the British Grand Prix?

TWENTY-SEVEN

Matt Straker watched as Arno Ravilious walked across the gravel and in through the front door of Stoke Place. No one came to the door to meet him. He disappeared inside. The engines on the Bell Jet Ranger were still running, as were its rotors.

'Is the chopper going to stay?' asked Straker.

'Doesn't look like it's in any hurry to leave or shut down.'

'Can we use the noise to conceal the drone and film the registration plates of those cars?'

The remote aircraft was soon moving again, hovering close to the ground, hidden from the house by the trees. Zooming in, it showed the back end of one black car. Jane caught an oblique but legible shot of the plate. Capturing the second proved difficult.

Straker noticed that the helicopter's rotors were starting to slow.

'Quick, the helicopter is shutting down.'

The pilot immediately dropped the drone onto the ground, and shut down its eight rotors to prevent its noise being heard above the quietening helicopter. The drone's camera, though – still pointing at the front door of Stoke Place – was able to keep filming.

Straker was engrossed. He continued to study the live image on his screen. After fifteen minutes of inactivity, he chanced using the PiP facility to look at the latest uploads from his watchers. There were no further pictures from Silverstone of course, but there were several shots from Belgravia and his two photographers at Biggin Hill.

Images from Ravilious's London house showed a small number of people arriving that morning, most likely making deliveries. A truck had pulled up outside. The name Broomhead Removals was painted down its side. A couple of men were seen climbing out and knocking on the front door. It was answered by an elderly man in an apron.

A conversation seemed to ensue for quite some time. One of the two men thrust a piece of paper at the elderly man. In response, the elderly man took a step back and firmly shut the door on the visitors.

As the pair walked back to their van, one of the men was on the phone. It seemed an odd encounter. Straker jotted down the time this had occurred and made a note of the removal company.

Why had they come to Ravilious's house in the first place? And on a Saturday morning? They clearly weren't there to deliver anything.

What had they come to pick up?

And why hadn't they been successful?

Straker flicked his eyes back to the drone's shot of the front door of Stoke Place, but found nothing had changed.

He turned to look at the pictures from Biggin Hill. His two photographers seemed to be working hard down there. A number of private jets had come and gone over the last 24 hours. The man up in the woods had shot over twenty aircraft landing and seventeen taking off. Straker bundled shots of their registration numbers and sent them to Sam Bailey at Quartech Aerospace, to see if one of their databases could identify their owners.

His other photographer, observing the airfield from the road out on the other side of the VIP terminal, had captured a series of people emerging after landing. Some of the faces were familiar. There was a well-known footballer, two actors, and, with a dozen or so similarly dressed young men, what looked like a cricket team. Straker was not prompted to research any of those further. But there were five individuals who did catch his eye.

Two of these looked like they were men of status: men who carried themselves with self-importance – appearing to demand that doors be opened for them and their luggage carried.

Bundling up the photographs of the five, Straker sent them to Tahm Nazar at Ptarmigan, Benedict Wasserman at the investment bank, Bernie Callom in Quartech's PR department and to Dominic Quartano.

Just after four fifteen, Straker was back on edge.

Over the loudspeaker of his laptop he heard a different noise.

A high-pitched whine.

Toggling quickly, he called up the drone's camera showing the front of Stoke Place. The helicopter was restarting its engine.

The Ringmaster appeared from the house. He could be seen walking down the steps onto the gravel. Another well-dressed man in his late fifties with neat dark hair emerged from inside. Ravilious stopped and turned. There seemed to be a formal exchange of words, rather than a conversation.

'Can we get a better view of the other guy?' Straker asked down the phone to Bailey.

'Not until the helicopter's rotors are turning, the drone might be heard…'

On the screen Straker saw Ravilious raise his left hand and spin his index finger. Within a matter of seconds the rotors of the helicopter were starting to turn.

Bailey, over the line, said: 'Okay, here we go … we can move now.'

Straker saw the drone retake to the air. In behind the silver birch trees, the pilot jockeyed the remote aircraft sideways to find a better position.

There!

The drone's camera had a clear shot; it happened, just as Ravilious shook hands with the neat man and then turned back towards the helicopter.

Jane, the pilot, zoomed in.

Clear as day, they were recording a full-frontal shot of the other man's face.

'With that clarity, recognition of this man shouldn't be difficult.'

But Straker's pulse was racing.

A surge of adrenalin was coursing through him before he realized why.

Then it struck him.

Toggling again, he dived into the Dropbox and called up the uploads he had just been sifting through.

Click, click, click.

There!

Straker stared down at the face from Stoke Place, and then at the picture taken outside the VIP terminal at Biggin Hill – showing one of the two men 'of status'. Weren't these two shots of the same man?

Then, aloud, he said: 'Got you … *Got* you … you bastard.'

'Sorry?' came the voice from the other end of the phone.

'Sorry, Sam – no, not you … I think we've got a match!'

'Brilliant. Which person do you want to follow?'

'Ravilious – stay on Ravilious.'

Straker kept an eye on the scene at Stoke Place. He went back to clicking through other photographs uploaded to the Dropbox.

Click, click, click.

He found the one he was looking for.

Thankfully, his photographer at Biggin Hill had stayed on the man with the neat dark hair and had continued to fire off shots as the man's car pulled away from the VIP terminal. One of his pictures had captured the registration plate of the car.

Straker picked the phone up: 'Sam, Sam? Can you give me the registration plate we took earlier off that car on the drive?'

'Yes, hang on.'

A minute later Bailey was on the line. 'It's…'

Within an hour Arno Ravilious had been flown back to Silverstone.

In the meantime, Straker had sent pictures of the dark-haired man to his identification committee. This had to be significant, didn't it? Within the last 24 hours, an unknown individual had arrived in the UK – via a private airfield, one closely associated with Arno Ravilious – and, a few hours later, had met Ravilious himself, surreptitiously – at a private house – midway through Qualifying for the British Grand Prix.

How could this set of incidents not be relevant to Motor Racing Promotions?

The question Straker was putting to his identification committee was clear:

'Who is this guy?'

But Nazar, Callom, Bailey and Quartano all fed back within an hour. None of them knew who he was. Straker's last hope was Wasserman. He emailed, texted and rang – leaving several voicemail messages – but couldn't reach the investment banker.

The day wore on. Straker had to know who this person was.

At five o'clock, Dominic Quartano rang him. 'Have you had any luck identifying that man?'

Straker explained his unsuccessful attempts to raise Wasserman.

Quartano sounded sympathetic. 'Not surprising,' he said. '*Shomer Shabbat* ... it *is* Saturday.'

'Forgive me. I hadn't thought of that.'

'Why should you? He's very discreet about his faith.'

Straker was soon distracted from his lack of progress. One of the photographers at Silverstone had a problem at home and needed to leave. With a quick shuffle of his team, Straker managed to cover the gap.

Just before looking at the next batch of uploads to the Dropbox, his phone went. Straker reacted quickly when he saw who was calling.

'Benedict, thanks for coming back. Sorry to have bombarded you with so many messages.'

'No worries. I'm here now. *Havdalah*. I've seen my three stars. I've just been through the pictures you sent me.'

'And?'

'I *can* identify the man – at the secret meeting with Ravilious.'

'Who *is* he?'

'Gabriel Barrus the Third. An American. Runs a company called Salt Lake Media.'

'Would he be relevant to Motor Racing Promotions?'

'Oh yes...'

'What?'

'He's serious trouble. Matt, you and Quartech need to be extremely careful.'

'*Why?*'

'He's a multibillionaire corporate raider. Doesn't give a shit about anyone or anything that gets in his way. And he's as litigious as hell.'

'Okay, Ben,' said Straker pulling a face and grunting. 'You called him a billionaire, so I'm guessing he could afford MRP?'

'Out of his back pocket. And it fits: Barrus owns several sports teams in the US … and he has cash- and asset-stripped them all.'

Straker rang Dominic Quartano.

'Well done, Matt, that's impressive work – truly strategic-level intelligence. You've given me something concrete to tell the Chinese. I'll also try and make contact with Mr Barrus, to see what he has in mind for F1. In the meantime, please keep this man and his company's identity on a very close hold … let's not give away our advance knowledge. I *don't* want the paddock to know; I'm happy we don't even tell Ptarmigan, okay?'

TWENTY-EIGHT

Having made some progress with his investigation, Straker felt a full-on buzz going into race day of the British Grand Prix.

The heatwave continued. By eight o'clock there wasn't a cloud in the sky.

The atmosphere was building.

The first spectacle was the drivers' parade. All 22 Formula 1 stars were driven round the Silverstone circuit on the top of an open double-decker bus. Waving to the crowds, they were granted a classic British welcome.

Just after midday, the first of the F1 cars fired up their engines. Anticipation fizzed as they emerged from the pit lane, heading onto the track. Using the slow lap for any last-minute adjustments, the drivers ran through a series of heavy acceleration, braking and swerving moves, hoping to generate last-minute usable data for their race engineers on the pit wall.

Rounding the track, the cars pulled into the pit straight, ready to take their starting positions. As the last one came to a stop, the grid was opened to the teams. In a matter of seconds, blocks of colour formed as groups of mechanics in their distinctive team liveries clustered around their cars. Trolleys were wheeled in close beside them, each loaded with a range of kit, spares and alternative tyres. An immediate priority was to grab the tyre blankets and wrap each wheel on the cars, keeping the compound at the right temperature for the start of the race. Drivers climbed from their cars and stripped off, trying to keep themselves cool. In a number of cases, the cars themselves were cooled by blowers plugged into the radiator pods and airbox.

Onto the grid came the media. Hundreds of TV, radio and streaming channels had their journalists and presenters swarming over the hallowed ground, there to whip up the excitement for their audiences back home. Microphones were thrust into the faces of the drivers, team bosses, the occasional well-known Formula 1 designer, engineer or tyre manufacturer.

A number of A-listers from Hollywood and the music world were also on the track, many attracting considerable attention. Lesser celebrities were also there in force, including several politicians – the local Members of Parliament and even the Secretary of State for Transport and the President of the Board of Trade.

Straker watched from the pit lane. A particular noise filled the air – not from the cars or anything on the ground. Straker looked up. He saw the diamond formation of nine scarlet Hawk T1 aircraft roaring across the sky at little more than 500 feet. The Red Arrows flew over in perfect formation, a matter of inches apart, their synchronization so tight they looked like they had been painted on a sheet of acetate being slid across the sky.

Even above all that hubbub and melee, there was suddenly a new spectacle on the grid.

Arno Ravilious appeared.

His entourage numbered fifteen to twenty people.

Photographers, TV presenters and camera crews jostled for position to record the progress of the Ringmaster's court around his bailiwick. Exciting the media to a frenzy were three of Ravilious's guests, each from the film world: two of them were the leading man and lady from Disney's latest fantasy franchise. Not only had the film's takings just topped $1 billion at the box office, but its two leading actors had become the latest portmanteau glamour couple, prompting their faces to be plastered across every tabloid newspaper and TV-on-a-page glossy magazine. The third film figure was the latest actor only recently appointed to play James Bond.

Matt Straker's photographers were in their designated positions. Between them, they were covering all points around his target.

Straker moved to the pit wall and joined the Ptarmigan team boss. The two of them walked through the narrow gap and out onto the grid.

'Have you got your people watching?'

Straker nodded.

'I owe you an apology, Matt,' said Nazar, 'I thought your approach to surveillance was nuts. The number of areas you've covered, and the awareness you've built up of Ravilious's haunts, is seriously impressive.'

Straker was gratified by the team boss's change of heart, particularly as he hadn't even shared his discovery of Gabriel Barrus as a potential owner of Formula 1.

Straker snatched another glance in the direction of Arno Ravilious – and then all around him to check that his reconnaissance screen was intact.

In a matter of seconds, though, none of that would matter.

There was a carnival atmosphere in the countdown to the British Grand Prix.

Twenty-two cars were lined up on the Silverstone track, but they were hidden by people. Hundreds were swarming all around them.

At 12:45, Straker heard the hooter go and saw the posting of the 15 minutes signal on the various boards.

Drivers started going through their drills, inserting their ear plugs, pulling on their fire-resistant balaclavas, doing up their race suits, pulling on their leather gloves and, finally, their helmets.

They were soon climbing into their cockpits.

The Ringmaster continued to walk among the throng on the grid.

Straker's attention was caught by a flash of movement.

A television crew dashed through a gap in the crowds, straight towards Arno Ravilious. A young female presenter thrust her logoed microphone under his chin.

Ravilious was in the middle of a conversation with James Bond.

The Ringmaster clearly didn't appreciate the intrusion. He turned to face the intruder.

Ravilious was about to say something when, with the reflex of someone losing their balance on ice, he thrust his right arm out to one side. After a couple of jabbed reaches, the Ringmaster caught James Bond by the forearm. The actor, shocked at the sudden pain, tried to pull back – until he looked round and understood what was going on.

Ravilious's balance was faltering, his left knee giving way. His long, slim body buckled as his shoulder dropped and he doubled over on his left-hand side.

Straker saw distress and fear in Ravilious's face.

The other knee gave way as it, too, started to buckle. Only the support of his right hand, locked around James Bond's forearm, prevented Ravilious from slamming down onto the ground.

Straker saw the Ringmaster's face turning a haunting shade of grey.

And then, taking Straker by surprise, the stricken man seemed to look him directly in the face.

All around them people were yelling.

A couple of shrill female voices started screaming.

Pandemonium broke out.

Officials – marshals – anyone with a radio started shouting into them.

A siren could be heard from the back of the grid.

The mass of people began to part, clearing the way for an ambulance. It could only creep down the avenue of F1 cars and through the throng to reach the stricken Formula 1 boss.

In the distance, Straker heard the whine of a jet turbine.

Then a chopping sound.

A moment later a helicopter could be seen overhead, banking steeply, flying in low over the Wing. It was looking to put down on clear tarmac, forwards of the front row of the grid.

The ambulance reached the scene of the stricken Ravilious. Three paramedics leaped out and ran to him.

A marshal, crouching down beside Ravilious, looked up and pointed to his own chest and rubbed his right hand down the inside of his left arm.

One of the medics, carrying an oxygen mask, leaned over the slumped body; a second tried to check for vital signs; a third was manhandling a stretcher, which was dropped onto the ground beside the lifeless body. Seconds later the medical party was lifting Ravilious onto it.

Heaving the loaded stretcher off the floor, the medics shuffled into a disjointed jog towards the air ambulance. The helicopter's rotors were still going at near maximum revolutions. Its side door was already open.

In one smooth motion, the paramedics lifted the stretcher up and onto the floor of the cabin. Before the doors were even shut, the pilot was lifting the helicopter into the air.

No more than six minutes had elapsed.

The Ringmaster was away – in the air and heading for emergency treatment, it was assumed, at the circuit's associated medical centre, the Northampton General Hospital.

No one had managed to get a close look at Ravilious during the evacuation.

No one had any idea of what state he was in.

No one knew whether he was going to survive.

TWENTY-NINE

One o'clock came. And went.

Twenty-two Formula 1 cars remained on the grid.

Stationary.

Silent.

No one seemed to know what to do. To run the race? To delay it? To abandon it out of respect for Ravilious?

The FIA, the GPDA, the BRDC, the broadcaster – all formed into a huddle. No one could decide what the fitting protocol was here.

Straker hurried back to the Ptarmigan motor home to call Dominic Quartano.

'Arno Ravilious has just collapsed on the grid of the grand prix. It looked like a massive heart attack. He went down, right in front of me. Was casevacked immediately by air ambulance. It all looked pretty serious.'

'Is he going to be all right?'

'No one has the slightest idea. There's no information. It's chaos around here.'

'I can imagine. Maybe the stress of all this has done for Arno, poor man,' offered Quartano. 'Let's hope he's okay. Without meaning to sound callous, this is going to play havoc with the fate of Motor Racing Promotions.'

An hour later Straker was in the Ptarmigan motor home when the team boss received an email from the FIA:

'The Fédération Internationale de l'Automobile and Formula 1 reports that Arno Ravilious has been taken into medical care with a suspected cardiac arrest. More news on his condition will be distributed as it becomes known. In tribute to him, the British Grand Prix will be run – in his name – but at a new start time of 3:00 p.m. BST.

We all wish Arno Ravilious a speedy recovery.'

That may have eased the immediate impasse, but it did nothing for the mood around the sport. For the second time in 72 hours, Formula 1 was thrown into turmoil. Now, there was not just the prospect of Arno Ravilious stepping down from his role; as of that moment, he was out of it in practice.

Even before the delayed British Grand Prix was started, speculation ran amok. Countless ideas were put forward as to how Formula 1 should handle this state of limbo. Suggestions were made as to which individuals could be appointed as caretaker manager, while others wasted no time in making recommendations on new structures, particularly those that involved new ways of distributing the spoils from Formula 1.

Around mid-afternoon Straker was rung back by Dominic Quartano. 'I've managed to make contact with Gabriel Barrus.'

'What did he say?'

'Very little. Was extremely cagey. Questioned me on why we thought he was involved with Ravilious at all.'

Straker smiled.

'But as he didn't admit he was involved in F1, he wasn't going to talk about any plans he might have for it.'

'Good grief.'

'With all of today's developments, we've got to plan our next steps. Come and see me at eight o'clock tomorrow morning in the office, would you?'

The Grand Prix was finally started at 3 p.m.

While it ran, word went round Silverstone that a news conference was going to be held. Suleiman Al-Megrahi declared that he had an announcement to make about the future of Formula 1 and particularly his plans for the sport.

'The *nerve* of the guy,' spat Nazar. 'Ravilious is lying on the slab and Al-Megrahi is already launching a power grab.'

'I thought, from what Andy was saying, Al-Megrahi has little standing in Formula 1,' replied Straker.

'He doesn't.'

'So in what capacity is he holding this press conference? As a sage? A guru? Someone else's front man?'

Nazar shrugged. 'We'll have to wait and see. Knowing Suleiman Al-Megrahi, it won't be from any position of humility.'

At six o'clock on the Sunday evening of the British Grand Prix, the International Media Centre in the Silverstone Wing was heaving. Jostling for position at the front were countless journalists, while along the back wall were banks of television cameras, at least three rows deep. A table was set up at the front of the room which had a banner draped over it:

A NEW BEGINNING – F1: 2.0

Nazar and Straker squeezed into the room at the back and waited for the arrival of Suleiman Al-Megrahi.

At five past six a side door opened and in walked a tall, physically impressive individual with black hair, ebony skin and, surprisingly, the bluest of eyes. He was greeted by a barrage of flashguns. In the stroboscopic lighting, the Tunisian held court for a moment, looking out at the room; his expression could have been read as that of someone relishing the pulling power of his name.

He sat down.

In heavily accented English, he said: 'I am, of course, saddened to hear of Arno Ravilious's health, and wish him a speedy recovery.'

'Like you could give a damn, arsehole,' whispered Nazar.

Al-Megrahi continued: 'With Arno announcing his retirement last Thursday, the time has come for us to rethink Formula 1 – particularly how it could be made to work better for all of us. And with Arno being indisposed, there is no time to be lost.'

Mutterings rippled across the room.

'I am proposing a reallocation of the revenues from Formula 1. I propose to tear up the Concorde Agreement and replace it with a more equitable participation in the revenues. I propose we set up a NewCo, which will own the rights to all aspects of F1 – the TV rights, the title rights, the advertising rights, the hospitality rights and the official merchandising rights. This NewCo will be "Formula 1 two-point-oh", if you will. And this new company will be owned by…'

'…Suleiman Al-Megrahi…' was shouted out.

The Tunisian's face hardened, looking unamused. 'F1 two-point-oh will be owned – *not by me* – but by the FIA, the teams, the circuits and, in return for its management, a team that I will lead.'

Further sounds came from around the room; not all were supportive. Al-Megrahi seemed to take offence at the reaction. His self-assurance and presence began to morph into arrogance.

'I suggest you take my ideas and suggestions seriously,' he said with a hint of menace. 'The consortium I represent already owns a minority stake in Motor Racing Promotions. You should know that I am a matter of days from securing a further stake in the company. The combination of those two holdings in MRP will … very shortly and very clearly … give *me* outright control of Formula 1.'

THIRTY

'He claimed he owned *how* much?' asked Quartano.

'It came just as much of a surprise to everyone in the room,' said Nazar into the iPhone resting on the table in the private cabin of the motor home.

'How in the hell has he come by a controlling shareholding?'

Straker responded: 'I've tried to get back to Benedict Wasserman again, to see if Ziebart Blauman had picked up any sign of this, but can't reach him. He can't have known about this transfer of control; he would have surely warned us?'

'I want him straight onto this, Matt – as soon as you make contact.'

'Okay.'

'Tahm?' said Quartano. 'What's your take on all this – how's Formula 1 going to react? How would the sport work if it was led by Al-Megrahi?'

The professorial-looking Indian listened to the question.

Straker, watching Nazar's face, had a strong idea of the team boss's answer before he replied.

'Suleiman Al-Megrahi would be a disaster, Dom. The man's utterly divisive. Relishes confrontation. F1, with him anywhere near the sport, would be fractious – argumentative. With Al-Megrahi in any position of authority – in this confounded *F1 two-point-oh* of his – it could only result in dictatorship. And who knows where such a petulant, egotistical, ambitious man would leave us?'

Nazar's reaction would be more widely shared in only a matter of hours.

Because of Ravilious's ill health, it might have been assumed the MRP deal would fall into a state of suspension; Straker, though, wanted to keep his team of photographers in place. The only exception to this was at Silverstone as tailing Ravilious was no longer relevant. Straker thanked his team for their efforts and stood them down.

Having also signed off with Ptarmigan, Straker headed down the M40 towards London. His mind was more engaged in the Formula 1 story than ever. Not even the setting sun behind him, bathing the full-leafed Oxfordshire countryside in a hue of glorious orange, could distract him from his thoughts.

His phone pinged as he reached the chalk cliffs of the Chilterns cutting. Chancing a look down, Straker saw Nazar had sent him an energetically titled email:

'URGENT – DQ AND MATT – <u>READ THIS IMMEDIATELY</u>!'

Checking via his mirrors and over the open back of his car that it was clear enough for him to pull over onto the hard shoulder, Straker braked and brought himself to a halt. He put on his four-way flashers.

Straker opened the message.

He saw it contained a link to a Twitter handle he'd never heard of, something called the @WhittleburyGroup. As Straker clicked through to the Tweet, he found a link to a website which carried a formal-looking statement:

FORMULA 1 TEAMS AND HISTORIC CIRCUITS
LAUNCH BREAKAWAY SERIES
'THE GRAND PRIX WORLD CHAMPIONSHIPS'

In response to the news of Arno Ravilious's forthcoming retirement and divestment of his company, Motor Racing Promotions – and the announcement this afternoon by Mr Suleiman Al-Megrahi of his intention to acquire a controlling interest in the commercial arm of F1 – a number of Formula 1 teams are formally announcing a collaboration with a group of historic grand prix circuits to form a breakaway series of elite motor racing.

Signatories to the Whittlebury Group believe the time has come to return Formula 1 motor racing to its traditional values and to refocus on the inherent skills of driver and car.

Signatories to the Whittlebury Group are listed below; invitations have been issued to all other similar entities to participate equally:

TEAMS	CIRCUITS
Massarella	Brands Hatch (Great Britain)
Lambourn	Magny-Cours (France)
Williams	Watkins Glen (USA)
Renault	Estoril (Portugal)
Red Bull	Imola (San Marino)
McLaren	Jerez (Spain)
Force India	Anderstorp (Sweden)
Sauber	Zandvoort (Netherlands)
Manor	Spa-Francorchamps (Belgium)
Haas	Nürburgring (Germany)
	Kyalami (South Africa)
	Interlagos (Brazil)

With the intention of re-embodying the historic spirit of the sport, the Whittlebury teams and circuits are fully committed to raising the funding to establish a complete rebirth of Formula 1 and to hosting its first full season next year.

'Holy crap,' said Straker out loud.

He put his car in gear and fed himself back into the traffic.

Switching his phone to hands-free, he called the Ptarmigan team boss.

'Arno Ravilious is out of action for a matter of hours and the sport is already feeding off his carcass.'

'It really is quite tasteless,' agreed Nazar.

'This breakaway group, though, clearly backs up what you said earlier – about the key players being unwilling to work with an Al-Megrahi-led F1?'

'We'd not even heard of the Whittlebury Group until two hours ago. It can only have been formed this quickly because of Al-Megrahi's announcement this afternoon.'

'It looks like he's shifted the tectonic plates, then,' said Straker. 'I noticed Ptarmigan are not named as a signatory? Have we not been invited to join?'

'We and Ferrari were the first two teams Lord Lambourn approached. DQ and I do not believe any such breakaway series will be plain sailing.'

'Why not?'

'First off, we have significant contractual agreements with Mandarin Telecom, which are entirely predicated on the Formula 1 brand. As long as that relationship lasts, we need to honour them. For Ptarmigan to break from MRP, we'd have to have prior agreement from the Chinese – and they weren't happy with things before the Ravilious crisis, so I doubt they would be willing to contemplate adding to the uncertainty. I would have serious doubts the breakaway group could fund itself to anything like the same level as current F1. The Whittlebury Group couldn't offer a fraction of what we can offer Mandarin Telecom through Formula 1. Not only that, the Whittlebury signatories all have a matrix of pre-existing contracted rights and obligations with Motor Racing Promotions, as, of course, *it* does with all the current circuits and TV. Any breach of those contracts would trigger a blizzard of lawsuits from any Al-Megrahi-controlled Motor Racing Promotions. It can only get extraordinarily messy.'

Straker continued on his way to London in a state of agitated silence.

While he was driving through West London to Putney, barely aware of the evening sun, he received another phone call.

'Matt,' said the unmistakable voice over the loudspeaker.

'Mr Quartano.'

'I need you to read an article that has just been posted online by the *Wall Street Journal*. It mentions your friend, Gabriel Barrus. We'll need to talk about this and all the other developments at eight o'clock tomorrow morning.'

The traffic was sticky down the Fulham Palace Road as Straker willed his progress over Putney Bridge and onto the waterfront. Parking up and hurrying back to his house, he opened the front door of the Georgian villa, shot upstairs, fired up his laptop and, as it was loading, made himself a jug of Pimm's, lacing it with ice. Taking the computer and his drink out onto his first-floor balcony, he sat at the garden table. Below him, in the warmth of the balmy summer evening, numerous boats and sculls were out on the water, taking advantage of the millpond conditions – but Straker paid the scene no attention. He was already clicking on a link to pull up the *WSJ* interview:

Gabriel Barrus III, one of America's foremost sports entrepreneurs – founder of Salt Lake Media and owner among other things of the NFL League's Golden Spikers, the NBA's Rushmore Riders and the MLB's New England Soulsearchers – is contracting to buy Arno Ravilious's stake in the multi-billion dollar Motor Racing Promotions, the commercial rights holder of Formula 1. In an interview with Marty Lowenstein, Barrus explains the rationale and his plans for entering a new sport:

ML: 'Why Formula 1? You've not had any interest in this sport before?'

GB III: 'I have previously owned an IndyCar team, and made money from it. Sports management is highly specialized but, in my experience, rarely sport specific.'

ML: 'You must see opportunities to improve the efficiency of Formula 1?'

GB III: 'Undeniably. Arno Ravilious, the founder of the commercial side of Formula 1, has been an outstanding creator – a true entrepreneur, if you will. The sport has been beset recently by issues to do with odd regulations and rules; the pursuit of a green agenda by the

FIA; budget caps, which limit inter-race testing and constrict innovation and which, therefore, render the racing highly predictable; there's been a tilt towards Pay Per View, which has undoubtedly diminished TV audiences; and, lastly, there's been an asymmetric distribution of the sport's revenues.'

ML: 'All those would seem to be political issues – rather than commercial ones?'

GB III: 'Welcome to the world of sports management! I have found one thing to be universal: Increase the commercial returns, and the politics will follow.'

ML: 'So what's your route to increasing the commercial returns?'

GB III: There are several instances of low hanging fruit. On the costs side, rationalization of the way teams are transported is a must. On the revenue side, the TV rights have grown in value recently – and these, through renegotiation, will be adjusted across all territories, countries and markets. Another adjustment will be the mix of circuits, and the scale of the fees they pay; currently, the rates are all over the place. I intend to go straight to the highest bidder, and so expect yields there to expand considerably. For instance, Saudi Arabia are expressing keen interest in hosting a grand prix and are offering nearly double the current highest level of fees.'

Straker finished the article.

He stayed sitting on the balcony for nearly fifteen minutes, without moving.

So much had happened in the last three days, and yet the most significant developments seemed to have occurred in the last six hours. Straker had witnessed the physical collapse of the Ringmaster and, with Ravilious being removed from the field of play sooner than expected, three groups had stepped forward to stake their claims over how Formula 1 should be managed: Suleiman Al-Megrahi, the Whittlebury Group and Gabriel Barrus III.

How was all this going to play out?

Straker remembered his meeting with Quartano, scheduled for the following morning. Answers to that question would inevitably be sought and discussed then. If Straker was to offer Quartano any kind of intelligent assessment, he needed a much fuller understanding of the characteristics, predispositions and likely behaviours of all these players. How could he possibly achieve that beforehand?

A thought struck him.

Straker jumped up and strode into the house, making for the weighty research tome he had been given by Benedict Wasserman, the investment banker. Picking up the Ziebart Blauman report, and thumbing through it again, he saw it offered what he was after: the first half set out a detailed history of Formula 1 and the rise of Motor Racing Promotions.

Needing sustenance before getting started, Straker ordered an Indian. While waiting for it to arrive, he took the chance to shower and change into looser clothes.

The distraction of eating gave him the chance to think things through.

How – in a matter of days, only a few hours, really – could the global leviathan, presence and seemingly unstoppable force of Formula 1 motor racing be on the verge of a factional war for control?

Were the forces and interests now ranging to claim control of F1 in any way credible?

Could these claimants ever address the problems they were citing, or would the sport be forever damaged if left with aggrieved parties?

Who or what, now, could restore order to – let alone save – the extraordinary sport of Formula 1?

Matt Straker settled down – and started to read…

BOOK TWO

KYALAMI

THIRTY-ONE

The day that changed Formula 1 was not like any other of 1972. It didn't provide that summer's balmy sunshine. It came with heavy cloud, torrential rain and blustery squalls. The bigger shock was the cold, made all the sharper by a biting easterly wind. The Formula 2 circuit at Thruxton, the repurposed RAF and USAAF D-Day air-field, was particularly exposed. There, the wind whipped across Salisbury Plain, seeming to carry the rainfall almost horizontally.

Ten men crouched in the downpour; their boiler suits drenched to the skin. Repeated attempts to sweep the rainwater from their eyes were made as they looked up the pit lane for the Ptarmigan Formula 1 car.

They could hear it coming, but not yet see it. The 450 horsepower 3.0 litre V8 Ford-Cosworth revved, screaming out on each down-shift, none of its sound being muffled by the weather. Finally honing into view, the pronounced wedge-like shape in British Racing Green emerged through the swirling rainwater. Ptarmigan's JJM5 had small front wheels, chunky and wider rear wheels, side-mounted radiator pods, front and rear wings – both as an extension of its overall wedge shape – and a tall, slim airbox above the driver's head.

For all the car's striking appearance, it was little more than a knockoff. As with most of that season's F1 cars, all their designers could do was try and keep up. Two years before, the mould had been shattered by the revolutionary black-and-gold John Player Special-sponsored Lotus 72: Colin Chapman having produced one of the most striking examples of change ever seen. Drawing the car's shape directly from the idea of form following function, the JPS celebrated the beauty of physics in a way never expressed so elegantly before, an expression that also translated into a quantum improvement in performance.

Since the '72, other Formula 1 teams had tried to copy its shape, some even authentically – but none was going to emulate the totality of Chapman's genius. It would take the pit lane a long time before they even learned about – let alone understood – the full majesty of Chapman's design: the inboard brakes, the anti-dive front suspension, the anti-squat suspension in the rear, or the full artistry of the aerodynamics.

Through the driving rain at Thruxton, Reno Solanki's Ptarmigan copycat sped along in front of the breeze-block garages, before he turned in and jolted to a stop.

The drill was on.

Raindrops created small explosions of steam as they hit the top of the burning-hot engine block, exposed through the open bodywork.

In the torrential rain, jack men – front and rear – heaved the car up off the ground.

Each wheel was attacked by a mechanic, each with a wheel gun. Central wheel nuts were hastily removed.

Four men, one to each wheel, heaved his wheel off and swung it out of the way.

Another four mechanics, each holding a new wheel, converged rapidly on the car, slotting the new ones onto the male nut of the hub.

The mechanics with the wheel guns lunged forward and started re-fixing the new wheels in place.

As each member of the team finished, he looked up and forward to the front of the car. There, another mechanic, holding out his arm, 'held' the car.

But his arm stayed out. It didn't drop.

Reno Solanki wasn't being released.

The rhythm of the drill was broken.

All eyes turned back, searchingly, to the four wheels. What was wrong? Why had the car been held? *Who* was holding it up?

A young, gangly man with long wet red hair straggling down his face hunched over the chunky right rear wheel. Wrestling physically with the wheel gun, he seemed to be fighting it – applying to it his entire-but-slight body weight.

'*OH for FUCK'S SAKE!*' was screamed at him.

JJ McKay, under a held umbrella, stood to one side of the car and was waving the stopwatch in his hand. On his head, the Ptarmigan team boss wore his habitual maroon peasant's coppola, and, against the weather, a knee-length embroidered sheepskin coat with large strips of fleece around both the lapels and cuffs. The length of McKay's coat was matched by the length of his hair down his cheeks; JJ McKay was right there with the Jackie Stewart/Elvis Presley/ Emerson Fittipaldi mutton-chop sideburns.

McKay bellowed: 'What the fuck's going on?'

Solanki revved the engine to urge haste, its noise shaking every bone around him.

The young redhead didn't reply, still investing himself – heaving and yanking at the wheel gun.

A mechanic standing beside him shouted: 'Hey, Ravilious?'

There was no response from the wrestling mechanic.

'Rav*ilious*!'

Still no answer.

The older mechanic kicked the ankle of the crouching man's boot.

Ravilious defiantly raised his right shoulder, as if to say 'leave off – I'm *doing* it'.

The wheel gun did begin to turn the nut. But slowly. Ravilious agitated the thing, heaving it off before eventually raising his right hand.

The mechanic's arm – at the front of the car – finally lowered.

With a surge of revs, the clutch was dropped and the Ptarmigan shot forwards. A matter of yards later, standing water was hurled into the air as the car disappeared into a cloud of its own spray down the pit lane.

The mechanics stood up, their body language indicating utter dejection. Rain continued to lash down, prompting them to move out of the weather, back into the garage.

Another couple of cars also testing that day roared by on the track.

JJ McKay was yelling at his people to converge on him, when his voice was drowned out by an ear-piercing scream of crunching metal.

No question: it sounded serious.

The mechanics rushed back out through the open front of the garage, out into the rain. Looking down the pit lane, their gaze followed the noise. Other mechanics, from garages nearer the apparent incident, were sprinting away towards it. The Ptarmigan mechanics quickly followed on.

As they ran, the reason for the commotion became obvious. One car had rammed another. A Ptarmigan had rammed a Marlboro BRM. The Ptarmigan's collapsed rear end was resting on the surface of the track; long gouge marks showed where its subframe had scraped along the concrete. The Ptarmigan's right rear wheel was missing; its nose had ridden up over the sidepods of Peter Gethin's grand prix car. Reno Solanki climbed out of the Ptarmigan. His mechanics ran towards him; he started screaming at them in a thick Italian accent. Audible even through his helmet. Gesticulating ferociously, he accused them of a crap pit stop. Looking at the damaged rear end of his car, he bawled:

'Who the fuck-a did-a my rear right-a wheel?'

The man in the maroon coppola and sheepskin coat was closing in, the blond girl holding JJ McKay's umbrella having to shuffle awkwardly sideways to try and keep the team boss dry.

Solanki's voice was lost in a surge of wind before he screamed again: 'Who the fuck did rear right?'

The team boss's attention focused on a tall lanky youth, his face streamed with wet red hair. 'You! – Well?'

'The wheel gun was wet,' replied the redhead in a surprisingly flat Northern Ireland accent. 'The nut was wet.'

'What do you fucking expect in the fucking rain?'

'The components are badly designed.'

'They weren't for the other three wheels,' JJ McKay shouted back. 'Who the fuck are you – what's your *name?*'

'It cross-threads *far* too easily,' came an unapologetic rejoinder. 'It gets stuck, far too easily.'

'The others didn't fuck up,' shouted the team boss. 'Hang on! ... *Hang on* – I *know* you ... that gobby lip? You're that new fucker ... fucking *Ravilious* ... you're that tit that fucked up last time?'

Ravilious was already coming back at him when McKay held up his hand: 'That's it ... that's enough, already. You fuck up in the dry ... you fuck up in the rain ... I'm fucked off ... you're fucking *out*.'

Ravilious only looked affronted and frustrated. He began to speak again, when McKay bellowed: 'Didn't you *hear* me – get the fuck *out!*'

Ravilious just stood there. Almost disbelievingly.

McKay ended up throwing a gesture of dismissal.

Finally, the lanky redhead started walking away, back up the pit lane.

His carriage was defiant. Unyielding.

Angry.

THIRTY-TWO

Arno Ravilious rode his early 1960s Lambretta back to Kirtlington Park in Oxfordshire; the Ptarmigan factory was housed there in the stately home's ancient stable yard. After two hours through the rain, Ravilious was still soaked and even angrier, brooding on his dismissal from the pit lane.

Walking into the converted barn, he was met with a wealth of sounds echoing around the unadorned space – hammering, a hissing oxyacetylene torch, the dentist-drill screech of an angle grinder spewing sparks across the floor. Josh Garrett, Ptarmigan's chief mechanic, was lying on his back beneath Shauni Brannigan's car which was up on a stand. All the bodywork had been removed. In that state, it lacked any dignity or elegance, looking completely homemade. It appeared little more than a riveted box made up of 10-, 12- and 16-gauge aluminium. Except that such a fragile-looking container was the driver's only protection against the heavy, muscular components all around him. In turn, those components looked like they were only there to try and control the power of the brutal-looking 3-litre V8 engine, which, even when silent, looked almost impossible to restrain.

'You're all back, then?' asked Garrett, as he resurfaced.

Ravilious grunted. 'Just me,' he said, as he rubbed a hand through his red hair, now dried slightly after being under his helmet.

Garrett looked up. 'Oh Christ, Arno. Not again – not another fuck-up?'

'I can't help it if the kit's crap.'

The chief mechanic shook his head. 'Jeez. You have a *way* with people, Arno ... you do know that the kit is mine ... *my* design?'

Ravilious seemed to give the chief mechanic a QED shrug.

'Did he fire you?'

Ravilious shrugged again.

'Well, until that's clear, you're not lazing around until JJ gets back and does it properly. You can sodding well earn your pay. A chore's come up, but I've had to work on this. JJ wanted me to call the Österreichring – like I need fucking paperwork – so you can damn well do it. The relief for all of us is that it'll keep you off anything mechanical. Get up to the office and do it from there.'

Garrett rummaged through a pocket in his boiler suit before holding out a scrap of paper. 'These are the details that need confirming. Olive will tell you how to get hold of the right guy.'

Ravilious took the note and unfolded the scrunched-up piece of paper. It was covered in oily thumbprints:

Details to be confirmed –
Date & timings of arrival
Accommodation – hotels / drivers & team
Appearance fee
Share of prize money

Ravilious's expression changed. 'What sort of arrangements should I expect?'

'*You* don't expect anything,' answered Garrett. 'All you've got to do is listen. Go through each of those items and just fucking write down what he says.'

Ravilious shuffled to the bottom of the steps. Still looking down at the scrap of paper, he started up the stairs to the manager's office.

'For fuck's sake, Arno,' shouted Garrett after him, 'look sharp about it.'

Ravilious still had his head down, and looked as if he was dawdling, but he was contemplating the contents of the note. He climbed the steps to the elevated office with its commanding position above the factory floor. Two storeys up, he reached the platform in front of the glass-fronted cubicle and opened the flimsy door, which rattled as he walked in.

Olive Cadwell, JJ McKay's secretary-cum-office manager, greeted him with a suspicious glance. 'Yes?'

'Mr Garrett's asked me to make a telephone call.'

JJ McKay's secretary looked a little disbelieving. After a pause she tilted her head in the direction of her boss's desk and phone. Ravilious had only been in here once before – during his interview. What he did remember was the mess. Papers were stacked feet high in places; layers of dust covered the shelves; while, even in here – away from the garage – there was the inescapable bitter smell of stale, dirty oil.

Ravilious circled the desk, turning sideways through the gap between it and a grey filing cabinet. Lowering himself into the creaking chair, he placed the scrap of paper on the only small clear area on the surface. 'Excuse me, mum,' he said across to Cadwell. 'How do I get hold of this bloke Ostering?'

Olive showed surprise at his style of address, which seemed to soften her. 'It's Öst-er-reich-ring, dear – and it's not a bloke – it's the name of a circuit. In Austria. You'll need to ask for a Mr Niklas Strolz.'

'Okay.'

Responding to Ravilious's rather vacant gaze at the phone on the desk, she said: 'Dial 100 and ask for the international operator. Then you read out this number,' as she reached across and handed him a business card; it, too, was adorned with oily thumbprints.

Ravilious nodded his thanks, lifted the heavy Bakelite phone and dialled. A stream of clicks sounded out as the wheel of numbers juddered back anticlockwise. After a sequence of clunks down the line, Ravilious heard a middle-aged voice wearily say: 'Exchange.'

'An international number.'

'Hang on.'

There were more clicks followed by silence. Then another voice came on: 'Country?

'Austria.'

'Number?'

Ravilious read it out.

All sorts of sounds came down the line, and a few seconds later there was a long continuous 'dring' in his ear.

'*Guten Tag?*'

Ravilious was thrown. In a panic he asked: 'Er, do ... you ... speak ... English?'

'*Ja*, a little.'

He sighed with relief. 'Can I speak to Mr Strolz?'

Disconcertingly, the line went silent.

Ravilious heard nothing for several seconds; he wondered if he had been disconnected when a deep Teutonic voice came on the line. 'How can I help you?'

'I'm calling from Ptarmigan, Mr Strolz – the Formula 1 team in England. I've been asked to confirm a number of details for when we come to your grand prix.' Ravilious read them out.

He hoped he had been understood. All he heard from the other end was a grunt, followed by something else, something that didn't fully register until much later: 'Ptarmigan, yes?'

'Yes.'

Ravilious heard a rustle of paper.

'Yes ... hello, Mr...?'

'Ravilious, sir. Arno Ravilious.'

'Mr Ravilious, then ... Ptarmigan's arrival is scheduled for the 9th of August. You can arrive at any time after twelve noon, any earlier and you will be charged. We've put your team up in the Gasthof Schönburg. Ptarmigan's appearance fee is ... 72,000 Schillings. Your team's share of the prize money is 4 per cent.'

With the receiver jammed under his chin, Ravilious hurriedly wrote it all down. He offered his thanks and replaced the handset.

That wasn't so hard.

Ravilious was about to collect his bits and pieces together and leave, but, as he stood up from JJ McKay's chair, he stopped.

How much, he thought, was 72,000 Schillings?

As it happened, he did have some acquaintance with foreign

currency: for a pittance in summer pocket money, he had been dragooned into doing chores around his father's parts business, spending God knew how many hours sorting through and settling invoices, mostly related to importing components from the continent. Old man Ravilious had drummed into him two endlessly repeated points: never settle bills immediately, as this was the cheapest source of credit going – and, because of Britain's crippling exchange controls, he was to disregard the currency in which they were quoted. Currencies were to be juggled in case settlement could be managed cheaper using other currency balances they might already have running at the time. For all his experience of those countless mind-numbing hours, though, Ravilious had never worked in Austrian Schillings. He lowered himself back down into the chair.

'Excuse me, mum,' he said to Cadwell, with a little more confidence.

'It's *Olive*, dear. Call me Olive!'

'Oh, okay. I'm Arno … Hi. What do you know … Olive … about Austrian Schillings? How many of them are there to the pound?'

Her expression changed slightly with his more assertive tone.

Without speaking, Olive Cadwell leant down, pulled out a rickety wooden drawer in her desk and extracted a small booklet. Ravilious caught a glimpse of the name Thomas Cook on the front as she opened it and laid it flat. 'As of the 1st of July,' Olive said, scanning the dates across the top and running her finger across the columns, 'there were … fifty-six Austrian Schillings to the pound.'

Ravilious grunted his thanks and jotted down the rate across the top of his notes. He did a quick division. 72,000 Schillings was £1,285 … so call it £1,300, give or take? Ravilious looked at this and immediately thought he must have got the numbers wrong. How could the amount be that low? He quickly redid the calculation.

'Olive,' he asked, 'are you sure that's the right exchange rate?'

Olive Cadwell exhaled irritably.

'Could I have a look at that booklet?'

'You don't believe me?'

Ravilious looked up and smiled openly. In a moment Olive Cadwell was disarmed – as if Ravilious had become someone else. His face had altered. The transformation was arresting. Suddenly there was something engaging about this slim, gangly young man with his shock of frizzy red hair.

'No, no, Olive,' he said. 'I trust *you* completely … it's Mr Strolz I'm not sure about…'

Cadwell accepted the qualification and handed over the book.

Ravilious resorted to the way his father had taught him to double-check his maths. Flicking through a few pages he managed to find a second exchange rate, that of US dollars into Austrian Schillings. He needed another piece of paper to scribble on; being unable to find one on the desk, Ravilious looked down and saw the team boss's overflowing wastepaper basket. A dead envelope lay on the top. Picking it up, Ravilious used the back of it to scribble down some numbers; he then cross-checked his estimate of the Schilling/Sterling exchange rate, recalculating it via US Dollars. In under a minute he had established a triangular rate. He was assured that there were, indeed, give or take, fifty-six Austrian Schillings to the Pound.

'Olive?'

The secretary stopped what she was doing this time and turned to face him.

'How does the team get to Austria?'

'By ferry to Calais, probably, and then driving down through France and Germany.'

Ravilious was already doing more calculations in his head and starting a tally. 'How much does the ferry cost to get our trucks across the Channel?'

Olive, beginning to be intrigued by the intensity of this young man, reached towards a shelf above her head and pulled down a dust-covered file from the jam-packed row. She flipped over several pages and soon reported: 'When we crossed over to Nivelles in June, the total ferry bill was 700 pounds.'

'And where was that?'

'Belgium.'

'Okay – and how much does the kit we carry for each race vary in weight and space?'

'Very little.'

'Getting across the Channel to Austria should cost us about the same, then, pretty close to 700 pounds?'

Olive Cadwell nodded.

Ravilious quickly jotted that figure down. He then made some more notes and started making estimates of a few more things. Three days' travel. Twenty guys travelling with the team. Hotel rates would be, what, £20, £30 a head on the way there, perhaps less if the rooms were shared? Then there were the room rates while they were at the race; finally, there were all the travelling and accommodation costs on the return journey.

While Ravilious was working this out, something Strolz had said suddenly bubbled to the surface; the man had said: *'Ptarmigan's* share of the prize money', hadn't he?

Why had he said that?

Why had he said *Ptarmigan's*? Why hadn't he just said 'the teams' share'? What did that specific attribution to Ptarmigan mean?

Ravilious was soon wondering: what harm could there be in asking?

Before he could stop himself, he had lifted the phone again, re-called the operator and re-asked for the Austrian number.

Olive Cadwell turned round in surprise.

Two minutes later he heard: 'Yes, Mr Ravilious. What can I do for you now?'

Very politely, he answered: 'Mr Strolz, I'm sorry to come back so soon. I was anxious, before I spoke to Mr JJ McKay, to check I'd written your figures down correctly. I don't want to upset him any further?'

To his surprise, Strolz chuckled in response.

'I've been looking at our costs for getting over to your grand prix in six weeks' time,' Ravilious explained: 'The ferry, the hotel rooms in Germany on the way down to you, while we're with you there, and on our way back, will cost Ptarmigan over 4,000 pounds – the equivalent, therefore, of 224,000 Austrian Schillings.'

Ravilious stopped talking, wanting to leave the number hanging in the air.

There was no response from the other end.

It started to feel embarrassing.

Ravilious decided to step in: 'Mr McKay is going to bite my head off, sir, if I can't cover the costs of competing at your race. Can I just check the number you gave me *is* for Ptarmigan?'

That question didn't induce any reply either.

Ravilious, in the meantime, was beginning to buzz: the Austrian could have quite easily told him to get lost…

…but he hadn't.

Ravilious was sure the number Strolz had given him *was* correct, but juxtaposing Ptarmigan's costs with the amount offered as an appearance fee – and the size of the difference – seemed to have made Ravilious's point for him.

Strolz finally came back assertively: 'That *was* Ptarmigan's figure I gave you…'

'You're going to think me stupid, Mr Strolz – as I am new to grand prix racing – but I don't see the logic of a team losing money in order to appear at your race?'

Ravilious stopped talking again.

He wanted the other man to fill the silence.

Nothing, though, was volunteered.

Ravilious's heart rate was quickening all the time.

Should he go for it?

He thought of his experience that morning in the pit lane, of his aptitude with the car; he thought of being soaked through and uncomfortably cold; finally, he thought about the humiliation he'd suffered – of being bawled out in front of the team. What the hell did he have to lose? Wasn't he all but out of Ptarmigan already?

'I'm just saying, Mr Strolz, that – after doing the numbers – Ptarmigan might not be able to afford to take part.'

Olive swung round and glared at him.

Ravilious's heart rate pounded, his demeanour tensing at the expression on Olive's face, which indicated serious disapproval.

Right then Ravilious's heart rate was shocked even further.

The glass-panel door of the office rattled loudly as it juddered open. Who should be standing in the doorway ... but JJ McKay?

Ravilious flinched. He half stood in a salute to a senior officer, partly feeling he should vacate his boss's chair.

Despite the pressure of the audience he now had, Ravilious said: 'As long as you don't think your spectators would mind seeing a reduced number of cars at your race.'

The moment McKay registered what was being said, he joined Olive in looking aghast.

Ravilious didn't respond, continuing to stand with the handset to his ear.

JJ McKay took a step forwards.

Ravilious held up his hand to the team boss: an outright gesture of defiance.

McKay was beginning to fume.

Ravilious, maintaining eye contact with his boss, said emolliently: 'I would be grateful if you could think about this for us, Mr Strolz,' and slowly lowered the handset.

'What the fuck are you *doing*?' screamed McKay. 'Have you just threatened a grand prix promoter with this team's absence?'

Ravilious surprised himself with his own calmness. He was standing at his boss's desk ... in his boss's office ... having just threatened to absent the team from the Austrian Grand Prix ... without authorization ... in front of his boss ... who didn't approve.

Ravilious said: 'Strolz was offering to pay us less – in fees and prize share – than it would have cost us to get there.'

McKay was on the verge of exploding; he took another step forward.

'Grands prix sell tickets to the public,' Ravilious said, 'by the bucketload. The race promoter gets to keep those proceeds. *He's* making money out of us being at his race. Ptarmigan *aren't*. I simply made the point it shouldn't cost us to provide Mr Strolz with his spectacle.'

'Get out!' bellowed McKay at Ravilious. 'Get the *FUCK* OUT OF MY OFFICE.'

Ravilious could have shrunk with the vehemence of the outburst. Instead, he made to leave calmly. As he walked closely past JJ McKay, towards the office door, he heard the team boss say:

'Olive, for Christ sake get Strolz on the phone … *immediately*.'

Ravilious turned around and said quietly: 'Is there any harm in leaving it for a while … let him come back to us? It might be worth pointing out, sir … Mr Strolz … didn't actually say no…'

'GET *OUT!*'

Ravilious walked out onto the platform at the top of the stairs. His attention was caught by those on the floor below him.

The factory was silent.

There was no activity in the workshop: no hammering, no welding, no grinding. Every pair of eyes was looking up. They had all heard McKay's outburst; how could they have missed it? All were watching the recipient of it as he made his way down the steps. His teammates were now all the more intrigued.

Instead of showing any embarrassment, Ravilious seemed to indicate a certain confidence. He was even offering a half-knowing smile.

His demeanour seemed to change the mood.

Somehow, the workforce knew it was not smelling blood any more. The youngster had been chewed up – twice – in rapid succession, but he looked far from spat out.

What else, then, *were* they sensing?

Garret watched him saunter back to Brannigan's car.

'Jesus, Arno, what the fuck have you gone and done now?'

Ravilious offered a shrug. 'I've just been pointing out the obvious, Josh. Whether the shortcomings of wheel-changing designs, or appearance fees, the obvious doesn't go down too well around here.'

'Oh my God,' replied Garrett, his voice trailing away in resignation. 'What the hell have you landed me in this time?'

He was about to think of something for Ravilious to do, to get him out of the factory, when a bellow came for Garrett from up in the rafters: '*JOSH!*'

It was JJ McKay.

The chief mechanic glowered at Ravilious as he made his way across the factory floor to the foot of the stairs.

Still no work was being done around the barn: everyone was waiting to see where one of the legendary JJ McKay tirades might take them all next.

Ten minutes later Josh Garrett reappeared at the top of the stairs. He made his way down onto the factory floor.

Ravilious was wheeling a dolly laden with boxes from the stores towards Brannigan's car.

Ravilious asked: 'How did that go?'

'You've *got* to learn your fucking place. I'm fed up taking the blows for your insolent behaviour.'

Ravilious wasn't convinced by Garrett's sternness.

'You're never to overstep your authority again, Arno – do you understand? JJ is livid.'

Ravilious's face broke into a smile. 'I notice you haven't fired me,' he said. 'Strolz's original offer was 1,285 pounds and 4 per cent of the prize money ... so what's he revised it to?'

Garrett looked like he was pausing to think how to tone his answer with some kind of message.

Ravilious suddenly realized something – why his heart rate had remained so high, despite the dressing down from his team boss.

He barely caught Garrett mumble something. 'Sorry, Josh, what was that?'

'Five thousand for our appearance fee and 10 per cent of the prize fund.'

THIRTY-THREE

The 1972 British Grand Prix at Brands Hatch was electrifying. Ptarmigan's Italian driver, Reno Solanki, mounted a determined challenge against the JPS Lotus of Emerson Fittipaldi. For most of the second half they clashed wheel-to-wheel through Paddock Hill Bend, down and up through the compression to Druids and then in repeated foot-to-the-floor drag races out through the woods up Hawthorn Hill. After 76 laps, Solanki was barely a second behind as the Brazilian crossed the line to take the chequered flag. Jackie Stewart, in his Tyrrell-Ford, was only a short distance behind in third.

Despite their performance on the track, the top three teams – and a couple of others – were far from content. Numerous gripes burbled along the pit lane. The key one concerned Ferrari. Yet again, the Italian team had been given special treatment. Instead of the accepted convention, of allocating pit lane garages according to standings in the Championship, Ferrari had been 'promoted' above their rightful position to a position of favour.

At the same time, JJ McKay was consumed by a gripe specific to Ptarmigan, causing him additional agitation. Ten minutes after the race, the stewards summoned him and his driver to appear; Solanki had been accused by another team of overtaking under a yellow flag. Were this to be upheld, the driver would be disqualified, depriving the team of its place and desperately needed prize money. Before going to the inquiry, McKay dispatched Arno Ravilious to fetch the team's set of rules from one of the trucks.

At the beginning of that week, Josh Garrett had sat Ravilious down.

'You are exasperating, Arno. You are no mechanic. JJ had been screaming at me to fire you.'

'Daddy's discounts too valuable, then, huh?'

Garrett ignored the quip. 'JJ's made it plain we have no job for you on the factory floor or at the trackside.'

Ravilious shrugged.

Garrett went on: 'JJ is many things, but he *can* spot talent. He was *staggered* by what you got out of that old goat, Strolz, at the Öster-reichring. As a ... last chance ... he wants to try you on something else – but you'd still be on probation.'

Ravilious's expression was impassive.

'Getting Ptarmigan more money from race tracks,' Garrett continued, 'would be a meaningful contribution to the team. JJ wants you to move up there,' he said, indicating the elevated office up the steps. 'He's going to give you six months to prove yourself. You'll be called "office assistant". JJ wants to try you out as the team's liaison with the circuits, to work on securing appearance and prize money for us for the rest of the season.'

Ravilious's smile showed a degree of triumph.

'The good thing about this new arrangement,' said Garrett with a smile of his own, 'is that *I* won't have the ball ache of trying to manage you.'

When the newly promoted 'office assistant' returned with the team's copy of the rules at Brands Hatch, JJ McKay and a handful of other team bosses were huddled in a small tent at one end of the pit lane. In the stiffening afternoon breeze, its canvas panels were billowing, occasionally cracking in the wind. Ravilious ducked under the flap and found eight men sitting in a small circle, all on plastic chairs on the grass.

'And don't start me on that American,' said the Earl of Lambourn, the owner, boss and founder of his own grand prix team. The peer's effortless bearing, confidence and charisma seemed to envelop the gathering.

Lambourn was aged in his early thirties. His manner, naturally voluminous hair, close-fitting cheesecloth shirt and orange silk cravat all added to his eye-catching presence. Tabloid newspapers described him as the 'playboy peer': fuelling the image, the young aristocrat was frequently photographed out with a succession of beautiful women, typically European film stars. But that was only one facet of him. Since his days in the nursery, cars and motor racing had been his passion. With the double-edged moment of inheriting young, he had been presented with an extraordinary opportunity to indulge himself. By his mid-twenties, the new earl had set up a team in his own name. Ten years on, even with moderate success, he seemed to be spending most of his family's money propping up the Lambourn Formula 1 team.

'And who's that appalling chap that runs Watkins Glen?' he asked. 'What's *his* name?'

'Brad Margesson,' spat Ken Tyrrell.

'That's him.'

'"Mayflower" Margesson,' added Colin Chapman with a smirk. 'Talk about a promoter who feels he acts with divine right.'

'I even know him – have done for a while,' said Teddy Mayer of McLaren, 'and not even a personal relationship makes any difference. The sod of it is that he knows nothing about Formula 1. He only knows NASCAR and IndyCar. It's a different world over there. Those teams have the backing of the huge motor companies. Money seems to be no issue for them.'

'Margesson wouldn't even know where Europe was,' added Frank Williams.

BRM's Tim Parnell shook his head. 'Precisely why he seems to have no idea how much it costs us to get over there!'

Inside the tent, Ravilious had to squeeze – side on – to get round behind the circle of chairs to reach his team boss. He handed over the folder.

McKay leant back to say something to him, but Ravilious's attention had been caught by the conversation.

'When I dealt with that Swedish guy,' Teddy Mayer was saying, 'he wasn't even going to offer McLaren travel expenses. I had to go back to Yardley, cap in hand, practically begging for more money.'

'And what about that *bliksem* in Austria,' said Eugene Van Der Vaal, the South African boss of the Massarella F1 team. 'That man Strolz is tighter than a duck's arse.'

The Ptarmigan team boss suddenly clocked why Ravilious wasn't responding.

Turning to face the chat going on around the circle, McKay suddenly realized the competitive advantage his team might have struck – and it seemed that he couldn't help himself crow; McKay declared: 'You should have heard what my young friend, here, said to him,' introducing Ravilious with a slap on the young man's shoulder.

All the other team bosses looked across to JJ McKay – and then up at the spindly young man with the shock of red hair. Given his appearance, they were curious.

'Why, what *did* you say?' asked Lambourn. 'Threaten to sabotage Ferrari?' The comment prompted a round of laughter.

Ravilious smiled back nervously. He straightened up and said: 'No, sir. I pointed out that his initial offer to Ptarmigan – for us to attend his grand prix – didn't cover our costs.'

Expressions around the tent changed in an instant.

With one sentence Ravilious had silenced the meeting.

'And you found that *that* made a difference?' Lord Lambourn asked.

Ravilious looked round the meeting of team bosses as they sat in a circle, on plastic chairs on the grass, as the tent flapped in the wind. He really didn't know if they were taking him seriously or not. 'Not immediately, sir, no. I left Mr Strolz with the thought that we were going to lose money by attending his race … and that, because of it, we might not even…'

Lambourn interrupted him with a laugh. 'What? … You threatened not to *go*?'

McKay was now laughing too. 'I was livid, I can tell you. I couldn't believe what he'd said. I was all for calling Strolz straight back – to put things right – to say there'd been a misunderstanding. Except this insolent young man, here, urged me to wait … to see if Strolz wouldn't come back to *us*.'

'And *did* he?' asked Lambourn incredulously.

JJ McKay nodded. '*And* upped his appearance fee from 1,285 pounds to 5,000, as well as raising our share of the prize money from 4 per cent to 10.'

'*Fuck*, no.'

'Good God.'

'Holy cow.'

'You're *kidding*?' said Parnell.

Ravilious was amazed. All of them – each of these grizzled old campaigners – appeared genuinely surprised by how he'd dealt with the Austrian promoter.

'That's extra*ordin*ary,' offered Lambourn. 'I have to say, dear friends, this whole system *is* dreadfully unfair. Hearing what you've just said, though, I'm embarrassed into making a confession; I have to admit that Strolz actually offered us more than the initial amount he offered you, JJ, not that we knew it then of course. He'd offered me 2,000 pounds and 7 per cent. But well done, Ptarmigan! Securing that kind of increase is a quite stunning improvement.'

'I'd been ready to cave,' said JJ McKay. 'It was all Arno, here.'

'Good on you,' offered Tim Parnell of BRM.

With a chuckle in his voice, Lord Lambourn said: 'Perhaps you should be negotiating for *us*?'

The team bosses started laughing.

McKay definitely was.

'Why not, sir?' said Ravilious, loud enough to be heard by the peer. 'Haggling with a promoter would be a whole lot easier if you're bargaining for more than one team.'

The laughter started to fade.

The tent fell silent.

Tim Parnell was soon shaking his head. 'That's got to be right, hasn't it? I've always felt shafted – traded off – played off against the rest. I've never felt I had *any* bargaining power, not like Ferrari's at any rate.'

'My friends,' said Lambourn, 'in all seriousness, I think we should consider what our young friend here is saying. Thanks to Colin, FɪCA brings us together for reasons to do with transportation; why wouldn't we come together for financial negotiation as well? It would *have* to give the circuits pause for thought – if we acted together – if we were represented together.'

Lambourn looked round the faces. 'Gentlemen, how about this? We've all had our issues with Watkins Glen, have we not?'

There were nods and murmurs of agreement.

'On behalf of my team,' said Lambourn, 'I'm prepared to give Mr … oh, please forgive me, young man – I don't know your name?'

'Ravilious,' offered JJ McKay. 'Arno.'

'How do you do, Mr Ravilious?' replied the peer with a genuine smile. 'Patrick Lambourn, but please call me Budge. I, for one,' he went on, 'am up for giving you a go at getting a deal for us with Watkins Glen. If *you're* up for it,' he said, looking at McKay for agreement, 'I'd be prepared, for that race, to pool Lambourn with Ptarmigan. I'd be happy to share, equally, in whatever extra Mr Ravilious might try and secure for us.'

Lambourn looked again to each of the others. 'Anyone else want to join in?'

'How do you know he'll do it right?' grunted the McLaren boss.

'We don't, Teddy,' Lambourn said, 'but our young friend could hardly do any worse than we have. At least someone else would be taking the strain,' said the peer turning to Ravilious and giving him a wink.

Teddy Mayer pulled a face. 'I'm not sure, Budge. He's only a kid.'

Lambourn shrugged. 'What about the others? Ken? Tim? Frank? Colin … Eugene?'

Ravilious followed Lambourn's roll call to see if any of the other team bosses might fall in. They took their time. But two more did.

'Okay, well there we are, young Arno,' said Lambourn, 'you have the support of four members of the FɪCA – Lambourn, BRM, Lotus and Ptarmigan. Let's see what you can do in getting us a deal in America.'

Ravilious's brain was working fast.

But so was his team boss's.

'Okay, okay, gentleman,' said JJ McKay with a smile, while adding a tone of reality: 'This sideline can't affect Arno's other duties for Ptarmigan.'

Ravilious chose this moment to step in: 'That's okay, Mr McKay,' he said, 'I'd be happy to do this out of hours.'

Which prompted something of a disarming nod from his boss.

'Would it be reasonable, though,' Ravilious asked the circle, 'to suggest something for my efforts?'

Lambourn made a moue but then smiled at the self-assurance. 'If this is to be done in Mr Ravilious's own time, rather than Ptarmigan's, that can only be fair, can't it? What did you have in mind, young man?'

'What about 50 pounds a team?'

Tim Parnell from BRM was quickly shaking his head. 'That won't work.'

'Why not, Tim?'

'Where's the incentive? – 50 pounds flat, he could just phone it in. Aren't we better to offer him a percentage?'

The counter suggestion prompted indications of agreement.

'How about that, son?' asked Chapman.

Ravilious was thinking through this possibility. 'That would be fine. How about, then, gentlemen ... 2 per cent of any offer that's accepted?' he said, showing the first sign of hesitancy.

With barely any hesitation the other way, one of them shouted: 'Done!'

Two of the others around the circle, who weren't taking part, seemed to smirk – as if to suggest Ravilious had settled too soon.

Ravilious, though, wasn't at all perturbed. Two per cent was an exceptional rate; if he had received 2 per cent of the deal he'd just pulled off for Ptarmigan in Austria, he would have earned 100 pounds – the equivalent of three weeks' pay.

Ravilious replied confidently: 'If that's an arrangement you'd be comfortable with, gentlemen, then so am I.'

'Excellent,' confirmed Lambourn as, graciously, he rose to his feet and took two steps across the tent to offer Ravilious his hand. 'You have yourself a deal, young man.'

'Okay, Arno,' said McKay, drawing the distraction of their meeting to a close, 'now back to work. Your day job still needs doing. Josh needs help getting everything back to the barn.'

Arno Ravilious was soon leaving the meeting. He was, though, in quite a state.

Only a short time earlier he had walked into that tent, performing the menial errand of fetching a copy of the regulations; and yet here he was, only ten minutes later, walking out with a commission from four of the leading Formula 1 teams.

Arno Ravilious had never felt so energized in his life.

THIRTY-FOUR

The team's departure from Brands Hatch had to be delayed by several hours, while the stewards conducted their inquiry. Reno Solanki *was* deemed to have overtaken under a yellow flag, forcing him to forfeit his place. The official result was adjusted: Emerson Fittipaldi retained the lead and Jackie Stewart was elevated to second.

JJ McKay was steaming.

On their way back to Oxfordshire, Arno Ravilious was just as wound up but for very different reasons; he was bursting to get started on his new commission. He didn't get home to his bedsit in Bicester until one o'clock in the morning; even so, first thing the next day he was bounding up the stairs of the barn and into the team boss's office. Olive was already in. Ravilious explained to her what he had been asked to do over the weekend and found her genuinely impressed.

'What I'm going to need, Olive,' he said, 'are the names, addresses and contact numbers of those three other grand prix teams, and whatever you can tell me about the American Grand Prix.'

'Of course,' she said.

'I need to write some letters, too,' Ravilious explained. 'When do you normally go home in the evening? Can I borrow your typewriter? Can I lock up the place for you?'

Arno Ravilious clock-watched all day; ironically, not for reasons of waiting for work to end so he could go home, but so that he could get started on his own block of work for the team bosses.

When everyone had finally gone home, and he was alone in the office, Ravilious set himself some priorities. His administrative work, even as a lowly clerk in the RAF, had taught him the basics of bureaucratic efficiency – ingraining the discipline of establishing clear trails of correspondence for what the Airforce had described as CYA. He saw the same procedure applying usefully here, but as a protection against misunderstandings among the bosses, particularly his own.

Olive Cadwell had put together a list of all the addresses he wanted. Ravilious's first task was to write to the four team principals at that Brands Hatch meeting, including Ptarmigan's, and record the agreement they had reached. Ravilious identified the grand prix promoter he had been asked to negotiate with; confirmed that they had given him the authority to negotiate on their behalf; and that he would be entitled to an arrangement fee of 2 per cent – on both the appearance money and the share of the prize money. Ravilious agonized about getting these letters just right. After three hours he had prepared four envelopes, addressed and stamped them – ready for them to go in the first post the next morning.

Ravilious looked out through the windows of JJ McKay's office into the blackness of the now-deserted workshop. He revelled in the idea of working on something while everyone else might be at rest.

He jotted down some thoughts on how he might approach Brad Margesson at Watkins Glen. Several minutes later he had a structure for his conversation. Looking at his watch, he worked out it was roughly mid-afternoon in upstate New York. Picking up the phone, he dialled 100 and asked for the international operator. He waited to be put through to America.

'Hello, Mr Margesson? I'm Arno Ravilious, sir, calling from the Ptarmigan Grand Prix team in England.'

'Oh yeah,' said the brusque voice.

'I am keen to discuss the arrangements for attending the US Grand Prix.'

'Okay, son. Which team was that again?'

'Ptarmigan – but actually, sir, I'm not just calling for ourselves. I have the authority to speak for three other Formula 1 teams, as well.'

'Oh yeah?' said the American. 'Which ones?'

'Lotus, BRM and Lambourn.'

Ravilious stopped talking, waiting for a reaction. Hearing none, he continued: 'I've been doing some numbers on getting us to America, and worked out some costs. May I share these with you? I've calculated that, to be cost-neutral for these four teams to attend the Watkins Glen grand prix, they would each need to be reimbursed to the tune of 10,000 dollars.'

'You gotta be kidding me, right?'

Ravilious decided not to answer.

He waited, letting the call go silent, to see if the American would fill the silence. Margesson ended up saying something all right: 'Fuck you. I don't even pay Ferrari *that* much.'

Ravilious suddenly found himself breathing heavily. He made sure to hold the telephone away from his mouth.

Somehow, subconsciously, he logged the information he'd just been told; somehow he knew it was pivotal, seismic, but he had no immediate idea why.

'Sure,' said Ravilious, 'I accept Ferrari is the leading name in Formula 1…'

'…don't kid yourself, son … it's the *only* name.'

'Is that right? Except, Mr Margesson, Ferrari aren't anywhere in this year's Championship. Lotus and McLaren are the two serious contenders. Watkins Glen is the last race of the year. Any end-of-season showdown is only going to involve those two teams, both of which, incidentally, have a strong American connection – both being powered by Ford engines. Ferrari will be lucky to be fourth. If you don't have the teams there that count, you're not going to have much of a show for the crowds.'

There was silence on the line.

Ravilious fought to hold his nerve.

'I'm not going to increase the payments to teams that America has never heard of. *Ferrari* sells tickets. Other teams don't. Ferrari gets the lion's share. So, Mr Ptarmigan – no dice.'

THIRTY-FIVE

Ravilious felt like he'd just been kicked in the stomach. His bargaining position, even for four of the teams, was nowhere near as strong as he thought it would be.

He picked up his envelopes, walked to the office door, turned off the light, shut the door behind him, locked it and went down the steps into the hollow empty workshop towards the barn doors.

For two days Ravilious lived with the frustration of his conversation with that guy at Watkins Glen. He was determined the rebuff wasn't going to stop him getting the result he wanted, but he had no idea how to get round it.

He tried to rationalize the situation. There were three months until the US race. He wasn't going to go back to Brad Margesson any time soon. Maybe the American might now be sweating a little himself? But Ravilious dismissed that possibility as wishful thinking.

Whatever the reality, unless there was a change in his bargaining position, he was adamant the other guy was going to be the one to make the next move.

A few days later Arno Ravilious was travelling to Nürburg, West Germany for the German Grand Prix. During the weekend, some of the four bosses asked whether he had got anywhere with the US Grand Prix. Ravilious played for time.

The American promoter had made no attempt to be back in touch with him.

The next race of the 1972 season was the Italian Grand Prix. Ravilious accompanied the team to Milan and then on to Monza.

The heart of Ferrari country.

Everywhere he went he was reminded of his disappointing conversation with the American at Watkins Glen. All Ravilious could see was the power of the *Tifosi*, the Ferrari fans and the mightiness of the Ferrari brand. How could any of the other Formula 1 teams ever compete with that extraordinary scale of following? How could they ever be worth the same to a race promoter?

On the second day of practice, though, Ravilious suddenly asked himself a different question … and his answer was a revelation:

Why was he seeing Ferrari as the problem?

Could there not be a way of turning Ferrari to his *advantage*?

After the practice session was over, he sought out JJ McKay in the garage. He wanted to ask his team boss for a favour.

'What?' responded McKay. 'Absolutely no fucking *way*! Why on earth would I do that?'

'Because I want to ask him his advice.'

'About what?'

'I'm *this* close to getting us three times the money for the American Grand Prix.'

McKay looked at Ravilious incredulously, as if to ask himself whether the flight of fancy he had pulled off with Austria had all but run its course. 'Christ, Arno. Haven't you got work to do?' asked McKay, as he turned abruptly and walked away.

Ravilious explained his request to Josh Garrett. The Ptarmigan chief mechanic told him sharply that what he had asked for would put McKay in an extraordinarily difficult position: no one would ever have the impertinence to ask to see *Il Commendatore*.

Arno Ravilious was liaising with the Monza circuit office when a member of the Ptarmigan team appeared. With a tone that sounded like a warning, the middle-aged mechanic said: 'JJ's *looking* for you.'

Ravilious made for the pit lane and found his team boss standing over Reno Solanki's car, where he was in the middle of a discussion with the Italian driver.

'Arno,' McKay said dismissively, not turning to face him: 'Mr Ferrari has offered to see you at 6 p.m. this evening … for 10 minutes … He'll be in the bar of the Principe … for fuck's sake don't be late.'

The rest of his afternoon was a blur. Ravilious had to pull off managing his duties, effect his escape, shower and change – all with enough time to make the five miles from the Parco di Monza into the centre of Milan for six o'clock. He managed to get to the hotel with ten minutes to spare.

Trying to calm himself before the meeting, Ravilious ran through his thoughts for the hundredth time; he believed he had worked out how to steer the conversation to the subject he wanted. *How* on earth, though, was he going to ask for what he wanted from the great man? What possible bargaining position did he have with Ferrari?

Il Commendatore walked in on the dot of six.

Ravilious felt the 74-year old's arrival, instantaneously. At six-foot-one, the godfather of Formula 1 was fractionally taller than Ravilious. As expected, Enzo Ferrari was wearing a nearly black suit, white shirt and, inevitably, his Persol Ratti dark glasses. Ravilious walked up and, as confidently as he could, introduced himself.

Ferrari looked the youngster up and down.

Gruffly, he stated: 'JJ McKay says you're a cocky young man.'

Ravilious tried to convince himself that if the godfather of Formula 1 was using the word 'cocky' pejoratively, he would never have been granted this audience.

'Thank you, sir,' he said, and smiled.

Ravilious's eyes never left Ferrari's face. 'Has Mr McKay told you about Ptarmigan's coup with Mr Strolz?'

Ferrari shook his head and growled: 'No.'

There was an awkward silence.

'*He* hasn't,' the godfather added drily. 'But Lord Lambourn has.'

Ravilious couldn't believe it.

Ferrari indicated Ravilious to a chair, called for a waiter and declared: 'That Austrian has been above himself for too long.'

The maître d', hovering to the side of the room – apparently in permanent attendance of this honoured guest – saw the signal. Snapping his fingers, he summoned a waiter to attend Signor Ferrari immediately.

The godfather looked at Ravilious: 'You're a young man – extra*ordin*arily young – to be scoring points like that against the likes of Mr Strolz.'

Ferrari loosened the middle button of his three-piece suit jacket.

'I drew Mr Strolz's attention to a breach of common sense, sir, that's all: I compared Ptarmigan's costs of getting to his race with the fee he was offering and let him work out the deficit for himself.'

'So, why do you want to speak to me?'

At that moment the waiter appeared to take their orders. It gave Ravilious some time to compose himself, to find his zone. 'To my – naïve – mind, sir,' he said, when they were alone again, 'the Formula 1 teams are subsidizing the race promoters.'

'I can't disagree with that.'

Ravilious suppressed a smile.

'How does that affect me?' asked Ferrari.

'Circuits and promoters have been able to take advantage of the fact that the teams are independent concerns. They are able to rely on one team being unaware of the amount other teams are being paid.'

He saw Ferrari nod his head, perhaps acknowledging that Scuderia Ferrari was the biggest beneficiary of that state of affairs.

Before Ferrari could counter, Ravilious added quickly: 'Yet the circuits are doing exceptionally well out of all of us: they make money on the gate, they make on their shops, they make from the food and drink they sell – even if it's inedible – and they make from the advertising around their circuits.'

'So?'

'May I dare to say, then, sir, that means the Scuderia is subsidizing these circuit owners and promoters the most? If Ferrari didn't appear at these races, there *would* be no spectacle ... there *would* be no crowds ... there *would* be no money for the promoters.'

Enzo Ferrari seemed to acknowledge this as an acceptance of fact.

Ravilious pushed on: 'I spoke to Mr Margesson at Watkins Glen, sir, along the same lines as I had approached Mr Strolz. I laid out the costs we would face of getting to his circuit in America. I explained to him that Ptarmigan's appearance fee would need to be 10,000 dollars, or we wouldn't even cover our costs of getting to America ... we'd lose money on the trip.'

The godfather was showing no sign of resistance.

'Would you like to know what he said to that, sir?'

Il Commendatore's expression hardened.

'He said, sir – and I quote: "Fiddle you ... *I don't even pay Ferrari that much*".'

Beneath the dark glasses, Ferrari's expression went from a bristle to a suggestion of mild offence.

'If your costs are anything like ours, sir,' Ravilious charged on, 'the Scuderia would *also* appear to be losing money when going to America, while Mr Margesson and his circuit are still making a substantial profit. It is not my place, of course, but should not Ferrari – the spirit of Formula 1 and the bringer of spectacle to races – be earning reasonable money from bestowing its favour on such a circuit?'

The waiter returned with a tray.

Both men were momentarily distracted as they took their drinks.

Slowly, Ferrari took a sip of his Cinzano. He said: 'I can see that there could be an improvement, but why should *I* care – the arrangement works for me. I am in a unique position. Why would I ever give away my advantage, let alone to the *garagistes*?'

'Forgive me, sir,' replied Ravilious, 'I am not suggesting – in any way – that there should be *any* dilution in the differential between the Scuderia and the other teams.'

'You're not?'

'No sir.'

'Then what ... *are* ... you suggesting?'

'That the Scuderia keeps your existing "premium", if we might call it that. Instead, we use the Ferrari team name, along with those of the other teams, to apply a little persuasion to raise *all* the teams' fees … in proportion.'

'But why would I help the upstart teams?'

'Because unless there are worthy teams there to challenge the Scuderia on the track, and so provide an opportunity to demonstrate Ferrari's majesty, sir, there *would* be no spectacle. They might as well just hire Ferrari cars to come and put on a parade, little more than a *concours d'élégance*. Under those arrangements, though, sir, I would hazard the Scuderia's fees would be highly unlikely ever to rise from their current levels.'

A formal figure was suddenly standing beside them. 'Mr Ferrari, sir,' said the maître d', 'His Grace the Duke of Modena has arrived as has his lordship, the Marquis of San Marino.'

Enzo Ferrari rose from his chair.

He said nothing more to Ravilious as he stood up.

Before he left, however, *Il Commendatore* offered his hand to the young man.

The handshake lingered perhaps four of five seconds longer than Ravilious had expected.

A moment later the godfather of Formula 1 had turned and was walking away.

THIRTY-SIX

Arno Ravilious heard nothing more about his meeting over the weekend. McKay did not mention it; there were no questions from him; no desire to find out how it went. Life went on as if the encounter had never taken place.

On the Sunday evening after the grand prix, Ravilious was busy loading the trucks, ready to ship the team out of Monza early the following day, when across the Ptarmigan section of the lorry park, he heard his name being called.

An official from the race track appeared and handed him a buff-coloured envelope. It was addressed to him personally. In ink, it said: 'Care of Scuderia Ptarmigan.'

On the back of the envelope was embossed a single word in brilliant *Rosso Corsa*. With trepidation, Ravilious opened the envelope.

The letter was handwritten in fountain pen, in English:

'I will try you in America. You may add the
Scuderia Ferrari to your negotiations, strictly on a
pro rata basis. E.F.'

Arno Ravilious was ecstatic.

The journey back to Britain, over the Alps and across France, seemed to go on forever. Ravilious was desperate to get back to England and to re-engage with Mr Brad 'Mayflower' Margesson.

On the Tuesday morning he faced another day-long wait before he could take up Olive Cadwell's vacated chair and make his call to America. Ravilious had received two responses from the four agreement letters he had sent out to the teams. Neither, though, was from Ptarmigan.

Six o'clock came.

The moment Olive left the room, Ravilious dived across to the phone and started the international calling procedure.

The drawling tone of the American phone system seemed interminable.

Finally, he heard his call being answered.

'Mr Margesson,' he declared to the promoter of the American Grand Prix, 'having not heard from you, I am pleased to be back in touch – about the appearance fees and prize money for some of the English teams to appear at Watkins Glen. I thought I should let you know that there's been a development. I have been appointed by one more Formula 1 team to discuss their arrangements with you. Perhaps we could revisit our earlier discussion?'

'Oh, yeah, and which team's that, then?'

'The Scuderia Ferrari, sir.'

Arno Ravilious did not see JJ McKay until lunchtime the following day; the team boss had been away from the barn. As Ravilious saw him appear through the window of the team's elevated office, he jumped up, ran down the stairs and strode across the floor of the barn to intercept him, immediately offering an update. They had not spoken properly since their frosty meeting in Monza.

Ravilious walked with McKay back into the stable yard of the stately home and then out under the stone arch into the grounds. McKay lit up a Players No. 6. They stood, looking out over the Kirtlington valley.

'I have some news,' Ravilious declared.

'Oh, God, what have you done now? How badly did you upset *Il Commendatore*? I knew that meeting was a mistake.'

Ravilious ignored his team boss. 'I've struck a deal with Watkins Glen.'

JJ McKay drew on his cigarette.

'As a reference point,' Ravilious began, 'Ptarmigan's appearance fee last year in America was 7,000 dollars with a 4 per cent share of the prize money. At the-then exchange rate, that would be the equivalent of 2,811 pounds.'

'So what's the new deal?' McKay asked.

'Ten per cent share of the prize fund.'

'That's better ... and what about an appearance fee?'

Ravilious paused. 'It's been upped too...'

'To what?'

'21,000 dollars.'

McKay saw the significance immediately. 'Which is ... *what*, though ... in today's money?'

'8,571 pounds.'

'Holy fucking cow,' he said. 'How the fuck did you *do* that?'

Ravilious smiled. 'I persuaded Enzo Ferrari to join our pool.'

'Holy, holy ... fuck,' blurted the team boss, seeming to exhale and laugh at the same time. Not only had Ravilious achieved a result in his negotiations, but this young man – a mere 25-year-old – had convinced the godfather of motor racing to follow his approach.

'How much did you secure for Ferrari, then?' he asked.

Apologetically but firmly, Ravilious replied: 'I am sure you wouldn't appreciate it if I told others what Ptarmigan might have been offered or paid? I will always try and keep individual team awards confidential.'

THIRTY-SEVEN

By the end of September 1972, when the Formula 1 circus arrived at Mosport Park north of Bowmanville for the Canadian Grand Prix, the paddock was buzzing. Nobody knew the full story, but rumours were rampant over Ravilious's deal with Watkins Glen. Fuelling speculation, Lord Lambourn was declaring Ravilious's achievement for his team as 'nothing less than a coup'.

Within hours of his arrival, emissaries appeared in the Ptarmigan garage – from McLaren, March and Williams, some of the teams that had declined Lord Lambourn's invitation to join the negotiating pool: each of them was now asking whether Ravilious could secure similar appearance fees and shares of the prize money for them. He rang Watkins Glen straight away and managed to secure an extension of his terms for the new teams in his group.

At the meeting back in Brands Hatch, the four pooling teams had only agreed to give Ravilious a trial run in negotiating with the United States Grand Prix. He was now being asked questions like: 'When are you going to start on getting us deals with next year's races.' Ravilious was thrilled with the goodwill he was creating, but suggested an ad hoc meeting with the participating team bosses to discuss some of the concerns he had. They all came, meeting in a hotel outside the circuit complex.

Once gathered, Lord Lambourn was effusive in his praise; he stepped in and offered his congratulations for what This Young Man had achieved for the American race. It set the tone far better than Ravilious could have wished for.

He stood up and addressed the meeting himself: 'For Watkins Glen, we now have 7 teams in our group,' Ravilious said, 'having been joined this weekend by McLaren, March and Williams. That means we account for 29 of the 46 cars on that grid. I am grateful for your recognition that this pooling and my negotiations with that circuit have increased your appearance fees and share of the prize money.'

'And *how*,' said Tim Parnell.

'You've played a blinder,' added Colin Chapman.

There came a few 'Hear, Hears' from other parts of the room.

'Incidentally, with so many cars in our syndicate,' Ravilious continued, 'I have also been back to our freight handler and can even improve on FiCA's transport rates by a further 20 per cent.'

More noises of approval were forthcoming.

After that the room fell silent.

One of the bosses then said: 'I think you've successfully passed the trial period Budge talked about at Brands Hatch, Arno. When are you going to start on getting us equally good rates and fees from circuits for next season?'

A series of nods seemed to seek the same answer.

Ravilious was inwardly rejoicing. 'If that's what you'd like me to do…' he said, but then he paused.

Lord Lambourn looked at him. 'Arno…?'

With a little more confidence, Ravilious said: 'If the current pool stands, gentlemen, for next year we're talking about 29 cars going to 15 races in 15 countries. Handling all those arrangements would take a much greater time commitment than it has so far. Mr McKay has been generous, letting me encroach on my working day with Ptarmigan for the US Grand Prix, but this operation would be a lot bigger than that.'

There were mumbles of understanding around the room.

'I could hire someone to help,' suggested Ravilious, 'except they would need to be paid. But, really, to handle this expansion and manage it properly, I would suggest you set up and fund a new company, perhaps calling it the Formula 1 Constructors Association Limited. And then, in it, you could all have an equal share. You could pool the cost savings, and share in the increased income from race fees, to cover any of the admin costs.'

Tim Parnell replied: 'What do you mean by "fund"? How much are you talking?'

'Not that much … just enough to pay the initial set-up costs and the administrator's salary.'

The room fell silent again.

'I'm not talking a large amount of money,' Ravilious added, as the room remained quiet, 'and all of you would share in any further savings the company made.'

There was no further response from any of the team bosses.

Tentatively, Lord Lambourn stepped back into the conversation. 'Arno,' he said, 'I think the issue, here, is that we're all racing teams. We're not interested in administration, as, frankly, I'm not sure any of us are any good at it. We all so admire what you've done. I'm pretty sure,' he said with a chuckle, 'we'd far sooner just have *you* keep doing it.'

Colin Chapman stated: 'We want you to do *all* of it – *we'd* all prefer to spend our energies and your hard-won cash on improving the cars.'

'I'd be happy to do it,' said Ravilious after a few moments, 'but I would still have to cope with the extra admin.'

His own boss then asked: 'How much more time do you think you need, Arno?'

'I'm not sure, yet, JJ. But it could easily be a day a week…?'

McKay looked like that was more than he was expecting.

'It wouldn't be fair on JJ to shoulder all the burden,' offered Lambourn.

'Mr McKay wouldn't have to,' answered Ravilious, 'if Ptarmigan no longer paid me for any days I spent on this.'

Tim Parnell of BRM said: 'If JJ can spare you, that's a generous gesture,' he said. 'But I'm not sure you should lose a day's pay a week for us.'

'Perhaps, then,' said Ravilious, 'we could look at this another way? You have already agreed my 2 per cent commission on the appearance fees I arranged for you in America; what if we raised that to 4 per cent? … After all,' he added quickly, before anyone could counter argue, 'I almost doubled the income you got from that circuit.'

Simultaneously, and without a heartbeat's pause, Lambourn and Parnell said: 'Done.'

Two other key developments occurred at the 1972 Canadian Grand Prix.

On the back of his bigger agreement with the FICA group, Ravilious still wanted to act for the largest team he had not discussed extending his relationship with. Having worked through the night on his approach, he went to the Ferrari garage the next morning to deliver a handwritten letter for onward delivery to *Il Commendatore*. In it, Ravilious intimated that with his enlarged and now ongoing negotiation pool he was confident he could achieve a significant uplift in Ferrari's remuneration from the other tracks and promoters across the Formula 1 season. Ravilious, was, of course, at Mr Ferrari's disposal, should his services be further required.

The second incident of the weekend involved the other Italian team, the Scuderia Massarella.

Ravilious had been making his way to lunch in the paddock's only food outlet, a mobile greasy-spoon diner, when he was intercepted by the brusque South African team boss, Eugene Van Der Vaal. Ravilious would never have expected the South African to eat with the hoi polloi; he had to believe the Massarella boss had been waiting there to catch Ravilious on his way to lunch.

'I gather you've secured a pretty good deal for Ferrari from the Americans,' said the South African, doing everything he could to sound unimpressed.

'I'm delighted to say that the people at Watkins Glen saw the logic of the case I put to them.'

'Massarella would be prepared to add its name to bolster your bargaining position,' said Van Der Vaal as he cleared his throat, 'for the same deal as you secured for Ferrari.'

'I'm afraid, sir, that the Watkins Glen promoter sees Ferrari as a special case.'

'Italy has a disproportionate significance in Formula 1,' said the

Massarella boss, looking at him with feigned nonchalance. 'You are young, and only just starting out; you should know, therefore, that Massarella and Ferrari are considered equal marques in the world of Formula 1 motor racing.'

'If *Il Commendatore* invites me to pool Massarella F1 with the Scuderia,' he said, 'I would be delighted to go back to Watkins Glen and renegotiate Ferrari's terms.'

The queue shuffled forwards as the breeze off Lake Ontario wafted the aromas of chargrilled meat and frying onions all around them. By the time Ravilious turned to face the Massarella team boss, he found Van Der Vaal looking defiant; insulted, even.

'Massarella will be treated the same as Ferrari, or not at all.'

'That's fine, sir,' said Ravilious. 'I'm sure Mr Margesson at Watkins Glen will be aware of that and be receptive when you negotiate your arrangements with him.'

Eugene Van Der Vaal grunted his dissatisfaction. And walked away.

Ravilious exhaled with relief.

Hadn't he just managed to dodge a bullet? At the very least he'd managed to duck having to say 'No' to the Massarella boss. Ravilious was pretty sure of one thing, though: Eugene Van Der Vaal and Massarella seemed like they could very easily be trouble.

A week or so later Ravilious received a curt but courteous telex in reply to his handwritten letter to Enzo Ferrari.

Il Commendatore was declining his offer.

Enzo Ferrari stated that his brand and standing in Formula 1 was unique. And while he might have been impressed by Ravilious's result with Brad Margesson, he was told:

YOUR HANDLING THE NEGOTIATIONS WITH WATKINS GLEN A ONE-OFF
BUT THANK YOU STOP THE SCUDERIA IS FORMULA 1 STOP WE DO NOT
NEED TO JOIN FORCES WITH OTHER TEAMS TO SECURE OUR DUES STOP

E FERRARI MARANELLO

THIRTY-EIGHT

Despite the disappointment over Ferrari, heading into 1973 Ravilious spoke for 7 teams in his FiCA negotiating pool – out of a total 18 – and, most assuredly, his teams were at the business end of the grid. The sport's race promoters knew they would have to take Ravilious seriously.

He soon realized, though, that what he was now selling had changed. Ravilious wasn't really selling 'teams' any more. He rationalized that he was negotiating the core 'content' of a grand prix. Without the block of teams he represented there would be no race. Consequently, his language and pitch needed to focus on the other significant benefits that would be enjoyed by the places that might host a race. He focused on the kudos of hosting a grand prix, the boost it would bring to the economy – not only local but national – and the positive commercial benefit to be enjoyed by the promoter of a grand prix. Ravilious began conducting detailed research into each venue's audience; its gate over the last few years; its support from local government; and the revenues the race would bring to the area – and then tailored his pitch specifically for each venue. To his surprise, the new arguments worked remarkably well. Circuits were putting up far less resistance to his increasing demands than he might have feared.

Arno Ravilious developed his bargaining technique further, particularly when he found two circuits in the same country vying for the honour of hosting a race. He tried this first in Britain. Brands Hatch and Silverstone were tendering to host the British Grand Prix. Ravilious quickly saw he could play the bid from one circuit off against the other. To Johnny Bradshaw, the chairman of the BRDC, he said sympathetically: 'Brands Hatch have so far offered X. If you would like the British Grand Prix to come to Silverstone, I am pretty sure I can arrange for them to be there for X plus Y.'

Up until this point in Formula 1, the circuits had been calling the shots; in a very short time, Ravilious found he was able to make the pendulum start to swing the other way, to be a little more favourable to the teams. Negotiating with a larger pool of seven teams, he found he could achieve a very different set of results.

Two things happened within Ptarmigan because of it. The increase in appearance fees enabled the team to move into a smart new facility on the outskirts of Bicester. The second was that JJ McKay was proud enough to start bragging of his 'boy's' performance to the other team bosses.

With this growing goodwill, Ravilious signed up two additional teams to his group: no lesser names than Tyrrell and Brabham. By the end of the first half of 1973, even Eugene Van Der Vaal had been prompted to join F1CA – no longer able to resist the financial benefits to his team.

Massarella joining F1CA brought Ravilious's pool of teams to ten.

At that point, only one name of any note was missing.

Negotiating the next year's prospective French Grand Prix in 1974, Ravilious had been dealing with Jules-Bert Macon at Magny-Cours, the circuit 40 miles north of Vichy. By then, the overall fees for his F1CA syndicate to appear at a European circuit were close to $400,000.

'Magny-Cours couldn't possibly pay that kind of money,' said Macon.

The French promoter counter-offered with $200,000, itself a rise of $50,000 from the previous year.

Ravilious said: 'No.'

Macon asked for some time to consider. Ravilious agreed and gave the Frenchman a deadline of two weeks hence.

Magny-Cours came back to Ravilious nineteen days later. Jules-Bert Macon declared, begrudgingly, that he *had* managed to amass the necessary $400,000.

When this new application was made, Ravilious turned it down flat. He told the promoter over the telephone: 'You've missed the deadline. I have, instead, awarded the race to the Circuit Paul Ricard.'

Macon exploded, almost beside himself with anger.

Word went round, though, that Ravilious meant business: if FiCA set a deadline, it was expected to be honoured.

The teams were delighted. Their fees continued to rise. It allowed them to spend more of their ever-growing revenues on research and development. It translated into the cars going faster. The spectacle on the track increased. More crowds came to see races. Circuit promoters made more money. And in turn, Ravilious was able to push FiCA's appearance fees higher ... again.

However, Ravilious was about to discover that Formula 1 had its very own version of Newton's Third Law; that, just as with physical objects, a political action tended to have an equal and opposite reaction. Ravilious was about to encounter Formula 1 politics.

And it wasn't going to be pretty.

Particularly when it came in the form of Salvador Makarios.

THIRTY-NINE

The Greek shipping millionaire, Belvedere Makarios, ran the world's largest fleet of supertankers in private hands. The sea, ships and shipping had been at the heart of the family business for centuries; but relatively recently, Belvedere, while still in his thirties, had managed to secure an epoch-defining deal that confirmed the name Makarios in the pantheon of Greek shipping families. Deputizing for his father, Belvedere had talked his way into a joint venture with Aramco, the oil company jointly owned by Saudi Arabia and the United States.

In the mid-1960s, the recently crowned King Faisal had set out to reduce his kingdom's reliance on America, determined to see more aspects of Saudi Arabia's activities opened up to other companies and countries, a priority for diversification being the shipping of Aramco's crude. Belvedere Makarios got wind of this potential change, camped out in Riyadh, worked his way into the court and created the opportunity to pitch for the main contract to ship Saudi Arabia's oil. His success in securing it created a rocket-like rise in wealth, position and power for the Makarios family.

A secondary boost to the Makarios fortune would come in 1973, from the Arab-Israeli War. America, responding to the Syrian and Egyptian invasions on Yom Kippur, entered the conflict indirectly – via its decision to supply arms to Israel. The predominantly Arab OPEC took offence at the US's partiality and announced an oil embargo against numerous countries, including the United States. In a matter of weeks, the price of crude rocketed from $3 to $12 a barrel; Aramco, sitting on colossal reserves, became the most valuable company in global history. Belvedere Makarios's contract with it began to create untold riches, enabling him to build the largest fleet of supertankers ever known. Old man Makarios lived just long enough to see his son's extraordinary achievement transform the family's wealth and status all over again.

Belvedere Makarios may have owned and run a bigger fleet, with a bigger deadweight tonnage and a bigger bank balance than probably Onassis, Lemos and Niarchos put together, but he never shared their thirst for the limelight. Belvedere had no interest in the sort of publicity that went with escorting world-famous opera singers, owning strings of racehorses to rival the Tsars or the Aga Khan, or bidding for old masters in the auction houses of New York and London. Belvedere Makarios was a private, modest family man; a simple devotee of the Greek Orthodox Church.

Despite his low profile, the world's media was still obsessed with the name of Makarios. Keeping them interested in it – and the Makarios shipping fortune – though, was Salvador Makarios, the elder brother. It had been an atavistic Greek tragedy: old man Makarios brutally preferring the younger Belvedere to succeed him as head of the family business. Salvador had been unceremoniously passed over.

It wasn't just a disinheritance from the helm. The first-born was not to be found any role within the Makarios empire either. Salvador's self-esteem, as well as his public reputation, took a massive blow. Despite his exclusion, Salvador Makarios was hardly going to starve: ensuring his financial security, the father established an impenetrable series of trust funds to hold his substantial shareholding in the family company. Adding further ignominy, these had been structured to strip Salvador of all voting rights; instead, a board of trustees was empowered to exercise every shareholder duty and responsibility attached to his sizeable block of shares. As far as Salvador's place in the family business was concerned, his only permitted activity was to receive the colossal dividends his trustees paid him on a quarterly basis.

Even with such vast wealth, Salvador Makarios got through it faster than it came in. With no responsibilities, he had nothing to do but indulge himself – which he did on an Olympic scale, whoring, snorting and gambling his way round the fleshpots of the world.

Salvador Makarios also spent a fortune on his passion, motor racing – even hiring a team so that he could compete all the way up to Formula 1. Millions of drachmas down, the reality hit him long after it had everyone else – that he was a long way short of being a natural driver.

Salvador Makarios soon involved himself, whether solicited or not, in political and regulatory issues of the sport. He blagged his way into a low-level role in the *Commission Sportive Internationale*, the CSI. Salvador may not have inherited any of his father's or brother's charm or business acumen, but something gave him an unbending belief in the rightness of his opinion. In a period of ten years, accelerated by his money and its ability to lubricate political wheels, Salvador Makarios bombasted his way up through the ranks of the automobile's international governing body such that, at the age of 53, he emerged as the President of the CSI, the arm of the *Fédération Internationale de l'Automobile*, the FIA, that governed Formula 1.

As president of a global sport, particularly with the prestige Formula 1 enjoyed, Salvador Makarios was granted – ex officio – status, esteem and a fair amount of publicity. Most observers saw this role as his salvation, saving him from indulging himself into an early grave.

Salvador Makarios took the CSI presidency seriously, becoming hugely protective of it – even territorial. His first act on assuming office was to reform the committee, ramming through a number of changes – most notably its name. He changed that to the *Fédération Internationale du Sport Automobile* – to be referred to as FISA – and then set about asserting its autonomy.

Hence where the politics began.

Formula 1 had always fostered an environment of tolerated chaos. Stakeholders argued constantly. When circuits and teams, the usual fault line, got into a spat, it created a heroic role for FISA to step in and play the magnanimous purveyor of wisdom and judgement. Salvador Makarios, as its president and the man with the final word, revelled in being called upon to save the day and pour balm on troubled parts of the Formula 1 landscape.

In a matter of months, Arno Ravilious had come from nowhere. Through his success with FICA, he was creating a very different order. Most crucially, he had created a form of stability – one that lessened the need for any kind of Makarios-style arbitration or avuncular intervention. In certain quarters, therefore, Ravilious's efficiency was considered a threat to the cosy old order.

As early as the second grand prix of 1973, Salvador Makarios received a petition from three of Formula 1's principal promoters, all three making a special trip down to Interlagos in Brazil for the sole purpose of submitting it in person. These were from Watkins Glen, Brands Hatch and Magny-Cours. The petitioners urged the president to take immediate steps to counter Arno Ravilious's interference with the F1 calendar and reverse the rapidly increasing appearance fees he was demanding for the teams. To the president of most governing bodies, a gripe of this kind would have been an unwelcome annoyance. Not to Salvador Makarios. Quite the opposite. He welcomed the petitioners with open arms. Their issue would give him a role and the chance to demonstrate his power.

Immediately after local hero Emerson Fittipaldi won the Brazilian Grand Prix, Makarios was on the case. He flew from São Paulo's Congonhas airport straight to Monte Carlo, heading for the principality with the intention of recruiting André d'Aumont, the promoter of the world's most prestigious motor race, to the cause.

D'Aumont took little persuading. Monaco had not had any direct experience of Ravilious's demands for higher appearance fees; even so, the Monegasque could see that if the current upward pressure on rates continued across the other races, at some point he too would be squeezed. He was more than ready to fight for the established political order in Formula 1, seeing the role of the promoter/circuit owner as the natural power in the sport. He did not want that influence to be challenged.

Salvador Makarios discussed the current state of play and shared his plan.

D'Aumont bought in.

Before Makarios had even left Monaco, d'Aumont sent out a press release – announcing that, for 1973, the Monaco Grand Prix would be reducing the number of Formula 1 cars on its grid from 26 to 16. No explanation was given – no justification was offered for such a substantial reduction in the number of competitors.

Its purpose, though, was simple:

To penalize one group of people and one individual – the British teams, each of which ran more cars than any of the continental teams, *all* of which were represented by Arno Ravilious. Makarios's move was very clearly designed to divide and conquer.

Suddenly, Ravilious found himself under immense pressure. Each of his FiCA teams was decidedly nervous. They may have enjoyed the benefits he had earned for them, squeezing other circuits for higher appearance fees, but Monaco was Monaco. *It* had an entirely disproportionate level of influence: every sponsor of a Formula 1 car would want their car to run in the Monaco Grand Prix. Prevented from being present there, of all races, could upset a lot of teams' sponsorship receipts. The teams would be hit financially. The teams couldn't *afford* not to go to Monaco. Tension started to grow.

Each of his teams lobbied Ravilious hard, insisting that their cars should not be the ones to be dropped. His stock reply was that there must have been some sort of misunderstanding: Monaco had never done this before. They had run 26 cars for years. Ravilious tried to reassure them he would get to the bottom of it.

After Brazil, the next race was the South African Grand Prix at Kyalami on the 3rd of March.

Ravilious came under further pressure from his own team boss, JJ McKay:

'You work for Ptarmigan; for fuck's sake, make sure we get to run all five of our cars at Monaco. Our client drivers are threatening all sorts if they don't get to go.'

Ravilious suggested he travel to the promoter of the Monaco race and talk to him personally; McKay even released him from going to South Africa, so he could get to Monaco all the sooner.

Ravilious flew to Nice and took a taxi into the principality. Even in cooler, crisp spring air, the atmosphere of the place felt otherworldly. He met André d'Aumont in the lobby of the Hôtel de Paris.

'Thank you for seeing me, Monsieur d'Aumont. I am sure we can sort out whatever your problem might be. After so many years of 26-plus cars on the grid here, why are you so keen to reduce the numbers? Have you changed the course – narrowed it? Is this because of safety?'

'We have had a rethink,' said the promoter.

Ravilious studied the man's face. He got a feeling that something wasn't quite right.

André d'Aumont started to look awkward. Uneasy.

Ravilious smiled to himself as he realized something had to be going on: d'Aumont had made a drastic change to the organization of his race, reducing the number of cars, and yet he was offering no explanation for it.

'André,' he said. 'You've given me no reasons for taking such a decision. I find that strange. I also find your decision to be arbitrary and unequal, André, as it will penalize the British teams. Therefore, I would like to leave you with one thought. Unless a proper reason is offered for the reduction you've made, none of the English teams will come to Monaco. None of them will race ... at all. Do you understand?'

André d'Aumont sat bolt upright. '*What?* You can't do that! You can't *boycott* Monaco?'

'You're trying to boycott the FiCA teams. If they're not worthy of your respect, let's see what the Monaco Grand Prix looks like with only Ferrari and a couple of backmarkers – if you're lucky, you might just get the American Shadows and the South African Lucky Strikes to come.'

'This was not my idea – I want Monaco to be a success – all the teams *must* race.'

'So there will be *no* reduction in the number of cars, then, André?'

D'Aumont shook his head.

Ravilious stood up and offered his hand. André d'Aumont reached out and shook it.

Despite the apparent resolution of their issues at that meeting, Ravilious came away with a feeling of deep disquiet. If d'Aumont had capitulated so easily, the drastic reduction in the number of cars racing at his grand prix couldn't have been his idea. In which case, whose was it?

And, more to the point, why had they put it forward?

Formula 1 moved on from South Africa to Montjuïc in the Catalonian Mountains for the Spanish Grand Prix. Mood ahead of the race was buoyant, particularly among Ravilious's FiCA teams – all being relieved to hear the result of his meeting with André d'Aumont in Monte Carlo.

Things, though, were about to kick off.

At the very next race after that.

The Monaco Grand Prix itself.

FORTY

Monaco was the jewel in Salvador Makarios's crown. Having been humiliated, dethroned as the heir to the world's greatest shipping dynasty, this was the one occasion on which he could hold his own. As president of the organization in whose name the grand prix ran, he could behave here as host of the world's most glamorous sporting occasion. Salvador Makarios could mix on equal terms with kings, presidents and the world's financial and social elite.

Arno Ravilious arrived in the principality with the Ptarmigan team.

All the preparations for the race, including Qualifying, proceeded without incident…

…at least until the day of the grand prix.

At seven o'clock that morning Arno Ravilious received a summons:

He was commanded to attend the FISA president at eleven o'clock in his suite in the Hôtel de Paris.

Ravilious asked JJ McKay: 'Why do you think Makarios wants to see me?'

Now fully acknowledging the young man's value to the team, the Ptarmigan team boss had taken on a role of mentor. 'You're doing things – new things, Arno. People – the establishment, the vested interests – are suspicious. At the same time, others don't like the idea of being screwed for more money or being squeezed out. Radical changes, like the ones you've been instigating, are going to get up people's noses.'

'So this isn't a social call?'

'Good God, no! Be well on your guard.'

Ravilious took a walk round the promontory, the site of the Prince's Palace, and then stood looking down on the sun-bathed Monaco harbour and the small flotilla of yachts below. He tried to think everything through.

Ravilious decided he was going to present himself as no challenge; as much of a supporter of the status quo as possible.

At just after eleven o'clock, Ravilious was shown into the president's suite.

The overweight, large and fleshy-faced Greek was sitting in an armchair in the middle of the room, facing the door.

'Ravilious,' said the FISA boss, 'it has come to my attention that you have pressured unreasonable appearance fees from a number of circuits and that you have altogether swindled others out of their right to hold a grand prix. This extortion is to stop immediately.'

Makarios had not offered his hand, or even got up.

There had been no pleasantries. No offer of a drink, any refreshments or even a chair.

Ravilious, fighting to hold his tongue, tried quickly to think how best to respond.

He decided to do so with a question:

'What rights do the teams have to choose where they race, Mister President?'

'They will have the rights that *I* give them.'

Ravilious was thrown by the bluntness. 'What about the money the teams need to race?'

'None of us are in Formula 1 for the money.'

Ravilious fought himself not to react. 'Then it's perfectly possible you may not have so many teams at your races.'

'Formula 1 is the pinnacle of motorsport. The World Championship is the most prized accolade there is. There will *always* be teams wanting to win it. Teams will come and go, that's just survival of the fittest. *I* will decide which teams will be granted those privileges.' Makarios's expression hardened. 'And it is my order that the Monaco Grand Prix *will* be limited to 16 cars – as per the decision announced on the 12th of February.'

Ravilious said as calmly as he could: 'I had a conversation with André d'Aumont. He withdrew that restriction, not least because he couldn't justify it.'

'Well *I'm* justifying it.'

McKay had not been wrong. This *was* the establishment offering its resistance…

There was a knock on the door.

Makarios barked over Ravilious's shoulder: 'Yes?'

'Catering service, sir.'

'Come.'

Keys jangled in the lock and the heavy door of the Churchill Suite was opened. A young woman dressed in hotel livery opened the door and an older man in black tie pushed a large trolley across the polished wooden floor towards the centre of the suite. 'We've had the dining requests from your guests, sir.'

'Both their majesties?'

'King Constantine and King Umberto, yes, sir. President Pompidou, as well. All your guests are happy with the lobster thermidor, sir – apart from Miss Minelli; Madame's requested a Caesar salad.'

'Out on the balcony, then,' ordered Makarios.

In a stronger tone to Ravilious, he said: 'We're done here. I have to get ready to host the President of France. You will reinstate Brands Hatch, Magny-Cours and Watkins Glen as grand prix venues. The teams will be paid the going rate, as determined by the circuits. And you can start putting things right immediately – with the Americans this weekend – by apologizing to Mr Margesson, who's here in Monte Carlo.'

As the large Greek heaved himself to his feet, Makarios gave Ravilious a wave in the direction of the door.

The young man didn't move.

To Makarios's back, as the man headed outside to supervise the hotel staff on the balcony, Ravilious said: 'I will be delighted to offer you the chance to eat your lunch in relative peace and quiet, Mr President … at least from the street below. The sound coming from the track will be considerably less: not one of the British teams will be racing unless all 26 cars are on the grid.'

Ravilious turned and walked to the door.

Makarios spun round, his face swelling with anger. 'You come here and threaten me, you lousy little upstart. *Sixteen* cars will race, do you hear? And for your impertinence, *Ptarmigan* won't be among them. Do you understand me?'

Ravilious did not turn around to face the bawling president.

Makarios shouted something else through the door as he left.

Ravilious was already thinking rapidly of other things: he had to get to JJ McKay – quickly – and probably Lord Lambourn.

He had to get to them before any of the FISA officials could get to them first.

FORTY-ONE

Ravilious sprinted down Beau Rivage towards the pits. He was soon badly out of breath. He made his way along Albert I Boulevard, the location of the temporary pit lane; here, all the Formula 1 cars were merely pulled over onto the side of the road and parked under the trees. In the Monegasque street, mechanics worked on their cars – while members of the public wandered up and down, peering at the teams, trying to engage some of them in conversation. Ptarmigan's spot was at the far end, down near the Gazomètre Hairpin.

Ravilious weaved his way through the crowds. He had to find his team boss.

There was no sign of him.

He ran back up the pit lane, looking for the Lambourn team.

He found the peer under one of his cars, working on the suspension of its nearside front wheel.

'Budge,' he said, as he exhaled between breaths, 'Makarios has overridden the race promoter. Everything's gone to pot. He's shutting the race back down from 26 cars to 16.'

Lord Lambourn stopped what he was doing and slid out from under the car. 'Good God ... *this* late?'

'I've just come from a meeting with the president. It's definitely Makarios who's behind the reduction.'

Ravilious was stressed. How was Lambourn going to react to this? He needed the peer to stay with him.

'What's JJ said?'

'I haven't found him yet. You're the first FiCA boss I've reached. I've come here straight from the meeting.'

Lambourn started to nod.

Ravilious was surprised. What did that mean? 'I am concerned,

Budge. If we go along with Makarios's diktat, where will this kind of interference end?'

Lambourn was still nodding.

Just then, the Ptarmigan boss walked past. Lambourn called out: 'JJ?'

McKay changed direction.

'Glad we've got you. We seem to have a bit of a problem. Our young friend, here, has been told by Makarios that the ridiculous reduction of cars from 26 to 16 has been reinstated.'

'What, *now*? After everyone's already travelled all the way here. The *bastard*. How can he do that so close to the race? There's only two hours till the start.'

'It's clearly some sort of brinkmanship.'

They both turned to Ravilious.

McKay asked him: 'What did you say in response?'

'I took a stand,' he replied. 'Makarios was being extraordinarily arrogant. I asked him what rights the teams had in regard to appearances and fees. His reply was: *"They will have the rights* I *give them".*'

Lambourn's eyes widened. 'He said that?'

Ravilious nodded.

'So what did *you* say?'

'That it would be 26 cars … or none.'

'You threatened to boycott the race?' asked Lambourn.

Ravilious paused then nodded.

This was it.

Crunch point.

If these two backed down now, who knew what Makarios would come up with next?

'Good for you,' said Lambourn, and he turned to McKay. 'JJ,' he said, 'we've got to persuade the others to support Arno's ultimatum. Makarios must be left in no doubt we're serious. Can you go and talk to Tim, Frank, Colin and Max – I'll go and see Ken, Eugene, Teddy and Bernie.'

Ravilious was amazed.

He had gone out on a limb – even threatened the FISA president – taking a huge gamble on whether the FɪCA pool would hold together. And now two team bosses were heading up and down the pit lane ready to do his bidding.

But would the teams stand firm?

The financial pressures on the teams to race in Monaco were immense. Sponsors would be mighty aggrieved if their cars were not on the grid. Would the teams be prepared to take this risk?

Less than one hour before the race, word spread down the pit lane:

'There're hundreds of police pouring into the pit straight.'

Ravilious shouted the news to McKay, who was talking to one of his drivers. Quickly breaking away, McKay and Ravilious rushed to the front of their pit area to look down towards the Gazomètre Hairpin.

A phalanx of policemen was indeed marching up the pit lane. They seemed to be adopting a pattern. As the posse drew level with a car, two policemen would peel away to stand opposite it, taking up position.

'Good God,' said McKay, 'they're armed. Are they there to stop us getting to our cars – or to stop our cars getting out?'

Ravilious found himself smiling.

'Whatever you might have started, Arno,' said McKay, 'is now happening.'

Lord Lambourn walked across to join them. There was a smile on his face too. 'This is all a bit rum, wouldn't you say?'

'What happens now?' asked McKay.

'We hold our ground,' said Ravilious. 'Monaco will want a race. Makarios cannot be allowed to get away with his ridiculous threat.'

Lambourn responded quietly with a: 'Quite right.'

Ten minutes later another posse appeared in the pit straight.

This time from the other end of it. From Sainte Devote.

It didn't take long for Ravilious to realize this group was something very different. Particularly as it seemed to be making a beeline for *him*.

It was led by two people whom Ravilious recognized. One was Salvador Makarios. The other person was only familiar to him because he had seen the man so often in the press and on television.

Over his shoulder, he said to the Ptarmigan chief engineer: 'Josh, quickly – go and fetch JJ and Lord Lambourn over here, would you?'

Josh Garrett could see what was happening and headed straight off.

Salvador Makarios marched to a stop right in front of Ravilious.

'Mr Ravilious,' he said, 'I would like to introduce you to His Serene Highness Prince Rainier – who wants to know why you're sabotaging his race.'

'How do you do, sir?' said Ravilious and offered something of a bow.

The prince seemed awkward. 'I hope we can resolve this and get the race on the way ... under the rules as laid down by FISA.'

'We're all looking forward to your race, sir. It's the highlight of the Formula 1 year.'

For a moment Prince Rainier seemed to react genuinely to the compliment.

Ravilious elaborated: 'Twenty-six cars raced here last year, sir. The same number of cars that raced here the year before that. Indeed, sir, you've had that number run here in Monaco for the last five years. We don't understand why President Makarios has decided to drop the number to 16, let alone within two hours of the race. I am pleased to inform you, sir, that 26 cars *are* here ... and everyone *is* ready to race.'

At that moment Lord Lambourn and JJ McKay closed in, approaching the discussion with due deference.

Prince Rainier's face broke into a broad smile as he saw the English peer approach.

'Budge,' said Rainier, offering his hand.

Lambourn shook hands and then, dropping his chin briefly onto his chest, saluted the royal head of state. 'Your Serene Highness, such a pleasure. Thank you, as always, for having us here. We can't wait to put on a good show for you.'

Ravilious watched their exchange, but was keeping a close eye on Makarios.

The Greek seemed to be scowling.

Lord Lambourn said: 'I'm sure we can overcome what is surely just a misunderstanding? Isn't that right, Mister President?'

Both he and Prince Rainier turned to look at Salvador Makarios.

Forty minutes later 26 cars formed up on the grid of the 1973 Monaco Grand Prix. To the outside world, everything seemed normal at the most glamorous sporting event on the planet. But behind the scenes, the battle for control of Formula 1 had well and truly begun.

FORTY-TWO

Ravilious came away from that 1973 Monaco Grand Prix deeply troubled. Salvador Makarios had him worried. During the confrontation in the Hôtel de Paris, the man's arrogance had been obscene; but it had been the pettiness and petulance of Makarios's actions that unnerved him most. What else might this man be capable of?

Ravilious might have won the skirmish on the streets of Monaco, but that didn't obviate the FISA president's order that he desist from negotiating with the circuits; it did nothing to countermand the instruction Makarios had given him to reduce his fees to Watkins Glen and reinstate Brands Hatch and Magny-Cours as grand prix venues.

In the aftermath of Monaco, Ravilious was clear on one thing: he was not going to comply.

Salvador Makarios may be using motor racing as some sort of social platform, but Ravilious was adamant Formula 1 had more to offer than that. How could he work to professionalize the sport and fulfil its commercial potential if such blazers were out to preserve an out-of-date status quo? He was not going to let Salvador Makarios thwart him.

Ravilious didn't brood on this for long. A chance conversation two weeks later in Anderstorp, south east of Gothenburg, for the Swedish Grand Prix set Ravilious's mind running.

At the end of a long day, he and several Ptarmigan teammates began talking about plans for supper, but there was no catering provided at the Swedish racetrack. A gaggle formed, ready to make for a tavern in among the brightly coloured wooden-clad houses of the town.

Ravilious's group found an eatery just off one of the wide,

unhurried streets – only to find it heaving with other members of the F1 circus.

On a trip to the pine-panelled bar to organize drinks, Ravilious was intercepted by a familiar voice. 'Arno, I'm so glad to catch you.'

Lord Lambourn's welcome didn't seem as easy or as generous as usual. 'Could I have a quick word?'

'Budge? … Of course.'

They sidled off to a quieter patch, towards the edge of the throng.

'It looks, Arno, like I might be losing Worldwide as my biggest sponsor.'

Ravilious was genuinely disappointed and sympathetic. 'How can that be? You're lying second in the Championship. You've had an enormous amount of press attention. Crowds are up. News coverage is up. How can they not be pleased with the publicity you've got for them?'

'Because, they say, there's been a "loss of clarity". I fear they might have a point. There are so many tobacco companies now in Formula 1. Worldwide resent spending all that money, only to find their name getting lost – particularly against the visibility of JPS, et cetera.'

Sponsors were always likely to come and go over time, but the principle behind Worldwide's complaint was serious. Ravilious was annoyed at himself for not having spotted this before.

'I'm so sorry to hear this. Would you mind if I talked to them?'

'Oh, would you?' said Lambourn. 'Their advertising guy, who's an American, happens to be coming here tomorrow – elements of his family are Scandinavian.'

Arno Ravilious and Lord Lambourn met the director responsible for Worldwide Tobacco's sponsorship in the Lambourn garage the next afternoon.

To Ravilious, Yoel Kahneman was a man who seemed unwaveringly pleased with himself. To get an idea of who he might be dealing with, Ravilious had sought out a bit of background. Apparently, the American had squandered an expensive education – his intelligence being more of a curse, enabling him to master subjects too rapidly for educators to keep him occupied. Kahneman's intellect rendered him quickly bored, while his underdeveloped emotional intelligence hadn't prevented risky behaviour. He was thrown out of Exeter Academy for possession of cocaine. Despite that blemish, his exceptional mind secured him a place at Princeton; except, there too, he never completed his degree: midway through his sophomore year he was sent down for dealing.

Yoel Kahneman was tall, boyishly good-looking, with a disarming manner. He had charm. As a natural for advertising, he talked his way into a succession of jobs, each more prestigious than the last, reaching the rank of SVP at Benson Mathias. Benson Mathias were as good as it got in advertising, acclaimed as the thought leaders of the agencies centred on Madison Avenue when Madison Avenue was Madison Avenue.

Kahneman had a nose for the accounts with potential. His first coup was to launch Freddie Laker's Skytrain in America, the world's first discount airline. Against all the odds, the campaign captured significant market share from the huge, established and far better-resourced flag carriers.

His success with Skytrain gave him considerable licence. Coup number two was to use it to pioneer a new, aggressive form of advertising. Yoel Kahneman was the man behind the first use of 'hidden cameras' – creating advertisements showing members of the public, in blind tastings, preferring Pepsi to the market leader, Coca-Cola. The shock results of such a 'negative' approach catapulted him into advertising folklore.

Kahneman had come across Formula 1 for the first time in 1972, the agency's London office already being modestly involved in the sport through Worldwide Tobacco's sponsorship of the Lambourn Formula 1 team. Kahneman had been invited to attend the US Grand Prix at Watkins Glen.

Emerson Fittipaldi may have already been World Champion before that race started, and retired midway through it, but

Kahneman couldn't take his eyes off his Lotus's JPS livery and the impact it had on brand promotion. His agency's biggest client was being smothered by John Player, which also, of course, happened to be one of Worldwide's biggest competitors. Kahneman understood the urgent need – as well as the opportunity – to neutralize JPS's monopoly of this sport. Approaching Lord Lambourn, he set about involving himself in his agency's relationship with Formula 1.

The conversation in the Anderstorp pit lane was taking place a few months after that.

'We are not getting standout,' the American told Ravilious. 'There's too much clutter at grands prix, particularly from other tobacco brands. We're not getting enough clarity for the money we're spending.'

Ravilious studied the man intently. 'Do you have any examples?' he asked.

Kahneman replied: 'Why don't you look at the hoardings at any trackside. Wherever Worldwide's logo on a Lambourn car is photographed, it's almost impossible not to see another tobacco company's name in the same shot. We're paying to help promote our rivals.'

Ravilious quickly saw what Kahneman was saying, but he couldn't help feel that there was something unnervingly superior about the American.

'Thank you for bringing this concern of yours to my attention, Mr Kahneman. Will you leave this with me for a week or two?'

Ravilious was anxious to get back from Sweden. The morning after Ptarmigan returned to Bicester, he headed off at the crack of dawn. Driving non-stop, he made his way down to Brands Hatch in Kent. In the still air and early morning sun, Ravilious got inside the circuit and walked out onto the track. He had with him a camera and notebook. For over two hours, Ravilious walked the entire site, making sketches and taking photographs from every angle – down the straights, into the corners, through the corners, out of the corners; then he looked at the site lines from each of the views the spectators were offered – from the grandstands, the bleachers, and all the other places people might congregate to watch the races. Finally, he walked out of the Brands Hatch complex along each of the approach roads. From a distance of three miles away, he turned round and walked back towards the circuit, again making sketches and shooting several rolls of film.

Two weeks later Formula 1 reconvened for the next grand prix, at the Paul Ricard Circuit in France. Ravilious found Lambourn and suggested they set up another meeting with Kahneman, saying he might have a solution to Worldwide's advertising concerns. The team boss sounded relieved and grateful.

'How about this as a concept?' Ravilious offered to Kahneman. 'It's going to cost you or your client a little more money,' he said, 'but what if I gave you unequivocal message standout?'

Ravilious pulled out his drawings and the photographs he had taken around Brands Hatch. He laid them out on a trestle table, weighing down his various exhibits against the breeze with an oily screwdriver and a couple of adjustable spanners. 'What if I provided you with advertising, like this, at the end of every sight line from, say, 80 per cent of the viewing or photograph-taking points around a circuit? It would, effectively, give you and Worldwide a monopoly of the branding at a grand prix.'

Kahneman's eyes were already glinting. 'What would you charge?'

'That would all depend, Yoel – on whether you want a one-off or whether you want to obliterate the competition?'

'Meaning what, exactly?'

'I *could* let you have the intensity of that 80 per cent exposure … not just at one circuit … but across the entirety of the grand prix season…'

Ravilious knew, right then, that he had him.

He could see Kahneman already thinking that this could be an extraordinary coup for Worldwide Tobacco – his client getting the chance to trump its biggest rival, JPS.

Arno Ravilious knew that he could pretty much name his price.

Kahneman replied: 'We'd do it for more than one season.'

'No, sir,' said Ravilious, 'I really couldn't hold you to that, in case it doesn't work. Happily, I'll offer you first refusal on year two though.'

Kahneman leant forward and said: 'Okay, so what's the number?'

Ravilious felt ready to push it; Kahneman was clearly sold. He went for a bigger amount than he had even been contemplating.

Without hesitation, Kahneman offered Ravilious his hand.

The boss of the Lambourn team was beaming. Ravilious had more than solved Lambourn's sponsorship problem: he had, literally, nailed his benefactor into the Formula 1 landscape.

'This is an extraordinary opportunity, Arno,' said the peer, expressing his gratitude through a follow-up handshake. 'Do let me take us all somewhere to celebrate this fantastic new arrangement?'

Ravilious nodded, but Kahneman's reply was soon to prompt him into another spiral of thought:

'A celebration would be a great idea,' said the American, 'but it's a ball ache we can't do it here; there's never anywhere decent to eat at the trackside.'

'Sorry,' said Ravilious, 'what did you just say?'

'Why don't we go and celebrate?'

'No, no – not that. The other thing ... about there never being anywhere decent to eat at the trackside?'

FORTY-THREE

During the next few weeks, while Formula 1 took its summer break and headed for the beach, Arno Ravilious worked even harder – and travelled further – than he had ever done in his life. In the four-week recess, he visited every circuit in the Formula 1 season, conducting the same kind of advertising assessment he had done at Brands Hatch. But following Kahneman's comment about eating at the trackside, Ravilious added a new segment to each of these audits.

Ravilious's priorities, though, were the grand prix circuits Makarios had mentioned in that appalling meeting in Monaco: Brands Hatch, Magny-Cours and Watkins Glen. If he was going to neutralize any political resistance to his activities, he specifically needed to bring those three race tracks back onside.

After a month of travelling, Ravilious reckoned he was ready.

Starting with Simon Gerrard at Brands Hatch, he said: 'I've been asked to be in touch with you by the FISA president ... Mr Makarios mentioned your unhappiness at not hosting the British Grand Prix next year.'

The phone call seemed to throw the promoter; he sounded hostile.

'I would like to make amends,' added Ravilious. 'It was wrong of me to hold the British Grand Prix up for auction.'

'Thank you,' replied Gerrard.

'I would *like* to reinstate the 1974 grand prix with you, at the same rate you were paying in 1972.'

Ravilious was surprised by the silence from the other end of the line.

He went on: 'If you agreed to that, there would be two extra things I would like to purchase from you.'

'What things?' Gerrard snapped.

'I want to rent from you – paid up front – all the advertising locations around Brands Hatch, and I want to lease from you a third of an acre of land.'

'At what sort of price?'

'For those two things together … leasing the advertising space and the land … I am prepared to pay you 10,000 pounds.'

The Brands Hatch promoter couldn't believe it. Not only was he looking at hosting the British Grand Prix again, but now he was also being offered a substantial sum of money for parts of his circuit that didn't make him any return.

Gerrard couldn't stop himself saying yes, there and then.

Ravilious worked the same routine with the two other circuits Makarios had mentioned in Monaco: the French and the American. His proposition was accepted by both with similar enthusiasm.

But as the confirmatory paperwork followed on behind, the promoters may not have noticed something new in Ravilious's contracts. The counterparty on the team appearance fees and prize money was FICA, as before – but the counterparty on the lease for the advertising locations and the small plots of land was a company they would never have heard of. For these, Ravilious was signing on behalf of a new entity called Motor Racing Promotions Limited.

The circuits never asked about this.

They were not to know that the only shareholder in this newly launched company was Arno Ravilious.

The Formula 1 community was astonished when it pitched camp at Watkins Glen in upstate New York for the last race of the 1973 season. Styled as the World Championship of Drivers and the International Cup for F1 Manufacturers, it was as if the entire experience of attending a grand prix had been revamped.

Driving in on the approach roads to the venue, visitors were hit by numerous 40-foot wide advertising hoardings to the left and right: Worldwide Tobacco's principal brand was displayed in vivid colour; a woman smoked a Flagrante cigarette, looking as savvy and self-composed as Lauren Bacall had in *To Have and Have Not*. Within the circuit, from anywhere in the stands, spectators couldn't escape the same large advertising images, which had been placed strategically in every sight line. No one could avoid knowing that Worldwide Tobacco was now the major sponsor of the United States Grand Prix.

Not only had the promoter resecured his grand prix at Watkins Glen, but Brad Margesson was now the beneficiary of substantial proceeds from the lease on the advertising sites and a third of an acre of unused land. Walking around his grand prix, Margesson looked like a man whose pride and status should never be doubted.

But he was not the only one who felt he had 'won':

Yoel Kahneman lorded his way around this grand prix, as if *he*, too, owned it – because of the scale of the trackside advertising he had secured for Worldwide Tobacco. Kahneman basked in the plaudits for having pulled off such a coup. Yoel Kahneman considered himself to have arrived in Formula 1.

There was another player buoyed by that year's grand prix in America:

Liaising in advance with FISA's headquarters, Ravilious confirmed that the president, Salvador Makarios, was certain to attend Watkins Glen. Ravilious then invited him to host thirty of his guests in something unfamiliar called The FISA President's Suite. The invitation described a gala lunch and offered a sample menu, listing some of the first-growth wines that were to be served. Ravilious's covering letter was at pains to stress how much he valued the FISA president's guidance, and how he hoped this lunch, held in his honour, would be a declaration of FISA's achievements in the development of Formula 1. The FISA president accepted.

The weekend of the grand prix, however, was soured irrevocably.

Midway through Qualifying, the sport suffered the loss of Jackie Stewart's teammate at Tyrrell, François Cevert – the man with the film star looks and the personification of French charm. Jackie Stewart was devastated. Already having sewn up the drivers' title for the third time, he withdrew from the race in tribute to Cevert and then announced the formal end to his driving career.

Despite the tragedy and that news, the race went ahead and still proved to be spectacular: Ronnie Peterson's Lotus was chased throughout the race, only ever a matter of feet behind him, by the eye-catching rookie: James Hunt in a Hesketh March.

Salvador Makarios arrived at the Glen on the morning of the grand prix.

He was invited to enter through the new VIP entrance to an area of the circuit that had only ever been scrubland and a storage area for tyres, spent oil drums and unused trackside barriers. This time Makarios found himself approaching a luxurious marquee with an awning tunnel, surrounded by freshly laid turf and a white picket fence.

Waiting for him at the end of the tunnel was Arno Ravilious.

The president of FISA was invited to accompany him along the red carpet and into the hospitality tent. Ravilious could see Makarios was impressed. Inside, the marquee was lined with white muslin and lit by a row of crystal chandeliers. Tables were decorated with floral centrepieces worthy of an RHS exhibition. Chairs were encased in silk covers; the tent was floored with a deep-pile carpet.

'Mr President, thank you for sending through your guest list,' said Ravilious. 'If you'd like to check everything is in order – your personal maître d', Franco here, will be ready to make any adjustments.'

Ravilious called forward a middle-aged man with a balding head and the bearing of an undertaker.

'In the meantime, Mr President, please let me show you to the President's Lounge and Balcony?'

Salvador Makarios looked around the venue and seemed to be growing in height.

Ravilious led the FISA president to the side of the tent, behind the President's Table. From there, a flight of steps rose within its own tunnel to emerge into a large enclosed room, one storey off the ground.

This lounge was also carpeted, containing a bar, several large sofas and elegant chairs. On the walls was a collection of paintings and prints of motor racing since the sport started. But what caught Makarios's attention most was the spectacular view of the track. A plate-glass window ran the length of the long wall. Makarios, followed by Ravilious, stepped through this and out onto the balcony. They were now looking directly out onto the Chute, Toe and Heel of the Boot.

'This, sir, is the President's Suite,' said Ravilious with a sweep of his hand indicating the tent. 'It is made up of the dining room downstairs, the lounge up here and this balcony. This will be set up for you at every grand prix next season.'

'You know, young Ravilious,' said Makarios, 'I was sure you would come to understand the significance and the worth of these traditional circuits.'

Ravilious thought to himself: 'Traditional circuits, my arse ... there is nothing *traditional* about anything that has been laid on at this grand prix.'

Ravilious thought the style of hospitality he had put together for the FISA president might have wider possibilities. He offered similar facilities to the teams, but none took up his offer – responding that, even at the cost-plus prices he was charging, they were far too expensive.

Ravilious was not deterred. He pursued the idea with sponsors.

Yoel Kahneman's reaction was completely different.

The advertising man stated his agency would buy every available cover on behalf of his clients. At Watkins Glen, Worldwide Tobacco ended up entertaining nearly 500 people in the tents and facilities Ravilious laid on around the paddock. Over the race weekend, the style, ambience, grandeur – and effusive reaction from the guests – were noticed by all.

As a result of the subsequent interest, Ravilious had to double the hospitality he had been planning to lay on for the next season.

High-end entertainment in the paddock looked like it was going to take off far quicker than he ever expected.

On the Sunday afternoon, Ravilious was approached by Kahneman who confirmed that not only was his client committed to their twelve-month advertising experiment, but declared: 'I am exercising my right of first refusal ... I want to extend Worldwide's commitment to this advertising – on an exclusive basis – to five years, right now.'

Ravilious was convinced his new marketing opportunities would appeal to a host of other advertisers. He decided he would be limiting himself if he sold them all that far ahead to just one client, so he declined the offer.

Indeed, eighteen months later at the start of 1975 – the first season after Worldwide Tobacco's exclusivity of this trackside advertising ended – Ravilious was earning five times as much from Worldwide Tobacco, even though he had reduced their rights to a third of the space at any one circuit. Ravilious subsequently found he was able to sell the other two thirds for the same sort of price. He was careful to choose brands that were not in competition with each other, and names that helped reinforce the prestige of the others ... as well as Formula 1. Trackside advertisers also demanded the opportunity to entertain their guests in his trackside hospitality...

The style and luxury of the companies now involved in his advertising, and the hospitality he was offering, had transformed the look and feel – the experience – of attending a grand prix.

It was only six months on from Arno Ravilious's unpleasant dressing down by Salvador Makarios in Monaco. He had handled the political confrontation from the three griping circuits by solving two other problems: the threatened loss of an F1 team's sponsor and the lack of anywhere decent to eat at race tracks.

Through his new approaches of monolithic advertising, Ravilious was now writing some big cheques to those circuit owners and promoters, which kept them happy, while, at the same time, he had used this new style of advertising as a vehicle to reposition Formula 1 as a high-end brand.

He had placated the FISA president, by offering him his own prestigious hospitality venue at grands prix in which he could play the grand host.

But his solution hadn't just led to Ravilious looking after one 'client'. He had taken the same format and, offering the same style of hospitality to all the other sponsors, found considerable demand for trackside entertaining – which became another contribution to the rebranding of Formula 1.

These innovations resulted in Ravilious being able to defuse the political tensions with the circuits, while, at the same time, create two brand-new revenue streams. Moreover, the new revenue was being channelled through a company owned entirely by him, Motor Racing Promotions Limited, which had no involvement from the teams or the governing body.

None of this could have been what Salvador Makarios, the FISA president, had intended for Ravilious after that odious meeting in the Hôtel de Paris during the weekend of the Monaco Grand Prix.

FORTY-FOUR

When Arno Ravilious met her, she was 21. Evangelina Amalfi was PA to Gianni Medici, the president of the *Commissione Sportiva Automobilistica Italiana*, the political patron of the Italian Grand Prix.

At the time, Ravilious was finding Medici particularly obstructive. Evangelina was having to field calls from an increasingly irate Ravilious, who was showing less and less patience with the Italian promoter.

He called in on the CSAI headquarters to see Medici, in person, a month or two before the 1975 Italian Grand Prix. That was when Ravilious met her. Evangelina Amalfi didn't look anything like the way she sounded on the phone. Her dark brown eyes, caramel-coloured skin, large but sculpted top lip and perfect white teeth made for an impression of angelic calm. Serenity.

Ravilious was captivated.

Evangelina Amalfi, too, had been surprised.

Most of the men she dealt with through the commission were chauvinistic, patronizing … lecherous. Arno Ravilious turned out to be a striking contrast. Her suspicions had been aroused by the way her boss talked about him, deriding him as an emperor – as grabbing – as getting above himself. She had fully expected to see Ravilious in those terms, and was well on her guard. In the flesh, though, she found him very different. Socially diffident; quiet. She found him polite, patient, and someone who took pride in his appearance but not to the point of making any kind of statement. In particular, she was struck by his passionate, almost encyclopaedic knowledge of motor racing, the *Commissione Sportiva Automobilistica Italiana* and the Italian Grand Prix. It even prompted her to start questioning her boss's judgement.

Evangelina's and Ravilious's professional relationship had been transformed.

Subsequently, his calls to Monza became occasions that were looked forward to. He made time to talk to her. Their conversation began to broaden out, giving him an insight into her family, her life and interests.

'Oh, no,' she said, in her heavy Milanese-accented English, 'I *never* go to the races. Cars just going round and round. The noise. All those men ... leering; it's no place for a self-respecting woman.'

'Why don't you come with me then – let me show you what it's really like?'

Evangelina accepted his invitation without hesitation.

That September Ravilious escorted her to the Italian Grand Prix at Monza. At the race, she saw him walking easily among the thick of the throng, greeting people and discussing snippets of business.

'All these people *know* you ... they all want to *please* you. What *are* you to them, some kind of boss?'

He smiled and shook his head.

The more she heard Ravilious's conversations, the more Evangelina became aware of his status. By the time they had walked along the pit lane and out onto the grid, she had put her arm through his.

At one moment she flinched, almost pulling him to a stop.

Evangelina was frozen. To the spot.

Ravilious turned to look at her, not understanding what was going on.

'Mr Ravilious,' said a commanding voice in a heavy accent.

He turned round. '*Il Commendatore,*' he replied, and held out his hand.

From behind his dark glasses, the godfather of Formula 1 said very little. 'I'm glad we managed to sort our recent issues. But, Mr Ravilious,' added Enzo Ferrari, 'I am not best pleased...'

Ravilious was immediately on edge.

He did not want to have disappointed the great man.

'...you have forgotten something...'

Ravilious continued to look blank.

'…you have not introduced me to your charming companion.'

Ravilious sighed before smiling in relief. With an expression that was now relaxing, he ceremoniously presented Evangelina Amalfi.

'*Mia signora*,' said Ferrari with a hint of musicality.

As he took her hand and raised it towards his lips, Evangelina Amalfi almost curtsied.

Over the phone a day or two later, she admonished Ravilious gently: 'You never told me you knew *Enzo Ferrari* … He is a god in Italy.'

'Not just in Italy.'

'My father wants to know who you *are*. How it is that, at your age, you are even known by a great man like Enzo Ferrari?'

'You've talked to your *father* about me?'

'Of course. You don't think I go out on dates with anyone?'

Ravilious paused, then sounded embarrassed: 'I didn't know that was a date.'

Evangelina chuckled, again with a hint of admonishment. 'Of course I'll forgive you, but only if you tell me where you're taking me next.'

Formula's 1's newfound self-confidence was soon to be noticed by the outside world. In 1976 it was catapulted to global status.

In that season James Hunt came of age. From an explosive start in the privately funded Hesketh, he had graduated to a fully competitive team: McLaren. Its tobacco sponsorship, hugely increased on the back of Ravilious's marketing strategy started at Watkins Glen, provided the vital resources to fund a material increase in innovation and development. Hunt was in contention from the off. He and his nemesis, Niki Lauda in a Ferrari, were destined to run each other down to the wire. The tragic accident at the Nürburgring should have ended the Austrian's campaign; a superhuman recovery saw him back on the grid six weeks later. It wasn't enough, though, to keep the gung-ho Englishman at bay.

The Mount Fuji Circuit in Japan, the last race of the season, was to be the Championship decider. Hunt came into it on 65 points, 3 behind. To take the title, Hunt needed to win outright or come at least two places higher than Lauda, the Championship leader.

In the build-up, and during the race, the heavens opened.

Through the rain, Hunt battled hard – but stayed out too long on a set of wets as the track dried deceptively quickly. He was forced to pit again with only 9 laps to run.

Even with so much to play for, Lauda bravely called it a day with only 2 laps to go, declaring the risk too great in the conditions. Hunt was left needing to score the 3 points or more, which fourth place would have given him: that would see him equal Lauda's point tally; despite the tie, the title would still have been Hunt's – he having the edge from the greater number of wins that season.

Crossing the line, Hunt thought he was fifth – thought he had blown it.

The results published by the organizer, though, showed he had finished third. Confusion ensued for ten minutes. After an agonizing wait, Hunt's position was confirmed.

Officially, he *was* third.

It meant he had scored 4 points, enough to clinch the title, ending up only 1 point ahead of Niki Lauda.

As a figure for people to idolize, James Hunt was irresistible. He was fearless, irreverent, temperamental and sexually devastating. He and his triumph caught the attention of the world.

Formula 1 had found its first global celebrity.

Behind the scenes, Arno Ravilious was busy stage-managing Hunt's fame.

While acting for F1CA, everyone knew about Ravilious's deals with the circuits, to secure increasing levels of appearance fees for the teams.

Very few knew that when Ravilious was securing the advertising and hospitality package at each track, he was acting for Motor Racing Promotions.

In Japan, he had gone one step further:

With the Mount Fuji Circuit, Ravilious had inserted a clause into their contract granting himself the rights to cover the Japanese Grand Prix on television. No one had asked him – neither the circuit nor its lawyers – whether such TV rights were the Fuji Speedway's to give away, let alone if they were Ravilious's to demand. No one asked what claim FISA might have to them, not least as the race was to run under their rules. No one asked such questions for a simple reason:

Television companies had shown no interest in Formula 1.

If the broadcasters weren't interested, what were the rights worth anyway? In Ravilious's contract with the Mount Fuji Circuit, he stipulated that the TV rights were to be assigned to Motor Racing Promotions.

With those rights in his pocket, Arno Ravilious went and talked to the European Broadcast Union – effectively the wholesaler of television programming to fifty-odd countries. But the EBU's enthusiasm for Formula 1 was underwhelming. The BBC, the British state television company, showed even less interest:

'Formula 1 is peripheral ... a bunch of rich yahoos going round in circles,' he was told. 'How could covering it come anywhere close to fulfilling the BBC's public service broadcasting responsibilities? In any case, we got a public hammering a few years back when one of the cars was sponsored by a firm that made French letters. We'll not be making that mistake again.'

With their interest at zero, Ravilious took an expensive punt. He offered the BBC a risk-free deal: 'If I produce a programme, entirely at my own expense,' he said, 'and then you think the story's worth showing, might you be prepared to broadcast it?'

With nothing to lose, the head of BBC sport offered his hand across the table.

Before leaving that meeting, Ravilious asked the BBC editor if he could recommend a good producer. He was given the name of one Howard Lloyd. The two men met, and got on immediately.

Under Lloyd's guidance, Ravilious hired a local production company to film the Japanese Grand Prix and demanded that they shoot it on 16 mm film stock. At the end of that race, the moment James Hunt was confirmed World Champion, Ravilious was on the phone to England – putting Lloyd on immediate standby. Reels of film were about to be loaded onto the Tokyo-London BOAC flight and Lloyd was to start sifting through the footage, to piece together a rough edit of the race. Ravilious would be back by Wednesday morning ready to supervise the final cut. By sunrise on Thursday, having worked an all-night session in a West London studio, Ravilious's film of the Japanese Grand Prix was finished. The timing proved immaculate. James Hunt, having been on a two-day bender to celebrate his World Championship win, had only just flown home. Photographers were waiting for him at Heathrow. His flamboyant shoulder-length blond hair was complemented by a Hawaiian shirt and a tall leggy blonde on each arm as he swigged from a bottle of champagne. The media went crazy. James Hunt was front-page fodder for every tabloid for days.

Before Ravilious had been back in touch with Television Centre in Shepherd's Bush, the head of BBC sport was on the phone begging *him* to show the film. It was aired on the BBC the following weekend. Formula 1 was a hit.

What made the programme was their choice of commentator – Ravilious and Lloyd having struck gold. Murray Walker, a former advertising man with a passion for motorcross, would have been able to put an audience on the edge of its seat describing a chess match. But when his voice, communication skills and pants-on-fire delivery were invested in Formula 1, it became a TV experience that no one had had before.

Through all this excitement James Hunt became a household name; a media star. Against the backdrop of drought, riots at the Notting Hill Carnival, endless bomb blasts in Northern Ireland, industrial strife, union militancy and yet another sterling crisis, a long-haired blond racing driver having a great time – with a mouth that 'told it how it was' – was an escapist shot in the arm.

Having successfully inserted the TV rights clause into the contract with the Japanese circuit, Ravilious now included the same stipulation in his agreement with every other grand prix venue. Instead of the assignee of those rights being the FɪCA or even Motor Racing Promotions, a new entity was named: Motor Racing Promotions TV. Once again, the owner of this company was 100 per cent Arno Ravilious.

FORTY-FIVE

During the fourth race of the 1977 season, at Long Beach in California, Ravilious's promotional work paid further dividends. He managed to attract a procession of Hollywood big shots to attend the United States Grand Prix West.

In March of the previous year, Ravilious invited a legendary chat show host to the 1976 grand prix as his guest. Johnny Carson had been fascinated by the Formula 1 circus. In the run-up to its return the following April, *The Tonight Show* host set up an ongoing theme. For three weeks, Carson commented on the glamour, excitement and appeal of Formula 1, describing the drivers as modern-day gladiators. He talked incessantly about the upcoming race, asking each of his A-list guests – with the Burbank studios being close to the Long Beach circuit – whether they were going to be at the grand prix. Guests were soon out of step with the mood if they said anything other than 'Of course!'

One journalist described the constellation of stars at that grand prix as a 'walking Hollywood Hall of Fame'. Every major name was there.

It was now the height of cool to be associated with Formula 1, and not just in the US. Tinseltown's longstanding connection with the glamour of the Riviera, particularly with Monte Carlo through Princess Grace, also gave the Monaco Grand Prix a rebirth, reconfirming it as the must-attend race in Europe.

Evangelina Amalfi was excited as the private jet landed at Nice airport. She was met by a waiting car, ready to take her along the Côte d'Azur to the principality. Evangelina was bowled over by the buzz ahead of the grand prix, the glamour of the people she and Ravilious met, and the attention Ravilious received from the great and the good. On the Saturday evening, after dining on a superyacht in the harbour, one of their party suggested they all go dancing.

'Oh yes, can we, Arno?'

Ravilious pulled a face.

'Oh come on,' she said, before turning to the host and saying: 'We'd love to.'

Ravilious soon lost his reservations. On the deck of a neighbouring yacht, under the warm summer night sky, Evangelina danced with abandon. He couldn't take his eyes off her. In a sky-blue dress, which set off her copper-toned skin so perfectly, he thought her a dream. She moved with effortless rhythm and joy. Unexpectedly, Ravilious was being drawn to her, more deeply than he could have expected.

Not long later she grabbed him by the hand and kissed him fully and sensually on the mouth. Still holding his hand, without saying a word, she led him off the deck. They found a spare cabin on the sumptuous yacht and, once locked inside, were soon ripping off each other's clothes. As he saw her slim, tanned, taut body for the first time, Ravilious was not just lusting in the moment – he was smitten. With something far more profound.

In the rising glamour of Formula 1, Arno Ravilious found sponsors approaching him in droves, but now interest came from large companies in very different sectors: drinks manufacturers, watchmakers … and then he had an enquiry from Rothmans.

The US tobacco giant was won over by the new guise of F1 – and was keen to get involved ⋯ on a massive scale. An association began that was to last for two decades.

But not everyone was pleased.

Yoel Kahneman was incensed.

Worldwide Tobacco, his client, were livid. Kahneman started spreading the word that Ravilious had betrayed him.

In the pit lane, Kahneman thundered at Ravilious: 'You've shafted me – after all the help I've given to your grubby little business.'

'Yoel, you and I took a punt on each other,' he replied. 'Your client's profile was amplified massively in those early days, repaying their relatively small investment many times over. Together, we have grown the sport. If you can match Rothmans' proposed budget, I'll gladly send them packing.'

Kahneman scowled at him: 'You know we can't.'

'Nothing stays the same, Yoel. Everything changes. I can't help it if people now see greater value in Formula 1. That's the way it is.'

But Kahneman wasn't in the slightest bit mollified.

FORTY-SIX

Arno Ravilious soon felt his own remuneration from what he provided the sport wasn't keeping up. He felt it was time to reposition himself with the teams. He came up with what he hoped would be a mutually beneficial arrangement.

He called a meeting of the bosses, all of whom were revelling in their hugely increased cash flows.

'FiCA has become fairly big now,' he stated, 'and really needs to change how it operates at this larger scale. I would like to offer you two options. One is a guarantee of more money to each team per race, while the second would be to offer each of you a stake in the operation that I run for FiCA.'

As Ravilious had expected, every face around the meeting room at the Heathrow Excelsior Hotel looked suspicious.

'Okay,' he said, 'let's start with the first of these: if you are prepared to commit to 18 races a year, I am ready to offer you each – guaranteed – a fixed appearance fee of 50,000 pounds a race.'

'Good God.'

'Christ.'

'Holy cow.'

'No fucking way.'

'Is that a problem?' he asked.

'Good God, no, Arno,' said Tim Parnell of BRM. 'That's no *problem*, mate. It's Nirvana – 50,000 a race is nearly double the amount you're getting for us currently.'

'I'm glad you're happy with that,' Ravilious replied, 'and what about 18 races?'

'If you're going to force us to take nigh on 1 million pounds a year guaranteed, we'll do whatever you need,' said another.

'Okay,' said Ravilious, 'but that's only one option. The second idea is that we launch F1CA as a standalone business – so that, from here on, it would handle all the negotiations with the circuits as well as organize the transport, flights, et cetera, to flyaway races. If we did it that way, each of the ten teams could participate as shareholders in F1CA, as an agency.'

'What sort of involvement would that mean?' asked Van Der Vaal.

'For a 10 per cent stake, the discounted sum would be 1 million pounds per team.'

Lord Lambourn drew on a large cigar and blew a plume of smoke. 'I'm in for all of it,' he said, 'but don't expect me to find that kind of capital. I'm sinking all I've got into the car.'

To Ravilious's surprise there was no interest in the idea of the teams becoming shareholders. He couldn't believe it. He was offering them a stake in F1CA Limited, which was projected, with the scale of the current cash flows, to pay back any outlay for shares within one season. And yet there were no takers.

'I'd be on for the 50,000 pounds a race deal,' said Lambourn.

'Okay,' said Ravilious, still disappointed that the teams hadn't gone for his shareholding idea.

'And the 50,000 is guaranteed come hell or high water?' added another boss.

Ravilious nodded.

'Then that's the option I'd go for.'

'Me too.'

'Hear, hear.'

Ravilious was amazed. They hadn't gone for his offer of investment, but were ready to obligate him – to put him on risk via the guarantees – to the tune of £500,000 per race.

'In that case,' he said, 'I'll draw up the agreements. Just so you know, the entity that will be paying you is a company called Motor Racing Promotions. While this will run in parallel with the F1CA, I, personally, will be underwriting the guarantees.'

Arno Ravilious was now substantially on risk to provide this new level of payout. Any failure by MRP to meet it would cost him personally, putting him in serious financial straits.

What Arno Ravilious did not discuss with the Formula 1 bosses at that meeting was anything about Motor Racing Promotions' involvement in the advertising and hospitality activities at grands prix, nor did he say anything about Motor Racing Promotions TV's role in respect of developing the sport's television and broadcast rights.

Now that he had formalized his relationship with the teams, Arno Ravilious felt everything was becoming more settled. It gave him the confidence to make a big decision.

He and Evangelina Amalfi were married on Sicily. Numerous Formula 1 dignitaries were there – drivers, team bosses, past champions. The occasion was covered extensively in the press, with the two of them hailed as Formula 1's golden couple.

Domestic life, however, was not straightforward. Evangelina was not keen to accompany her husband to races, and he was travelling constantly in between. To try and mitigate his absences, they ran an apartment in Milan and a townhouse in Kensington, West London.

Evangelina, though, became fascinated by the political issues he faced in Formula 1, perhaps beginning to feel that any challenge to Motor Racing Promotions was now a threat to her own interests.

Ravilious found it strange, sometimes awkward, to have someone with whom he could discuss his problems, let alone to have an ear into which he could sound off as yet another issue flared up. But Evangelina became a prop, someone he could look to for support, someone with whom he could try out ideas.

As the 1977 season got going, all the media metrics for Formula 1 went off the scale. Its popularity and following ballooned. Column inches in the press exploded. Audiences at races almost doubled.

The momentum enabled Ravilious to bargain even harder with the circuits. The amount he asked for in appearance fees almost trebled in two years. FICA's – now Motor Racing Promotions' – receipts were soon well above the amount he had guaranteed the teams.

Once they had been paid their £50,000 per race, though, the

guarantees meant they were not entitled to any more: Motor Racing Promotions was entitled to keep any sums earned above that figure.

And it didn't stop there: demand for on-track advertising rocketed, while that for hospitality increased so quickly Ravilious had to quadruple the capacity he was laying on at grands prix to fulfil it.

Everything was looking good for Arno Ravilious.

Or so he thought.

He was about to feel the effect of Newton's Third Law again.

Except, this time he was going to feel it on multiple fronts.

FORTY-SEVEN

It didn't take long for people to become aware of Ravilious's financial coup, although no one knew exactly how much money he was making.

Isolated points of disgruntlement began to emerge.

The first came from the circuits. Ravilious's demands for appearance fees continued to rise dramatically. With growth in all audiences, media coverage and sponsorship, more circuits became interested in hosting a grand prix, which forced existing circuits to bid ever higher to retain a grand prix at their venue. Some, run by the more clubby types, were scared off by the sums that Motor Racing Promotions was now asking. Those that were ready to stump up the additional amount became resentful, particularly when they realized the scale of the ancillary rights they were also expected to sign away – for the advertising, hospitality and TV. Before long, the only income left for the circuits was the gate money and whatever they could make from their on-site shops and concession stands.

Salvador Makarios was lobbied hard.

'Formula 1 belongs to the FIA,' he was told repeatedly.

'Why, Mr President, aren't you laying down the law? Why isn't the FIA managing the calendar – and setting the fee scales?'

'And who is Arno Ravilious, anyway, to be setting these terms in *our* sport?'

Yoel Kahneman, the advertising director for Worldwide Tobacco, had been smarting since Ravilious had brought in Rothmans.

At Monaco in 1977, things came to a head.

On the Friday morning, Yoel Kahneman held a press conference.

In the ballroom of the Hôtel de Paris, he appeared in front of a sizeable press corps flanked by Brad Margesson of Watkins Glenn,

Jules-Bert Macon of Magny-Cours and Simon Gerrard of Brands Hatch.

Kahneman declared: 'We are launching, today, a new championship – as an alternative to Formula 1.'

The room was aghast. No one had expected anything like this.

'Formula 1 has become too corrupt – too greedy,' Kahneman went on. 'With the backing of Worldwide Tobacco, we are forming the World Championship Racing series, the WCR. Six circuits have signed up already, including Watkins Glen, Magny-Cours and Brands Hatch – representatives of which are here today. The WCR is in discussion with several others, including Anderstorp in Sweden, Zandvoort in Holland and the Juan y Oscar Gálvez Autodrome in Argentina. The prize money at each of these WCR races, underwritten by Worldwide Tobacco, will be 2 million dollars.'

An audible gasp came from around the room.

Questions were then yelled at Kahneman:

'Does the WCR have the support of the FIA?'

'Yes.'

'Are you sure the teams will compete at WCR races?'

'Yes.'

'Will you allow them to compete in Formula 1 grands prix as well?'

'No.'

'Will you be allowing other sponsors in alongside Worldwide Tobacco?'

'Yes, although WWT will retain a veto over any rival tobacco brands.'

'How do you expect Motor Racing Promotions to react to this challenge?'

Yoel Kahneman replied: 'Arno Ravilious needs to realize that motor racing existed before he came along – and that it's a sport with numerous stakeholders.'

'How *do* you expect him to react?'

'If the FIA, the circuits, the teams – and their sponsors – think the

WCR is the way forward, Arno will have to fall in behind. I am here to serve the true interests of the teams. Mr Ravilious will have to accept that, to all intents and purposes, I am running motor racing now.'

News of the press conference was fed back to Ravilious almost immediately. Lord Lambourn, Tim Parnell and JJ McKay met him in the Ptarmigan garage in the pit lane.

'It's not looking good,' said Lambourn. 'Kahneman seems to have got things pretty well sewn up.'

'He's not only got three of the largest circuits on board,' agreed McKay, 'it's rumoured Colin Chapman and Frank Williams are talking to WCR, and that Eugene Van Der Vaal has already gone over.'

'I'm so sorry, Arno,' said Parnell. 'What do you think you'll go on to do after Formula 1?'

The three team bosses were surprised when they saw Ravilious smile.

'That question,' he replied, his Northern Irish accent at its edgiest, 'is the one you should be putting to Yoel Kahneman.'

Arno Ravilious returned to his motor home, locked the door and started swearing. But ranting wasn't going to solve anything. There had to be a way back from this. He forced himself to calm down.

Sitting in one of the sumptuous chairs in his mobile headquarters, Ravilious looked through the smoked-glass windows at the pastel-coloured houses spread across the hillsides of Monte Carlo and then down at the Monaco harbour at the rows of superyachts that now came to this race.

Before, when he'd come up against a political issue in Formula 1, he'd managed to solve someone's problem – typically financial – or he had played on an individual's weakness. Yoel Kahneman, though, was shrewd, capable and sly. Almost immediately, Ravilious resigned himself to not going after the man.

But what about his support?

He needed to disrupt Kahneman's base – the elements that might be giving the American his seat of power. Ravilious thought about this and started to smile.

Working at a manual typewriter, he drafted a press release. Having run off numerous copies, Ravilious walked out into the paddock and hand-delivered them to each member of the press pool:

```
Motor Racing Promotions announces the 1978 Formula 1 season
        For next season, the calendar of Grands Prix
             will be reduced from 18 races to 12.
```

That was all it said. It did not specify which six of the scheduled races were going to lose out.

Then Ravilious went to work. He knew there was a contingent of Dutchmen in Monaco that weekend. He set out to find them. He tracked down Adriaan Bakker, the promoter and circuit owner of Zandvoort.

'What's all this about you going with WCR?' Ravilious asked him.

Bakker began to look sheepish.

'What have you agreed with Kahneman?'

'Yoel asked some searching questions ... about you ... and then, because I wasn't sure, Arno, where Zandvoort stood with the grand prix next year I said if things didn't work out with the grand prix schedule, we *might* be open to a discussion.'

'So you haven't signed anything yet?'

Bakker shook his head.

'Okay, Adriaan, I understand. It's my fault – I should have been much clearer. Let me be so now. How would you like Zandvoort to host the 1978 Dutch Grand Prix?'

Bakker's eyes widened before he smiled with relief. The Dutchman wasted no time sticking out his hand. Ravilious took it.

Bakker shook it but not with 100 per cent gusto.

'My word is my bond, Adriaan,' said Ravilious, without letting go of Bakker's hand.

The Dutch promoter's rate of handshake started to increase.

On his way to the next person Ravilious wanted to talk to, he ran into Valter Lindström of Anderstorp. The Swede was agitated.

'What's all this about next season being reduced from 18 races to 12?' Lindström asked. 'After all the money we have put into the Formula 1 teams' facilities, we'd go bust without the race. You *can't* drop us from next year's grand prix.'

Ravilious liked the Swedish promoter but gave the impression of being unmoved. He knew Lindström to be a close friend of Antoine Vermeulen, who ran the Zolder Circuit in Belgium. 'I tell you what, Valter,' said Ravilious, 'if you can persuade Antoine to host the Belgian Grand Prix, I will guarantee both Zolder and Anderstorp remain on the Formula 1 calendar next year – and for the next two years after that.'

Lindström looked relieved. It was all Ravilious could do to shake the man's hand before the Swedish promoter was off, presumably to go looking for the Belgian.

Arno Ravilious made two more interventions before he was accosted by Johnny Bradshaw, chairman of the BRDC.

'You'd better not be dropping Silverstone from the F1 season,' said Bradshaw.

'Well I don't know, Johnny,' he said. 'Simon at Brands is causing me trouble. If he runs off to WCR, then I'd have to win him back somehow.'

'Why wouldn't I go with WCR, then?' asked the Silverstone boss.

'Who, *then*, would underwrite your £500,000 loan from Motor Racing Promotions?'

'You wouldn't call that in?'

'Loyalty and support cut both ways, Johnny.'

'Okay, okay,' replied Bradshaw. 'I won't go anywhere near WCR.'

Ravilious offered his hand to the BRDC chairman, who shook it keenly.

'Thank you, Arno.'

'I stand by the idea that loyalty cuts both ways, but you know what would cement our friendship?' Ravilious asked.

'What?'

'I need you and Brands to come to some kind of arrangement. I can only have one race per country per year, and I need—'

Bradshaw interjected: 'Why?'

'Sorry ... why what?'

'*Why* can you only have one race per country per year? IndyCar doesn't – all of its races are in *one* country, for God's sake. You're the boss of this thing, aren't you, Arno? Why limit yourself to such an arbitrary restriction?'

For once it was Arno Ravilious who was prompted to pause.

In the pit lane, Ravilious managed to track down Jorge Morales, the promoter of the Argentinian Grand Prix. The Argentine, too, looked sheepish as Ravilious approached. He was about to say something when Ravilious spoke over the top of him:

'Jorge, after all I did to revive your circuit – committing the Argentinian Grand Prix to you – you go and repay me by siding with Kahneman and his bullshitting WCR. You know what, when I announced a reduction of races next year from 18 to 12, the Argentinian Grand Prix was the first of the six to go. Congratulations, Jorge – you've just hosted your last grand prix.'

The Argentinian did not protest but replied: 'Kahneman is serious, Arno.'

'Well that's just as well for you then, isn't it, Jorge. You realize *none* of the teams are going to commit to the WCR, or whatever he calls this thing?'

Morales offered him a hurtful smile. 'I wouldn't be so sure about that, Arno.'

FORTY-EIGHT

Ravilious did not like what he heard from the Argentinian promoter. As he set about trying to counter the WCR breakaway series, Ravilious hadn't been concerned about the teams. He decided to switch tactics immediately.

One of the first people Ravilious wanted to talk to about a suspected defection was keeping his distance. He couldn't find Colin Chapman anywhere. Ravilious bumped into Eugene Van Der Vaal, whom he found to be even more smug than usual.

'You may have been sharp to go after the circuits,' said the gruff South African, 'but you won't be so lucky with the teams. Greed finally *will* show itself to have its costs,' grunted Van Der Vaal. 'The amount you're taking out of the sport, on the backs of the teams, can only end up getting us all pissed off.'

Ravilious walked away with a feeling of unease.

He expected Van Der Vaal to goad him, but what if he were right? Ravilious might well find that there were enough circuits still vying for a grand prix, despite the temptations of the WCR, to allow him to play one off against the other. But Ravilious could not afford a split in the teams: his entire bargaining power, from the very beginning, had come from them all showing up together and putting on the performance of grand prix.

Right then, Ravilious decided to make a concerted effort to get round all the team bosses that weekend. But very quickly he sensed trouble.

He couldn't *find* them.

Were they avoiding him?

Could the odious Eugene Van Der Vaal of Massarella be right? Could Ravilious actually rely on the teams any more?

By the Saturday afternoon of the Monaco Grand Prix weekend, Ravilious was seriously troubled. It helped him make his next key decision. He was ready to leave Monte Carlo, immediately – if he was given the chance to speak to one man.

For over an hour, Ravilious badgered the hotel operator, repeatedly asking her to give him an outside line – having her keep trying a particular number.

It took a while, but finally Arno Ravilious got through.

Within an hour of securing his appointment, Ravilious had chartered a plane. Three hours after that he had flown out of Nice airport and was heading for Bologna.

Arno Ravilious arrived at Enzo Ferrari's house at 7 o'clock that evening. Despite the distance Ravilious had travelled, *Il Commendatore* kept him waiting for 45 minutes.

He was finally ushered into the presence of the Great Man.

The godfather of Formula 1 was wearing a silk smoking jacket; Enzo Ferrari remained standing and did not offer his visitor a seat.

Without preamble, Ferrari asked: 'Why shouldn't the Scuderia go with WCR?'

Ravilious took a breath and looked into the dark glasses ranged across the craggy face. Was this legendary old man really going to abandon such an extraordinary heritage on the say-so of a tobacco salesman?

Ravilious decided to take a punt: 'You must have met Yoel Kahneman,' he said, more as a statement.

Ferrari paused for half a beat.

And then said: 'There is a general concern that the balance of authority in Formula 1 has been altered.'

Ravilious knew he'd scored his first point:

Clearly, *Il Commendatore* had *not* met Yoel Kahneman.

'Do you deny, sir, that the teams are better rewarded, now, for the effort they make?'

Another momentary hesitation from Ferrari allowed him to feel emboldened; Ravilious quickly added: 'To prove the might and the power of the Scuderia, Ferrari has to have worthy adversaries *and* your team has to be at the pinnacle of motorsport. What, sir, if I arrange for the cars that remain in Formula 1 to be raced noticeably faster than those in the breakaway series? The WCR will be seen to be second rate. How could that not diminish the Ferrari name?'

'Circuits and traditional practices,' Ferrari answered, 'are being threatened by an unattractive pursuit – the pursuit of ever higher appearance fees and prize money.'

Ravilious was beginning to feel less concerned. Ferrari had not answered any of his questions so far, nor had he responded to his provocative comments. More to the point, *Il Commendatore* had not challenged or levelled a direct threat against him. Ravilious felt emboldened to go further:

'Motor Racing Promotions and the grand prix format,' he said, 'would, quite clearly, be diminished without Ferrari – but I also presume to say, sir, that Ferrari would not be the same without the F1CA teams as rivals.'

He paused.

'To demonstrate the relative value of the Scuderia to Formula 1,' Ravilious added, 'are we not able to come to a suitable "arrangement"?'

Ferrari's hauteur was back, as if any discussion of money could only lower the tone.

Il Commendatore, though, rotated his right hand – in the manner of a royal wave.

As an invitation to continue?

'How about this?' said Ravilious. 'Should Ferrari agree to stay fully committed to Formula 1, we could agree a 10 per cent increment in the Scuderia's appearance fees – *and*, sir, what if I were also to inform Mr Makarios that you have asked me, personally, to see him – to discuss the supremacy of the FIA and the relative balance of power within Formula 1?'

Enzo Ferrari looked at the younger man with a strange expression. Nothing more was said.

All Ravilious received in acknowledgement was a discontinuance of the wave and the slightest nod of Ferrari's head.

The audience was over.

Arno Ravilious was going back through Bologna airport within the hour, and had returned to Monte Carlo by 11 p.m. that evening. The moment he reached the Hôtel de Paris he asked the concierge to pass a message to the president of FISA, whom he knew to be staying in the Churchill Suite. The message, deferentially toned, asked if Makarios would be open to discussing the WCR.

An answer came back – delivered by a page slipping a note under his door – almost by return. Salvador Makarios would grant Ravilious five minutes at 9 o'clock the following morning.

Trawling the bars, Ravilious sought out several of the team bosses whom he'd struggled to find earlier. As word got round that he'd met with Enzo Ferrari, they started agreeing to see him.

At nine o'clock the following morning Arno Ravilious was shown into the President of FISA's suite of rooms in the Hôtel de Paris.

'Now, Ravilious,' drawled the Greek billionaire, 'I trust you realize that we, the FIA, can bestow our patronage wherever we see fit. The WCR is now the vehicle we wish to use to deliver the Formula 1 season and championships.'

Arno Ravilious replied: 'Before we get down to business, Mr President … may I … pass on a message?'

Makarios frowned slightly, thrown by the calmness of the tone and the unexpected comment.

'Sir … *Il Commendatore* … sends you his regards.'

Referencing the Great Man was a very clear indication that Ravilious had been busy.

Makarios's face immediately set.

What had been discussed?

What had been agreed?

Ravilious took advantage of the Greek's hesitation: 'The Scuderia is fully committed to Formula 1 and will not participate in your WCR. Furthermore, Brands Hatch, Magny-Cours and Watkins Glen have each confirmed that they will be holding grands prix, and not WCR races, next season. Colin Chapman has reconfirmed that Lotus will stay in F1, where he says he belongs. Van Der Vaal has also capitulated, which means that the entire F1CA group will remain with Formula 1 as currently structured.'

Salvador Makarios stood in the centre of his grand suite in the Hôtel de Paris, having prepared himself to act as lord high executioner on Ravilious's career. In the space of three minutes, it became painfully clear that Ravilious had taken fewer than 24 hours to dismantle Kahneman's breakaway series and had neutered any leverage FISA may have had over him. Salvador Makarios had been outmanoeuvred.

Rapid pulsation became visible in the arteries of the man's neck.

His eyes started to bulge.

Veins were proud across Makarios's face, particularly down the centre of his forehead.

'Get out,' he screamed. 'Get the fuck out!'

Taking his time, Arno Ravilious walked out of Makarios's suite. Ravilious could feel his hands shaking as he reached to press a button for the lifts. As he rode down, he was aware that he had beaten yet another deliberate attempt to thwart him – to cut him down – even to force him out.

Ravilious *had* beaten off FISA and Kahneman decisively.

As he walked across the lobby to the main entrance, and out into Place du Casino, though, he wasn't punching the air. For the second time in a few years, the president of the sport's governing body had tried to damage his business, both times in Monaco. From the man's reaction just now, Ravilious knew that this was never going to be the end of it. He had no doubt Makarios would be back at him again all too soon.

As Ravilious walked down the pit lane to the Ptarmigan garage, he caught sight – in the distance – of Kahneman lording it among the cars and A-listers out on the grid. From his demeanour, it was clear that he had not yet got the news about the WCR from Makarios. Ravilious had no desire to tell him: it would be much more effective for him to hear about it from somebody else.

After the grand prix, Yoel Kahneman did come looking for him.

'You slimy *bastard*,' he yelled into Ravilious's face. 'Dirty deals, *under*hand deals – deals behind people's backs. And that's the way you think this sport should be run? What a cunt. This isn't over, Ravilious; this *isn't* over.'

FORTY-NINE

Ravilious's dismantling of the WCR brought him some unexpected acclamation. Shortly afterwards, he was asked to take on the presidency of FiCA. He had no need to, as his influence and business lay with Motor Racing Promotions, but he accepted the honour – given that it would, at the very least, deny the post going to someone else who might use the position to cause him trouble.

Ravilious began his tour of duty with an unusual proposal: he suggested to the team bosses that they change the name of the body to the Formula *One* Constructors' Association and the acronym: FOCA.

'What's the point of such a trifling adjustment?' asked one of the team bosses.

'Whoever coined FiCA is not much of a linguist,' Ravilious replied. 'Evangelina giggles every time she hears us pronounce it 'feecka'. The name's a joke in Italian … sounding like their slang word for fanny.'

Some looked embarrassed at not having been aware.

'The change of name to FOCA is obviously a good idea, then,' said Lambourn, 'although I'm not sure that'll free us entirely from slang-related connotations.'

The restoration of peace led to a period of stability and a resurgence of growth. Team sponsors' cash flowed into Formula 1. In turn, that sparked technological advance. Teams were soon pushing ideas in all directions to gain advantage on the track. Among the engineers, there was an added incentive – motivated by pride. There was the need to catch up with the brilliance of Colin Chapman, who always seemed to be one step ahead of the game, ever since the days of his Lotus 49.

With that design, he had the radical idea of making the engine block an integral and central part of the chassis, attaching directly to it the gearbox and rear suspension. Such a revolutionary configuration saved weight, space, as well as transforming the balance and handling of the car. After that, other teams had been desperate to prove their worthiness to be in Lotus's company.

More recently, one team had struck out with an idea to improve their aerodynamics. Tyrrell saw the front wheel of an F1 car – a tall, wide, head-on profile to the oncoming airflow – as a source of too much drag. What if they could reduce it by using smaller wheels and tyres?

The physics made sense, except that reducing the tyre's diameter would also reduce the tyre's contact area with the track, and so cost them grip. What, then, if they built a second front axle of similar small-diameter wheels – to recover some of the lost contact area with the road? In other words, four-wheel steering.

The accompanying mechanical drag created a few new challenges, but it seemed to work – particularly when the profile of smaller wheels could be smoothed further by the aerodynamics around them. Tyrrell created an unbroken airflow from the leading edge of the front wing, up its 'ramp' and over the tops of the front wheels, which were now flush with the radiator pods behind. The benefits did indeed prove significant.

The six-wheeled Tyrrell A34 was an eye-catching design, even iconic. Jody Scheckter and Patrick Depailler raced it in 1976, achieving a one-two finish in Sweden. The design ultimately fell short, though, as its mechanical complexity required heavier components to ensure reliability and, in a straight line, the size of the rear wheels still dominated the drag profile. By the end of 1977 the Tyrrell had reverted to four wheels.

Other teams also experimented with a six-wheel format – March, Williams and Ferrari – except their versions had the second axle to the rear. This configuration prompted the March to be referred to as a 2-4-0, invoking the Whyte Notation used in the classification of steam locomotives.

None of these six-wheelers, though, were to reach a competitive pace, even where, to reduce the drag profile, the teams ran with six small wheels. Sometime later the experiment with additional axles and wheels was formally brought to a close: the FIA stipulated, in 1983, that a Formula 1 car could only have four wheels.

These developments had indicated adventurousness and innovation, except none of them was successful enough to be political. A sea change in technological advance, though, was coming. No one had the faintest idea at the time that it would ultimately precipitate the political clash that would define Formula 1 for the next 35 years.

It started in 1978 – with another act of genius from Colin Chapman. His background was that of a trained structural engineer, added to which he had a passion for flying. As a result, he was always asking his team to push the envelope, particularly in the development of aerodynamics. Their latest idea was to convert the underside of a car into an inverted wing. Airflow beneath the Lotus 78 was designed to generate a low-pressure zone that effectively sucked it down onto the track. In combination with the other wings and aero surfaces around the bodywork of the car, this development created an extraordinary level of downforce. The Lotus had been given an ability to corner at considerably higher speeds. Where genius was truly shown, though, was in the team's recognition of – and then countering of – a very specific problem: the wing-tip vortex.

The Lotus was generating lift, albeit inverted, by using the effect of a typical wing's aerofoil shape – with a rounded top side, to increase the distance the air has to travel between its leading and trailing edges. To make up this extra distance, the air speeds up and, in doing so, creates an area of low pressure. Airflow over the other – flatter side – of a wing is also altered slightly and inevitably it, too, creates an area of low pressure, but a smaller one than on the 'lift' side of the wing. Nature's attempt to equalize the imbalance between these two low-pressure areas creates the lift and causes an aeroplane's wing to rise. Bernoulli's Principle. But Chapman was all too aware that nature often has other plans.

At the tip of any wing there is a chance for the two pressure areas to balance more easily, by simply bleeding round the end: All hail the wing-tip vortex. This can lose a wing a significant amount of lift; the wider the span, though, the lower the effect of that overall loss. Modern attempts to address this phenomenon are readily spotted on aircraft with small vertical fins at their wing tips. Such small devices can increase, by a material degree, the efficiency of even sizeable wingspans.

Colin Chapman found that, on his Formula 1 cars, the wing-tip vortex was all the greater because of the narrowness of his 'span' – his 'wing' being only the width of the car. The desired low-pressure imbalance was too easily equalized by air bleeding into the underside of the car from the sides, significantly degrading his downforce. Colin Chapman and Lotus solved this problem with considerable elegance.

They thought to mount panels down either side of their cars, between the front and rear wheels. By doing so, they were able to create their own wing-tip fin of the modern airliner, finding a way to block the wing-tip vortices. These side panels hugely increased the efficiency of their inverted 'wing'.

The lower these panels could be, the greater the benefit. Chapman could see that the best results would come if they achieved a zero gap, with the panels actually in contact with the surface of the road – but how could they get round the friction that that would create? They didn't want such a component to slow the car down.

Genius was shown by Lotus when the edge of those panels was coated with a low-friction runner, the best results coming from ceramics; therewith, they had discovered the tightest seal with the lowest friction they could.

Colin Chapman's brilliance had improved the ground-effect car by inventing the 'skirt'.

The 'sealed' tube running underneath the car was now also capable of creating a Venturi effect, where accelerating the air under the car would create a low-pressure area beneath it – having the effect of sucking the car into the ground.

Before this approach was adopted more widely, another team demonstrated a dramatic innovation – more to do with the interpretation of the rules than the laws of physics. Brabham introduced a variation of the skirted car with a twist. The BT46B had its own version of skirts, sealing the space under the car, but it also had something else … to assist with its 'cooling'.

The rear of the car was shaped like a backward-facing cowling. Set in this was mounted a large fan, linked directly to the output of the Alfa Romeo flat-12. As the engine revved, the fan rotated. The faster it went, the greater the 'cooling' effect, the fan serving to extract air from under the car. But, because of the skirts, it also created something of a vacuum – which, coincidentally, happened to suck the car down onto the road. While Chapman had created an inverted wing, Brabham had, in effect, created an inverted hovercraft. All this, though, rested on an imaginative interpretation of the regulations.

Under the F1 rules, aero surfaces were not permitted to be variable, so there had always been a trade-off between downforce and drag – the more the downforce, the more the drag. When the angle of a wing was set to provide meaningful downforce through a corner, it inevitably created unwanted downforce – and drag – when travelling at speed in a straight line.

Technically, the blades on Brabham's fan were fixed and were not geometrically variable, so they did not infringe the rule prohibiting variable aero surfaces. The speed of rotation of the fan, though, clearly was variable – so the forces exerted by the fan were most certainly not fixed. It all came down to how much the fan *was* there for cooling purposes. Perhaps, understandably, the fan car caused controversy, being objected to by the other teams. For a range of reasons, it was soon withdrawn.

In the meantime, Colin Chapman's skirt successfully created a quantum leap in downforce. His Lotus 78 left the competition almost standing. Within a couple of races, other teams incorporated their own version of what Chapman was doing and enhanced their own performance. In short order most of the England-based teams had adopted the ground-effect concept and were almost unstoppable.

Which was when the technology became political.

Salvador Makarios, the president of Formula 1's governing body, never stopped criticizing Ravilious, FOCA and Motor Racing Promotions, constantly finding fault with his operation.

Ravilious's power base, built by aggregating the interests of the smaller Formula 1 teams that Enzo Ferrari had once derided as *garagistes*, was largely English. The president of FISA believed his best way of countering this increasingly powerful block was to favour the continental manufacturers: Ferrari, Alfa Romeo and Renault, none of which had adopted the ground-effect principle and so had been losing out badly.

As the Formula 1 circus turned up at Zandvoort in Holland for the 1980 Dutch Grand Prix, Makarios – without warning – announced an arbitrary ruling. He declared, claiming the full authority of FISA, that the skirt was a violation of the regulations and that cars had to run a full six centimetres above the surface of the track.

A meeting of FOCA team bosses was hastily called.

One of them said: 'What on earth's he playing at? There's nothing in the rules about ride height.'

'We've got to lodge an objection, en masse,' said Lambourn.

The FOCA teams went ahead and did just that.

It didn't produce a favourable outcome.

Makarios wouldn't concede any ground over the skirts.

Formula 1, once again, reached an impasse.

In the build-up to that year's Dutch Grand Prix, Salvador Makarios had extended an invitation to the newly crowned Queen Beatrix of the Netherlands to join him in his Ravilious-supplied President's Suite. Other dignitaries had also been invited, including, significantly for Makarios, his younger brother Belvedere – the man who had been preferred over him to run the family shipping empire. Zandvoort was to be *the* showcase with which the FISA president would display the status he had achieved in his field.

Makarios refused to back down over the banning of skirts.

Ravilious was getting more and more irritated, and, as the clock counted down to the start of the race, he went on the attack – announcing a boycott:

'The English teams,' Ravilious stated, 'would not be racing in the Dutch Grand Prix.'

Pandemonium broke out.

Makarios was seen all but running from the hospitality area down into the pit lane. Ravilious later learned the president had made straight for the Lotus garage, trying to do a deal with Colin Chapman over the skirts independently of FOCA. Next he tried Williams and, finally, JJ McKay at Ptarmigan.

None of the bosses showed any readiness to concede.

The English teams were holding the line.

The clock, though, was still counting down.

The Queen of the Netherlands was due to arrive in 10 minutes.

Through gritted teeth, Makarios realized he had to concede. In a tone of panic, he shouted: 'Let them race. Let the *fucking* English race.'

But he made sure there was a sting in the tail:

'This race, though, will not count towards the Championship … I declare it is no longer an official grand prix.'

Makarios was not done. Before the end of the Dutch Grand Prix weekend, the president went on to decree:

'Only the FIA has the power and authority to declare the Formula 1 calendar – it alone will decide where races will be held – and the terms that are negotiated with the circuits.'

This was a direct attack on Ravilious's business.

Under this policy, FIA-negotiated fees would inevitably be lower.

Ravilious, though, would still be on the hook, obligated to pay the teams their guarantees. The margin squeeze would be felt entirely by Motor Racing Promotions, meaning Ravilious personally. The FOCA teams were just as concerned, but more about the unpredictable and subjective influence on the sport.

Lord Lambourn and Ravilious made repeated attempts to get a meeting with Makarios. The president would not even acknowledge their request.

'It's no good if we are going to be hostage to such a whimsical interpretation of the rules,' said Williams.

'How does this ever get any better,' asked Tyrrell, 'when Makarios is so clearly biased towards the continental teams – the manufacturers?'

Ravilious had come to a conclusion. It was going to be radical; he would have to pick his moment carefully.

It came sooner than he expected.

At around 8 p.m. that evening, after several hours of angst within the FOCA camp, he found the moment to say: 'I think we should break from FISA.'

His timing was good. There were barely any expressions of concern from the team bosses; their responses, if anything, were practical.

'How could we afford it?'

'We need the sponsorship, the money, to keep going,' said another.

'I hear you,' Ravilious said calmly. 'This, therefore, is what I propose...'

In the next three hours, Ravilious got busy. Calls were made. Costs were calculated. Availability was confirmed.

Throughout the evening, Ravilious put in repeated requests to see the FISA president. Makarios finally deigned to meet him and Lambourn, but not until midnight.

They were shown into his presence – in the President's Suite. The Greek billionaire was on edge.

'This has to stop,' he barked at Ravilious, 'FISA – *I* – run Formula 1 ... *not* you. No race will be staged without *my* express approval. And

… the television rights to each grand prix will sit with FISA – *not* you, *not* the teams, *not* FOCA. With me.'

Ravilious forced himself not to respond.

At least not yet.

Makarios suddenly looked less sure of himself and was about to speak again when, barely above a whisper, Ravilious said: 'Mr Makarios, this meeting is useful as it confirms how relations within our sport have broken down. Relations between the governing body and the teams are so poor that Formula 1 is over. Lord Lambourn and I are here to tell you that FOCA is forming the World Federation of Motorsport, the WFMS, which will see us compete for the World Professional Drivers' Championship, the WPDC. Our first race will be held at Kyalami in South Africa on the 7th of February 1981, which was scheduled to be the first race of next year's F1 season. Whether you like it or not, Mr Makarios, Formula 1 – as a result of the progress we have made recently – is a business, a business with significant obligations and commitments. It cannot be interfered with as it has been this weekend with last-minute rule changes and "asymmetric" adjudications.'

Makarios's large-featured face concealed nothing. His frustration broke through. 'Go ahead, you jumped-up car mechanic, go right ahead,' he screamed, 'because you will fail. The puppets you think you can manipulate in fucking FOCA will follow you, but you *won't* have the manufacturers – and what you don't understand is *they* are the heart of Formula 1, not the jumped-up privateers. You won't get the sponsors – who are not drawn to the teams but to the prestige of Formula 1 – to the prestige of FISA. And one more thing,' said the Greek as he faced off against Ravilious, 'you're not coming back, do you hear me? Don't expect to be welcomed back into FISA when you've all gone to shit.'

FIFTY

A week after Zandvoort, Evangelina found she was pregnant. Ravilious was overjoyed. He rushed home to Kensington to be with her as they delighted in their news. But it was not an easy pregnancy. Evangelina was laid low with severe bouts of morning sickness. It never seemed to let up.

While he was at home, Ravilious had to make a start on planning the breakaway race. It was hugely time consuming, requiring him to be on the phone for hours at a time.

Evangelina couldn't keep anything down. She lost a lot of weight.

During that time, Ravilious also experienced a flare-up in America. Watkins Glen, the venue of the United States Grand Prix, was in financial trouble and looked like it might pull out: it was due to host the fourteenth and last race of 1980, so its cancelling would have left a bitter taste at the end of the season. Ravilious did not want to lose the commercial asset of a race in America; at the same time, he refused to discount FOCA's fees, fearing it would set a dangerous precedent.

For several months negotiations between Brad Margesson and his bankers had seemed to be going round in circles. As much as Ravilious tried to handle it by phone, it wasn't enough. He had to fly to America to sort it out. To keep an eye on Evangelina, he asked her mother to come over to be with her daughter. The elder Milanese made it clear she was not impressed that her son-in-law was not to be at home by his wife's side. Ravilious received instruction on what his husbandly duties should be. The stress began to take its toll, shown in his hairline. It started to recede. Within months Ravilious had lost his fringe and the crown of his head was no longer covered by his instantly recognizable red hair.

Towards the end of September, when Watkins Glen looked like it would be able to host the grand prix after all, Ravilious flew home. But his spousal absence was never forgotten. He was guilted into attending every antenatal appointment – check-up, test and briefing. Ravilious's mind, though, was more often than not elsewhere: Kyalami and the breakaway race went on causing him considerable stress.

Three weeks after his return, the breakaway race reached a crisis point. He had managed to secure a healthy appearance fee from the South African National Party government, and a local TV company to film the race, but he couldn't raise sponsorship. Because of apartheid no company of any size would take it on.

Ravilious realized he had to make a momentous decision.

He'd reached the point of do or die.

If this gambit was to go any further, he would have to meet the uncovered costs of the Kyalami grand prix out of his own pocket.

Evangelina was beside herself: 'How can you sacrifice everything – our home – in the name of that sport's future? Life has got to be more important than this.'

In February 1981 Ravilious's group of FOCA teams turned up at the Kyalami Race Circuit, a short distance north of Johannesburg, for what should have been the first grand prix of the year.

The National Party government received the motor racing visitors lavishly, keen to welcome rare international sporting guests – this despite FISA declaring the race unofficial and that it would not be a recognized part of the Formula 1 season.

Its status didn't bother Ravilious. He and Lambourn renamed the race The Formula Libre. What mattered was that they were there to make a different point. But Ravilious soon had other concerns.

For all the publicity the breakaway race had garnered in Europe, its significance was not registering in South Africa. Virtually no spectators came to the practice or Qualifying sessions.

There was no publicity from local TV, which barely mentioned it.

Ravilious feared the spectator turnout for the race itself was going to be dire. Making things worse, extra seating had been erected by the owners in anticipation. If empty stands were shown in any film coverage of the race, Ravilious's gamble with FISA would be sure to backfire.

As the clock counted down, Ravilious jumped into a jeep. He asked to be driven, at speed, to each camera position around the circuit. Climbing out, he issued instructions to every single operator:

'Whatever you do, don't shoot the stands in your arc of the track – *only* shoot the cars … like you're only ever looking at them from the waist down!'

The start of The Formula Libre race was signalled.

Ravilious held his breath.

If he couldn't rely on any atmosphere coming from the crowds around the circuit, he had to pray for some fierce competition out on the track. Except, of course, that dynamic was completely beyond his control.

It turned out to be a thrilling race – a showdown between Carlos Reutemann, the Argentinian, and Nelson Piquet, the Brazilian. In a true nail-biter, the on-track battle went down to the chequered flag. At one point, Ravilious even found himself forgetting his concerns – forgetting to watch for camera angles and editing opportunities – finding himself completely wrapped up in the race itself.

He knew he had been saved.

Immediately the chequered flag fell, Ravilious went to work with Howard Lloyd – selecting specific camera angles and then editing, cutting, splicing the footage frame by frame. When, at 2 o'clock the following morning, he and Lloyd were ready to watch it back, Ravilious was buzzing. They realized they had a blockbuster: supreme wheel-to-wheel action – two hours of a gripping motor race. Once again, Murray Walker's commentary engaged the viewer by adding another level of excitement to the already high drama on track.

Prints of the film were shipped off to television stations around the world.

One of the copies arrived in France. Because of the intensity of the sporting drama it depicted, France's second TV channel – *La Deuxième Chaîne* – chose to air the film in its entirety the following weekend. Salvador Makarios, sitting in his Monte Carlo apartment, couldn't resist watching it. As the film rolled on, he became more and more frustrated.

His anger and loathing of Ravilious's grip on motor racing rose like bile in his throat.

Lord Lambourn rang Ravilious: 'Arno, my friend – congratulations. What a *fantastic* film. Better still, it absolutely launches the WFMS brand – screaming quality and excitement.'

'How do you think Makarios is going to react?'

The team boss replied: 'After that? The only way he can; he's either got to lose us – or concede.'

A few weeks later, Salvador Makarios as the President of FISA sued for peace, offering to sign a deal with Arno Ravilious.

On the 11th of March 1981 an agreement was struck.

Having negotiated the terms in FISA's headquarters in Paris, Makarios asked that the document be named after the FIA's address. Lambourn put a hand on Ravilious's shoulder and said: 'Let him have it, Arno – anyone who knows the real story knows the truth.'

The Concorde Agreement was born.

Makarios had conceded on a number of fronts: the principal one being that the FISA could not authorize grands prix unless they satisfied the terms that Motor Racing Promotions had negotiated with the circuits.

In return, MRP, acting for the Formula 1 Constructors' Association, acknowledged FISA's authority to make, change and enforce the rules set out in the Formula.

Another major concession was FISA signing over Formula 1's TV rights to Motor Racing Promotions TV; from these, there were to be three beneficiaries. FISA was to receive $1.25 million per year for the rights themselves; then there would be an equal three-way split of the royalties generated, net of costs, going to the FIA, the teams as a block and Motor Racing Promotions TV.

Ravilious was convinced his Kyalami gamble had paid off. There was now a formal, contractual and publicly acknowledged organizational split between the rule-setting governing body and the commercial interests of the sport.

Arno Ravilious had finally arrived.

FIFTY-ONE

In her third trimester, Evangelina knew something was wrong. She felt weak; lethargic. She started to feel disorientated.

Evangelina woke one morning and tried to get up. She felt light-headed as she tried to move. Needing to make herself comfortable, she had to make for the bathroom. But lost her footing on the bedroom floor and stumbled.

She misjudged her hold, trying to rely on a swinging door and crashed onto the floor tiles of the bathroom. She never knew how long she was unconscious.

As she came round she could feel an area of warmth between her thighs and down her legs. She saw the pool of blood and somehow knew what had happened.

She started bellowing with a heart-wrenching scream.

Ravilious rushed home from Rio de Janeiro after the Brazilian Grand Prix at Jacarepaguá. Arriving back in London, he sped to the hospital. Evangelina lay like a cadaver on the bed. She was gaunt, haggard, exhausted. She barely had the strength to indicate the small bundle beside her.

He looked down at the lifeless body of his son.

At that moment Ravilious's soul was cleaved in two.

He tried to comfort Evangelina, but didn't know how. How could he console her when he himself was inconsolable?

Evangelina was to suffer another blow: she was then hit with a deep bout of postpartum depression.

Trying to help her was all Ravilious could think about. It distracted him from his business. But after three weeks, she showed no sign of responding. For all Ravilious's wealth, which should have denied them nothing they could ever need, it showed itself to be completely inconsequential. Nothing was going to dull this pain.

Nothing seemed to ease the heartache.

Nothing could come close to assuaging Ravilious's feeling of guilt.

Even prioritizing his commitment to Evangelina, there were issues in Formula 1 that could no longer be ignored. For a while some of them could be dealt with at home. Howard Lloyd, Ravilious's editor on the films of James Hunt at the Japanese Grand Prix in 1976 and the breakaway Formula Libre race in South Africa, seemed to camp out in Ravilious's home for most of April.

To capitalize on the TV rights secured via the Concorde Agreement, Ravilious found himself on a steep learning curve. He needed to master a new set of skills, and quickly. They had managed to sell the two previous films featuring Formula 1, but those had been one-offs. He had no experience of producing regular content for television companies. Howard Lloyd went through the process in detail; between them, they decided to go back to the European Broadcasting Union. Lloyd believed the EBU would solve Motor Racing Promotions' TV distribution challenges, as it already supplied 90-odd countries with TV content.

The BBC liked the film from Kyalami and were keen to hold it up as a standard for future storytelling and production values. The corporation told Ravilious: 'You have to assure us you'll provide the same level of quality and watchability, going forward.'

Lloyd's view was that the only way to safeguard quality was for them to control the production of the coverage themselves. Motor Racing Promotions' production facilities were set up within six weeks. All the equipment needed was bought in. A base with ready access to transport links was needed. Lloyd knew people in Kent. He and Ravilious arranged space at a little-used airfield down there called Biggin Hill.

The next race in the middle of May was the Belgian Grand Prix at Zolder near Hasselt. It was shambolic.

An innovative hydraulic system had given Brabham an advantage, but it sparked accusations of rule infringements.

Carlos Reutemann ran over a mechanic, prompting a drivers' strike over the levels of mechanics' safety.

At the start of the race, an Arrows stalled on the grid. A mechanic ran out to try and restart it only to be hit by the other Arrows car. And because no red flag was flown by the race officials, cars continued to stream by the injured man who lay unconscious on the track with two broken legs.

The consequences of all this lingered for days.

Ravilious decided he had to step in to try and sort out the mess. But in going to Belgium, he had to leave Evangelina for the first time since the loss of their son.

The problems at Zolder took longer to sort out than expected and, inevitably, while he was there, new problems emerged.

When Ravilious found the time to ring Evangelina in London, there was no reply. He kept trying.

Beginning to get worried, he rang her parents in Milan.

'Of course she's not there,' said his mother-in-law in her heavily Italian accent. 'She's not been there for five days. She's come home to us now.'

Arno Ravilious boarded the first flight to Milan, a matter of hours later.

'You are failing in your duties as a husband,' his mother-in-law told him severely.

Ravilious couldn't argue. What he never told them, and they wouldn't have expected, was the pain he was in, harbouring a sense of loss he could never express to his wife or her family.

He, himself, had suffered a miserable childhood rooted in an unstable family. Ravilious had been yearning to make amends – to 'put things right' – imagining that, with the luxury of wealth, he could give a child of his anything he or she could ever have wanted. Now, he felt that the opportunity to achieve closure on his own childhood was lost. Not least as Evangelina was no longer able to bear them another child.

FIFTY-TWO

In 1984, someone unexpected came onto the scene – a new force who would light up Formula 1, not just to diehard petrolheads but to the world:

Ayrton Senna, né da Silva.

On his first outing, in an unreliable backmarker car – a Toleman-Hart – Senna's engine blew in front of his home crowd at Jacarepaguá. He clocked up his first ever Championship point in his second grand prix, at Kyalami in South Africa – a result he repeated at the Belgian Grand Prix at Zolder three weeks later – before failing to qualify for the San Marino Grand Prix.

By the time of the sixth race of that season, at a rain-soaked Monaco, people realized that Ayrton Senna was special. Qualifying 13th, he passed Niki Lauda in a vastly superior McLaren to take 2nd place on lap 19. He'd been catching Alain Prost in the other McLaren at a rate of 4 seconds a lap when, on lap 31, the race was stopped for safety reasons. Senna even passed Prost on the winning line of that lap but, under the rules, the result was taken from the end of the last lap completed by every driver, meaning the lap before – which gave Prost the win. Senna, though, had scored his first podium … in an inferior car … in treacherous rain … at his fifth ever grand prix.

It wasn't long before the mainstream media were excited by this prodigious talent, hailing him as a superstar.

Despite this boon, Ravilious was frustrated.

He and Howard Lloyd were finding it almost impossible to sell their TV coverage of Formula 1.

Evangelina was showing little sign of recovery. For nearly a year she had continued to suffer from postnatal depression. Nothing Arno suggested had any effect. The more Evangelina struggled to recover, the more her mother seemed to hold him responsible for the loss of her daughter's only child. Struggling at home Ravilious found solace in the one thing that could mend his soul: the development of Motor Racing Promotions.

In 1989, a backmarker Italian team was bought by a company no one had heard of and was immediately rebranded with their name. No one had heard of the man put in to run it, either: a Tunisian called Suleiman Al-Megrahi.

'Ali Baba', though, quickly showed his ability to weave a social magic. A combination of his brilliant blue eyes, ready smile, and a style of listening during conversations that was almost hypnotic, rapidly dispelled any suspicions. His acceptance began with women, who saw him as something of a fantasy figure. Gradually, his nickname changed to Omar. But who was he? Where had he come from? And who and what was Calabria?

Calabria, people were soon to learn, was a Mediterranean hotel chain with numerous outlets across southern Europe and North Africa. Suleiman Al-Megrahi, it was thought, was the company's marketing director. No one could recall any previous appearance by him at a Formula 1 race, or pinpoint a track record in any form of motorsport. People were sure they would have remembered. From a motor racing point of view, no one expected anything from such a neophyte.

The establishment was in for a shock.

The pit lane became aware of – and then alarmed by – Calabria's presence. Al-Megrahi began enticing key technicians from other Formula 1 teams, as well as hiring from the IndyCar series in the States. He hired Alf McBride, the acclaimed chassis designer from Williams; Sam Wylye, generally considered the best engine man, from Ferrari; Codie Farr, the pioneer of active suspension at McLaren; and his biggest scalp, which finally drew public attention to his programme of recruitment, was to win over Stitch Dungannon, Lotus's aerodynamics genius. Al-Megrahi didn't stop at technicians. He enticed the two fastest F1 drivers of the previous season, Shauni Brannigan from Ptarmigan and Carl Salzburg from McLaren – their departures significantly upsetting the fabric and chemistry of both those teams.

But Al-Megrahi's crowning achievement was to source engines from Ferrari which, for the preceding three years, had been the most competitive on the grid. This coup got everyone wondering. How had he persuaded the Scuderia to sell him engines? Countless teams and sponsors had approached Maranello, but every application had always been rejected with short shrift. There was a well-worn axiom: 'Ferrari only supplies Ferrari.'

With such an accumulation of talent, assets and attention, the paddock looked forward to Calabria's humiliation. Except the team started to perform. After three races, Al-Megrahi's team gained their first podium; after two more, famously at Spa in Belgium, the team won their first grand prix.

Calabria's presence at grands prix was huge. Money seemed no object. Calabria's hospitality was far more lavish than even the well-sponsored championship-winning team of the year before. Calabria hired the best chefs, commissioned *the* in designers of the moment to dress their hospitality tents, and entertained five times as many guests at races. A-listers and celebrities came flocking. In a short time, Calabria was setting a standard for style, luxury and glamour – and not just within Formula 1. Their presence started dominating the pages of the world's glossy magazines.

Suleiman Al-Megrahi was no longer an outsider, but a man of exoticism. He became a 'rock star' – managing to cross the colour barrier, as had Muhammad Ali and O.J. Simpson.

Calabria's cars weren't just a spirited drive ahead of the next best team; they were three or four seconds a lap faster. Many put their superiority down to the brilliance of the personnel Al-Megrahi had recruited; others weren't so sure. Frank Williams and Ken Tyrrell, both of whom had outstanding technicians of their own, could never accept Calabria's success was simply down to brainpower.

'At the very least they've got to be running something dodgy,' said Tyrrell.

Ravilious, too, was concerned by the abnormality of the results, but for very different reasons. Such predictability in races was damaging the appeal of grands prix to the television channels. The technology of the cars needed to be changed. But after the showdown with Makarios in Holland over the skirts dispute, Ravilious knew none of his teams would get anywhere if they took a technical challenge against Calabria to the FISA president.

In 1990, at the end of only its second season in Formula 1, Calabria won the Constructors' Championship and Shauni Brannigan became World Champion.

The team started to spend even more money.

Through its achievement, Calabria became a household name, projecting success, high-end style, glamour and élan.

Ravilious, however, was deeply frustrated. The TV companies still weren't biting.

FIFTY-THREE

In the spring of 1991, the most powerful and yet discreet media figure in the United States entertained a party of twenty on board his superyacht in the Mediterranean. Lying just off Cephalonia, a perfect ball of orange sun was lowering towards the horizon; the air, warm from a day of unbroken sunshine, was almost body temperature.

After coming aboard, Lord Lambourn said to Ravilious. 'Arno, I'd like you to meet our host – Gabriel Barrus the Third.'

Ravilious shook hands with the American who was immaculately groomed and dressed in a white linen 1920s-style suit.

'Gabriel is a pioneer of sports management,' Lambourn explained. 'Golf, but he also owns a couple of American football teams and a baseball series.'

Ravilious didn't know what to expect or how to read Gabriel Barrus when the man said: 'I'm interested in any sport that gives me a 20 per cent IRR. I'm prepared to amortize costs of an acquisition over five years. If a deal can clear both those hurdles, I'll give it a second look.'

Ravilious just assumed he was hearing the wordy guff he heard from most Americans.

Barrus added: 'I'm impressed with what you've done to rebrand Formula 1.'

Ravilious nodded half-heartedly at the compliment.

Lambourn was invited to meet someone else, and as Barrus and Ravilious were left together, the American said: 'What are you doing about pushing your TV coverage?'

'I'm working on it,' replied Ravilious. 'We've had some success with a few broadcasters but, so far, they've only gone for highlights shows. Their view is that grands prix are too long, and no one knows what's going on after the first couple of laps.'

'Who are your distributers?'

'No one in the US, if that's what you're asking. I've got a relationship with the European Broadcast Union over here.'

The other man sucked his teeth and started shaking his head.

'Is something wrong?' Ravilious asked.

'The EBU're an institution. Bureaucratic, at least by American standards. Okay for stock programming, I guess – where everybody knows what's coming. For me at any rate, they're not proactive, not nearly entrepreneurial enough.'

'How should I be distributing F1 in Europe, then, Mr Barrus?'

'Bypass the EBU – go to the TV companies direct. This advertising you've got going at the racetrack is fantastic; it *screams* commercial. If it were me, I'd talk to all of the sponsors you've got already. Ask them if they'd have any marketing dollars to support TV programmes. If they say "Yes", I'd go and talk to the TV companies: if you can show them you've got a load of advertising already lined up, the broadcasters will listen. I'd start with the commercial channels though.'

Ravilious was paying careful attention; he particularly liked the linkage idea: of going to the TV companies with a bunch of advertisers who had *already* committed to supporting the programmes.

'For a sport to be commercial,' Barrus went on, 'you've got to remember one crucial factor: The product of a sport is *not* the race … and the customer is *not* the spectator.'

'They're not?'

'No, no, no. A sport's product is the *audience* … and the sport's customer is the *advertiser*.'

Ravilious seemed to freeze for a moment, and then started nodding slowly.

He was logging all this away.

The American continued: 'If you bring the advertising revenue with you, you would have the leverage to push the TV stations to give you two hours of non-stop coverage for each grand prix. If your audience got to see Formula 1 in its entirety, it would grow – I reckon you'll be needing to beat off advertisers with a stick.'

Ravilious pondered.

'Oh, and one other thing,' said Barrus, turning to face him. 'You've got to control the content of your coverage. *You* know which bits make for an exciting grand prix. Whatever you do, don't leave the editing to producers who have only ever covered tennis or football: they'll *kill* it. Above all, you've got to have a commentator that can present the complexity of a grand prix to the mainstream and engage the audience. Someone truly distinctive.'

Barrus, feeling he had offered more than a conversation starter, said: 'Now, Arno, if you're looking for a partner in Formula 1, I'd be very interested. I'm ready to buy in.'

'That's kind, Mr Barrus,' said Ravilious, and was about to decline, when Luigi Tonnini, one of the two Captains Regent of San Marino approached, ready to introduce himself.

Gabriel Barrus's ideas, though, had set Arno Ravilious's thoughts on fire.

When the yacht berthed in Monaco two days later, he made straight for the paddock. Within hours, through a number of FOCA teams, Ravilious had secured meetings with their largest sponsors – suggesting that he had a way of helping them reach a much bigger audience via Formula 1.

In a few months, with several sizeable sponsors' support, Ravilious and Lloyd were ready to test if they would be able to distribute TV coverage outside the EBU. During their first direct interaction with a TV company, they were astonished. Bundesadler TV, one of the three private networks in Germany, was truly intrigued. Clinching their interest was the collection of letters Ravilious produced from three of Formula 1's biggest sponsors – each stating their readiness to buy ad time if grands prix were broadcast live. But, at Ravilious's instigation, the sponsors also indicated that they would only be interested in doing so if each race was shown in its entirety.

Ravilious summarized: 'I am, therefore, bringing you content to fill two hours of your air *and* I'm bringing you the supporting advertisers. I am bringing you ready-made content, audience and revenue.'

Discussions of a deal progressed rapidly with Bundesadler in Germany, as did some promising talks with a French station. And that was when Ravilious made the decision to stop those negotiations. Immediately.

At the Hockenheimring for the German Grand Prix at the end of July, Arno Ravilious asked for a meeting with the FISA president. He said he wanted to discuss renegotiating the Concorde Agreement's relationship with the European Broadcast Union. Ravilious was emboldened to meet Makarios, having been spurred on earlier that weekend by an off-the-cuff remark from Shauni Brannigan.

'Watch yourself,' said the Irish driver to Ravilious. 'I heard about your possible renewal with the EBU. I have told President Makarios to be careful. The French station, *La Cinq* – one of the biggest contributors to the EBU – is on the verge of collapse. TV revenues to the EBU from France, therefore, are likely to fall badly.'

In his meeting with Makarios, Ravilious said: 'I appreciate FISA's desire to minimize fluctuations in revenue. I am anxious to do what I can to help. Under the Concorde Agreement, Motor Racing Promotions has paid FISA approximately 3.75 million dollars as its share of the TV revenues over the last 3 years.'

Makarios nodded.

'I am prepared to offer you, Mr President, an increased – fully *guaranteed* – amount of 6 million for the next three years and a *guaranteed* amount of 9 million for the three years after that.'

'Are you sure you can afford that much of a hike ... *guaranteed?*' asked Makarios.

Ravilious nodded before saying: 'I've been talking with France's *La Cinq* who, as you probably know, are the biggest contributors to Formula 1 via the EBU deal. I think,' he said, looking the Greek in the eye, 'there are some exciting things about to happen there.'

The Greek kept smiling.

In that moment, every opinion Ravilious held of Salvador Makarios was confirmed.

You odious bastard, thought Ravilious. *You know, because Brannigan's just told you, that the EBU's takings are about to take a serious hit – as La Cinq's about to go under. And yet, here you are, still prepared to screw me by accepting the guarantees I've just offered.*

Ravilious went on: 'As these would be guarantees to FISA, Mr President, I feel it only right to offer the same guarantees to the teams. I will offer them the same sort of undertaking. They have been splitting 2 million dollars between them. I will increase this, in the same proportion as FISA's uplift, to 3.2 million for each of the next three years and will take that up to 4.8 million for each of the three years after that. That way, the teams, too, would have predictable income, no longer fluctuating from one year to the next.'

Makarios was now smiling broadly. Presumably, thought Ravilious, because my liability will be all the greater when *La Cinq* collapses.

'And I feel, Mr President, that *I* should underwrite those guarantees myself … that I, *personally*, should bear any losses. Consequently, I am proposing that it's only right the counterparty to our deal should be a company of which I am the sole financial underwriter.'

Ravilious saw an extraordinary expression on the face of the FISA president. Makarios was already offering his hand across the table.

'So we have a deal?' Ravilious asked unnecessarily.

'Oh, you most certainly do. I think this is all *very* generous of you.'

'Oh, Mr President,' said Ravilious, 'I wouldn't say that.'

FIFTY-FOUR

Ravilious may have got the deal he wanted, but he couldn't get over Makarios's readiness – fully knowing about the dire situation at *La Cinq* – to see him screwed. What kind of person did that? How could such petty-minded vindictiveness consume someone, let alone someone supposedly responsible enough to run a global sport with a GDP of nearly a billion pounds a year?

The more Ravilious thought about it, the angrier he became.

He had built up that value within the sport, and yet this was how Makarios was ready to repay him. Ravilious may have knocked the Greek back after each attempt to do his business harm, but Salvador Makarios was still a threat. And during that meeting, the man had shown his malicious intent had not been dimmed at all – that he had simply been waiting for the next battering ram to come along.

Ravilious spent the weekend making the same pitch to the teams, offering them a hike in their TV receipts – from their current $375,000 a year to $600,000 for the next three years and then $900,000 each for the three years after that. There was no rejection, hardly a surprise given the magnitude of the increases being offered – let alone that these higher amounts were also to be guaranteed.

The guarantees did, though, put Ravilious seriously on risk. If MRP TV failed to receive enough income to cover these amounts, he would have to make up the shortfall personally. The pressure was on for Ravilious and his producer, Howard Lloyd, to increase their TV sales substantially. And quickly.

As soon as Ravilious had got signatures on all the documentation to amend the Concorde Agreement, he and Lloyd went straight out to work, reactivating their campaign to talk to TV companies on the basis of their new advertiser-based model, as suggested by Gabriel Barrus on his yacht off Cephalonia.

Over the next eight weeks, so by the time of the Portuguese Grand Prix on 22 September 1991, Motor Racing Promotions TV had struck fifteen deals in different parts of the world. All of these involved a full two hours of coverage for each race; all would show adverts from existing Formula 1 sponsors; and each deal involved a multiple uplift in TV rights fees.

Via those fifteen deals, Ravilious had managed to lock in enough revenue to cover his first three years' worth of guarantees to FISA and the F1 teams. In fact, the fees MRP TV was now receiving were already enough to secure the following three years of guarantees as well. Ravilious was in the clear.

In the previous Concorde Agreement, after paying out to FISA and the teams, MRP had only enjoyed a minority proportion of the TV revenues cake. With the new 'guaranteed' deal, the amounts enjoyed by FISA and the teams were a lot higher, but the key difference was that these payments were now fixed – capped. Any revenues received over and above those guarantees, therefore, would accrue to MRP TV. The company's percentage share of the Formula 1 TV revenues began to rise.

It soon exceeded 55 per cent of the total receipts.

Not only that, Ravilious had managed to increase the overall size of the cake to boot.

With the added buoyancy he now felt, Ravilious took some time out from the season to be with Evangelina. His whole psyche felt like it was expanding. Motor Racing Promotions, in its various guises, was pounding ahead and, to his untrammelled joy, his wife seemed to be re-engaging with the world ... and with him.

He still had the impression that she held him responsible for the loss of their son, feeling Evangelina's resentment was only ever just below the surface.

He managed to get her out of the house, away for a holiday. She started to make progress, even asking him about the business.

'That's an amazing deal you pulled off with the TV rights,' she said. 'How much money *are* you making?'

Towards the end of that 1991 season, the Tunisian – Suleiman Al-Megrahi – started to cause trouble. His drivers and cars were dominating both championships. On the back of the recent increase in TV coverage around the world, and the enormous surge of public interest it brought to motor racing, Al-Megrahi began to claim he and the Calabria team were more responsible for Formula 1's popularity than anyone else. His dissent started with little things.

The Tunisian complained about travel arrangements ... about the facilities at grands prix. Then his complaints moved on to more managerial matters and finally on to financials.

Al-Megrahi was soon briefing the press, sniping about the asymmetric receipts of revenue within the sport. He declared that he was not participating in the increased affluence of the sport as much as he should be; he started asking questions:

'Who has control over Formula 1 revenues?'

'Who gets what percentage?'

'What does Motor Racing Promotions do – and what does Arno Ravilious get out of all this?'

'Surely, the sport is good enough to sell itself – why do we need such an expensive middleman?'

Arno Ravilious began to feel the heat. Until then, he had been able to operate discreetly, talking to the different stakeholders on a bilateral basis – never allowing a situation where one party was likely to talk to another and compare notes. Suleiman Al-Megrahi set about drawing attention to some of the deals and arrangements MRP had set up.

Then something strange happened.

The figures and data that Al-Megrahi was quoting became very specific and surprisingly accurate.

Ravilious could only reach an unnerving conclusion.

He became convinced Al-Megrahi's 'facts and figures' had to come from an insider. They could only have come from FISA – in fact, they could only have come from one source. The president himself: Salvador Makarios.

It then appeared that Al-Megrahi had recruited another ally.

The Tunisian's rantings had been music to the ears of another disgruntled player whom Ravilious had driven from the field of play. It looked like the tobacco man, Yoel Kahneman – the man behind the WCR breakaway championship series – was back.

Also, by reintroducing Worldwide Tobacco as a substantial sponsor of Al-Megrahi's Championship-dominating Calabria Formula 1 team, Kahneman had created a brand-new platform for himself.

Ravilious was soon to face an ongoing threat from a combination of three aggrieved players – Salvador Makarios, Suleiman Al-Megrahi and Yoel Kahneman.

And then the whispering campaign began:

'Do you know how much Ravilious takes for administering the teams?'

'Who owns the hospitality and advertising revenues at race tracks?'

'How did Ravilious ever get control of the TV rights?'

'How much now comes in from TV?'

'How much money *is* Arno Ravilious making out of Formula 1?'

At a meeting of the FOCA team bosses at the end of 1991, Lord Lambourn said:

'I think, Arno, you're going to have to do something about this. The money you bring in for us all is extraordinary, but the politics are not helpful. We worry that so much shit-stirring – from the likes of Al-Megrahi and co. – is corrosive. It's affecting the perception of the sport.'

There were noises of acknowledgement from the other bosses.

Ravilious, though, welcomed Lord Lambourn bringing this up. 'The criticism that's being levelled at me, Budge, is not what it seems.'

'It's not?'

'Al-Megrahi and his poodle Kahneman may be making a lot of

noise, but none of it's originating from them. It's all coming from one other place.'

Ravilious paused. He was anxious not to sound biased or paranoid. 'Each of those critics is using statistics and figures to attack what I am doing.'

Lambourn said: 'They are, which is what's doing us all harm.'

Ravilious nodded his understanding. 'And their figures are accurate.'

'Indeed they are.'

'But there's only one person who's in possession of *all* that information … only one person who *should* know that information,' said Ravilious.

The team bosses suddenly saw what he was saying.

Ken Tyrrell sighed: 'The president of FISA…'

Ever since Kyalami, ten years before, Ravilious had suspected the FISA president of being a threat. The question had now become: How to deal with Salvador Makarios once and for all? But Ravilious was anxious not to be the one to start that conversation.

Fortunately, unprompted, Lord Lambourn obliged that evening.

Inwardly, Ravilious rejoiced. But having got them this far, he didn't want the idea to lose any momentum. He decided to drop a pebble into the pond by asking: 'What would you say is the basis of Makarios's power?'

'Above being a billionaire?' said Tyrrell.

'Within Formula 1?'

'He's been elected.'

'But only as president of FISA – he sort of walked into the presidency of the FIA.'

'Fair point. So how are presidents *normally* elected to the FIA?'

'Through its electoral college.'

A relatively new boss asked: 'How does that work?'

Lambourn replied: 'One vote per affiliated country, and there are about 115 of those. Then there's a slew of affiliated clubs and associations, who are also entitled to a vote.'

'About 200 electors in all,' Ravilious summarized.

'What are you saying – we could never stand anyone against him,' said Tyrrell. 'Makarios is the darling of the national federations – of the committees – of the blazers.'

'He is,' added another team boss. 'He'd win any FIA-wide election, hands down.'

Ravilious paused before saying: 'Are we so sure, though, that that would still be the case – after the ridiculous 26 to 16 cars fiasco in Monaco, and then the arbitrary banning of skirts in Holland?'

'I fear it is,' said Lambourn. 'Formula 1 sits in a bubble. Only a tiny proportion of FIA's countries participate in it. It's highly *un*likely anyone outside the pit lane would have reason to be dissatisfied with him.'

'Maybe not publicly,' offered Williams. 'But some of those we might expect to be his supporters will be aware of what's been going on and probably wouldn't be that comfortable with it?'

'I guess there's only one way to find out,' suggested Lambourn, who then used a term made known during the recent dethroning of Margaret Thatcher. 'And that would be to run a stalking horse.'

'You mean someone actually *does* challenge him for president?'

'When's the next election due?'

'At the end of this year.'

'A stalking horse won't work,' retorted Ravilious. 'That wouldn't dislodge him. It could be counterproductive, might even make people feel they should come to the aid of the system – the blazers might just vote for him out of loyalty to the FIA. His position could be strengthened. No, if he's going to be challenged, it would have to be by a substantive candidate ... a viable alternative as a president of the FIA.'

'But who could we get to stand?' Lambourn asked.

Frank Williams looked at the peer: 'Why don't *you* stand, Budge?'

'Why not?' chimed another enthusiastically.

Ravilious was nodding. 'It makes absolute sense, Budge. You're the *perfect* candidate – a team boss, with years of experience – and everyone adores you.'

A week later Lord Lambourn announced he would stand in the election for president of the FIA when the term of the current president was up for renewal.

Salvador Makarios was incensed.

At the time the challenge was announced, the press coverage was substantial. To the column inch, it declared that support lay with the incumbent. But as the short campaign went on, Makarios's comments became increasingly outlandish. He lashed out at the FOCA teams – and at the British for always causing trouble; against Lord Lambourn, as a self-interested opportunist – who would be subject to huge conflicts of interest if he stayed on as a team boss; and, in particular, he lashed out at Arno Ravilious who, he said, was the one really behind this insult.

By contrast, Lord Lambourn's campaign was diligently put together.

Ravilious focused on the FIA statutes and made sure he was clear on the voting procedure. It was reassuringly simple, with little chance of discretion exercisable by the FIA. With just two candidates, it would be a straightforward first-past-the-post election, irrespective of the number of votes cast.

Ravilious made a point of analyzing past elections.

He found the average turnout rarely exceeded 40 per cent of those eligible to vote. That meant a probability of around 80 votes being cast. To win, whatever the number of contenders running, a candidate would need 45 votes to be comfortable of victory – 45 countries or affiliated institutions would have to be won to the cause. Quite a number. Several team bosses were far from convinced Lambourn could do it.

But Ravilious was building the campaign step by step.

There were 16 countries scheduled to host a grand prix in 1992. Ravilious rang each of the race promoters and suggested that they might persuade their national federations to support Lord Lambourn for the presidency of the FIA, or they would be asked to rebid for their race. A week later he rang the chairman/president of each of those same national federations, expecting them to have been softened up by the possibility of rebidding for their grand prix. Ravilious asked them how they felt about Lord Lambourn as the next president of the FIA. He secured a pledge of support from all 16.

Ravilious contacted people on committees in other selected national federations and started hinting that they *could* be awarded a grand prix if certain conditions were met. In a number of cases, they responded: 'We couldn't afford it … or … we couldn't afford the infrastructure investment you would demand.' Ravilious explained that he had already come to arrangements, even with several well-established circuits, to provide them with funding help, and that he could be in a position to do the same for them, should they need it.

In under a fortnight, Ravilious was feeling confident he had secured a further 13 pledges of support. Lambourn was delighted.

The candidate reported that, having been working the phones himself, he was sure of at least 16 pledges from other national federations and associations.

However, could they rely on the 45 votes they believed they had been pledged?

The secret ballot was held in October.

The 'returning officer' announced that 82 votes had been cast; the split of support turned out to be 48 to 34…

…in the challenger's favour.

Lord Lambourn had been elected to be the president of the FIA. Arno Ravilious's diligent approach to the campaign had secured his victory for him.

Via that election, Ravilious had finally managed to rid himself of Salvador Makarios – the meddlesome, biased and trouble-making president of Formula 1's governing body.

FIFTY-FIVE

Ravilious should have been pleased, but he was still vexed by the remaining members of that critical triumvirate: Suleiman Al-Megrahi and Yoel Kahneman. Ravilious concluded Kahneman was little more than a parasite, latching on to whatever body happened to pass by. The real threat was Al-Megrahi.

Ravilious reckoned that if he could take care of the Tunisian, he would more than likely take care of Kahneman at the same time.

Al-Megrahi continued to criticize Ravilious at every turn.

Ravilious wanted to find something to take Al-Megrahi down a peg or two; he scoured the FIA statutes for possibilities. But there were no facilities to hold the Tunisian to collective responsibility.

As the new president of FIA, one of Lord Lambourn's first undertakings was to revamp the organization. He did away with FISA, bringing Formula 1 under his direct control as president of the FIA. His second task was to review Formula 1 regulations for the next season. Ravilious offered him some advice: wasn't it time to clean up the whole skirts controversy?

Lambourn, for 1992, announced significant changes to the 'Formula'. The FIA announced it was maintaining the ban on turbochargers, stating in the new rules:

> *'Engines may not be fitted with turbochargers, nor may there be enhancements made to the normally aspirated output of a car's engine.'*

As this technology had largely been the preserve of the continental manufacturers, Lambourn, to show his even-handedness, also included a clause concerning skirts:

'Apart from the tyres, cars must show 6 cm of clearance of the lowest part of the car with the road surface.'

These changes were intended to level the playing field and diffuse the politics.

Al-Megrahi cried foul. He accused vested interests of targeting Calabria. He called out Ravilious as being behind a deliberate attempt to damage his team, his chances and therefore his ability to criticize Motor Racing Promotions.

No one could understand why Al-Megrahi was getting so heated: Calabria cars were not running skirts, and, as for turbochargers, they were banned anyway, so how could barring them affect Al-Megrahi either?

Unless…

Despite the significance of the changes to the Formula, the Calabria team romped off at the beginning of the 1992 season. Five races in, Shauni Brannigan was leading his teammate Carl Salzburg by a handful of points – and the two Calabria drivers were a sizeable distance ahead of the next challenger in either Championship. So much for levelling the playing field.

People, though, were becoming suspicious.

Other teams started asking how the Calabria cars could be so much faster than the rest?

Rumours started circulating. Al-Megrahi had to be running some sort of illegal device. He had to be using one of the add-ons that had been prohibited. The other teams – mechanics, journalists – all tried to get close to the Calabria cars and photograph them, to find out what was going on. But no one was allowed to get anywhere near them. Every time the Calabrias were out of their garages, they were covered in tarpaulins – right up until they drove out onto the track. Even while they were on the grid they were covered. And the moment they were back in the pit lane they were hurriedly wheeled into the garage and the doors were shut.

At Magny-Cours in July 1992, a gripping three-way fight ensued for the lead between Mansell's Williams, Schumacher's Benetton and Salzburg's Calabria. It was thwarted around Lap 11 by torrential rain, which became so bad the grand prix had to be stopped. The race was then restarted with one of Lord Lambourn's safety innovations: the first time a safety car was used in Formula 1. But then the rains returned. Before Salzburg could be called in to switch back onto wets, he lost control at high speed – aquaplaning through the exceptionally fast corner, Estoril, Turn 3. He ploughed headlong into the wall of tyres. Salzburg was bruised but unharmed. While he was led away to the medical centre, the wreck of his car was impounded, as, by law, it had to be examined by the French authorities. When they published their report, it included numerous pictures of the car's components, laid out as if they were part of a post-mortem. Something in them, though, caught the attention of the pit lane. It looked like a fan ... about the size of a saucer. Attached to it was, possibly, a fair-sized electric motor. The images were pored over, everyone trying to work out what this might be for: no other cars were running anything like it.

Thus the 'Fangate' conspiracy was born.

As with any conspiracy, it only takes one comment – even an inadvertent one – to blow the whole gaff. In a Malmedy bar late one night, during the weekend of the Belgian Grand Prix seven weeks later, a Calabria mechanic had had one too many. At 2 o'clock in the morning he let something slip: he boasted his team had developed a clutch fan, which could be triggered by the throttle. Powered by a small electric motor, they could accelerate the airflow through the ram-air intake above the driver's head. When activated, the fan increased the air pressure into the intake manifold. The inebriated mechanic claimed it was adding ten brake horsepower to their cars.

It seemed Al-Megrahi had introduced a device that, while technically not a turbocharger, performed much the same function and, being electrically operated, was intended to get round the prohibition.

Immediately the FIA became aware of this, the president launched an investigation. Suleiman Al-Megrahi was summoned to the FIA headquarters in Paris and asked to explain himself. During the hearing it became clear that two seasons' worth of Championship points, and the corresponding Concorde Agreement payouts, had been illegally 'won' by the wrong drivers and the wrong teams.

Al-Megrahi's defence was: 'They, Calabria, were well aware that turbochargers were banned, but this, by definition, was not a turbocharger: it didn't take energy from the exhaust – it didn't directly enhance the pressure of the fuel air mix into the carburettor.'

Lambourn answered: 'The rule, Mr Al-Megrahi, states: *"nor may there be enhancements made to the normally aspirated output of the engines."* Your fan in the ram-air intake is clearly designed to enhance the output of the engine, not least as, by adding a fan, you've departed from the engine being "normally aspirated".'

Al-Megrahi fell silent.

The Tunisian's next line of defence was: 'Okay, this fan device may have been on the car, but the FIA needs to prove it was being used.'

Lord Lambourn stared back at him. 'So what you're saying, Mr Al-Megrahi, is that the fan may have been attached – but you weren't using it?'

Al-Megrahi nodded.

'So,' added Lambourn with a half-smile, 'you may have had a fan, but you didn't inhale?'

Even Al-Megrahi couldn't help smirk at the Clinton defence.

Lord Lambourn and his close advisers were not convinced. As the new president of the FIA, he decided to come down hard and meted out the largest fine ever handed down by the Formula 1 governing body in any of its previous guises – the CSI, FISA or the FIA. Al-Megrahi was castigated for having broken the spirit of the rules and sentenced to a three-month suspension from Formula 1.

Ravilious was ecstatic.

Salvador Makarios had been seen off as a threat, and now Suleiman Al-Megrahi, his other principal detractor, had been branded a cheat, seriously damaging the man's credibility as a critic of Formula 1 and Motor Racing Promotions. As expected, shortly thereafter, Yoel Kahneman ran for the hills.

Ravilious finally found himself in a position to pursue the development of his business in relative peace.

But not for long.

Disaster was about to strike.

FIFTY-SIX

Evangelina had been continuing to show progress in her recovery, but without warning she started to regress. Becoming withdrawn. Quiet. Tetchy, again.

Ravilious became alarmed. Everything seemed to have been improving. He was concerned, but found himself with no time to ponder it.

The year of 1994 became Formula 1's annus horribilis.

Three races into the season, Roland Ratzenberger and Ayrton Senna died over the same weekend at the San Marino Grand Prix. To the world of motor racing, and to many elements of the wider public too, Senna's death was a John F. Kennedy moment. A charismatic young man had been cut down in his prime when most people felt he was infallible. The grief became even greater than the shock.

To the leadership of Formula 1, the aftermath was emotionally charged. Ravilious wanted to attend the funeral in São Paulo, but there were signs in Brazil that he might not be welcome. There were no accusations against Ravilious, directly, but as the pre-eminent figure in Formula 1, he was increasingly being held responsible for anything that went wrong. Tensions over the loss of Senna continued to rise. It was soon decided, given the size of the vigils and the crowds they saw building, that Ravilious shouldn't go to Brazil. Instead, he flew to Salzburg where he was able to pay his respects to Roland Ratzenberger. During moments of the well-liked Austrian F1 driver's funeral, Ravilious mourned the loss of both drivers.

There could never be any sense of recompense from such a tragic weekend, but the mood did serve to create a step change in attitudes to safety and driver protection. Compared with the number of fatalities in the 1960s and 70s, it would be an impressive 21 years before another driver would succumb to a fatal accident at a grand prix.

By 1997, Formula 1 was a cash machine. Revenues were pouring in. Everyone was getting richer. Teams became more and more lavish in their spending: investment in technical innovations ran at a frenetic pace. Performance on the track was ever improving. Money was being spent in significant amounts on corporate hospitality at grands prix. Formula 1 had become *the* international sporting series with which to be associated.

Press articles celebrated the noticeable transformation, examining how this peripheral sport had broken into the big league, now turning over billions of dollars a year. People were fascinated with how all this had come about, even more so by whoever had made it happen. Attention was directed at the man the media identified as the mastermind behind this extraordinary success. How had Arno Ravilious, someone entering Formula 1 as a lowly mechanic, managed to emerge as the commercial powerhouse of the sport and make so much money from it?

On the back of this publicity, Ravilious was soon attracting attention from unfamiliar sources. While at the Nürburgring in September, during the new and oddly titled Luxembourg Grand Prix, he drifted into a conversation with someone from an investment bank. Ravilious was not sure what that was. Tex Brubaker, an American, introduced himself as head of 'EMEA' for a firm called Klyman-Messner. When Ravilious still looked bemused, Brubaker illustrated what he did by explaining that he had recently handled the IPO for the internet sensation, Amazon.

'What's an IPO?'

For a moment the investment banker's expression indicated surprise – as if to say: *'How could you head up such a sizeable commercial operation and not know about things like IPOs?'*

'Initial Public Offering,' Brubaker replied. 'It's how Wall Street, and now the City of London, Mr Ravilious, describes the floating of a business on the stock exchange – when a company's shares are offered openly for sale to the public and institutional investors for the first time.'

'And this I-P-O valued Amazon at how much?'

'Four hundred and thirty-eight million dollars.'

'Good God. I didn't think that company had been going very long?'

'It hasn't – about three years.'

'How on earth was it worth so much so quickly?'

'Investor confidence is strong at the moment, Mr Ravilious,' replied Brubaker. 'Also, Amazon has particular appeal as a company making money from the internet. It's attractive to a lot of private investors who have already built up a personal relationship with the company. Another factor is that stock market investors are always hungry to invest in companies with no immediate competition; they take significant comfort from knowing that no one else is going to come in and undercut their pricing. All of these things applied to Amazon, but,' he said, noticing Ravilious's interest, 'it would be my immediate assessment that Formula 1 could easily fall into the same category.'

'You're not serious?'

'I am,' said the banker.

'What do you think F1 would be worth then?'

'Formula 1 would certainly be considered free of any competition,' replied the banker. 'Given the uniqueness of the sport, and the significant commercial development of it, you would get institutional interest – but I would also expect, if there were a public share offering, considerable extra sizzle ... because of the passion of the fans. In previous sport-related flotations, it's been important not to underestimate how much the fans want to be involved and own a part of their sport. I don't know any of the specific numbers to do with Formula 1, only those I've seen in the press, but from what I can see this weekend, I could easily see a valuation on the commercial side of Formula 1 being anywhere up to 1.5 billion...'

'What ... 1.5? You're not serious?' he stammered.

The banker nodded.

Ravilious was stunned.

The banker, sniffing a percentage fee, said: 'Why don't you come and see me when you're next in London? I'd be happy to talk though the possibilities?'

'But if I sell, I'd no longer be in control of the business?'

The banker shook his head. 'That's not an inevitability at all. Control depends entirely on the proportion you decide to sell. Amazon raised 54 million dollars by selling only an eighth of the company on America's more junior exchange, the NASDAQ. For the main market, the minimum proportion you would need to sell would be 25 per cent, but even if you did that you would still retain 75 per cent of the shares in the company ... which, of course, would keep you very firmly in control.'

'So I could sell a *proportion* through this IPO thing?'

'You could. On my finger-in-the-air valuation, if you were to sell a 25 per cent stake, you could still release north of a quarter of a billion dollars. That money would then be available for you to reinvest in the business, if you needed capital for expansion or the acquisition of another company perhaps, or, of course, you could take it as the personal rewards from many years of hard effort.'

Ravilious had no idea his activities in Formula 1 could have created so much worth. He said to Brubaker: 'How about I come and see you on Tuesday morning?'

From the Nürburgring, Arno Ravilious flew to Milan. He was keen to tell Evangelina the news of his conversation with the man from Klyman-Messner and what this might mean for the two of them.

To Ravilious's bafflement, she seemed almost indifferent. 'We have enough money, don't we?' she said, barely meeting his eye.

'It would make quite a statement, though,' he replied. 'It would make Motor Racing Promotions one of the biggest businesses in the world, let alone in sport.'

Evangelina was still unmoved.

At the end of the weekend, Ravilious was making plans to go back to London when he was surprised by her change of heart. Evangelina asked if she could come. He was thrilled. It had been quite a while since he had felt that much of a connection.

On the following Tuesday, Ravilious instructed his driver to pull up outside the offices of Klyman-Messner in the newly thriving Canary Wharf complex in the East London Docklands. Ravilious was familiar with high-rise buildings and skyscrapers from his numerous trips to America, but he never thought to see a similar skyline in Britain. Canary Wharf, as this entire district was incorrectly called, had a very un-British, un-London feel. A collection of tall, glass-sided offices in close proximity to each other was making a powerful statement about London's place in the world.

Ravilious's car pulled up outside 15 Cabot Square. Three people were waiting on the pavement to greet him. One of them was Tex Brubaker, the other two were colleagues of his: for them to see Brubaker outside on the pavement, ready to meet a guest, was unheard of.

Rising in the lift through the grandiose neo art deco-style building, Ravilious was shown onto the 20th floor and into one of the investment bank's spectacular meeting rooms. It had a view westwards along the Thames towards Tower Bridge, the City of London – with its lower buildings – and on towards Westminster in the distance. Big Ben could just be made out through the mist.

'Thank you for sending me some of your papers, Mr Ravilious,' said Brubaker, as he indicated a chair at the conference room table. A total of five junior Klyman-Messner executives sat some way down each side of it from the two principals. 'On the back of your information,' said the investment banker as coffee was offered, 'we have had to make a slight adjustment to the projected valuation I put on Motor Racing Promotions in Hockenheim. If I may, I'd like to make sure I've got things right, before discussing a way forward?'

Ravilious, uneasy in such surroundings, was not made any more comfortable by Brubaker's opening remark. How much of an adjustment? Had he been brought here under false pretences?

'It would seem that your business, Motor Racing Promotions, is split into three obvious segments,' Brubaker said. 'The agency business, which negotiates with the circuits and which handles appearance fees and prize money for the teams, appears to turn over 90 million pounds a year.'

Ravilious nodded.

'Then there's the business which sells advertising and hospitality at grands prix; that would appear to turn over approximately 40 million pounds a year.'

Again a nod.

'And then there's the division that handles all the TV rights, TV production and TV sales; it appears to be turning over 155 million.'

Ravilious acknowledged Brubaker's numbers from memory.

'A total of 285 million, then,' Brubaker summarized. 'On the costs side, these seem to be tightly controlled. The principal outgoing is the fixed payment under the Concorde Agreement, by which you offer the teams and governing body, the FIA, circa 120 million.'

'That sounds about right.'

'Which leaves your businesses with a net profit of about 165 million pounds a year.'

Ravilious said nothing.

'With a few specific exemptions, Mr Ravilious, companies quoted on the stock market tend to be valued on what's called a multiple of their earnings. Currently, London is trading on an average multiple of roughly 11 times earnings. As I mentioned to you at the Nürburgring last weekend, Formula 1 would not have any immediate commercial competitors and so we could see investors being prepared to pay a slightly higher multiple than normal.'

The Ringmaster sort of nodded.

The investment banker continued: 'I could see your business trading possibly as high as 15 times.'

Ravilious started to frown, as he did the maths.

'Meaning,' said Brubaker, 'if we multiply your net profit of 165 million by 15 we get...'

Ravilious said: ' ...2.5 billion...'

Brubaker, beginning to pick up the stronger scent of a possible deal for himself and a double-digit percentage fee for Klyman-Messner, said: 'Indeed; forgive me for having been a little conservative at the grand prix over the weekend.'

'Good God,' said Ravilious.

'There's no rush for you to make any decision, Mr Ravilious,' said Brubaker. 'Please take as much time as you need to think about all this. If you do end up looking to take a stock market launch further, we would need to go a little deeper into each segment of your business, and assess the nature of each part. Depending on certain factors, we may need to make further adjustments to the estimated valuation I've given you, maybe a little down or a little up.'

Ravilious came away buoyed by his meeting. £2.5 billion!

Arno Ravilious suddenly realized he was now rich beyond his imagination.

Even if he received a tenth of that amount, he'd be richer than he thought possible. Except, a sum of money on that scale didn't really mean anything. How could it? No normal person could comprehend the scale of such wealth. Arno Ravilious certainly had no idea.

He rushed home to tell Evangelina. What would she say to the £2.5 billion? What would his mother-in-law say to that? Maybe all this might go some way to proving himself worthy of her daughter.

Little could Ravilious know that the conversation with that investment bank would bring Formula 1 to the very verge of collapse.

FIFTY-SEVEN

On 1 October 1997, a little known mayor of Pisa was catapulted from obscurity to a position of continental significance. Rialto Bocelli, a 50-year-old greengrocer from his home town in Tuscany, had been on the city's council. After 15 years of service, he was elected mayor and served the mayoralty as he had every other role to date: with a characteristic lack of impact.

The Italian Minister of Economy and Finances had been trying to push through permission for a large hotel in the city. There had been considerable local resistance. The minister approached Bocelli personally to see what could be done. Shortly afterwards full planning was granted. Six months after that Bocelli found himself nominated as Italy's Commissioner to the EU, becoming a member of the executive arm of the European Union.

Once Bocelli got to Brussels, he was feted, revered, consulted and courted as a man of influence. He had never known anything like it. For the first time in his political career it looked like he had been granted power to make things happen.

At four o'clock in the afternoon of a dreary Friday in December, a handful of journalists took their seats in a badly ventilated conference room in Brussels. All of them looked as if they had drawn the short straw, all looking like they should have been heading off for the weekend hours ago.

None of these hacks had any idea that this meeting would have them present at the moment of the butterfly's wingbeat that would lead to a political tsunami for Formula 1.

Rialto Bocelli announced a policy that would affect Europe for the next 20 years:

'As the recently appointed EU Commissioner for Health and

Food Safety,' he said, 'I am launching today a plan to ban smoking in Europe.'

The assembled journalists had heard pronouncements like this before, and remained unanimated in the stuffy, fluorescent-lit conference room.

'I won't be able to achieve this in one go,' said the commissioner.

No kidding, thought the hacks.

'So it will be phased in. As a first step, in a year from now – on 1 January 1999,' Bocelli announced, 'all tobacco advertising of any kind will be banned across the EU.'

None of the jaded journalists even batted an eyelid.

'I have an undertaking,' Bocelli said, 'from the President of the European Commission, the President of the European Council, as well as three quarters of the EU Commissioners.'

At that point, some of the scribblers did look up.

'This means that I have a chance to make a serious contribution to the health of our people. Legislation has already been drafted and submitted to the Chancellor of Germany and the President of France. I have been told by the President of the Commission that my bill will be tabled before the European Parliament in the next few weeks. Should it pass, it will be subject to ratification by QMV, Qualified Majority Voting – rather than unanimity – by the member states. I am hopeful, therefore, that this will allow us to start the process of stamping out this antisocial, health-damaging.habit which is ravaging our continent.'

Pencils, pens and fingers now started to twitch in earnest.

Five days later Arno Ravilious was under siege.

Screaming from the front page of the weekend's *Sunday Telegraph* was an eye-catching scoop – including a full exposé of Formula 1, revealing his proposed flotation of Motor Racing Promotions on the London stock exchange. Ravilious was incensed, and felt utterly betrayed. Everything negative he had ever thought about self-important money people had been confirmed. How had this story got out? Only five days had passed since he had talked – in private – with that investment banker. Ravilious read and reread the article:

> 'Arno Ravilious's Motor Racing Promotions, the commercial engine within the sport of Formula 1, is in early preparation for a flotation on the London stock exchange. Sources close to the sport suggest a valuation of £2.5 billion has been put on the company. This, according to other City analysts, would not be unreasonable given the strong cash flow and pivotal position of MRP within Formula 1.'

'Who the fuck could betray a confidence like this?' yelled Ravilious, into the empty room of his house.

A short while later on that same Sunday morning he received a call. It was Tex Brubaker from Klyman-Messner.

'Mr Ravilious, I can absolutely guarantee you that Klyman-Messner had nothing to do with that article in the *Sunday Telegraph*. Our entire business is based on client confidentiality. We have Chinese walls, firewalls, and rigorous codes of conduct for handling client information. You may not believe me, sir – and may decide to take your business elsewhere – which is entirely your prerogative – but on my professional reputation and that of Klyman-Messner, your affairs have not been discussed with anyone outside this bank.'

Ravilious wanted to believe the investment banker. But if the leak hadn't come from him, where the hell had it come from?

The moment Arno Ravilious appeared in the paddock at Suzuka for the Japanese Grand Prix in the middle of October, he was accosted by journalists. Team bosses came charging over whenever they spotted him.

'We're calling a meeting,' declared Frank Williams. 'You're going to have to account for yourself, Arno...'

A particularly hostile Eugene Van Der Vaal blasted: 'How the fuck have you taken a business worth that much out of Formula 1?'

'What kind of revenue *have* you been taking as your own?' asked a recently returned Suleiman Al-Megrahi.

'You've gone and fucking stolen F1, that's what you've done,' spat Van Der Vaal.

Ravilious was in unknown territory. For the first time other people could see what Ravilious had been up to, could see how much money the Ringmaster was making. Throughout his development of Formula 1 and Motor Racing Promotions, he had sought to operate discreetly, managing to keep everything private. He never went public with any one person's arrangements with anyone else. This, now, was very strange and very uncomfortable.

Arno Ravilious withdrew to his motor home. Eugene Van Der Vaal was even shouting after him as he went: 'You've finally been found out for what you are, Ravilious,' he yelled.

Lord Lambourn approached Ravilious's sanctuary an hour later. He did not have an appointment. The moment Ravilious saw who it was, he let him straight in.

'How are you holding up?' Lambourn asked. 'The mood's getting pretty ugly out there.'

Ravilious shrugged, not at all comfortable.

'Congratulations, by the way,' said Lambourn.

'On *what*?' asked Ravilious.

'On creating a business that the City values that highly. It's an extraordinary achievement.'

'You are the only person who could ever say something like that, Budge. Why aren't you as het up as everyone else?'

'There's a very simple answer to that,' said Lambourn, 'and one that's very personal to me. You saved my family's heritage and inheritance, is pretty much what you've done. If it hadn't been for the wealth you created through MRP, I would have overreached. Amesbury Hall and the Lambourn estates would have been stripped bare, and more than likely sold off. The magic you weave, pulling in and paying out these huge sums of money, has been my salvation. You saved me from destroying myself, from destroying my family's 400-year history.'

Ravilious had never heard the peer speak like this before. 'How the hell do I get out of this? Even if the flotation is cancelled, everyone now knows how much money Motor Racing Promotions and I am making.'

'People are upset, sure – but mainly because they've been taken by surprise. They *will* calm down. The others are more likely to be pissed off with themselves: I remember you offering us – the teams – joint participation in the FOCA agency business, but we turned you down. You later offered each of us a 10 per cent stake in your business, which admittedly would have cost a tidy sum, but you offered it at a fair price – which was backed by more than enough cash flow at the time, but we turned you down. The others are pissed off because they feel stupid that they didn't have the vision or judgement to take you up on those offers.'

'What *can* I do to calm things?'

'First, you should never be prevented from enjoying the fruits of your efforts. Second, do not apologize to anyone – you have nothing to answer for. Third, do *not* feel you need to make up for any wrong decisions others have made. No one else took the risks you did; no one else, therefore, deserves to share in the reward. As it happens, though … I do have an idea.'

Ravilious looked at the peer expectantly.

'You couldn't hope to spend 2.5 billion in ten lifetimes … I doubt whether you could spend 2 billion in that time?'

Ravilious's face creased, not knowing where Lambourn was going.

'Why not say to the teams that you're willing to cut them in?' said the peer. 'See it as a bonus pool. It could be a shareholding, rather than cash, but why not offer them collectively a grant of, say, 20 per cent of the shares? You might be saying goodbye to 500 million, but you would still keep the bulk of the business. 500 million split between the teams would yield them each a windfall of 50 million, which, I'd say, would be more than enough to keep them happy.'

Ravilious was feeling slightly relieved. He looked at Lambourn intently. 'Maybe a 20 per cent bonus is not an unreasonable amount to offer? Do you think it'd be anywhere near enough to keep the teams on side?'

'You can only try – it would represent more money than they could have ever expected.'

Arno Ravilious invited the team bosses to a meeting that weekend in Japan. He braced himself for hostility. Straight out, he proposed the idea of the 20 per cent bonus. It seemed to change the mood.

But not for everyone.

Eugene Van Der Vaal and Suleiman Al-Megrahi sounded affronted.

'Why should the backmarker teams get the same as the bigger teams, when we have spent so much more to create the spectacle at the front of the grid?'

Ravilious was soon screaming to himself: *'Oh, for fuck's sake.'*

Al-Megrahi added: 'You have still taken for yourself huge swathes of Formula 1 without anyone's permission. Taking something, without consent, amounts to theft.'

Lord Lambourn stepped in, addressing the meeting as a whole rather than Al-Megrahi specifically: 'On two separate occasions, Arno has offered us a chance to participate in his activities. I don't remember any of us taking him up on those, do you?'

For once there was silence around the table, even from Eugene Van Der Vaal and Suleiman Al-Megrahi; if only for a few moments.

Lambourn asked: 'Will you consider accepting Arno's offer, Suleiman?'

Al-Megrahi replied: 'I want to meet the investment bank and negotiate the terms.'

FIFTY-EIGHT

Arno Ravilious, at Lord Lambourn's encouragement, arranged a meeting with Klyman-Messner for the team bosses; six said they would come. Ravilious had a sense of how explosive this was likely to be; he resolved to have a plan. He thought everything through before briefing Tex Brubaker.

Assembling in the investment bank's palatial Canary Wharf meeting room, Suleiman Al-Megrahi and Eugene Van Der Vaal seemed to have a permanent sneer on their faces. Their disapproval intensified as the meeting went on – as the team bosses were made fully aware of the extent of Motor Racing Promotions' business activities, revenues and profitability.

'The gulf between what Ravilious earns and what we, the teams, receive from the Concorde Agreement,' exploded Van Der Vaal, 'is colossal. It's a fucking disgrace.'

Brubaker was taken aback.

Lambourn stepped in. 'Hang on, Eugene, let's keep a little decorum here. There is a matter of effort and reward in all this. It's taken significant effort to make Formula 1 a success. How much money have *you* invested to make this work?'

Van Der Vaal didn't seem to be moved.

Before the Massarella boss could speak again, Suleiman Al-Megrahi asked: 'Mr Brubaker, you say the company is valued at 2.5 billion pounds – and that it's proposed the teams are offered 20 per cent in shares as a bonus pool?'

'That is the current offer. Each team's share would be approximately 50 million.'

'But not all in cash?'

'No. A fair proportion of it would be. There's a plan to sell 39 per cent of the company, so each team would receive just short of 20 million in cash; the remainder of each team's allocation would be in MRP shares.'

Some of the team bosses started to think about how much this could mean to them.

Ravilious scanned the room, trying to read the mood. Looking across to Brubaker, he judged it was time to give the investment banker the signal.

Brubaker opened a file in front of him. 'Given that we have the most senior figures in Formula 1 here, it would be an opportune time to discuss an issue that could trouble the financial health of the sport. At the moment, sponsorship funding for 7 out of 12 of your teams, not to mention a good proportion of trackside advertising at grands prix, comes from tobacco companies.'

There was little reaction on the faces of the F1 personnel.

'There have been recent pronouncements by Rialto Bocelli, the EU Commissioner for Health and Food Safety,' Brubaker added, 'on his intention to ban smoking across the European Union. His first step, scheduled for 1 January 1999, is to ban tobacco advertising in the EU…'

There was still no response from the team bosses.

Brubaker was surprised. 'Are you not concerned?'

His face seemed to say: 'Apparently not.'

Looking down at his notes, Brubaker went on: 'Under proposed Directive … 1998/33/EC … there is the intention "*to protect public health by regulating the promotion of tobacco*". In Article 1, Section 1 (d) of this proposal, it talks about "*tobacco related sponsorship*". In defining "sponsorship", Article 2, subsection (c) defines it as: "*any form of public or private contribution to any event, activity or individual with the aim or direct or indirect effect of promoting a tobacco product*". While Article 5, Section 1 states: "*sponsorship of events or activities involving or taking place in several Member States or otherwise having cross-border effects shall be prohibited*".

'What this means,' Brubaker continued, picking up a clutch of photographs lying on the table in front of him and then holding each one up in turn, 'is that these advertising hoardings at grands prix, and these liveries on your cars, will be banned ... no Rothmans ... no Marlboro ... Mild Seven ... West ... Worldwide Tobacco ... Benson and Hedges ... Gauloises. As I understand it, gentlemen, tobacco sponsorship forms the bulk of your income. After 1 January 1999, it will be a crime in the European Union for your cars to be sponsored by a tobacco company; you won't be able to enjoy any revenue from any company in this sector.'

'But we're a global sport,' said Frank Williams. 'The TV pictures go all over the world. The European zone is a fraction of where we go and who sees us.'

Suleiman Al-Megrahi stepped in: 'And all the TV coverage of races around the rest of the world will be "allowed" to show our cars with tobacco liveries and advertising.'

'A fair point,' said Brubaker. 'Under Commissioner Bocelli's pronouncement, those *will* be okay – but only for another two years – until 2001. After that, they, too, will be banned.'

The room fell silent.

'If we go ahead with a flotation of MRP,' said the banker, 'Formula 1 will need to do some work on this. Investors will be concerned about the impending drop-off in revenue in the sport and, therefore, the ability of the teams to keep performing commercially, at least as well as they do currently.'

Ravilious stepped in: 'So not only will the teams attract less income through direct sponsorships, but the share-out from the flotation wouldn't be as high as 50 million – because MRP's overall valuation would be lower.'

Brubaker's expression indicated agreement. 'If the tobacco advertising ban is implemented in full, I'm guessing we'd be looking at a drop in MRP's overall value from 2.5 billion to below 1 billion, given the proportion of sponsorship and advertising that Formula 1 currently enjoys from tobacco.'

'What can we do about this?' asked Al-Megrahi.

Brubaker laid the photographs back on the table. 'First, I'd say your priority is to try and replace your tobacco advertisers with non-tobacco firms.'

'But they wouldn't be anywhere near as generous,' replied another team boss. 'We've been earning well in recent years, precisely because the tobacco companies have been restricted in their marketing elsewhere. We've enjoyed the benefits of being one of the few outlets the tobacco companies still had open to them.'

'That's as maybe,' replied Brubaker, 'but other sports are sponsored to significant amounts by non-tobacco companies.'

'None of them are as capital intensive as F1,' said one of the other team bosses. 'We need substantial sums of money to fund our development. What *other* approaches could we adopt to tackle this?'

Brubaker shrugged with his face. 'The announcement by Commissioner Bocelli is only a proposal, at this stage. The EU is notoriously full of hot air, with ideas being bandied about all the time. You should definitely try lobbying. Make a case for the negative economic impact on certain countries, regions – employment – if the ban went ahead. A special dispensation for things has been granted in the past. Some kind of exclusion might be possible?'

For all the significance of this discussion, Ravilious was intrigued. Suleiman Al-Megrahi did not look the slightest bit concerned. If anything, he looked like his mind was already somewhere else.

The Formula 1 team bosses left the conference room an hour later, leaving Ravilious in a private meeting with Brubaker and the Klyman-Messner staff.

'You were absolutely right, Arno – to raise the tobacco ban. It was an excellent point of leverage. It seemed to focus their minds.'

'For a while.'

'Before this meeting, though, I hadn't understood the *need* for it,' said the banker. 'But … good God – did you hear them? How they spoke to you – how they spoke to each other. How the hell do you control such a bunch of vipers?'

Ravilious shrugged. 'They're not called the Piranha Club for nothing. Every decision affecting them ends up being a transaction. That's why I was keen to apply some leverage on the flotation.'

'Well, you've managed to corral them for this long. In the meantime, I can report that we've gone through the additional information you sent us. We do have a few concerns over the operation of Motor Racing Promotions, some of which have been confirmed by that display from the team bosses.'

'Okay.'

'First, generally speaking, the City – Wall Street – doesn't like companies that are one-man bands. They carry too much risk. In the case of incapacity, illness, death, et cetera – who would run the show? You could address this by instituting a proper board; at the very least, you would need a chairman or president who would, notionally, sit above you. Most importantly, you need a named successor, someone investors can have faith in, should you no longer be around.'

Ravilious's face set. 'I'm not having people interfere. I give my word and that's it. I've never gone for processes and procedures. Either someone is worth doing business with, or they aren't.'

'That's fair enough, of course; I'm just telling you how investors in the City and on Wall Street look at things. You don't *have* to play by their rules, of course; but that would mean you might not get to play at all. Institutional investors like everything to be clear, clean and concise.'

'What are the other concerns?'

'The Concorde Agreement,' Brubaker said. 'This grants you a licence to operate the Formula 1 TV rights, which you remodelled when you offered those guarantees to the FIA and the teams.'

Ravilious nodded.

'It appears the TV rights are only yours, though, for a period of three years?'

'If you knew what I had to go through to get them, you would be embarrassed to say "only".'

'For such a sizeable proportion of MRP's revenue,' said Brubaker, 'this *would* cause investors concern. Three years isn't long enough.

Investors like predictability; any uncertainty over renewal would become a serious risk to confidence in the business.'

'But the FIA is on side. A renewal is all but a given.'

'Maybe, now, Arno, but what happens if you have a change in the leadership of the FIA, someone who wants to put some of the organization's activities out to the open market – to see if they can get a better deal? You could lose out.'

'I'll make a few enquiries.'

'Good.'

'Anything else?'

'We would need to have all your existing relationships properly set out in legally enforceable agreements, those with the circuits, suppliers, et cetera.'

'I work on a handshake.'

'Such agreements *would* need to include any between MRP and the teams…'

Ravilious exhaled loudly and smiled. '*That's* not going to happen … you saw the nature of the bosses. Some of them are completely bloody-minded … barely even think rationally.'

'Investors will want to do significant due diligence on your business. If they can't be sure of the integrity of the players, let alone the reliability between them, their confidence, again, will be hit.'

Ravilious nodded unenthusiastically.

'But, to me, the biggest issue of all,' said Brubaker, 'is the European tobacco ban. If the sport is denied that source of income, you could all be seriously damaged. Unless you're able to replace that revenue, Formula 1 as a whole will end up in serious financial trouble.'

'*If* the ban goes ahead…'

'Sure. But if it does – and, as a consequence, you don't have the same number let alone quality of teams racing – you won't have a TV programme. MRP's income could be devastated. You had better hope, Arno – whether there's a float or not – that, on tobacco, the EU does end up changing its mind.'

FIFTY-NINE

As he was driven away from the City, heading back to Biggin Hill in Kent, Ravilious called Lord Lambourn from the car.

'I don't think that went too badly,' said the peer. 'Van Der Vaal's always a difficult sod. I don't think even he would turn down 50 million, just to stop you going ahead.'

'I'm not so sure.'

'It looked like Al-Megrahi came round. I think he saw the benefit of taking this forward.'

'I'm glad you think so. Budge, there's something I've been prompted to talk to you about. Brubaker went through some of the housekeeping he needs for the flotation; I need to tidy up some of the contracts and so on.'

'Sounds about right.'

'He's concerned the contract for the TV rights in the Concorde Agreement is too short – he wants to be able to show investors there's a longer-term relationship than that.'

'Did he say how long?'

'Not specifically ... I'm guessing the longer the better.'

'How about going for ten years?'

'Sounds good.'

'But, Arno, you have to understand – I can't just sign stuff away. I would have to make it look like a good deal for us.'

'You mean I'd have to pay for something like this, after all the value I've created within F1? It'd be pretty galling to be asked to buy back the results of my own efforts. What sort of number are you thinking?'

'I would start with a knockout figure ... a nice round number. Off the top of my head, how about a million a race?'

'And I'm guessing that you wouldn't want any risk – so guaranteed?' countered Ravilious wearily.

'I'm pretty sure that would clinch it.'

'But if there's no downside for the FIA, Budge,' said Ravilious, 'there can't be any upside either.'

'Fair enough. Sixteeen million a year would set the FIA up beautifully. We'd have certainty over covering our administrative costs, as well as being able to fund a whole load of other projects. Leave it with me, Arno – but, in principle, I'd be happy we had a deal.'

Ravilious spent the next month attempting to formalize the pre-flotation housekeeping points made by the investment banker. Some counterparties responded well, keen to put their existing arrangements on a more formal footing.

Towards the end of October, as Formula 1 was making its way to Jerez for the European Grand Prix – the teams, the FIA, Formula 1 generally, as well as Tex Brubaker at Klyman-Messner – were all completely thrown.

Commissioner Rialto Bocelli was calling another press conference. In Brussels.

His proposed tobacco ban was attracting considerable attention.

This time, the room was packed.

The commissioner took everyone by surprise with his opening line:

'I am, today,' he said, 'announcing a suspension of the proposed tobacco advertising ban in Europe on the 1st of January 1999.'

There was an audible gasp in the room.

A fusillade of flashguns went off, the shutter clicks rattling like hail stones. Then, 300 journalists started screaming their questions.

Bocelli held up his hand. 'Instead, I am proposing that a ban will be phased in. Physical advertisements will be permissible until 2005. Sporting events, where tobacco brands are publicized, will be exempt until 2008. Television broadcasts that involve tobacco branding and advertising from outside the EU will not be banned until 2010.'

Before he had finished speaking, Bocelli was being barracked. Journalists, commentators, activists for public health were screaming questions – even abuse – at him.

During the weekend of the season's final grand prix, Formula 1 came in for a savaging in the press. An investigative reporter for the *Guardian*, Gareth Pound – also the author of an unauthorized biography of Ravilious – had pieced together a story. A double-page spread ran on the Saturday; the journalist posited the benefits of Commissioner Bocelli's change of mind were so significant to certain interests – namely Formula 1 and the proposed flotation of Motor Racing Promotions – that the EU commissioner could only have been 'got at'.

The press across Europe latched onto the same idea.

Around Formula 1, the political storm with the EU was all most people could talk about. It overshadowed the heart-stopping down-to-the-wire showdown between Villeneuve and Schumacher, even when it looked like the German might reprise his earlier 1994 shunt with a championship contender in the closing stages of a title-deciding race.

Across all media, Arno Ravilious was singled out as the principal beneficiary of the volte face by the European Union on its anti-tobacco stance. Ravilious had the most to lose: £2.5 billion was at stake. Why wouldn't he have intervened to get the ban altered?

After 48 hours into the trial by media, Ravilious's guilt was all but assumed.

Commissioner Rialto Bocelli also came under intense scrutiny. Every aspect of his life was brandished across the media. His private bank accounts and net worth were investigated; every misdemeanour and indiscretion he had ever committed was blown out of all proportion, making this former provincial mayor sound like an ethical black hole. His integrity was savaged.

Tex Brubaker at Klyman-Messner was keen to reassure Ravilious that, despite the furore in the media, the delay of the tobacco ban meant there was no reason why the stock market flotation should not be viable again.

Arno Ravilious, in any case, was looking through the flak of the tobacco ban politics, pushing on with the opportunity it had thrown up: of establishing a longer tenure agreement on the F1 TV rights. Whatever else was going on, the extension of it to 10 years was too good a chance to miss. Ravilious was even ready to make the first year's payment of £16 million to the FIA to consummate the deal.

The investment banker's remaining issue of concern around the flotation was the governance structure of the MRP's holding company. 'Who would you like on your board?' Brubaker asked Ravilious at a meeting in early November.

The Ringmaster sighed: 'No one who's going to get in the way.'

'This,' said the banker handing him a list of names, 'is what we would see as an ideal composition. It's been put together to include representatives from all the different stakeholders within the sport.'

Ravilious skimmed down the list:

A representative of the FIA
The chief executive of a grand prix circuit (Monza)
The chief executive of a podium team (Massarella)
The chief executive of a backmarker team (Lola)
The chairman of the Grand Prix Drivers' Association
The chairman of NBC Europe (non-exec)
The chairman of a top-10 Formula 1 sponsor (non-exec)
A non-Formula 1 finance director
A non-Formula 1 HR director

He almost threw the sheet of paper back across the table. 'I'm not having people like that anywhere near me. Didn't you see how the team bosses behave? If Formula 1 had been left to them, they'd still be racing round disused airfields, surrounded by straw bales with commentary coming from a bloke with a megaphone on the back of a hay lorry. Every one of those people only ever thinks about their own interests. No gathering of people like that could agree what time to have *lunch* … let alone what to eat.'

'The City/Wall Street needs to have clarity, Arno.'

'What could be clearer than having a business run by someone who knows what he's doing and gets things done? I'm the only person who knows how to get the most out of the circuits – the only person who knows how to maximize the advertising and hospitality at racetracks – who understands programming and sales, to get the most out of TV stations. You people might want clarity, but bring any of those self-centred morons into the mix, and you won't *have* clarity. You won't have a business at all. How clear is that?'

'I am sure investors would say that that's fair enough, but they're not going to risk 2.5 billion on a one-man band.'

By now Brubaker was familiar with Ravilious's stridency on certain things; he had learned to jockey his position and come at the same point from a different angle. 'Why don't I arrange a meeting with some key City investors, so that you can hear their views for yourself?'

A few days later a Mercedes-Benz S-Class carrying Arno Ravilious and Tex Brubaker pulled over in Eldon Street near Liverpool Street Station. Brubaker led the Formula 1 boss into the distinctive Broadgate complex, past the ice rink and towards the entrance of Number 5: the offices of the Japanese banking giant, Yoshi Securities.

Up on the meeting-room floor they were shown into a large room. Twenty people were already sitting around a boat-shaped conference table. As Ravilious sat next to Brubaker at the beamiest part, Samuel Robbins, head of Yoshi's equity research, introduced the other people present: among them were senior investment officers of Standard Life, Mercury Asset Management, the Commercial Union, Fidelity and the Pru, as well as fund managers responsible for the equity portfolios of the British Rail, Unilever, Shell, Quartech International, Royal Mail and British Airways pension funds.

Brubaker made a presentation setting out the Motor Racing Promotions business profile, outlining the profit and loss projections, the balance sheet and the key investment metrics. 'Now that the EU has withdrawn the severity of its ban on tobacco advertising,' he said,

'Motor Racing Promotions TV is expected to grow by 15 per cent, compound, over the next five years. Race fees are forecast to increase, as new circuits are continuing to come forward to host grands prix. Demand for trackside hospitality and advertising is projected to rise, both in turnover and profitability. Finally, MRP's TV rights are forecast to increase by between 15 and 20 per cent.

'Formula 1 is unique,' stated Brubaker. 'There are *no* competitive forces threatening to discount any of these profit projections. As a consequence, we feel Motor Racing Promotions should be valued as a concept stock. We will be looking to price the IPO on a multiple of between 12 and 15 times earnings, giving a market valuation of between 2 and 2.5 billion pounds.'

The room had been attentive throughout. Notes had been taken. When Brubaker finished, the floor was opened for discussion. Every question, though, had a similar theme:

'Who is your chairman? Your president?'

'Who is on your board?'

'Who holds you to account for business decisions?'

'Who is your finance director?'

'Who is your risk officer?'

And the question the room kept referring back to was:

'Who is likely to be your successor, Mr Ravilious?'

SIXTY

On the morning of the 2nd of January 1998, a squad of four police cars came to a halt halfway down a leafy suburban street in the Brussels district of Woluwe-Saint-Pierre. Dismounting in Avenue Marquis de Villalobar, a group of eight policemen walked across the pavement and up to the front door of one of the detached houses in the road.

'Commissioner Bocelli?' asked the Walloon Aspirant-Commissaire Bernard Demotte.

The figure from within nodded.

Hesitantly, given the magnitude of the moment, the police officer said: 'Commissioner Bocelli … I am here to arrest you under the Belgian Criminal Code … you are being charged with the acceptance of bribes and corruption in a public office.'

Elite guests of the Charles III Hotel in Monte Carlo expected to be insulated from the tawdrier aspects of life. It was to their consternation, therefore, that a posse of armed policemen should march into their lobby, particularly when the officer at its head demanded to be taken to the room of a guest in the hotel.

One of the concierges accompanied them up to the third floor and knocked on the door of the suite. It was opened by a man in a white bathrobe. The guest was addressed without preamble: 'Monsieur Yoel Kahneman?'

There was a bewildered look on the American's face.

'I am Chief Superintendent Jean-Paul Marot of the Division de Police Judiciaire. I am here to arrest you under a European Arrest Warrant for the bribery of a public officer.'

Bocelli and Kahneman were arrested, placed in handcuffs and led away to police cars waiting outside their respective dwellings.

Within hours the two men were formally charged.

Both men were told they should prepare themselves for trial.

The arrest and charging of an EU Commissioner and a prominent figure known to be associated with Formula 1 prompted the media to enter another of its feeding frenzies. They were now able to make a direct link between a political decision, the politician who made it, and a prominent figure in the world of Formula 1. News outlets went to town, able to infer that F1 had quite clearly been up to no good. After all, the arrests indicated the authorities believed there to have been interference in the proper process of government that could affect the lives of 500 million people across the European Union.

Fuelling editors' zeal was the use of the word 'bribery' in the statements issued by the arresting authorities in both Belgium and Monaco. Within 24 hours, the words 'Formula 1' and 'bribery' had appeared together in countless headlines.

That, though, was only the start of the EU malaise for Arno Ravilious.

Three days later, Aniela Kucharski, another EU Commissioner – this time a former *voivode*, a provincial governor, of Lodz in Poland – made an announcement that served to tarnish Motor Racing Promotions on a completely different level. This European Commissioner, for Competition, declared:

'The EU Commission has received an application from Motor Racing Promotions Limited for permission to float on the London Stock Exchange. On reviewing the application, I am announcing today that permission for this has been denied. My department has responsibilities for commercial competition, cartels and anti-trust issues. In particular, our objection centres on infringements of Articles 101 and 102 of the TFEU – in respect of anti-trust concerns, dominance, and contract duration. Specifically, Motor Racing Promotions has entered into an agreement with the *Fédération Internationale de l'Automobile*, the FIA, over the contracting of Formula 1 television rights for 10 years. EU law prohibits contracts in excess of 5 years. Motor Racing Promotions is, therefore, in breach of EU competition law. Consequently, MRP does not qualify for permission to float in its current state. As a result of this infringement coming to our attention, however – and the other issues it raises – I am going further: I am, today, announcing that we are launching an official investigation into the entirety of MRP's relationship with the FIA and its compliance with EU law.'

'What kind of bureaucratic bullshit is this?' Ravilious bellowed down the phone to Brubaker. 'Christ, the interference into my business since I started down your path to flotation has been a fucking disaster.'

'These are the standards within which all businesses have to operate in Europe, Arno.'

'Christ, how does anybody get anything done with these idiotic restrictions? No fucking wonder we're losing all our trade to the Far East. Chinese businesses don't have to contend with this kind of crap.'

Two days later Ravilious wrote to Aniela Kucharski, the European Commissioner for Competition. He declared that he would move Formula 1 – particularly all its revenues, employment and business opportunities – out of the EU:

'*There are 115 member countries affiliated to the FIA,*' he wrote, '*and only 15 of them are in the EU. Moreover, Europe represents at best 20 per cent of F1's global TV audience. Formula 1 – Motor Racing Promotions – is an international operation that generates taxes and jobs around the world. It will not be distracted by a small minority of its audience and members.*'

That weekend the spat turned ugly. A significant feature appeared in the *Financial Times* discussing the recent issues to do with Formula 1 and Motor Racing Promotions. It was written by Rosa Grant, the *FT*'s Investigation Editor. All aspects of Ravilious's dealings with Formula 1 and the FIA were laid bare. Business interests, revenues from each activity, percentage shares of each revenue between each stakeholder and the total per annum profits made by Motor Racing Promotions.

In a rant to Lord Lambourn, Ravilious said: 'That Polish cow Kucharski and the other one at the *Financial Times* have gone and disclosed facts, figures and statements – particularly to do with the 10-year TV deal – that were completely confidential; they were between us – between you and me.'

In fewer than four months since he had started talking to Klyman-Messner – about selling Motor Racing Promotions on the stock exchange via an IPO – Ravilious had had enough. The flotation was off.

But the issues it had brought to public attention, through the unwanted disclosures, wouldn't go away. In the late spring of 1998, Aniela Kucharski, the European Commissioner for Competition, handed down a scathing judgment, having investigated and confirmed a number of serious infringements of EU competition rules. It concluded:

'By dint of the 10-year contract with the FIA over television rights, a monopoly had effectively been created in favour of Motor Racing Promotions (MRP). It is the European Union's ruling that the FIA may no longer assign TV rights to MRP. Furthermore, any and all agreements made to date between these two parties are deemed to be ultra vires. Unlawful.'

SIXTY-ONE

Arno Ravilious had never felt so demoralized. He could not comprehend this scale of intervention. One consequence of the political interference did at least provide some comfort. For the first time, a number of Eurosceptic media outlets started criticizing the EU for damaging a world-class British business and success story.

Unusually, Lord Lambourn was not immune from criticism in the press and the paddock:

BRITISH PEER SELLS FIA'S FAMILY SILVER, ran one headline with a picture of Lambourn and Ravilious toasting each other with a glass of champagne somewhere glamourous. All attempts to explain that Motor Racing Promotions was now paying over the odds for the TV rights – and that because of it Ravilious was providing the governing body with a guaranteed income – failed to gain any traction with the press. Lambourn, the FIA, Arno Ravilious, MRP, Formula 1 were all being written up as EU law breakers, tarnishing the sport all over again.

The EU commissioners ruling was not a trivial matter.

The FIA was about to find itself in dire financial trouble: if even the existing TV deal with Motor Racing Promotions was to be declared illegal, the FIA would no longer be allowed to receive the income it was currently taking from MRP for the F1 TV rights. That meant an enormous hole had opened up in the governing body's finances.

'What can we do about this?' Ravilious asked Lambourn.

'I guess it would be different if you owned the TV rights, Arno, but I don't think I can sell them to you. Not now, anyway.' Almost as an afterthought, he said: 'Let me have a word with a lawyer friend. I'll see whether there's anything else we could do, for *all* our sakes.'

Yoel Kahneman was extradited from Monaco and transferred to temporary custody in Brussels. His trial, and that of Commissioner Rialto Bocelli, was held in Belgium's Court of Assize during the summer of 1998. To indicate the gravity of the offences – bribery and corruption in a public office – it was even held in the Arrondissement of Brussels-Capital.

Coverage of it by the continental media was described as the closest Europe had come to the saturation coverage of the recent O.J. Simpson trial in America. One blessing for the TV viewing public was that, in Belgium, TV cameras weren't allowed in the judicial chamber.

The trial was heard in front of three judges and a 12-person jury.

As part of his case, the leading prosecution lawyer, Alberik Janssen, set about twisting the knife in what the public already saw as a sordid affair. He went for the emotional jugular. He started with the workings of the tobacco industry, the legal issues facing it, the reasons why tobacco was evil, the number of people who died from smoking-related diseases, what their ailments looked like – in gruesome detail – and how governments the world over were right in restricting the cigarette companies' outlets for marketing their heinous products.

Next came his history of Formula 1.

The Belgian prosecutor called Arno Ravilious as a witness. Under cross-examination, Janssen asked him about the way he and Motor Racing Promotions operated; he asked about how deals had been done and how Ravilious had become so influential in the sport.

'And what is your opinion of the proposed smoking ban, Mr Ravilious?' asked the prosecuting lawyer.

Ravilious had been given some steer on how to deal with this kind of question: 'I don't smoke myself. It's entirely up to others to decide for themselves, provided they are given the facts. If elected politicians believe there would be popular support for such a law, then who am I to disagree?'

'So you don't object to the ban on tobacco advertising?'

'No.'

'Mr Ravilious, what was Motor Racing Promotions going to be

worth at the time you were planning to sell your company on the stock exchange?'

'About 2.5 billion pounds.'

'And how much of Motor Racing Promotions do you own?'

'All of it.'

'So selling MRP on the stock market meant that you, personally, were going to be worth 2.5 billion pounds?'

'Not the full amount, no – there were going to be other beneficiaries.'

'Some of the teams were to receive a windfall, were they not?'

'Yes, 20 per cent of the company.'

'So, all together, they were going to get about 500 million pounds?'

'Yes.'

'So, as the main shareholder, your holding was *still* going to be worth approximately 2 billion pounds.'

Ravilious nodded.

'Sorry, Mr Ravilious, please answer verbally in order that the court records may reflect your response.'

'Yes.'

'So you were destined to own a stake in your company valued at approximately 2 billion pounds. How much of Formula 1's overall revenue comes from tobacco advertising?'

'Probably around 70 per cent.'

'And what was likely to happen to Formula 1's revenues if the ban had been enforced?'

'They would have fallen, inevitably.'

'By about 70 per cent then?'

'Not exactly, we have other sponsors ready to take their place.'

'So would a 50 per cent fall be a surprise?'

Ravilious shook his head.

Once again, he was instructed to verbalize his answers.

'No.'

'No, Mr Ravilious – a 50 per cent fall in MRP's revenues would not be a surprise,' Janssen confirmed: 'Nor, then, would it be a surprise to see a similar fall in the value of MRP, as a result of the proposed tobacco ban?'

'Hypothetically, no.'

'No … so, in terms of an effect on your shareholding, the tobacco advertising ban was likely to have cost you, personally, about 1 billion pounds.'

'I suppose so.'

'You suppose so, and yet, Mr Ravilious, you are saying to this court that you *don't* object to the ban on the tobacco advertising?'

'No.'

'So losing 1 billion pounds … doesn't bother you?'

Ravilious looked the lawyer in the eye. 'If you are trying to establish a motive, Mr Janssen – for me to have interfered with EU policy, in order to safeguard my interests – you will be unsuccessful. I was never party to, let alone privy to, any conversation with Mr Kahneman. I have never met Commissioner Bocelli. I had nothing to do with any discussion about altering the EU's political proposals.'

'That is not what Mr Kahneman says.'

Ravilious's expression changed sharply, the lawyer's claim having pulled him up short. Ravilious paused, trying to weigh up what he might say next. Some interpreted this as the Ringmaster looking conflicted. Finally, he said: 'I think the record shows that Mr Kahneman and I have had some rough dealings in the past.'

Responding immediately, the prosecuting lawyer went through the issues Ravilious might have been referring to: his switch of sponsor from Worldwide Tobacco to Rothmans, after all the work they had done together setting up trackside advertising; and then the threatened breakaway group, the WCR, which had come to a head at the Monaco Grand Prix in 1977.

But the F1 boss declined to elaborate.

After five minutes of awkward persistence, the prosecutor finally said: 'Mr Ravilious, your lack of candour about your relationship with Mr Kahneman will have been noted by the jury. Is that the way you wish to leave it?'

Ravilious scowled at the prosecutor but said nothing more.

SIXTY-TWO

Over the weekend of the German Grand Prix in August 1998, Suleiman Al-Megrahi called an ad hoc meeting of Formula 1 team bosses. Two hours later he announced there would be a press conference held that evening.

With all the goings-on in F1 recently, there was no shortage of interest in what might be the next chapter in this soap opera. To a packed room of journalists and all kinds of other media, Al-Megrahi announced:

'Because of the bad press coverage and other troubles in our sport, various interests in Formula 1 are prompted to make amends. We are, today, forming a new Association: the *Association des Constructeurs Européens d'Automobiles*, the ACEA. This is being established to break away from the current Formula 1 and aims to reform and restructure the entire business model of motor racing. All the teams are showing interest. A formal agreement will be drawn up and signed at the Belgian Grand Prix at the end of August.'

Ravilious was seething with the teams, but more at how his fateful conversation with Tex Brubaker – about trying to sell his business – had opened up such a can of worms. None of the issues he was now facing had been in place before the discussion to float Motor Racing Promotions. All of these current troubles had been completely avoidable.

After Hockenheim, Arno Ravilious received a call from Lambourn.

'I *think* I may have found something, Arno,' said the president of the FIA. 'A possible way round the EU accusation of our creating a monopoly in respect of the TV rights.'

'I'm ready for any news that might not be negative.'

Lambourn explained: 'No contract we draw up, now, looks like it would be workable with the bureaucrats – and, having taken sound-ings, there's no appetite within the FIA to sell you the freehold, as it were, of the TV rights … however, I've had it on good advice that the FIA *could* sell you a lease on them, would you believe?'

'You're not serious?'

'Apparently, I am. A lease, it seems, would fall outside the EU's restrictions on competition. It should get you off the hook with the EU Competition tsar, Commissioner Kucharski.'

'Sounds extraordinary … would *you* be happy to go with some-thing like this?'

'If it's a way of restoring the FIA's income from its TV rights, then absolutely.' Lambourn then added: 'There would also be another enormous benefit to taking this route.'

'Which is what?'

'Signing a longish lease, say for 50 years, would in all likelihood scupper the chances of the ACEA breakaway group ever being able to get off the ground.'

Ravilious didn't seem to sound enthused: 'After all this, Budge, are you sure you wouldn't prefer to deal with the teams anyway?'

'Good God, no,' said Lambourn. 'I could never work with the teams. They're all out for their own competitive advantage. Collec-tive decisions would never get made. No, believe me, Arno – I'd far rather deal with you.'

'Okay, but if that means a lease would be doing the FIA a favour, make it a 100 years and you're on.'

'Listen, Arno, there would have to be a quid pro quo here.'

'Such as?'

'You and MRP would have to declare, explicitly, that the FIA owns the intellectual property of Formula 1 … and that you recog-nize the FIA's power to regulate the sport autonomously.'

'I would only pay you a fixed amount.'

'And the lease fee gets paid up front.'

Ravilious grunted. '200 million.'

'300…'

'250.
'Pounds…
'Dollars…'
'Done.'

News of the lease agreement was not made public in advance. A letter was sent by Lord Lambourn to the EU competition commission outlining the deal as a fait accompli.

Lambourn and Ravilious were certain that, in response, the EU would be throwing every lawyer across Europe at this transaction to get an opinion against it, desperate to give the Commission a way of blocking the arrangement – particularly as it was such a flouting of their authority.

But nothing happened.

The EU Commission said nothing more about it.

It couldn't.

Extraordinarily, a business relationship for 100 years, when structured as a lease, *was* acceptable within the European Union's own laws.

Lord Lambourn continued to feel the heat of the FIA/MRP relationship. He had been accused of being too close to Arno Ravilious. After news of the 10-year TV rights deal was revealed, those accusations intensified. Now that he had engineered the 100-year lease, he felt it would only be a matter of time before that, too, became public and the haranguing started all over again.

Lambourn rang Ravilious at the end of the summer break in 1998 and told him he had decided to step down. Ravilious was bitterly disappointed; he tried everything to persuade him to stay, even though he understood the peer's reasons.

It brought to an end an extraordinary relationship – a partnership almost.

Four months later Jehangir Banyan, the president of the Federation of Motor Sports Clubs of India, was elected to succeed Lambourn as president of the FIA.

In September 1998, Yoel Kahneman and Commissioner Rialto Bocelli were found guilty of bribery and associated offences of corruption in a public office. Each man was sentenced to 15 years in jail. To most people's surprise, nothing unfavourable was said in the judgment about Arno Ravilious. Even so, the trial had subjected Formula 1 and him to brutal exposure, especially during cross-examination. The identification of guilt and the sentencing severity drew attention to the seedier goings-on in some aspects of the sport.

Ravilious may have been battered and tarnished by the previous 12 months, but, bizarrely, he had emerged at the end of it in a significantly stronger position. Securing the 100-year lease on the most valuable element of his business, gave it – for the first time – real stability and longevity, while at the same time he was now established in the public's mind as a world-class entrepreneur.

For all that, Ravilious had been made aware that he owned and controlled a business theoretically valued at around £2.5 billion, and yet he had been stymied from releasing any value from it – thwarted from taking any of his money out.

SIXTY-THREE

At the Grand Prix Charity Ball in Grosvenor House, Park Lane – just before Christmas 1998 – Tex Brubaker introduced Arno Ravilious to another financier, Count Hanfried Von Wittelsbach from the German bank, Frankfurt Capital. The Formula 1 boss bristled the moment his role was described. 'I've had quite enough of bankers. Your lot have caused me nothing but bullshit.'

'In that case, I hope what I propose might be different,' said the aristocratic Wittelsbach. 'I am sure I *can* solve a key problem for you.'

'I'm not interested.'

Somehow, Brubaker's body language urged him to have patience. 'I think you might be interested to hear what Hanfried has in mind.'

Ravilious stopped himself from turning away.

'You're keen to release some of the value you have created in your business,' said the German. 'You have had issues, let's say, in finding investors who understand it, and who understand you. I *do* have a solution.'

Ravilious found his resistance abating; there was something about this man that demanded attention.

Wittelsbach said: 'I would be prepared to advance you a loan of 1.5 billion pounds against a block of your shares in Motor Racing Promotions.'

Ravilious wasn't sure what that meant.

Brubaker explained: 'Hanfried's approach, Arno, would allow you to release 1.5 billion – in cash – from MRP.'

Wittelsbach paused as he saw Ravilious was now studying him intently.

'I've looked at the cash flows,' said the banker. 'They are extraordinary. Your business's income would cover the interest charge on such a loan several times over.'

'Why would you want to do anything like this, when other investors have only ever found fault with what I do?'

Wittelsbach smiled. 'First of all, I own and run a private bank, and so I am prepared to back my own judgement: I am not thwarted by the bureaucracy common to stock market-related institutions. Second, since the conversations you had with them, something material has changed in your company's favour. You've created stability and appeal by securing that 100-year lease on the TV rights…'

Brubaker re-entered the conversation: 'Frankfurt Capital is one of the finest banks in Germany. Hanfried's approach, Arno, is a workable solution – *and* you wouldn't even be selling shares. You'd receive a cheque for 1.5 billion pounds – and, at the same time, remain the 100 per cent shareholder. You would stay in full control of everything.'

Things seemed to resolve themselves unexpectedly quickly. By mid-January 1999, Motor Racing Promotions entered into a loan agreement with Frankfurt Capital and, in exchange, MRP received £1.5 billion in cash. It was an incomprehensible amount of money.

It prompted Ravilious to do some things for Motor Racing Promotions that he might not have funded from earnings. He invested a chunk of the proceeds in buying equipment to film, edit and transmit higher quality finished programmes; Biggin Hill was kitted out as a state-of-the-art TV production facility; to transport all this new equipment to flyaway grands prix, he leased two Boeing 747 freighters; and to serve as his headquarters, he bought a lease on an office building in Berkeley Square.

Arno Ravilious also paid himself a bonus. With it, he bought two houses – a townhouse in Belgravia and a manor house in Oxfordshire. The arrangement Ravilious felt most self-conscious about, though, was to do with his car – not the extravagance of buying a brand-new Bentley, which had seduced him each day as he passed the Jack Barclay showroom next to his new office, but the hiring of a chauffeur to drive him around in it. Ravilious continually felt he had to justify this to himself on the basis that it allowed him to keep working, even when he was on the move.

Motor Racing Promotions' higher quality TV production created a noticeable difference. Within a matter of months it enabled him to expand his presence in twice the number of markets. On the back of that new business, MRP's overall receipts increased substantially, enabling him to earn back the investment he had made from the proceeds of the windfall loan, as he called it, within just two seasons.

And then, three months later, something unimaginable happened.

Without any warning, Ravilious's problems with Brussels vanished. In an instant. And completely.

In March 1999, Aniela Kucharski, the European Commissioner for Competition – who had tried to outlaw MRP's relationship with the FIA – resigned from her post. She, along with the entire 'Santer Commission', were forced to stand down after allegations of corruption against the European Union.

With a total clearout from the EU bureaucracy, the vendetta against Motor Racing Promotions went with it. There was an immediate end to the suspension of MRP's relationship with the FIA; no investigation of Ravilious's business dealings; and no longer any impediment to MRP's stock market flotation.

For the first time in quite a while, Arno Ravilious found himself able to operate without any outside interference at all.

SIXTY-FOUR

In 2007, the Concorde Agreement, which set the distribution of Formula 1's commercial income to the various stakeholders, was due to expire. All hell broke loose. The F1 teams were determined to force MRP to share out a far bigger proportion of the receipts in their favour.

Things came to a head.

The teams launched another breakaway group, this one called the Grand Prix World Championship, the GPWC.

Count Wittelsbach, unused to the posturing that went on in Formula 1, became seriously spooked. He feared that any fragmentation of the sport, let alone any loss of income to MRP, could fundamentally damage Motor Racing Promotions' capacity to service the interest payments on his £1.5 billion loan. With so much at stake, the banker felt he had to be proactive, even attempting to intervene by trying to broker a deal between the teams himself. Wittelsbach approached Ferrari and offered the Scuderia a disproportionate incentive to stay within the Concorde Agreement framework. Ravilious got to hear about this unauthorized intervention, and was incandescent. To counter it, he leaked details of Wittelsbach's Ferrari side offer to someone he knew would divulge them to Massarella. Eugene Van Der Vaal was so incensed by MRP and the other teams that he immediately broke from the GPWC and announced the launch of his own breakaway group.

The Concorde Agreement was still unsigned a year later when the credit crunch hit in 2008. By early 2009, many businesses worldwide expected an economic contraction; most feared a depression. Companies started cutting costs. Credit had underpinned so much of the Western economy, nowhere more so than in the mass-produced car market, new cars having rarely been bought with cash – instead being paid for by some form of financing or leasing arrangement. As the banks seized up, credit-financed car purchases crashed. No one was going to be buying new road cars any time soon. The car makers were facing Armageddon. Manufacturers started laying people off in their thousands.

Several global car firms – BMW, Honda, Renault, Toyota – had been spending substantial sums on Formula 1 teams. The millions they were spending on F1 became indefensible. The new FIA president, Jehangir Banyan, was faced with the stark prospects of a sizeable reduction in the number of teams competing in Formula 1. He was motivated to make a unilateral decision and announcement:

'From 2009, there will be a budget cap – a fixed limit – on what each F1 team can spend during the year. To further reduce costs, inter-race testing – save for a small number of formal sessions during the course of a season – will be banned.'

The non car-making teams objected. To coordinate their resistance to the FIA diktat, they formed a new group, the Formula 1 Teams Association, FOTA. Ravilious could only smile wryly: for the first time in Formula 1 history, a protest group had been launched without the express purpose of taking him on.

FOTA refused to sign up with the FIA, or to enter their teams for the next Formula 1 season, unless the governing body changed its proposed rules. As a tit-for-tat, the FIA set a deadline after which it would refuse to accept registrations from any FOTA team for the next year's F1 season.

As the brinkmanship intensified, two of the FOTA teams broke ranks, running off to sign up with the FIA – worried about securing their entry and thereby satisfying some of their sponsorship obligations. Those capitulating teams were then rounded on by the FOTA group and suspended from it. Invoking a golden oldie from the Formula 1 playbook, the core of the FOTA group then threatened to form another breakaway group.

The president of the FIA, Jehangir Banyan, also seemed to be pursuing a wider automotive agenda. Formula 1 had long claimed that it benefited the automotive industry as its innovations trickled down to road car design. At the same time, Banyan was anxious to show that motorsport was contributing to the environmental debate. Instead of F1 asking: 'How much power can we get from a given amount of fuel', he switched the ethos to: 'How much energy can be extracted from a finite quantity of fuel.'

Engine design became extremely complicated and, ironically, a lot more expensive. Under Banyan's regulations, engine size – its cubic capacity – was reduced. As some compensation for the power loss, teams were allowed to run turbochargers again but, on the reduced amounts of permitted fuel prescribed by this new Formula, no existing F1 car would have been able to reach the end of a grand prix. Engine manufacturers were compelled to go green and focus heavily on energy recovery. Instead of cars dissipating energy as heat and light under braking, engineers had to find ways of recycling some of that 'lost' energy. Generators were fitted to their drivetrains, while complicated electronics had to be developed to intermesh the retardant effect of those generators with the hydraulic brakes as the cars were decelerated. The age of the hybrid engine was born.

The engine manufacturers, though, managed to achieve something remarkable:

Formula 1 teams, working with considerably smaller engine capacities, had almost miraculously created engines that could, in brake horsepower and torque, outperform the earlier larger engines – and with much less fuel inefficiency.

Banyan's changes to the Formula were seismic. Manufacturers and teams had had to undertake huge development efforts and costs to comply with them, but not every team was lucky to have an engine manufacturer that got it right first time. Which, because of the ban on testing, denied the laggard teams any chance of subsequently catching up. At the beginning of the season, a pecking order was established – but, with no testing permissible, the order barely changed throughout the rest of the year.

In came the years dominated by Red Bull and then Mercedes.

The era of Formula 1 as a procession had begun.

All this, it seemed, had been brought about by decisions taken for political and environmental reasons, and nothing to do with the sport of motor racing.

In 2010, Tex Brubaker of the investment bank, Klyman-Messner, was back in touch with Ravilious.

'Arno, I have a way of releasing some more of MRP's value to investors for you.'

'If it's an IPO, you can fucking forget it.'

'No,' said Brubaker. 'A trade buyer.'

'Who?'

'An Italian television company … *Dramma Sportivo TV*.'

'Never heard of it.'

'The guy who runs it is a close friend of Silvio Berlusconi's. He, too, is a multi-billionaire. Sees huge potential in expanding F1's media presence. He's very close to FIAT/Ferrari, so there could also be some useful political influence. He's keen to buy a stake – a *minority* stake so you would retain full control. He's ready to offer you 1 billion pounds for a roughly 30 per cent shareholding in MRP … in cash.'

Ravilious's attention was suddenly held.

'One billion in cash, clean, for 30 per cent, Arno. That would give Motor Racing Promotions a clear … unequivocal … identifiable … overall value of 3.2 billion pounds.'

'I don't want any bullshit this time,' said Ravilious. 'It's absolutely take it or leave it. No changes … no adjustments … no boards … he buys, or he walks.'

Brubaker replied: 'The deal is as good as done.'

In early 2011 the deal was agreed, albeit for a slightly different-sized stake. Previous valuations of Motor Racing Promotions had been put at around £2.5 billion, but they had only been theoretical. Now that *Dramma Sportivo TV* had paid hard cash for MRP shares, the valuation of Motor Racing Promotions was real and north of £3.2 billion. Not only that, Arno Ravilious had succeeded in releasing – to himself personally this time – substantial proceeds from the company he had created.

It made him more than just a paper billionaire: thanks to *Dramma Sportivo TV*'s purchase, he had that actual amount of money in his bank account. At the same time, he retained 68.5 per cent of the company, firmly keeping himself in corporate control of it.

Matt Straker closed the Ziebart Blauman report on Motor Racing Promotions and exhaled deeply. In just that short illustration of Arno Ravilious's career, he found himself with all kinds of feelings. The sheer intensity of the man's history was extraordinary.

But a number of things now bugged him.

The Ziebart report was dated three years before, so didn't cover the recent past. How had Formula 1 in that short time gone from dominating the zeitgeist to its current catastrophic decline?

Another matter that disconcerted Straker was the corporate control of Motor Racing Promotions. If Ravilious was still CEO and the majority shareholder, holding 68.5 per cent, it was clear that Gabriel Barrus could have bought Ravilious out and taken control.

But if that was the case, what was Suleiman Al-Megrahi talking about?

How could he be claiming to own a minority stake in MRP and that very shortly he would gain outright control of F1 – as he stated up at Silverstone that weekend?

How did that make sense?

Also, Straker had had little idea of Formula 1's history before he had read this report. He was now aware of what Ravilious's 'career' said of the man himself and more importantly about his character...

As a result of that, something else here just didn't seem to fit.

BOOK THREE

SHOWDOWN

SIXTY-FIVE

Needing to clear his head, Straker changed into his running kit and set out along the towpath as the humid evening gave way to night. He was preoccupied: he was due to see Quartano at 8 o'clock the following morning. At that meeting, Straker would be expected to discuss his understanding of Motor Racing Promotions and his ideas for furthering the investigation into MRP's future. But, as yet, he had nothing to offer.

Back at the house, he showered, pulled on a bathrobe and poured himself a whisky. Grabbing a blank piece of paper he tried to order his thoughts – in the way he preferred – by visualizing the different components. Across the top of the sheet, he scrawled a title: 'Share Ownership of MRP'.

In the middle of the page he drew a large circle. Segmenting roughly into one third and two thirds, he wrote beside the smaller segment: *'Dramma Sportivo TV'*. Into the remaining two-thirds segment Straker wrote Arno Ravilious and, outwards from this into an empty part of the page, he wrote: 'Sold to Gabriel Barrus?' That was the ownership of MRP as he had inferred it from the report.

Where, on this chart though, should he write Al-Megrahi's name? Where was Al-Megrahi's shareholding? Straker had no idea. He ended up writing the man's name across the bottom of the pie chart followed by a series of question marks:

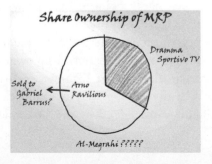

Straker had to speak about this to Benedict Wasserman, Quartech's investment banker at Ziebart Blauman. But it was far too late on a Sunday evening.

Leaving the house at half past five the following morning, Straker reached his desk in 20 Cavendish Square by a quarter past six. Expecting Wasserman to be on his way into the City, Straker rang both of the investment banker's numbers, but his calls were diverting to voicemail. Leaving messages on each phone, he stated the urgency that they speak.

In the quiet of his 9th floor office, Straker looked out over the roofs of the West End. Being midsummer, it was already light, the sun breaking above a bank of cloud to the east, an orange tint filling the sky.

Somewhere within this conundrum around the ownership of Motor Racing Promotions, he thought, somebody somewhere had to know something.

But who?

One answer was pretty obvious, wasn't it: Arno Ravilious would have to know?

Gabriel Barrus would have to have some understanding, as he was supposed to have an agreement with Ravilious?

And Al-Megrahi must know something, given that he claimed he was about to take control of MRP.

The straightforward solution would be to ask one of them, except his prime target – Arno Ravilious – was thought to be unconscious, recovering from a heart attack, while the other two had positions in this corporate fight, so were hardly going to divulge anything to anybody.

Straker growled at his lack of inspiration.

If he wasn't going to get anywhere with people within Formula 1, who else might be in a position to know who owned what?

Straker reverted to the Ziebart Blauman report and history of MRP. He turned to the bibliography in the back. It contained a summary of all the sources used by the investment bank in the composition of the 'history' section. Straker then noticed something. Several journalists as well as a documentary film-maker were mentioned multiple times. Each of them, at one time or other, had produced in-depth works on Motor Racing Promotions, Formula 1, Arno Ravilious or the FIA.

Shattering the quiet of his empty office, Straker's phone rang. With some relief, he saw that Benedict Wasserman was returning his calls.

'I've gone through your history of Arno Ravilious and Motor Racing Promotions, Ben, but I don't understand something. With the shareholding structure you've described, how can Al-Megrahi come close to claiming any control of MRP? Have there been any share sales since?'

'Not that we know of, although we can't know everything,' replied the banker. 'Our best information, at the time we wrote the report, suggested that Al-Megrahi didn't, then, have any shareholding at all.'

'How do I get to the bottom of this?'

'With difficulty, I'm afraid. As I said when we saw each other last Friday, we're talking about a private company. We're not given anything like the same access to its affairs as we would be with a public/listed one. Allied to that, the information we want is likely to be scarce; most of MRP is offshore. And in the case of Arno Ravilious, we are dealing with a very private man who's a genius at secrecy and misdirection. When we put that report together, we had to extrapolate and interpolate a lot more than we would like. No one, other than Ravilious himself, is likely to know the whole picture.'

'I'm due to see DQ in ten minutes – and I'm going to have to come up with some way of filling in some of the gaps, Ben, but I don't have any idea where to start. Which of the outside sources you used would be the most authoritative on MRP?'

'Depends on what angle you're coming from: Gareth Pound, the investigative journalist for the *Guardian*, has made a pretty good career out of hounding Ravilious, having written what most consider to be "the definitive biography".'

'Okay.'

'Rosa Grant, the Investigation Editor at the *Financial Times,* has written a number of finance-related think pieces on F1, mainly analyzing the corporate aspects – the commercial performance of Formula 1 overall – and financial health of Motor Racing Promotions.'

'Right.'

'From a gossip column perspective, which we only touched upon for background colour in the report, we contacted Shally Gazzore.'

'*Shally?*'

'Gazzore.'

'Him or her?'

'Still not sure. Shally, though, works for *Hello!* ... *OK!* ... or one of those, and gave us some of the background references – things like Ravilious's marriage, home life and various houses. Oh, and we also spoke to AT McGuire, an investigative TV documentary maker, who used to be a producer on the BBC's *Panorama* programme; he was the one who dug the dirt on the delayed implementation of the tobacco ban which led, eventually, to the EU bribery trial. All those sources are in our bibliography at the back of the report.'

'I'd spotted them, Ben, thank you. Who among them did you meet?'

'All, but some more cursorily than others.'

'Sorry, Ben – I'm going to have to go.'

Matt Straker walked into Dominic Quartano's office at 8 o'clock on the Monday morning. It had only been the previous Thursday evening, three and a bit days before, that Arno Ravilious had shocked Formula 1 by announcing his unexpected sale and retirement.

Quartano greeted Straker with: 'I have already had Mandarin Telecom on the phone this morning. Their concerns have multiplied, not just about the future of Formula 1 but about our present sponsorship arrangements. The cost – and lost opportunity – will be disastrous if this sport pulls itself to pieces. The Chinese are fast losing confidence. What conclusions have you drawn since we spoke last night?'

'I've gone a fair way into Ravilious's background, and built up a clearer picture of his career.'

Quartano studied Straker's face intently and paused before saying: 'Okay, so what's troubling you?'

Straker had to smile as he felt he had been read. 'There are a few things in all this, sir, that just don't feel right.'

'Like what, exactly?'

'For one, there's a major corporate anomaly. Gabriel Barrus, the American sports tycoon, is claiming to have agreed the purchase of a controlling interest in Motor Racing Promotions.'

'But not an outright takeover?'

'Correct ... as Ravilious's own shareholding has already been reduced to around 69 per cent, having sold a 31 per cent stake to *Dramma Sportivo TV*, an Italian media company, in 2011.'

'Okay, so?'

'I can't, therefore, work out how Suleiman Al-Megrahi can have any claim to be "within days" of controlling MRP?'

'Could he have done a deal with Barrus?'

'It's not impossible ... except Al-Megrahi's statement on Sunday was unequivocal – he only talked in the first person singular – there was no reference to anyone else – no talk of a joint venture.'

'Okay ... but we *do* need to clarify this.'

Quartano noticed the expression on Straker's face. 'What else is bothering you?'

'Ravilious's career has been extraordinary. He's managed to navigate his way through the politics of this vipers' nest for 40 years. He's fended off countless challenges to his position and beaten everyone who's ever come at him.'

'So?'

'The man has always shown extraordinary resolve in the face of most problems, and seems to have dodged any bullet, always finding a way to do what he wanted.'

'And?'

'I don't get why he's selling up and stepping down *now*? Ravilious could have sold up and walked away at any time in the last 10 years.'

'Maybe he's had enough?'

Straker shook his head. 'I'm not claiming I know Ravilious well, as all I've done is read about him. But my impression is that this is a man who lives for the role. Running Formula 1 is his life's work. His religion. His identity. Most people expected Arno Ravilious to die at his post.'

'Okay. Maybe there are other valid reasons for him to be stepping down now ... Formula 1 has been through the doldrums in the last two years ... maybe he doesn't believe F1 can recover quickly enough for him to get out at a better price.'

Straker accepted the point, but not enthusiastically. 'The moment Arno Ravilious realized *any* proceeds from MRP, he was in receipt of more money than he could ever spend.'

'Maybe it's a health thing then? Let's not forget he collapsed yesterday ... most of the press coverage since has talked about a heart attack. What if he's been diagnosed with a serious condition, and was warned what was coming?'

Quartano saw that his younger director was still not persuaded. The tycoon looked serious. 'I've learned to take your hunches seriously, Matt – Buhran, the Massarella affair, French Guyana, Moscow. You obviously think there's something going on here. What are you going to do?'

Of course Straker had known that this question was coming. Without missing a beat, he said: 'Benedict has explained that finding out anything about private companies is a major challenge ... he's also talked me through the challenges of getting access to privileged and price-sensitive information from any company ... he's briefed me about fiduciary duty. I am nervous about overstepping any mark here, causing Quartech any kind of embarrassment.'

Quartano didn't respond.

There was no hint – no wink – no nod.

Nothing.

Straker, therefore, was clear.

'It's going to be a challenge,' agreed Quartano. 'But you've dealt with bigger ones before ... You've dealt with bigger challenges for Quartech.'

So, thought Straker, that was his brief: he was expected to try and uncover corporate secrets of a private company – without breaching corporate ethics.

Quartano said: 'Mandarin Telecom are seriously nervous. I need to be able to reassure them as soon as possible. Please keep me abreast of your progress every six hours.'

SIXTY-SIX

Straker left Quartano's office – returning to his desk – feeling pumped up and daunted in equal measure. His assignment was clear but, in practice, hugely complicated. By the time he got back to his desk, Straker was hit with something that ramped up the stakes even further.

Bernie Callom, Quartech's PR director, had sent him an email with a link to the Sky News website. Callom had flagged it up:

'URGENT. *Watch this bulletin. People in F1 aren't hanging around…*'

Straker clicked on the link. It triggered a video. It looked like some sort of outdoor press conference. From the time bar at the bottom, Straker saw it was quite recent: broadcast at 8 o'clock that morning, BST.

Gabriel Barrus was speaking:

'I am here today to make a special announcement,' said the American sports mogul, standing behind a branded lectern. His eyes were squinting against a near-blinding glare. *'I am honoured to declare that I have just confirmed with His Royal Highness Crown Prince Fahd,'* and bowed in favour of the man standing in Arab dress beside him, *'that Saudi Arabia are to join the Formula 1 family. Under my ownership, Formula 1 will hold its first grand prix here, in two years' time, at the King Abdulaziz Circuit, to be built where we are now standing, on the outskirts of Riyadh.'*

The cameraman zoomed out. The well-groomed Barrus was wearing a dark suit. Beside him was the Crown Prince dressed in a brilliant white abat and a red-and-white chequerboard keffiyeh. The camera zoomed out again. The two men were standing in the middle of what looked like a considerable expanse of sand. Behind them, a heat shimmer seemed to dance like flames in a grate. Barely perceptible in the distance – almost as a whitish strip along the horizon – was a collection of buildings. A sheen of silver covered parts of the ground in between, the mirage reflecting an inversion of those buildings.

At the front of the picture, below the level of the lectern, a sizeable object was covered by a sheet of green silk, which moulded itself to the shapes and contours of what lay beneath.

'*The Kingdom of Saudi Arabia,*' Barrus announced, '*will be a most welcome host and a prestigious contributor to Formula 1. I have been discussing plans with His Royal Highness. The King Abdulaziz Circuit will be the most extensive grand prix venue in the world. It will set a new standard for circuit design and economic stimulation.*'

The two men stepped forward, moving out from behind the lectern. At Barrus's invitation, the Royal Prince took hold of a corner and started to pull the green silk sheet towards him. It undulated as it slid over the shapes before revealing an extensive architect's model underneath.

'*The King Abdulaziz Circuit will be more than a race track; it will be the heart of a vast complex.*'

Barrus reached for a lightweight pole and began to indicate different parts of the display. The camera zoomed in and followed the end of his pointer. '*The complex will have two seven-star hotels, here and here; an engineering university; a range of manufacturing and light engineering facilities; a series of test tracks; accommodation – for staff, students and employees; three mosques; and, over here in this three-square-mile area, a car-oriented theme park. We intend this to be nothing less than the world centre for … automotive excellence, learning, research, development, manufacture and entertainment. This complex will be, in effect, a citadel to the automobile.*'

Barrus added: '*This is a physical representation of the management and culture of the Formula 1 organization under my ownership. I will push Formula 1 as an economic, social and academic force – to embrace the future and its technological development further than ever before. I look forward, particularly with prestigious new partners like His Royal*

Highness and the Kingdom of Saudi Arabia, to seeing the sport reach new heights in earnings, commercial growth and cultural contribution.'

The video clip ended.

Straker picked up the phone to Bernie Callom. 'Thanks for the news item. DQ's tasked me with trying to find out what's going on with MRP. Are you able to put me in touch with Rosa Grant at the *Financial Times?*'

The Quartech PR director scoffed: '*She* won't take part in one of your surveillance jobs, I can tell you that.'

'No, she's written several grown-up pieces in the *FT* about the corporate side of Formula 1 – I want to talk to her about Ravilious.'

'With all the news about Formula 1 going on, she'd have to be up to here writing follow-ups. I doubt I'd even get through, let alone be able to get you any time with her at the moment.'

Straker replied: 'Between us – and Ziebart Blauman – we'd have to have some clout, surely – some chance of getting her attention?'

'Let me talk to Benedict; I'll see if we can't work something out.'

Straker realized this situation was going to be fast-moving. With Barrus's press conference, he felt the urgency of his task even more. He went back over the notes he had made from the Ziebart Blauman report. A thought struck him.

He *had* missed something.

There was another entity, heavily exposed to Formula 1 and Motor Racing Promotions, whose involvement was deep, not least as they had gone to the trouble of filing an injunction against the sale of MRP: Frankfurt Capital. Their perspective on all this would *have* to be telling. Straker wondered on what basis he could ever get the chance to meet the German bank and ask them questions.

He thought about making a direct approach, but then discounted the idea: he was a complete unknown, and barely involved in Formula 1 enough to have any credibility. Tahm Nazar might have some clout as a Formula 1 team boss, but possibly not enough from a corporate perspective to prompt a meeting. Because Frankfurt

Capital's involvement was finance related, perhaps he could get Benedict Wasserman at Ziebart Blauman to front him, but that might be seen as an enquiry from a rival investment bank and make Frankfurt Capital cautious. Straker concluded that any approach needed to be from a heavyweight. And that could only be one person.

He spent ten minutes drafting an email to his chairman and then half an hour composing a suggested wording Dominic Quartano might use to approach Frankfurt Capital. Picking up the phone, Straker rang Jean, the tycoon's PA to explain what he was sending up.

Quartano responded within twenty minutes, blind copying Straker in on his email to Hanfried Von Wittelsbach. With only a few minor alterations, Quartano had used the core of Straker's draft.

A matter of minutes later Straker was copied in on a second email from Quartano. This one was to someone called Amelie Hesse. The name didn't mean anything to him. As Straker looked at her email address, though, he realized contact with Frankfurt Capital had been made. In the second email, Quartano stated that his representative, Matt Straker, would make the arrangements to travel to Germany at Frankfurt Capital's earliest convenience.

Straker's approach had worked.

He was in.

Straker's phone beeped again.

A text had just come in from Dominic Quartano. All it said was: 'Take the jet.'

Straker followed up directly with Amelie Hesse to set the arrangements. He got the immediate impression that he was onto something. The Frankfurt Capital investment officer was offering to meet him at any time from that afternoon onwards: yet another indication of extraordinary urgency.

Liaising with Quartano's PA, Straker found the Quartech Falcon was available and on the ground at Northolt. He arranged to meet with Hesse at 5 p.m. that afternoon.

The Quartech Falcon covered the distance from the west London airport to Frankfurt in just under an hour and a half. A car was waiting for him. Straker headed straight for Frankfurt Capital's offices. It wasn't long before his car was turning into the end of Kaiserstrasse. And that was when Straker saw the first signs.

At the far end of the street, a police cordon had been set up, around the entrance to one of the buildings. A host of blue flashing lights strobed angrily, reflecting off the window glass along the urban canyon. Straker's car slowed.

'Where's the address I'm looking for?' he asked the driver.

'It's up there, sir – where all those police are.'

It was clear they weren't going to get any further along Kaiserstrasse. Straker said he would get out and walk the rest of the way.

But as he walked towards the cordon, he found the street was completely blocked by heavily armed police. They physically stopped him passing.

'But I have an appointment further along.'

'Which company?'

Straker replied.

The policeman seemed to bristle. Putting his hand to the radio on his lapel, he spoke in German over the air. Straker looked over the uniformed officer's shoulder and was able to see into the half-lit mouth of a garage. Inside it were half a dozen ghostly figures, each wearing a white plastic suit, white hat, white gloves and white overshoes. The figures were moving slowly, crouching down, some on their knees. In the middle of the garage was the wreckage of a car.

Straker asked himself if it was a BMW – an i8? Its windows had been blown out. Its roof, too. The scissor doors were missing. Its bonnet, now a gaping hole, was edged with jagged, ripped metal where the engine and front wheels had been blasted away. Even at that distance, from outside the building, Straker could smell the sharp, acrid smell of burnt plastic and rubber. He had seen all too many scenes like this in Kabul and Basra; he didn't expect anything like this in Germany.

The policeman waved him through.

Straker passed through the cordon and walked towards the main entrance.

Five minutes later he was shown to the top floor of the Frankfurt Capital building. As he emerged from the lifts, Straker was taken aback. Two men were standing on either side. Dressed in black, they wore body armour and webbing: balaclavas covered their faces. Each man carried a Glock 17 pistol; the other weapon Straker recognized immediately as a Heckler & Koch, and, with only one glance, was pretty sure they were MP7s. He didn't catch sight of any insignia on the men's uniforms, but he would have sworn they were GSG9. What the hell were they doing there? Did their presence have anything to do with the wrecked car in the garage?

Straker was greeted by a well-turned-out middle-aged woman with dark hair and brown eyes. She was doing everything she could to suggest there was nothing untoward going on. 'Colonel Straker?' she asked.

He nodded and offered his hand.

'Amelie Hesse. Count Wittelsbach will see us now.'

As Straker walked into the chief executive's office, several synapses sparked like fireworks. He was looking at a 60-year-old man with white hair, a powerful face and no-nonsense eyes – whom he recognized instantly. This was the unidentified man he'd seen in the photographs having that altercation with Ravilious in the Ferrari garage at Silverstone on Saturday. Straker had another strong sense that he might be onto something.

'Colonel Straker, come in ... please excuse our little distractions.'

'What's been going on?' he asked.

Wittelsbach gesticulated dismissively with his hand before indicating a seat. 'A little inconvenience, I fear. Let's not allow that to distract us. Now, Colonel, I gather from Mr Quartano, of whom I am a great admirer, that you wanted to discuss the goings-on in Formula 1?'

'Thank you, for seeing me, sir, ma'am. I come with my chairman's compliments and our gratitude for this chance to meet. I'm keen to point out that I do not wish to pry into your affairs, and to state that everything we discuss will be held in the strictest confidence – save that I would like your permission to report back to Mr Quartano and some of his key advisers.'

Wittelsbach nodded.

Straker continued: 'Perhaps I might start by declaring that we have a mutual interest in the political stability and commercial health of Formula 1. My employer owns the Ptarmigan Formula 1 team, and we currently enjoy the largest sponsorship in the sport's history from the Chinese giant, Mandarin Telecom. Because of recent events, we are in danger of losing this sponsor – unless, that is, Formula 1 can hold itself together.'

'We, too,' said the German banker, 'have a material interest in the health of Formula 1 and so, to that extent, I think we can see our interests are aligned, certainly not in conflict.'

Straker nodded his thanks for the acknowledgement of common ground.

Wittelsbach added: 'So what is it that you wanted to talk about?'

'We would like to sound you out, sir, on Arno Ravilious's decisions and actions over the last 96 hours. We'd be interested to hear what you felt about the apparent bid for Motor Racing Promotions from the Gabriel Barrus organization; the rival claim of control from Suleiman Al-Megrahi; and the possible breakaway consortium of the teams and historic circuits.'

'Such fragmentation is of serious concern to us, and a significant threat to the value of our loan to Motor Racing Promotions. That said, I am afraid, Colonel, we do not know enough about the third-party players at the moment to form a reliable judgement – or to say, with any certainty, how this chaotic situation might be resolved.'

'Would you be prepared, sir, to share the reasons for launching your injunction?'

'Frankfurt Capital,' replied the German slowly, 'were the first outside corporate participant in Motor Racing Promotions. We were well aware of Mr Ravilious's business style, his way of working, and of his obsession, shall we call it, with "confidentiality"? By the standards and style of normal business practice, he is unorthodox, to say the least – but we *were* happy to accept that Formula 1 was not a normal business.'

Straker nodded, offering a half smile.

'We were aware of his attempted IPO through Klyman-Messner,' Wittelsbach continued, 'and understood the reasons why that didn't succeed. We became involved in MRP because we saw real value in the company. We were prepared to lend a sizeable amount of money to Arno Ravilious's business, in order to participate ourselves.'

'Certain press articles, sir, put your loan at 1.5 billion pounds; would that be anywhere near the right figure?'

'Yes, 1.8 billion euros,' said Wittelsbach with a nod before adding: 'Because of the nature of the deal we struck, we expected to play a part in management decisions of the company going forward, particularly given our conversion rights. Since Thursday evening, we have been keen to discuss Mr Ravilious's plans with him, before any deal went any further…'

'I can't claim to know Mr Ravilious,' said Straker, 'but I suppose, then, neither would most of my Ptarmigan colleagues. None of us can understand why he is stepping down and selling out *now* … it appears to be so out of character. He could have sold out at any time over the last 15 years, and at far higher prices.'

'We don't understand that either.'

For the first time Amelie Hesse contributed to the conversation. Quietly, she said: 'We think there are forces at work.'

Straker turned to her. He didn't understand the expression on her face. 'In what way, ma'am?'

She didn't answer immediately, but he spotted Amelie Hesse's eyes flash through the office door to the hallway outside.

Straker was intrigued: what was she was 'saying'?

'Mr Quartano,' he went on, 'is keen that we each see ourselves on the same side. We are not sure yet how, but if there is any way we could be of assistance, he would be flattered if you were ready to ask us.'

Amelie Hesse seemed to have regained her focus.

'We appreciate the sentiment,' said the banker. 'Although I am not sure *how* you could help us. Even so, I am delighted we are now in contact, so let's please keep a dialogue going in future.'

Straker stood and thanked the two directors for seeing him.

Hesse showed him to the lifts as Straker made his way back down through the building to the ground floor. He happened to walk out through the police cordon at the very moment the wreck of the BMW i8 was being hoisted onto the back of a recovery truck.

As he left Frankfurt Capital's offices, Straker found himself saying: 'Holy hell.'

SIXTY-SEVEN

Straker wanted to be sure of his privacy before ringing in. As soon as he was out of earshot of his German driver, he called Benedict Wasserman in the City.

'Oh, Matt,' said the investment banker, 'it's good that you've rung; I've just secured a meeting for you with Rosa Grant of the *Financial Times*. Lunchtime tomorrow. As Bernie feared, it wasn't easy – she *is* flat out on all sorts of Formula 1 stories.'

'How did you manage to wangle it then?'

'Bernie Callom's done a bit of bartering. He's offered her an interview with Mr Quartano.'

'Good grief. That's extraordinary. Mr Q never talks to the press. Thank you, Ben – really helpful. On other things, I've just come out of my meeting with the loan holder in Motor Racing Promotions.'

'Frankfurt Capital … saw you?'

'Indeed.'

'Their seeing you at all is really interesting.'

'I got the chance to question them about their injunction, not least as it would have to say something about their views on Ravilious's announced sale.'

'Did you learn anything?'

'They were pretty cagey. It doesn't sound like they have been consulted by Ravilious at all.'

'Wow, MRP must be in quite a state.'

'They used a phrase I didn't understand, Ben – and was hoping you could explain it?'

'Sure.'

'When talking about Frankfurt's loan to MRP, the CEO said something like: *We expected to play a part going forward, particularly given our "conversion rights"*.'

'Holy shit!'

'What?'

'Wittelsbach used that *exact* phrase … "*conversion* rights"?'

'He did … Why? … What does it mean?'

'Well done … and you were right to notice that … that's *dynamite*.'

'How come?'

'It means they've got a very specific kind of loan,' said Wasserman.

'I don't understand.'

'Okay … in outline … let me quickly explain. Loans can have different characteristics, and can take different forms. As a starting point, a bank can lend what we call "unsecured", meaning that there's no collateral behind the loan – the thing's just based on faith, faith that the borrower can service the interest and repay the sum borrowed out of profits. When such a loan *is* unsecured, and the company can't pay it back or it goes bust, the amount of the loan remaining to be paid back is at risk; the lender might only get a fraction of their money back from what's left after the business is broken up, the assets are sold and the other creditors paid off.'

'Okay.'

'So that's pretty risky,' added the banker.

'Got it.'

'The most secure way to lend,' Wasserman continued, 'is for the borrowed money to be legally attached to – or charged against, as we call it – a valuable asset of some kind: something like a building – an airframe, if it's an airline – or the hull of a ship, if it's a shipping company.'

'Like a mortgage?'

'Precisely. As loans go, therefore, those are the two principal types – loans that are backed by assets and those that are not.'

'Okay.'

'Between those two there can be other arrangements, a range of hybrids. With one such, instead of identifying a specific asset, the lender may be prepared to take a chance on the company as a whole; it might take, as collateral, shares in the company or even shares as repayment of the loan itself. It's quite a statement of belief in the business, though – and there has to be an inherent expectation that the shares will hold their value. We call this kind of arrangement a convertible loan.'

'So why the "holy shit" comment when I repeated what Frankfurt Capital told me?'

'Because it means their loan to MRP is *potentially* a shareholding.'

'So Frankfurt Capital *could* own part of Motor Racing Promotions?'

'If they converted it then, yes; conversion would entitle them to be issued new shares in the company. The frustrating thing, though, is that because it's a private company, we would be hard pushed to know how many shares they might be entitled to. We *can* be sure, though, it would not be more than 50 per cent.'

'How's that?'

'If they *were* entitled to more than 50 per cent, their new shares would reduce – dilute – the existing shareholdings proportionately. They wouldn't have needed to launch their injunction – they could have simply declared their intention to convert the loan and vote their shares against the proposal to block it. When the Frankfurt Capital loan was made, there was press speculation it might have been about 1.5 billion pounds in size.'

'They mentioned a similar amount – the equivalent in euros, at any rate – of 1.8 billion.'

'Well done for getting them to confirm.'

'Does that mean they would have an equivalent proportion of the company?'

'Not so easy to say, sadly,' replied Wasserman. 'It depends on the loan agreement and what the company was valued at when it was arranged; in other words, what proportion 1.5 billion might have been, at that time, of MRP's overall worth. Even so, the conversion is likely to be permissible under certain circumstances, for instance if MRP doesn't honour the interest payments, or when the share price reaches a certain level. But it would be fair to assume that conversion rights are only appealing to a lender if they promise an equivalent amount of financial security.'

'So Frankfurt Capital could be a fairly big holder of MRP shares if they "converted", although they don't seem to have a big enough stake to take control?'

'Perfectly summed up,' said Wasserman. 'Good work, though, Matt – you've just found out a significant detail of MRP's corporate structure that is *not* widely known.'

Straker was about to tell him of the police presence at the Frankfurt Capital offices, when something told him not to.

Straker climbed aboard the Quartech Falcon and made ready to return to England. Having settled in the cabin, he put a call through to Quartano. The tycoon's PA reported the chairman was in a meeting and couldn't speak; she was sure he would ring the moment he was out.

Straker was offered dinner; a sizeable chunk of the day had slipped by without his noticing. He was brought an avocado pear with smoked salmon and cream cheese filling, followed by a chorizo risotto. He hadn't realized how hungry he was.

Twenty minutes later he was dabbing his mouth with one of the plane's embroidered napkins. As Straker's tray was removed, he decided to check the photo surveillance Dropbox. To his amazement there had been over a thousand new photographs uploaded since that morning. Straker was in the process of editing them when his phone went.

Quartano was on the line.

'How did it go with Frankfurt Capital?'

'I've a number of things to report back.'

'Go on…'

'First, I asked them about their injunction. The impression I gained was that they filed it because they were not consulted by Ravilious before or after his sale announcement.'

'MRP is in a fair old state, then.'

'Second, it appears, Mr Q, that Frankfurt's exposure to MRP is via a convertible loan.'

'Good grief,' replied Quartano. 'Well done for finding that out. MRP's corporate structure is even more complicated than we thought.'

'The third piece of news though, sir, is more intriguing.'

'Go on…'

Straker explained the police presence at Frankfurt Capital's offices, the police cordon, the heavily armed GSG9 anti-terrorist police outside the CEO's office and the destruction of the BMW i8 in the garage.

'Good God,' replied Quartano. 'Germany's been having their problems. Did they think it was ISIS, or a local bunch of nutters?'

Straker paused. He wanted to make sure he got the tone of his reply right. 'No, sir. I have no proof, but Frankfurt's investment officer, Amelie Hesse, offered up what I think was a "tell".'

'"Telling" what?'

'It happened immediately after I suggested we didn't understand the timing of Arno Ravilious's sale and retirement, and that his unexpected decisions seemed out of character. She replied by saying: *We think there are forces at work.*'

'What did that mean?'

'Well, sir, that's the intriguing bit. As she said it, she looked fleetingly out of the office door – towards the policeman standing guard outside.'

'Good God, you think someone's putting the frighteners on Frankfurt Capital?'

'In light of Amelie Hesse's facial "tell", yes, sir – I would say she *was* linking the car bomb and police presence in their offices to their involvement in Motor Racing Promotions.'

SIXTY-EIGHT

Quartano's last comment was: 'Who the hell *are* these people? Matt, you've got to find out – but, for God's sake, be careful!'

The more Straker thought about the attack on Frankfurt Capital, the more pivotal he thought the German bank must be to the future of MRP. If the company continued with the injunction, wouldn't that heighten interest in Frankfurt Capital – from whoever it was that was threatening them?

Straker realized he needed to know more about injunctions; he reached again for his phone.

'Stacey Krall,' answered a deep voice. 'Hey, Matt. How are you?'

Straker brought Quartech's head legal counsel up to date with his case and explained what he was doing. 'So a *loan holder* has filed a claim against the sale of MRP going through?'

'Why do you say it like that?'

'I'd be amazed if that succeeded. Injunctions to block the will of the majority shareholder can only come from another shareholder.'

'Even if the loan has conversion rights?'

'Yes, because essentially it's just a loan – it doesn't have any voting rights – until it's fully converted into shares.'

'So Frankfurt's ploy won't work?'

Krall grunted in the negative.

'If this injunction was filed last Friday,' he asked, 'how soon is there likely to be any action on it?'

'Pretty soon – these are normally urgent decisions, a matter of days for a hearing on something like this. I'll check the Business List, see if I can find anything on its current state of play?'

Straker rang off and went back to checking his Dropbox. After more sifting, he found a surprising sequence of photographs.

Judging by their different aspects, these were taken by the two photographers outside Ravilious's house in Belgravia. Arno Ravilious, of course, was still up at Northampton General Hospital. Why, then, were there five large removal vans pulling up outside his London house?

Straker flashed through the pictures: a stream of items had been carried out by the boiler-suited men and loaded onto the trucks.

Looking at the shots from about two hours into the sequence, the removal men started carrying out a very different set of belongings. It looked like they were bringing out upstairs things, starting with a succession of dress carriers, hatboxes and ornate luggage. Then came a bed.

Just one.

How many bedrooms did this house have? It would have to be many. Why would only one bed be carried out? Had he missed any of the others? Or were the removal men just being selective?

If the items being extracted *were* being selected, who was doing the selecting?

He must have missed something.

Going back to the beginning of the removal-van pictures, Straker worked out the trucks had arrived just after 11:30 that morning.

He then clicked through all these pictures in rapid succession. There was no indication of anyone else arriving at the house during that time. Deciding to go back further in time, he went to the very first pictures taken outside the house that day. The two photographers had both been on site by 6:00 a.m., that being the timecode on the first photograph each had uploaded. Straker started clicking forwards. Finally he found something of interest.

A large black car with smoked-glass windows was shown pulling off the street and stopping in front of the gates to the house at 7:30. Reaching for the intercom, its driver had obviously spoken with someone inside. With little delay, the car had been let into the grounds. Straker tried to find any clear photographs of the person inside it.

'Damn,' he said, even though he found a sequence of six photographs showing the passenger climbing out of the rear seat. All he could see was the person's back. It was quite obviously a woman, given the design and colour of the clothes; whoever it was seemed fairly large and, from the way she walked, probably middle-aged. Straker saw nothing of her face. She had walked straight into the residence.

Straker clicked through the other pictures covering the black car. At the timecode of 12:16 Straker's pulse rose.

It looked like three photographs had picked up the departure of the unknown visitor. A figure appeared from inside the house. Large dark glasses covered most of her face and a voluminous scarf covered the rest of it. But just then a double-decker bus passed in front of the camera, precisely when the unknown woman was walking to the car. By the time the bus was out of the way, the passenger was concealed once again behind the smoked-glass windows.

Shit!

Who the hell was that? It couldn't be Mrs Ravilious, could it?

Straker loaded 'Evangelina Ravilious' into Google Images. Pages and pages of pictures appeared showing Mrs Ravilious with her husband – on red carpet receiving lines, at charity events, on various yachts, in art galleries and, occasionally, at grands prix, mainly Monza. From the first image that came up Straker was certain, even with the poor clarity of his own photograph, that it wasn't Mrs Ravilious coming out of that London house. He attached the two pictures he had to an email and got ready to send it. As their descent into Northolt was announced, he called the Ptarmigan F1 team boss.

'Have you heard any more from the paddock, Tahm, about the MRP sale or the rival bidders?'

'No, there's just a load of bullshit and blather,' said Nazar. 'The only bit of news is that we've been approached, again, by the Whittlebury Group.'

'I've not had any breakthrough either. How well do you know Evangelina Ravilious?'

'Pretty well – we don't hang out, or anything.'

'But you'd recognize her?'

'Sure.'

'I've got a couple of photographs here I would love you to see.'

'Fire them over.'

A minute later Nazar was back on the phone: 'There's no way that's Evangelina.'

'I need to know who this woman is. Is there anyone who would know enough about Ravilious to say who it could be?'

'We could try Budge Lambourn,' Nazar replied. 'Do you want me to ask him?'

By the time Straker was being driven along the Great West Road towards Hammersmith his phone was ringing.

The Ptarmigan team boss was feeding back: 'No good. Budge says he couldn't be sure who the mystery woman is from looking at those pictures.'

SIXTY-NINE

To smooth things along for Matt Straker's meeting with Rosa Grant the next day, the Ziebart banker had suggested the meeting be held nearby, somewhere close to the *Financial Times* offices on Southwark Bridge. They had agreed on Sweetings in the City. As the restaurant didn't take reservations, it was decided they should aim to be there early.

Straker arrived in Victoria Street for 12:30. He immediately warmed to the place, getting from it an old-fashioned vibe; Sweetings reminded him of Rules in Covent Garden. White tablecloths covered bar-like tables, which ran down the two outside glass walls, while properly dressed waiters wearing waist aprons greeted him with old-world politeness. In any case, an establishment specializing in fish had to be more sophisticated than most of the eateries in the City. He was shown to two spare places, along one of the bar tables, where a few well-dressed City types were already eating.

At 12:35 a fortysomething woman in a shapeless dark suit, no jewellery or make-up, walked into the restaurant. She moved with determination, her dark eyes scanning the room. They rested on Straker.

He stood as she approached.

Rosa Grant's handshake was firm. He indicated the places he had arranged.

She replied: 'I'd prefer to sit at a table, away from the window.'

They were shown down the steps, towards the back of the restaurant, to a standalone table; before the waiter left, Rosa Grant ordered a Black Velvet.

'You've got to have one too. They're a Sweetings tradition.'

Seeing that she was taking charge, he agreed.

'I haven't got long,' Grant said. 'The Whittlebury Group's press conference is scheduled for 3 p.m. this afternoon.'

This was news to Straker. 'What do you expect them to say?'

Rosa Grant looked down at her phone and scrolled through several emails. 'They've already announced their first Grand Prix World Championship race at Imola, San Marino – 1st of September. We might get to hear what they've lined up by way of sponsorship and TV support.'

'Who are you *expecting* to support them?'

'They'll most likely get support from people disaffected by the status quo. But that won't be the story,' she said.

'It won't?'

Grant shook her head. 'The story's going to be how long it takes for the first writs to come flying.'

'From Gabriel Barrus?'

Rosa Grant's face was suddenly a picture of disdain. 'No,' she said with a shake of her head. 'Suleiman Al-Megrahi.'

'Even though he's not a shareholder?'

'I suppose I shouldn't have expected that much from a marine…'

Straker interjected: '…*Royal* … Marine…'

At his tone, Rosa Grant, for the first time, looked taken aback.

Then, as if nothing had happened, he added: 'I am no corporate expert, Ms Grant, which was why I was keen to ask you for your advice.'

There was an interruption by the waiter as he presented their drinks. Straker took the offered flute from the tray but couldn't make out what was in it. A pale wine bubbled in the bottom half, while the top half was dark brown and opaque. The waiter, seeing Straker study it as if for the first time, explained: 'It's a Black Velvet, sir. Champagne in the lower half and Guinness on the top. Enjoy.'

Straker raised his glass to Rosa Grant; he half smiled, took a sip and immediately uttered: 'Yuk.'

Grant's expression changed instantly. Straker sensed his reaction was being taken as a rejection of her recommendation.

'A friend of mine would love this, though,' he said with a smile, trying to restore relations, 'Remy only ever drinks Guinness.'

The look on Rosa Grant's face changed again at Straker's apparently closer connection to the world she followed.

He put the glass down before saying: 'I would be grateful to know how Al-Megrahi came by his shareholding in MRP.'

As a marginal concession, Grant shrugged. 'He only came by it last week. He bought it from the administrator, when the Italian media company, *Dramma Sportivo TV*, went into administration—'

'So he's picked up *their* 31 per cent…'

Straker was buoyed: a sizeable gap in his understanding had just been filled. 'So that would be Al-Megrahi's premise for litigation against the Whittlebury Group,' he said, almost to himself.

Rosa Grant seemed to acknowledge, somewhat begrudgingly, one of Straker's comments as correct.

'But then,' he asked, 'how does Al-Megrahi have the right to claim that he is days away from securing a further stake in the company – which, he has stated, would give him outright control of Formula 1?'

'Suleiman Al-Megrahi is deeply unreliable – a chauvinist, a cheat, a coke head … why shouldn't he be a fantasist too? Maybe he's gone and done a deal with Gabriel Barrus?'

As Straker walked out of Sweetings, he called Tahm Nazar at Ptarmigan.

'What do you know about a Whittlebury Group press conference this afternoon?'

'It's at 3 p.m., in the RAC Club in Pall Mall. We were invited, but aren't going. We're definitely *not* joining their breakaway series.'

'I'd like to go, but not as anything to do with Quartech; is there any way I could get in?'

'I'm sure they'd say the more the merrier – in any case, it's more than likely to be open to the public.'

Straker looked at his watch. He could just about make it. Luckily, he didn't have to wait long for a black cab – there were several plying in both directions along Queen Victoria Street. As he set off for Pall Mall, he saw his phone had a missed call and voicemail message.

Stacey Krall had tried to ring him: *'Matt, I've tracked down Frankfurt Capital's injunction. It looks like they've filed an Unfair Prejudice claim ... I can fill you in on what that means. Crucially, they HAVE been given the go-ahead for the application – a hearing is listed for Thursday, the day after tomorrow.'*

As the taxi dropped down onto the Embankment to head west along the Thames, Straker rang Krall back.

She said: 'I really am surprised they have been granted any right to claim, though, Matt.'

SEVENTY

Straker's cab pulled over in front of the Royal Automobile Club in Pall Mall. A small crowd of people had formed around the entrance; a number of photographers were waiting to catch some of the more well-known Formula 1 figures as they arrived.

In front of the main door of the RAC, two liveried members of staff filtered the flow of strangers. Straker explained he was there for the Formula 1 conference; to his relief they invited him straight in.

This was London clubland at its finest.

He walked across the magnificent ovoid vestibule, which reached up past the columns around the first floor gallery to the domed sky-light two floors above him. Other new arrivals were streaming deeper into the building. He and they entered the sizeable lounge. This room, too, reached up two floors to the ceiling. An exhibition stage had been erected at one end of the long thin room and was lit by spotlights. Flanking it were two large panels for projecting closed-circuit TV images of the speakers or video footage. Set at the front of this space was a table, with three chairs, and a lectern to one side. An unfamiliar logo, bearing the name World Championship Motor Racing Series, was prominently displayed in three different places. Thirty rows of chairs stretched back from the stage.

By three o'clock, every seat was taken – the room was packed.

As the lights lowered and the spotlights brightened, Lord Lambourn appeared from the side of the room, leading out three other figures. They were received with a substantial round of applause.

'Ladies and gentlemen, thank you for coming,' opened Lambourn, his air of welcome as easy as if he were offering a guest a drink in his own home. 'While my friends beside me today need no intro-duction, I will out of courtesy present them to you. I am delighted to welcome Brad Margesson, the promoter of Watkins Glen in the

United States; Seve Montesino, the new team principal of the Massarella Formula 1 team; and Mr Avel Obrenovich, the owner and chief executive of Obrenovich Oil and Gas, Massarella's owner and principal sponsor.'

The room offered the three men another round of applause.

'It is of course a sad reason we need to be meeting at all, particularly as the man who has done so much for Formula 1 is fighting for his life after his collapse on Sunday. I would like everyone to know that we hold Arno and Evangelina Ravilious very close to our hearts at this difficult time for them both.'

There was a further ripple of applause.

'The truth is that we don't know what the current state of play is with Motor Racing Promotions. Last Thursday, Arno stated his intention to sell what is effectively the commercial heart of Formula 1, as well as his intention to retire. This came as a surprise to us all. There has been no clarification, no detail, on whom he is selling to and who is likely to be running F1 from now on. Unfortunately, we have major reservations about the two apparent bidders who have since emerged for MRP.'

Lambourn said tonelessly: 'We regret to say that we could not see the sport under Suleiman Al-Megrahi being anything other than fractious and unharmonious. Sports organizations are notoriously political. We could not see Formula 1 being run by someone who is considered to be a political troublemaker. We don't see MRP thriving in those circumstances, and such a state of affairs can only be described as business critical by those of us who run teams. We rely heavily on the way the commercial rights are managed and the revenues that they generate.

'The other apparent claimant,' Lambourn went on, 'is Mr Gabriel Barrus the Third, for whom we have huge admiration. He is one of the most successful businessmen in sport since Mark McCormack – but we feel he is precisely that ... a businessman. He would, undoubtedly, drive the sport to make more money, and we have to acknowledge that his proposed tie-up with Saudi Arabia is hugely impressive. We understand the fees they are expected to pay are eye-watering, which – via the Concorde Agreement, of course – would in part trickle down to us. But,' Lambourn added, with a hint of apology in his voice, 'there is a factor involved with the Saudis that Mr Barrus has *not* mentioned. Under Saudi law, women are forbidden from driving … motor cars…'

There were murmurs around the room.

'One of our sport's greatest stars is a woman Formula 1 driver. We would like to know where that would leave Remy Sabatino? I'm not sure being a team owner vests me with the right to take any kind of moral stance, but I *can* be proud of the fact that Formula 1 enables a woman to compete on equal terms with a man. I think, however, that all of us *are* qualified to safeguard the principles and essence of our sport. On that basis alone, we would find it unacceptable that Formula 1 could race in a country whose government prevented one of our drivers from racing. At the very least it would render the F1 season unequal. I notice Mr Barrus has not been challenged on this; it would be a shame if Formula 1 was run in such single-minded pursuit of profit that the fabric of the sport might be damaged in the process.

'Ladies and gentlemen, the Whittlebury Group was formed to make sure the 80-year heritage of elite open cockpit, open wheel racing is preserved. If one distils Formula 1 down to its atomic elements, it is relatively uncomplicated. It is composed of its drivers, its cars and its racetracks. By launching the World Championship Motor Racing Series, the WCMRS, we intend to focus on and celebrate the core of what makes this sport unique and what makes it one of the most exciting in the world. We believe that the Whittlebury Group, comprised of teams and circuits, is innately best placed to recapture and reinstate the spirit of Formula 1.'

With a flourish, Lambourn said: 'That is the rationale for our existence. Now I would fully expect you to ask, if we are to break away cleanly, how we are going to fund ourselves? That is the reason for our being keen to talk to you today. We are announcing a backer who has undertaken to secure our future.'

A murmur of commendation came from the room.

'We are all delighted that we will be supported by a sponsor who shares the same passions we do and who wants to see the perpetuation of the core values of our sport. We are proud to announce that Formula 1's proven friend, Avel Obrenovich – having sponsored the Massarella F1 team for eight years and supported the Moscow Grand Prix – has undertaken to be our financial guarantor.'

A substantial round of applause broke out across the room.

The Russian oligarch, a man who famously shunned the limelight, rose from his chair on the stage. He was a figure in his mid-sixties with a markedly angular face. Obrenovich's forehead, nose and chin all seemed to protrude to a common point, while his receding hairline created a sizeable bald patch over the crown of his head. What hair he did have, to either side, was long and grey. He scanned the room briefly, the glare of the spotlights causing his eyes to look particularly beady, before he sat down again.

'Avel has offered to underwrite the entire project,' Lord Lambourn went on, 'until such time as we establish ourselves and can attract a new family of sponsors who wish to align their brands with our values.'

Lord Lambourn was about to ask for questions when the conference was suddenly brought to an end.

An alarm rang out...

Shattering the quietness of the room.

The double doors set in the centre of the long side of the lounge then burst open.

A man in a dark, formal three-piece suit with gold trim around his collar barged in. He swiftly moved to the left of those doors and threw a number of switches on the wall. The room's main lights burned brightly.

'Ladies and gentlemen!' he said loudly and urgently.

'Is something wrong, Jerry?' Lambourn asked.

'Yes, my lord,' replied the club steward, as he strode across the room – squeezing himself between two rows of seated guests towards the heavy curtains on the opposite long wall. Pulling them violently back in one sweep, he banged his hand down on the grand door handles of the large French windows and pushed them wide open to the outside.

Turning back to address the room, the club steward said: 'Ladies and gentlemen, I would ask you please to evacuate the club immediately, taking refuge out here in the garden. As quickly as you can. I am obliged to tell you that we have received a bomb threat. The police are already on the premises and taking maximum precautions. For your own safety, I would please ask you to make your way into the garden – without delay.'

Noise emanated from around the room as people climbed to their feet. With an air of restrained panic they hurried towards the doors.

Matt Straker, sitting at the back and on the garden-side of the room, quickly got up and pulled back another pair of curtains; he went to open one of the other sets of French windows to prevent a bottleneck. The club steward had moved quickly to do the same with the third set at the other end of the room.

Gravel crunched underfoot as the attendees moved away from the building, soon spilling out into the manicured garden to the rear of the club – under the elegant gazebo, and between the potted trees and bushes.

Expressions of alarm were written on the faces of the guests.

Above the gentle rumble of traffic that could be heard out there, came the timbre of a familiar voice:

'Dear friends,' said Lord Lambourn, all the more reassuringly for his hands-in-the-pockets style of delivery and tone. 'Since we are all still here, and we obviously haven't got anywhere to go, I was wondering whether you might have any questions about our new series?'

The bomb alert remained in place for quite some time.

Straker, along with the other attendees of the conference, was only allowed to leave the RAC Club two hours later. He made his way back to Cavendish Square. As he walked away, he wondered whether that had been a random threat – one of those things to be endured in the post Arab-Spring-ISIS world – or whether this was too much of a coincidence? No information was given on whether anything bomb-related had been confirmed at the club. But what if the police or bomb squad *had* found something?

More pertinently, what if there were a link between the threat of this bomb and the one that had gone off in the garage under the offices of Frankfurt Capital in Germany?

Straker was frustrated he had no status that would enable him to question the law enforcement agencies and get official answers. He wouldn't be able to resolve his concerns without new information; reluctantly, he decided he had to park this line of thought for the time being.

Trying to be productive, he cast his mind back to the last material step forward in his investigation – his conversation with the *Financial Times* journalist. She had helped explain one piece of Al-Megrahi's claim to be a shareholder in Motor Racing Promotions: his picking up a 31 per cent stake in MRP from the *Dramma Sportivo TV* receiver. That had sounded plausible. But where, then, had Al-Megrahi's further stake in the company come from?

SEVENTY-ONE

As Straker crossed Oxford Street, his eye was caught. Outside a newsagents was a display board and dispenser for the *London Evening Standard*. It showed a notice written in the paper's characteristic felt-tip-pen-like font:

'BARRUS'S F1 INSTITUTIONALLY SEXIST'

Straker took a copy off the newsstand. Unfolding it, he saw a picture of Gabriel Barrus; it looked like it had been taken during his press announcement in the desert that morning. The accompanying text, though, was a report of the Whittlebury Group's conference at the RAC Club. There was no reference to the bomb scare, so this must have been filed during the early part of that meeting. Its first paragraph said:

> 'REMY SABATINO, THE MOST SUCCESSFUL FEMALE F1 DRIVER, would be barred from competing in one of the Formula 1 season's motor races if Gabriel Barrus's deal with Saudi Arabia goes ahead. The questionable Middle East kingdom, a long oppressor of women's rights, would apply the same ban on women driving to the grid of a Formula 1 race if that country hosted its own grand prix.'

Straker had to smile at the Formula 1 politics behind this article. For all his old-world charm and chivalric behaviour, Lord Lambourn had just fired a sidewinder into Gabriel Barrus's campaign. He had raised the issue of gender during a press conference – held in one of the cultural bastions of the old world – to make an irrefutable point aimed entirely at the new. Scanning the rest of the article, Straker saw the *Evening Standard* had sought quotes from numerous women's groups and prominent feminist politicians. He smiled again. He'd wager most of those people had never given Formula 1 a thought before now, yet here they were readily jumping onto an obvious political bandwagon.

Having been delayed by the bomb scare, Straker got back to his desk much later than he expected. But the walk back had given him time to think and plan his possible next steps. He went straight for the notes he'd made while reading the report on MRP and picked up the Ziebart Blauman's document again to study the sources they had used, set out in its index and bibliography. He was looking for a name that had popped up in numerous places – in connection with a BBC Television documentary: *Panorama*'s exposé of Formula 1: *Cutting Corners*. This was the investigative programme that had made assertions of impropriety at the time the EU's proposed tobacco advertising ban was delayed. One of Straker's thoughts suggested it might be worth knowing more about the people who'd made it.

He rang Bernie Callom in Quartech's PR department.

'I don't know anything about that programme,' replied Callom. 'But leave it with me – I'll make some enquiries.'

Straker returned to the latest uploads from his photo surveillance. A further 800 or so pictures had been sent in. After the incident of the removal vans in yesterday's batch, Straker was keen to study any photographs taken at the other Ravilious house in Oxfordshire. Might something similar have been happening there?

As he went for one of the files, he saw the uploads from Biggin Hill were mounting up too: his photographers in Kent were being kept busy. Straker realized he would not have the opportunity to scrutinize all these himself. He needed to speed up this process.

'Karen,' he said to his assistant, 'from now on, I'm going to need you to sift the pictures that have been uploaded. Could you weed out those that aren't clear or don't show enough of anything to help us identify people, planes or other happenings?'

'Okay, Matt – but I'm not going to know any of the people in them.'

'That's okay. We have a growing list of people we now know to be involved. Perhaps, as a start, you could put together an image directory of these as a reference. We're looking for senior people at the FIA, MRP, any of the team bosses, any of the key circuit owners – as well as, obviously, Gabriel Barrus, Suleiman Al-Megrahi and Evangelina Ravilious. I'd imagine there'd be no shortage of pictures of each of them on the web. Then, for those with whom you can't make an obvious match, you could send them on to the identification committee.'

Just before Straker was ready to leave for the day, Bernie Callom rang with news. 'I've got hold of your documentary producer for you.'

'Thank you.'

'He's called AT McGuire. He's an independent but does a lot of work for *Panorama* and the BBC. I've spoken to him. He'll see you for a lunchtime bite tomorrow, but only if you go to him, I'm afraid – says he's very short of time.'

The following morning Straker was driven out of London in the Quartech Mirage along the A40 to Iver Heath, arriving at his destination by 11:30. Pulling up to the main gates, he could see the Pinewood Studio complex looming before him. The car drew up to the grand entrance booth. After some confusion and several inward phone calls to the studios, the security guard acknowledged the meeting and gave his driver directions:

'You're heading for TV Two, driver, off Broccoli Road – next to the 007 Stage. When you've dropped your gentleman off, you can wait in P1 – in the North Car Park – just over there.'

They pulled forward under the roofed entrance.

Straker alighted at the specified TV studio.

Forty minutes later AT McGuire appeared from within, 20

minutes after their appointment. The TV producer wasn't exactly what Straker expected. AT McGuire looked more like an out of work geography teacher. From Straker's Google findings, though, he was aware of McGuire's considerable career in TV and films.

'I'm in the middle of an edit, so I've only got time to grab a sandwich, I'm afraid,' said McGuire, as he turned and walked back into the building.

The two of them made their way down a painted breeze-block corridor. Large pictures of well-known TV faces were spaced along the walls down each side. McGuire stopped, opened a door and showed Straker into a dimly lit production suite. Inside, he was met with a bank of television screens, a mixing desk and two people working.

At the back of the suite was a sofa and a low coffee table illuminated by a solitary spotlight set in the ceiling. A plate of sandwiches and a couple of cans of fizzy drink had been laid on. McGuire invited Straker to sit as he ripped the cling film off the tray.

'You wanted to talk about Arno Ravilious?' McGuire said through a mouthful of sandwich.

'I do, thank you,' said Straker, 'particularly about the documentary you made – *Cutting Corners* – the one in which you exposed the Formula 1/tobacco ban scandal at the European Union.'

'Fat lot of good it did me,' he said, biting another chunk of sandwich. 'I got my arse sued big time. Had to sell my house – and was forced to declare bankruptcy – because of it.'

Straker's eyes widened. That hadn't been mentioned anywhere in the Ziebart Blauman report, or online.

'Good God,' he said, 'Ravilious sued you?'

SEVENTY-TWO

A harassed-looking man barged in through the doors with a set of headphones hanging around his neck. Carrying a wad of papers in his hand, he walked straight over and interrupted:

'Eighty, the writers are having a fit ... apoplectic with the Blair-at-the-Chilcot-Inquiry section. They say you're under-politicizing the scene.'

McGuire said: 'God save me from these zealots – we're not the fucking Crown Prosecution Service.'

'They're threatening to walk...'

McGuire nodded dismissively. 'Sure they are. We've got plenty more where they came from.'

The man started to leave.

Calling him back, McGuire said: 'No, Jack, no – wait – *don't* tell them that. Tell them I'll come and see them in ten minutes.'

The man withdrew.

Straker now knew his time was severely limited. Not wanting to waste this opportunity, he prompted the producer: 'You were saying that you were sued by Arno Ravilious ... over that documentary?'

McGuire's face looked incredulous. 'No, *no* – I wasn't sued by Ravilious.'

'You weren't. Who by, then?'

'Al-Megrahi.'

'Suing you for what?'

'Defamation, can you believe it? How can anyone lose a defamation claim from that crooked son of a bitch? *Any* honest description of him could only paint him as a dishonest scumbag, and yet my barrister couldn't convince a jury – even on the evidence-based facts I was quoting.'

Straker was thrown by this new information. How wasn't this a game changer? Straker, though, now only had ten minutes until he lost McGuire to the agitating writers. He wanted to grab this opportunity. He forced himself to think quickly.

'If I were to find myself up against Mister Al-Megrahi,' he said, 'what do you suggest I be aware of?'

'Everything ... watch your back. Al-Megrahi's the most vicious, driven, self-centred arsehole I've ever come across ... and *I* work in television.'

'Could you help me with something, then, Mr McGuire? Where did Suleiman Al-Megrahi come from? No one seems to have any idea.'

'Please, call me "Eighty",' he said, 'and that's most definitely not true. People *do* know about Al-Megrahi – they *do* know. They're just too scared to say.'

'Really?'

McGuire nodded knowlingly. 'He's a Tunisian, but calls himself Carthaginian – romanticizes about being derived from the Phoenicians – even the Berbers, as in the Barbary Pirates. Who knows? The reality is that he's from a well-to-do family that runs a successful import business.'

Straker looked at McGuire as if to say: so, what's scary about that?

McGuire replied: 'How well do you know Italy, Matt?'

Straker paused and said he didn't.

'I want you to think about the very south, right down in the toe of the boot.'

'Okay?'

'The region of Calabria.'

Straker nodded.

'You've heard of the mafia, I take it?'

Another nod. 'Of course.'

'Well, you may or may not know that there are several different strands, of noticeably different potency,' said McGuire. 'Forget the Sicilian version, the Cosa Nostra. You can forget the Camorra, from around Naples, even though they're seriously harder core – being the group that spawned Al Capone and John Gotti. *Calabria* hosts the most vicious criminal society of them all … the 'Ndrangheta.'

'The what?'

''Ndrangheta – *En-drang-get-ta*.'

'Never heard of it.'

McGuire seemed to tilt his head, leaning over one eye – almost as a warning. 'If you are going to have anything to do with Al-Megrahi, then you had *better* have heard of it. *'Ndrangheta*, apparently, means loyalty or courage – from the Greek word *andragathía*. We don't hear anything about it because the old mafia values of *omerta* rigidly still apply.'

'The culture of silence?'

McGuire nodded. 'Because of *omerta*, the 'Ndrangheta is never talked about in the media, because people dare not say anything about it. Its most high-profile act was probably the kidnapping and ransom of John Paul Getty III, as long ago as 1973. Disturbingly, it hasn't been seen as such a threat since then, even though its power is colossal. Today, it's estimated that the 'Ndrangheta accounts for 3½ per cent of Italy's GDP.'

'That's extraordinary. I take it you've mentioned this because Al-Megrahi's involved with it somehow?'

'There is no proof that he is … While making that documentary, though, it became pretty clear his connections with it are far more than just circumstantial. The 'Ndrangheta's power comes from its huge wealth, principally from smuggling. Calabria is close to the bottom of Italy, and so is in easy reach of the North African coast; their geography has engendered a specialization across the Mediterranean for over 800 years. Today, they are involved on a gargantuan scale. They effectively control the region's main port, the Port of Gioia Tauro, which ranks first in Italy for container traffic and sixth largest around the Med. They move all manner of items through there, with complete impunity.

'Their heyday was back in the 80s, when they exploited the boom product of the age … cocaine. Estimates put it that, when coke was at its height, as much as 80 per cent of Europe's supply came in through the 'Ndrangheta. The money they made was eye-watering.

'In the 1990s, as cocaine use became almost endemic, European governments were desperate to clamp down on the organized crime behind it. The authorities went after the money. Preventing drug money entering the banking system – at all – was their principal strategy; any bank found to be accepting funds without establishing their full provenance was going to receive fines that hurt. Overnight, the drug cartels were faced with a significant problem. They could no longer turn up at a bank and deposit large sums of unexplained cash from a suitcase. Under the new regulations, banks were not allowed to accept cash, and certainly not in the volumes the 'Ndrangheta were dealing in. From that point on, to play it safe, the banks would only accept funds through bank transfers. The cartel's attempts to get their cash-based proceeds into the financial system were blocked. Getting quantities of cash into the *first* bank account, therefore, became their biggest challenge. Once they could get their money into a bank – *any* bank – it could then be transferred, bank to bank, with far lower chances of questions being asked. In practice, by the time any such money has passed through a third account, it has effectively been cleaned ... legitimized ... laundered. *This* is where we come onto the possible involvement of Al-Megrahi in the 'Ndrangheta.'

'Okay.'

'Tunis, as one of the closest points to Italy along the southern Mediterranean coast, has always been one of the 'Ndrangheta's principal smuggling routes from Africa into Europe. Somewhere, and at some time, Suleiman Al-Megrahi must have come into contact with the 'Ndrangheta – done some work for them – run errands for the society, or something. It appears he started doing more and more, earning their trust ... I have it on reasonable authority that, despite being very unusual for a non-Italian, he rose to the rank of *Quintino*.'

'Which means?'

'A very senior figure in the society – *Quintino* is thought to be one down from the *Capobastone*, the boss. It seemed that Al-Megrahi emerged after the very bloody Second 'Ndrangheta War, which ended in the early 1990s. To safeguard the peace, the warring families set up a commission – *La Provincia*. I was told Al-Megrahi was appointed to this body as something akin to the 'Ndrangheta's treasurer, although I doubt they'd ever use such corporate titles. Apparently, trying to get the drug cartel's dirty cash into the financial system fell on him.

'Al-Megrahi, though, is something of a genius,' said McGuire. 'He managed to work out a brilliant way to launder the 'Ndrangheta's cocaine money, and on an industrial scale. He needed a legitimate front, a business that would not arouse suspicion as a handler of cash desposits. So he focused on buying ordinary, middle-market seaside hotels around the Mediterranean – which he immediately declared were casinos. Incidentally, I found no trace of his first five "casinos" ever having been awarded a gaming licence; as far as I know, they were never applied for. We are, after all, talking here about a branch of the mafia, so I imagine any local official or busybody poling up and asking too many questions probably found themselves either bought off or dead. Why, though, did he go for hotel/casinos? Because they could be used as a perfect money-laundering entry point:

'Hotel guests, anywhere, frequently pay for hotel rooms in cash; but the critical element is that no one would question the idea of punters in a casino buying their chips with cash. With the takings from the accommodation and the casino's vig – vigorish, the house's cut – a business of that kind would, on a daily basis, be expected to be taking sizeable quantities of cash. A bank, therefore, would be far less likely to question such an entity on where its large cash receipts were coming from. Hey presto, those cash deposits became the cartel's – unchallenged – entry point into the banking system. And how easy would it be to inflate the number of punters they had, the number of chips they bought – or how much their punters were losing at the tables or in the slot machines? Meaning that volumes of cash could therefore be expanded. Sackfuls of cocaine money could simply be poured into the *caisses* of those casinos. The 'Ndrangheta had created for themselves an ability to feed God knows how much dirty cocaine money into the casino coffers, and then pay it straight into their unsuspecting bank account.

'But then, to legitimize these hotels, Al-Megrahi latched onto the awakening in the 1980s and '90s of the obsession with designer labels. Soon, he applied his genius for "brand". First of all, he decided on a name as the front for the 'Ndrangheta's chain of hotel/casinos, calling it after his region of Italy – Calabria – to invoke the same exoticism of other regional names like Tuscany, Umbria and Lombardy. Next, he saw the glamour of the world of Formula 1, and set out to harness it for his own ends. He went as far as buying a backmarker Formula 1 team that had been on the verge of going bust – and changed *its* name to Calabria.

'Apart from the branding potential, just think for a moment about the operational aspects of a Formula 1 team... the organization is global – it crosses borders – it shifts huge amounts of equipment and material – in big trucks and freight planes. Can you imagine a better cover for moving supplies of drugs around? But Al-Megrahi had designs to extract far more from Formula 1 than just logistics. He had a much more sophisticated plan.

'Spending millions on building his team, he was brilliant at creating an eye-catching lifestyle around the Calabria team. Lavish hospitality – huge parties – A-list celebrities – beautiful people. Calabria became *the* name to be associated with for the affluent and the people who wanted to be thought of as affluent. But then he backed up all this presentation with substance.

'He started hiring the best people from the pit lane – managers, designers, drivers – even sourcing engines from Ferrari, for heaven's sake. And so, surprise – surprise, his Calabria cars started to perform. Al-Megrahi won the Constructors' Championship in only his second year, making Shauni Brannigan World Champion. That success created an even bigger awareness and buzz around the Calabria name, associating the brand with elite achievement and international high-end acceptability. Before long, the Calabria brand was legitimized.

'Al-Megrahi had managed to engineer the perfect, vertically

integrated cover for a drug cartel. It's hard not to credit him with a remarkable flair for organization, marketing and brand.'

'And Calabria ... now?'

'As you no doubt know, it doesn't have the F1 team anymore, but it still has its hotel and casino chain. Calabria have since expanded big time into real estate, owning a huge portfolio of properties all over the world. Also, as the sums of money they deal in have grown, they have needed bigger ways of moving funds around. Their latest venture is leasing substantial assets that can move – so financing ships, aeroplanes, et cetera. The idea, here, is that they can fund a substantial asset in one place and then physically move it to somewhere else and sell it there – for a banker's draft, of course – so that they can then insert their illicit proceeds into another country's banking system without arousing suspicion. Yet another "legitimate" way to move substantial sums of money into and around the world banking system.'

'And what sort of scale are we talking about...?'

'I could never get a full answer during my research, not least because of *omerta*, their silence thing – but also because any published report and accounts for Calabria are only going to be bollocks. Once the 'Ndrangheta gets its money laundered, it doesn't show much willingness to part with any of it in tax! The accounts, therefore, are meaningless, not least as they get round their tax liabilities by having the bulk of their assets off balance sheet. But, from what I gleaned, if they were worth less than 40 billion dollars I would be amazed.'

'And Formula 1 helped them get there.'

'Inadvertently ... yes, it did.'

'So how did the 'Ndrangheta react when Al-Megrahi was disgraced, when he was suspended from F1 – after the Fangate scandal?'

'Not well, except the 'Ndrangheta were hardly likely to exercise their usual remedy.'

'He wasn't dealt with for letting the 'Ndrangheta down?'

'If Al-Megrahi had gone to sleep with a bullet in his ear, it would have sparked feverish press speculation about his background and connections, which could then have tarnished Calabria. The brand Al-Megrahi had created probably came as his salvation; the drug cartel would have had far too much tied up in that name to damage it intentionally.'

'After Ravilious's announcement last week, do you see Al-Megrahi being on the war path to capture MRP?'

'Without question.'

'And there's still enough cocaine money looking for a home, meaning the 'Ndrangheta would have funds enough to back him in buying Motor Racing Promotions?'

'Many, many times over.'

'And, commercially, you'd say there was a good case for Calabria taking Formula 1 on?'

'Good God, yes – even with the internal political challenges of running the sport. The brand enlargement for the 'Ndrangheta would be invaluable, not to mention, of course, the extra distributive cover that a fleet of aircraft that visits over 20 countries a year would offer an organization that has a need to shift large amounts of product across borders. And that's long before you get on to the money laundering and money transferring opportunities. Formula 1/MRP would be Calabria's – a smuggling organization's – wet dream.'

McGuire looked at his watch. 'I'm going to have to go, Matt – I'm sorry. Got to pacify those cock-sucking writers.'

Straker stood as his host rose from the table. 'Thank you, Eighty, for your time. I had been hoping to ask you, though, about the bribery scandal at the EU.'

McGuire wiped his mouth with a paper napkin. Shaking his head, he replied: 'The one thing you need to know is that Yoel Kahneman didn't do any of the bribing. He was completely set up to take the fall for Al-Megrahi.'

'Al-Megrahi?'

'Watch this space – you're likely to hear some amazing things from Kahneman ... and soon.'

'How come?'

McGuire had got as far as the door. 'Ravilious's retirement has thrown Formula 1 and Motor Racing Promotions into play. Kahneman, having been set up, hates Al-Megrahi with a vengeance. The last thing he wants is to see the man who put him in jail taking over F1. Kahneman's about to do a full exposé.'

'How do you know this? I thought he was *still* in jail?'

'He is. Somehow he managed to ring me, last Friday morning … said he's ready to give me the full lowdown on Al-Megrahi, on Calabria and on the whole MRP story. Sorry, mate, I'm really going to have to go,' and with that he opened the door, stepped through, closed it behind him and left Straker standing alone in the production suite.

Straker came away from Pinewood with more images flying through his head than if he had been watching one of the studio's films. If he could rely on what McGuire had told him, he'd just been offered a completely different insight into the world of Formula 1 … a side he had never been aware of.

But, for that matter, who was?

As Straker walked back to find his car, he found himself saying: 'Holy cow.'

SEVENTY-THREE

The following morning, Thursday, was the scheduled start of the court hearing. Straker wanted to be in the public gallery for the Frankfurt Capital injunction; this had every chance of being the crucible in which the next act of the MRP takeover could take place, and he was anxious to see it at first hand. He had, though, no official or preferential pass to be there. Stacey Krall, Quartech's head legal counsel, advised him places would be available on a first-come first-served basis. Not wanting to take any chances, Straker gave himself ample time to make Fetter Lane by 11 o'clock.

Arriving at the new Rolls Building three hours early, his spirits sagged. The streets and pavements around the courthouse were heaving. Media vans were parked alongside the kerb. A crush barrier had been erected around the entrance to the building and hundreds of journalists, cameramen and TV reporters were amassed behind it. Staff working in the building, and other people with business in the courts, had to run the gauntlet of media scrutiny as they entered or left the building, each of their faces studied by hundreds of pairs of eyes – in case any of them might have something to do with Formula 1 and Motor Racing Promotions.

Straker fell in with a gaggle of office workers as they gathered to make their pass in front of the intimidating wall of media.

Inside the modern entrance hall, he saw it was just as busy: were all these people trying to get into the MRP hearing too?

Queueing for ten minutes at the reception desk, he finally spoke to a court official.

'Yes, sir, as a member of the public, you can take a seat in the public gallery.'

'It's not going to be full already with press, is it?'

'Not if they are press, no, sir. *They* can only get in with an official pass.'

As Straker made his way through the ultra-modern Rolls Building, which had none of the Victorian grandeur of the Royal Courts of Justice in the Strand, he saw another mass of people waiting halfway down one of the corridors. Were they all waiting for Court 23? How many of them would fit inside?

Straker milled with them for over an hour before there was any activity.

A court official was spotted through the glass panels of the doors at the back of the courtroom. He was soon unlocking them.

Straker moved forward and, without barging, inserted himself into the group of people moving into the room.

He managed to get inside before anyone stopped the flow.

At a quarter to eleven, all sections in the public gallery were crammed to capacity. As a commercial court, the seating for the public wasn't spacious. Straker found a space at the end of a row, which gave him a side-on view of the courtroom.

Court 23 was stark with no windows. Its decor was utilitarian, with white walls lit by banks of fluorescent lights and furnished with modern office-type furniture, finished in a pale wood-like veneer. It also felt as if the room was configured side on: a raised judicial bench ran the entire length of the long wall, midway along this was a white silhouette of the Royal crest. Directly below it was the judge's chair. Facing the bench, at floor level, were two long rows of tables that also ran the entire width of the room with only a couple of walkway gaps through them. Easily twenty or so chairs were spaced out behind each of these tables. Straker presumed the parties involved in a case would sit there, the barristers sitting along the row nearest the bench.

There was movement in the court. New people came into the room from the corridor. The arrivals made their way to a section of the tables. A barrister wearing a wig, gown and the two white bans from his collar was showing them to their places. Straker studied the party.

Two of the figures he recognized: the white hair and distinguished bearing of Count Wittelsbach; beside him was the dark-haired Amelie Hesse, Frankfurt Capital's chief investment officer.

Not long after that another group appeared, also accompanied by a barrister. Straker had only seen Gabriel Barrus on television, but he wasn't difficult to recognize. Not a hair out of place, he seemed to walk as if he had a smell under his nose while, bizarrely, wearing a self-satisfied smile.

The players were assembling.

Straker anticipated the arrival of the other key contenders? Arno Ravilious? Suleiman Al-Megrahi?

He continued to check the doors to see if either of them was coming in.

Then it happened.

The matador-like Suleiman Al-Megrahi appeared.

Here was the man himself.

If the TV producer, Eighty McGuire, was to be believed, this was one of the world's most vicious and ruthless drug lords – a key player in a $40 billion cocaine drug cartel. The size of such an operation would make it one of the biggest 'commercial' entities on the planet, and yet here he was standing in the heart of the British legal system. Would such a thug, or his people, ever be bound by the civilized solutions such an institution handed down?

Straker waited for the man to take his seat.

But he didn't move forwards to sit at the tables.

Al-Megrahi moved to the back, to sit in the public gallery.

What? What did that mean?

Wasn't he a shareholder? Shouldn't he be at the front of the court-room, fighting his legal corner?

Straker was buzzing.

Keeping an eye on Al-Megrahi, he looked out for the appearance of any party representing Arno Ravilious.

As eleven o'clock approached there was a new arrival.

In among a last-minute surge of what looked like legal staff entering the courtroom, was another face Straker was sure he recognized. Dressed in conservative colours, but still wearing her large fashionable dark glasses, was the striking presence of Evangelina Ravilious. He expected her, too, to move towards one of the rows of tables and sit with her husband's group of lawyers, whichever they were. But that's not what she did.

Instead, she turned and made for a seat in the public gallery. Before Straker could think through the significance of that, it all started. A clerk announced the court was in session.

There was a loud scuffling noise as the packed courtroom rose to its feet. From one of the side doors, behind the bench, a short 60-year-old man appeared with grey hair swept back off his forehead and wearing a black gown. Mr Justice Boorman walked along the raised section towards his chair. Looking out at the packed room he bowed before taking his seat. Proceedings began with the reading aloud of a court notice:

'*Frankfurt Capital GmbH vs Mr Arno Ravilious,* my Lord; a petition for unfair prejudice brought under Section 994 of the Companies Act 2006 to prevent the proposed sale of Motor Racing Promotions Ltd.'

That, by itself, was intriguing: officially, the court was recognizing Ravilious as the principal shareholder and not, despite his claims, Suleiman Al-Megrahi.

Before the clerk had sat down, one of the four barristers – now evenly spaced along on the front row of tables – was on his feet.

'My Lord,' he said in a voice that demanded attention. 'I challenge the grounds of this claim brought by Frankfurt Capital on the basis that it disadvantages my client, Mr Gabriel Barrus. Frankfurt Capital are not equity holders in Motor Racing Promotions. They are lenders. It is unprecedented for a lender to invoke a petition available only to shareholders.'

Mr Justice Boorman looked at the barrister wearily, as if he had seen and heard it all before. 'Mr Bradman, good morning. I am comfortable that, on the basis of the Solitary Share attaching to that loan, Frankfurt Capital has, contractually, been granted such rights. I am, therefore, happy to allow the claimant to be heard.'

Bradman was back on his feet. 'But the disproportionality of these rights, my lord, were never consented to by the other shareholders in MRP.'

'Mr Bradman,' replied Justice Boorman, 'as I understand it, the only shareholder at the time the loan was taken out was Mr Ravilious himself, so he clearly gave *his* consent. The only shareholding since acquired in Motor Racing Promotions is that by *Dramma Sportivo TV*, which has been since acquired by another investor. The rights offered to Frankfurt Capital would have – *should* have – come out during *Dramma Sportivo's* due diligence, ahead of their purchase. I have no reason to see the acquisition of their stake as anything other than consent to the existing arrangements, including the Solitary Share; otherwise, Mr Bradman, it would have to be a case of caveat emptor.'

Before Bradman was given the chance to think about this any further, the judge was addressing the wider court.

In response, another barrister rose to his feet: Mr Denzil Attwell QC, Frankfurt Capital's barrister.

He – quietly, confidently and without any courtroom theatrics – laid out the German bank's claim.

'We are not seeking to harm the majority shareholder's freedom of movement, my lord, or diminish his ability to optimize the value of his company.

'However,' said Attwell, 'my client has not been consulted on what is proposed. All Frankfurt Capital is asking for is to be privy to the terms and conditions of the deal, and to be able to raise concerns – in the expected manner for any corporate constitution – before it is struck. However, my lord, to this very concern, my client is troubled not to see the majority shareholder in attendance today. This petition has been invoked entirely because, hitherto, Mr Ravilious has been unresponsive to my client's attempts to communicate with him. We would ask the Court for comfort that any judgment handed down by your lordship will indeed be heeded by Mr Ravilious.'

Mr Justice Boorman looked at Bradman for a three-beat pause before looking across to another barrister sitting at a different section of the front row of tables. 'Mr Samuelson, might I suggest you address this point?'

A heavyset middle-aged man in a wig that seemed to perch on the top of his head rose and addressed the bench.

'Thank you, my lord. I have already disclosed to the court, and my learned friend, that Mr Arno Ravilious is currently in hospital, having collapsed last Sunday at the British Grand Prix. I have a Lasting Power of Attorney which I have submitted to all the parties and to yourself, my lord. Mr Ravilious has granted that Lasting Power of Attorney to myself, which I am pleased to fulfil for the purposes of this trial.'

Straker felt like he'd been hit by a train.

He looked away from the bench – and the barristers – towards someone in the gallery…

…Evangelina Ravilious…

…Mrs *Arno* Ravilious…

Why, under the circumstances, had *she* not been appointed with her husband's lasting power of attorney? Wouldn't that have been normal?

For the next hour, the barristers rose and sat down as they fought their respective client's corner.

The moment an earlier point was repeated, Mr Justice Boorman raised his hand and said: 'I fear we are in danger of going over old ground. I thank you for your observations and arguments. Corporate governance should not be difficult between consenting adults. From hearing this case, I find that there is no fundamental objection to the idea that Mr Ravilious might wish to enter into a transaction to sell Motor Racing Promotions; as the majority shareholder, he would be entitled to do so. However, I do find that Frankfurt Capital has a legitimate expectation to be consulted in respect of its rights as a shareholder in the company. So, Mr Attwell, perhaps there is an easy remedy to this; does your client have a proposed course of action?'

Mr Attwell rose to his feet. 'My client does, my lord.'

Mr Justice Boorman gesticulated with his hand, inviting the barrister to elaborate.

'My client would suggest, my lord, that there be an opportunity for full communication with Mr Arno Ravilious.'

There was a fair amount of noise around the courtroom.

Mr Justice Boorman looked up and glanced at the people present; the noise subsided quickly. 'Please continue, Mr Attwell.'

'Frankfurt Capital, my lord, submits that an EGM be ordered – attended by entitled parties – the moment that Mr Ravilious feels fit enough to attend and participate fully. My client does not feel a decision of this magnitude, the selling of potentially a multi-billion dollar company, should proceed under a power of attorney when, however learned my friend Mr Samuelson might be, he is not a businessman or conversant with the complexities of Formula 1.'

In turn, each barrister rose to have their say, standing up and sitting down as the arguments were batted back and forth. After 10 minutes, Mr Justice Boorman declared: 'Gentlemen, I have reached my decision. It is the finding of the court that the petition brought by Frankfurt Capital for Unfair Prejudice be upheld and that, by way of remedy, an Extraordinary General Meeting be ordered, chaired by Mr Arno Ravilious, at such a time as he is competent to conduct it.'

The courtroom's reaction was noisy, from people on both sides of the case.

With Ravilious still unconscious and in hospital, the result of this hearing meant that the proposed sale of Motor Racing Promotions was now effectively on hold ... until such time as Ravilious recovered ... and who knew how long that would take.

Gabriel Barrus looked particularly disgruntled.

Straker couldn't resist casting an eye across to Al-Megrahi. The Tunisian was smirking. What did *that* mean? Why wouldn't he be disgruntled too – when he was supposed to be taking control of Formula 1?

Straker was baffled all over again.

SEVENTY-FOUR

For the time being, the status quo in Formula 1 would stand – the jockeying for position to control Motor Racing Promotions was set to continue. It restarted on the steps of the courthouse.

First outside was Gabriel Barrus. News of the judgment had already reached the media corps. The moment the American businessman was spotted, questions were yelled across at him. Barrus walked over to the barrier and made a statement:

'This decision is unjust and I have instructed my lawyers to appeal the decision. This injunction thwarts a legitimate transaction. I have a deal with Mr Ravilious – to buy his controlling stake in Motor Racing Promotions – and so this hold-up is an annoying inconvenience. Nothing will stop me from pushing on with my plans to modernize Formula 1. In addition to the Saudi Arabian project I announced Monday,' he said, adding somewhat defiantly, 'I have another game-changing plan that I will now be bringing forward. You should all be ready for that.'

'What happens if Mr Ravilious is unconscious for a long time – or he never recovers?'

'As the court was told, Mr Ravilious has signed over powers of attorney to his lawyer. If Mr Ravilious is not compos mentis soon, I will return to this court and press for the deal Mr Ravilious has legally struck to be honoured, with or without the approval of the minority share- and loan holders.'

Back in the office in Cavendish Square, Straker studied the news coverage of the injunction hearing. He was watching a clip of Barrus's press statement on his laptop.

In the background of the shot, walking out from the courthouse, Straker caught sight of the figure in the hearing that had intrigued him the most ... Suleiman Al-Megrahi.

Why hadn't *he* been represented in the hearing as a 31 per cent share-holder in MRP? And then there was also Al-Megrahi's relaxed expression as the judgment was handed down … what was all that about?

Before Straker could think about this further, his phone started ringing.

'How did the hearing go?' asked Quartech's head legal counsel.

Straker stood up and turned to look out of the window. London appeared gloomy; it was an overcast day with diffuse light rendering the outlook grey. 'The court upheld Frankfurt Capital's petition.'

'Was Ravilious there?'

'No … he was represented by his silk, who holds a lasting power of attorney.'

'And what was the judgment?'

'The court ordered an EGM when Arno is competent to hold it.'

Stacey Krall sounded as if this was not what she had expected. 'The prospective buyer will try to appeal that, he would have to.'

'Has already said he will.'

'Everything in the meantime, then, gets put on hold?'

'It does, which is not what Mr Quartano wanted. For the sake of Mandarin Telecom, he wants a resolution.'

'Does this put your investigation on hold?'

'Not entirely,' said Straker, who proceeded to bring Stacey Krall up-to-date with his new understanding of the shareholdings in Motor Racing Promotions.

The head legal counsel asked him: 'What contribution did Al-Megrahi make to the hearing?'

'Interesting you should ask. It's been vexing me ever since … he was completely passive. Disinterested.'

'Even though he claimed to be close to controlling MRP?'

'I couldn't understand it either,' said Straker. 'I have a strong feeling, though, that Al-Megrahi's up to something.'

'Like what?'

Straker explained the man's background, as told to him by the TV producer, Eighty McGuire.

'Good God, you mean this guy's some kind of mafioso?'

'The trouble is that my imagination keeps wanting to make connections.'

'Such as?'

'I keep thinking about the "mafia" in connection with the car bomb under Frankfurt Capital's office in Germany, and the bomb scare at the RAC Club during the Whittlebury Group's press conference.'

Krall made a sound of alarm. 'Those activities are *not* far-fetched, if you imagine how the mafia might behave.'

'Except I don't want to make assumptive leaps on the basis of imagination, or some kind of Hollywood inference.'

'How can you test your assumptions?'

'Ideally, I'd go to another – dependable – source.'

'And you can't?'

'I'm not sure, which is why I'm feeling stuck.'

'What kind of stuck?'

'There's virtually no transparency in this; I have no idea who would know anything anyway. I'm not sure who to approach, certainly not without giving Quartech away.'

'That part you mentioned, in your conversation with the TV producer – when he said there was going to be an exposé…'

'Yoel Kahneman?'

'The guy in jail?'

'Ah huh.'

'Can't you go and see him?'

'I've been wanting to see him for a while.'

'But you haven't … because you think it would compromise us?'

'No, because he's in jail and my approaches to his lawyers haven't produced a result.'

'Let me have a go – let's try lawyer to lawyer. Let's see if they won't connect with me.'

Despite the court ruling, the scramble for Formula 1 still continued to heat up. Articles were published – from the great and good down to the fan groups – discussing F1's current malaise. Some talked about the rules governing the sport: the 'Formula'. Much was made of increasing the noise made by the engines. Some talked about the sport's commercial development. Some about the scale and sources of the money involved. Others about where that money was going, and where it should be going. The centre of gravity and focus of attention within each article depended on the constituencies or demographics each one was addressing.

Then there were the activities of candidates. Gabriel Barrus gave an interview to the *Wall Street Journal*, emphasizing the business potential he was planning to unlock, evidenced by his prospective Saudi Arabia deal.

Suleiman Al-Megrahi launched his digital blueprint, announcing an initiative to develop the social- and interactive media coverage of Formula 1.

The consortium of the teams and historic circuits, the Whittlebury Group, published their projected dates and emphasized their intent to see Formula 1 return to its golden age. They advocated a return to bigger engines, more noise, more reliance on mechanical grip as well as a return to circuits with character, rather than the concrete clones of the last 10 years. At the core of their message was the aim to provide all-inclusive family entertainment.

Not long after the positive arguments had been made, the competing camps began drawing attention to what they considered to be the shortcomings in their rivals' proposals. Before long they were exchanging brutal attacks on each other.

To anyone observing the sport, let alone trying to make sense of where it was going, Formula 1 was in a state of self-destructive chaos.

The last grand prix before the summer break was run at Hockenheim in Germany. Despite the glorious summer sunshine and weather at the circuit, it felt as though a soul-sapping cloud had descended. One of the legends of the sport was interviewed on the grid. He managed to sum up the atmosphere for everyone:

'Formula 1 has always been political, but we've always prioritized the racing. Fighting for the two World Championships has always kept us focused. Now, we seem to have become even more political – like politicians. Each group is promising us the Earth, always in the name of the sport, when it is blatant the parties are out for themselves. I've never known anything so depressing as Formula 1 this weekend.'

As the jostling for position went on, Dominic Quartano was telephoned daily by Dr Chen of Mandarin Telecom. The Chinese were growing nervous for the future of the sport. Their investment in it was teetering on the edge.

Even the outcome of the German Grand Prix didn't change things.

The moment the chequered flag had fallen, the different camps were back to campaigning, back again at each others' throats.

At least – that was – until 6 o'clock that evening.

SEVENTY-FIVE

As the grand prix circus was starting to pack up from Hockenheim, to begin its summer break, the holding of a press conference was announced.

It was going to be held in New York; at City Hall.

The mayor of New York City, Django Brandenburg, had something to say.

At six o'clock Central European Time, from behind a City Hall podium, the mayor of New York declared:

'We are, today, launching a motor racing first...

'On November 30th this year, New York City will play host to something new; something we are calling the Undisputed World Motor Racing Championship.'

People's attention was caught.

'New York,' the mayor continued, 'is inviting the top eight drivers from Formula 1 and the top eight drivers from IndyCar – the world's two leading series of open-cockpit, open-wheel racing – to compete against each other. The distinction of this race will be striking. They will all be driving the exact same open-cockpit, open-wheel car.

'As is known, IndyCar is already a one-design series. Choosing it as our car would advantage the eight drivers already familiar with it. Therefore, once this season's Formula 1 Constructors' Championship has been decided, sixteen copies of that winning machine will be manufactured. In these identical cars, the 16 drivers will race each other for the title of *the* Undisputed World Motor Racing Champion. They will compete around a circuit created right here in the heart of New York City, in and around the Island of Manhattan.

'The drivers will be handsomely paid for taking part. There will be substantial prize money to the first five competitors. At stake, though, will be something much more significant. The cars, already proven to be the fastest anyway, are all going to be identical – and, to make it entirely random, they will be allocated to each driver by lot. They will be serviced by teams of mechanics in the pit lane – also drawn by lot. Everything will be unfamiliar to everyone – so equal for all. The *only* variable on the track, therefore, will be the skill of the driver. The Undisputed World Motor Racing Championship will live up to its name. The winner will *not* be the driver in the fastest car. The winner of this race will, unquestionably, be the fastest *driver*. For the first time in history, there will be no technological advantage … one car to another … one driver to another.'

Mayor Brandenburg went on to explain the format:

'There will be a limited practice session around the circuit in Manhattan before Qualifying, so the drivers can familiarize themselves with the car. Then, on the same day, the Championship will be run over 500 miles comprised of three races – 166 miles long – each separated by an hour. This, therefore, is going to be all of and the best of … a grand prix … an endurance race … and a *Grande Épreuve*. The winner will be determined by the aggregation of their times across the three races. There will be no in-race refuelling, and no mandatory pit stops. The organizers will be supplying a compound of tyre that will last and continue to perform uniformly throughout the duration of each leg of the Championship. In other words, the drivers will have no need to leave the field of play and will gain nothing by doing so. It is simple: this Championship will be entirely won or lost … out on the track.

'And what a track we have…'

The lights were lowered.

A video of a three-dimensional fly-through simulation of the proposed circuit came onto the screen. It was spectacular. It showed the circuit going past the Plaza Hotel, Carnegie Hall, through Times Square, Central Park and down 5th Avenue past the Metropolitan Museum of Art.

As the lights came back up, Brandenburg concluded: 'Ladies and gentlemen, the Undisputed World Motor Racing Championship will be the ultimate test of racing driver skill. The competition will be like nothing motor racing has ever seen before. We have no doubt it will be spectacular to watch; consequently, we say to the world: Come to New York City and witness it! Come and see – what will be one of the greatest events in sporting history – for yourself.'

Everyone was astonished.

And not just within Formula 1.

It seemed an extraordinary concept.

The journalists in City Hall starting yelling their questions. The mayor tried to calm the room by choosing one at random:

'Why should *any* of the drivers come?'

'Those that don't won't have the chance of showing how fast they are compared to the rest of the world,' said the mayor

'How much is the city of New York spending on this?'

'We're providing the infrastructure and civic support. All the rest is sponsored.'

'By whom?'

'A range of commercial firms.'

'Why are *you* doing something so radical and unprecedented as this?'

'First, because New York *should* be setting the lead with innovative concepts…'

The journalist followed up: '…I mean specifically in bringing Formula 1 and IndyCar together?'

The mayor replied: 'That's just it, isn't it. This interaction is neither radical *nor* unprecedented. Races have been held between these two open-cockpit series – Formula 1 and IndyCar – *before*.'

The journalists fell silent for a few seconds.

'They have, you know,' said the mayor. 'Go and look it up! *The Race of Two Worlds*, they were called. Two contests were held – between F1 and IndyCar – in 1957 and 1958. Both were held at Monza in Italy. The concept, back then, was given a portmanteau name … known and celebrated as Monzanapolis.'

Journalists were clearly being told things they didn't know.

'Crucially,' the mayor continued, 'both races were won by Americans, Jimmy Bryan and Jim Rathmann.'

'What about the unfamiliarity of the cars for this New York race?'

'First, it'll be the same for all drivers. In music, the ultimate test of musicality is the ability to sight-read. The format of the Undisputed World Motor Racing Championship will be the motor racing equivalent. It will test a driver's innate ability to tune into and get the most out of an unfamiliar but known-to-be-fast machine.'

'What about the driver who wins in the Formula 1 car you choose as your single-design standard?'

'What *about* him ... or her?'

'Won't they have an advantage over the other drivers? They'll know the car better than the rest.'

'Oh, I don't think that'll be an advantage at all, do you?' said the mayor. 'Think about it for a second. He or she will be under *more* pressure than the others. If he or she doesn't win, everyone will know it was the *car* that won him or her their title.'

With the next question, the mayor saw his answer as the moment to end the press conference:

'Mr Mayor, you mentioned the earlier running of this Two Worlds Race…'

'…*The Race of Two Worlds*,' Brandenburg corrected.

'…in the 1950s ... Monzanapolis?'

The mayor nodded.

'Do you have a name, then, sir ... for this one?'

'Yes indeed we do,' he said, pausing for maximum effect. 'This race, here in New York, will be known as ... Manhattanheim.'

The prospect of drivers competing to be the Undisputed World Motor Racing Champion finally took peoples' minds off the civil war going on for position and control within Formula 1. In no time, though, people were asking:

Who on earth is behind this?

Speculation was intense. It was concluded, very quickly, that it had to be Gabriel Barrus. The race was in America ... he was American ... with vast sporting interests in America ... and ... hadn't he declared to the press after the Motor Racing Promotions injunction hearing that he would be bringing another game-changing plan forward.

The assumption was reinforced when Suleiman Al-Megrahi went on the attack: 'This man Barrus is clearly no devotee of Formula 1,' he said. 'How can he be – if he's prepared to draw attention away from F1 and diminish the end of its season as radically as this?'

Other commentators were intrigued, but more by the different reaction of the Whittlebury Group, the consortium of teams and historic circuits:

'*As teams,*' responded Lord Lambourn in an article in Britain's *Daily Telegraph, 'we strive to produce the best cars we can within the technical restrictions. So often in Formula 1, the skill of the driver gets overlooked. Either he's only winning because his car is faster, or he is a great driver but his car is letting him down. At the very least, this Manhattanheim format will see the* driver *hailed once more as the true sportsman.'*

Despite the shock of the new, and the media's scepticism of the unfamiliar, press and public opinion were surprisingly quick to form a consensus.

Everyone seemed to get behind this idea; extraordinarily quickly. A true sense of anticipation took hold.

SEVENTY-SIX

At 8:55 a.m. on the Monday following the announcement of the Manhattanheim race, Straker was on the Eurostar heading for Brussels. He had two hours on the train without being interrupted to prepare his thoughts for this strange meeting.

Arriving at Brussels Midi, Straker transferred within the station to the platform for trains to Ghent. Half an hour after that his connection pulled into Sint Pieters Station. He emerged from the Gothic revival building and walked across the tramlines, hailed a cab, and took a short taxi ride through the East Flanders capital to reach the prison in Nieuwe Wandeling. He arrived just before 2 p.m. The Gothic style of this building offered a very different statement from that of the station.

Straker had travelled this far to see one of the men imprisoned following the EU tobacco ban bribery scandal.

Even on the production of emails, Straker's certified forms of ID and explicit written authorization from Yoel Kahneman's lawyers, it took an hour for him to be formally admitted. Eventually, Straker was led through the brutal prison complex to an austere room. Thick bars on the windows. A bare concrete floor. A steel table bolted to the floor. Two button stools, also fixed to the concrete. Across the middle of the table was a steel bar running three inches above its surface; presumably, he thought, as an anchor point to restrain a prisoner. After five minutes in this room on his own, Straker was beginning to feel disturbed. Just the awareness of such restraints reminded him all too starkly of his treatment by the CIA. Colonel Matt Straker was beginning to sweat.

Not a moment too soon the door banged open.

Dressed in an orange boiler suit and flanked by two prison guards, Yoel Kahneman – the former advertising genius, sponsorship director for Worldwide Tobacco and the co-architect with Arno Ravilious of trackside advertising at grand prix circuits – was escorted into the room. Beforehand, Straker had looked at numerous photographs of this man; most had been taken in Kahneman's heyday. They showed him to be tall, boyishly handsome and cocky-looking, not afraid to strut as he interacted with the Formula 1 hierarchy up and down the pit lane and on the grid. Now, in front of Straker, was someone who appeared completely deflated.

Straker moved across to introduce himself when the guards intervened, marching Kahneman briskly away – all but pushing the prisoner down onto one of the button stools. They locked the chain, between his cuffs, to the steel bar across the middle of the steel table. As they did so, Straker sensed there was still a spirit of defiance in the man.

The guards left and the door was shut.

Straker was alone with the prisoner.

Kahneman's eyes flashed as he stared up at the visitor. 'Were you followed?' he asked.

The question slightly threw Straker. He moved to sit down opposite him. 'Who might be following me?'

Kahneman's expression was one of instant derision.

Straker saw it and added quickly: 'No, Mr Kahneman … no, I *wasn't* … followed.'

'Oh, you can't be that sure. They'll be out there. They'll be out there, all right.' His mouth flashed briefly with a smile which was followed by rapid, intense eye movements. 'I don't know why I'm still alive. I don't why they've let me live.'

The man was clearly in quite a state.

It gave Straker cause to think. He wondered how he should question him. He decided on a particular tack and tone. Straker said quietly and deferentially: 'I have come, Mr Kahneman, to ask for your advice … I'd like to know what you think's going on in Formula 1?'

Kahneman stooped forwards and laid both his hands flat on the steel table. 'It's that cunt Al-Megrahi … that's what. That bastard's within inches of getting control… '

Hoping to be encouraging, Straker offered: 'The *Dramma Sportivo TV* holding certainly set him up?'

Kahneman's flash smile reappeared. 'Al-Megrahi's had his eyes on that since 2011, ever since Ravilious sold them the stake. All that shit the Al-Megrahi people have caused DSTV…'

Straker stiffened slightly; he didn't know about this. What was Kahneman talking about? Trying to keep the conversation going, he took a wild guess, following up with: 'You mean … apart from the … union troubles?'

There was a loud noise from outside the room.

The prisoner ripped his hands off the table and tried to envelop his chest with his arms. The chains, checking his movement, clanged as they snapped taut against the anchor point on the table.

Straker fought himself not to flinch. 'It's okay, Mr Kahneman; that was just a door being shut.'

Then, Kahneman tried to raise his arms above his head.

The orange sleeves of the prison uniform fell back from Kahneman's wrists, halfway down his forearms towards his elbows. All across the softer – paler – flesh down the inside of his arms were angry red slashes, scabs and scar tissue. Self-harm aroused considerable pathos, the prisoner's fragility causing Straker deep concern. Whatever Kahneman might have done, his state of mind – which he assumed had been exacerbated since being imprisoned – was punishing him far more than any loss of physical freedom.

'Yoel … help me deliver a blow to Al-Megrahi … something he won't forget.'

Suddenly Kahneman seemed taken by surprise. His face froze. His eyes swivelled to meet Straker's. The prisoner lowered his arms. His whole form began to tremble. Kahneman started emitting a deep sound from the pit of his stomach.

'You can stop him, you know, Yoel,' Straker said.

Kahneman inhaled deeply.

Quietly, Straker asked: 'Are you able to help me?'

He couldn't work out if Kahneman was listening to him. The man in the orange boiler suit wasn't reacting at all.

Straker waited. Very softly, he asked: 'Where have Al-Megrahi's other shares in Motor Racing Promotions come from, Yoel… ?'

Straker paused, hoping he hadn't asked too much.

As Kahneman reached the end of a breath, he lowered his head, bending his body forwards. Into the surface of the table, almost as a whisper, he said: 'Evangelina Ravilious…'

But that was all.

Straker held his breath.

He was desperate to know more.

'How?' he asked gently. 'How does he get his shares … from *her*?'

Another pregnant silence.

'Al-Megrahi's been banging her for years,' came the muffled reply.

Kahneman slowly raised his head. His eyes followed, rising up to be level with the visitor's. They were widening rather than squinting with the stare.

What the hell was Kahneman about to do now?

'Evangelina's divorcing Arno,' he said. 'She'll get half his holding in MRP, won't she?'

Kahneman's hands stopped trembling.

Then he whispered: 'Al-Megrahi's gone and promised to marry her … If she votes with him, Al-Megrahi gets control of Motor Racing Promotions…'

Twenty minutes later Straker was leaving the prison in Ghent. Emotionally, he was spent – and heavily conflicted. He had just witnessed the residue of a broken man. At the same time, though, he might just have learned some extraordinary things for his investigation.

SEVENTY-SEVEN

Because of the prisoner's disturbed state, Straker was anxious to cross-check what Kahneman had told him before he was prepared to accept any of it, let alone act on any of it. He needed third-party verification. The moment Straker was back on the Eurostar heading for England, he fired up his laptop and loaded '*Dramma Sportivo TV*' into Google. Would there be any corroboration out there to make sense of Kahneman's claims and accusations?

Straker couldn't believe it.

Kahneman's assessment, if anything, had been a significant understatement. Straker glanced through the first few references and found a remarkable history:

2011   *Dramma Sportivo TV* acquires 31 per cent of Motor Racing Promotions

2012   Labour union trouble for *Dramma Sportivo TV* – the station is forced off the air in a series of 48 hour strikes; considerable damage is done to relations with advertisers

2012   Studios belonging to *Dramma Sportivo TV* are destroyed in a fire engulfing the station's production facilities, including €10 million worth of equipment

2012   Ten outside broadcast trucks belonging to DSTV all mysteriously catch fire while they are parked at the *Stadio Friuli* for the European Champions League match between Udinese and SC Braga

2013   Dino Quintacelli, the *Dramma Sportivo TV* chief executive, is seriously hurt by a car which rams him as he drives out of the station's TV studio complex. Because of it, Quintacelli is thereafter confined to a wheelchair

2016 DSTV's bank forecloses on the television company's substantial loans. The station is unable to refinance the debt and is forced to put itself into administration

'Wow,' said Straker to himself, as the train sped him across Flanders. On a piece of paper, Straker drew a visualization of how this latest information might fit into his overall investigation:

Suleiman Al-Megrahi buys a backmarker Formula 1 team

Spends a fortune on people and wins the
Constructors' Championship

Al-Megrahi becomes a significant player in F1

Constantly criticizes Arno Ravilious and Motor Racing Promotions

Al-Megrahi humiliated out of F1 for cheating

Dramma Sportivo TV harried and harassed into insolvency

DSTV's stake in MRP picked up from
administrator by Al-Megrahi (+31%)

Al-Megrahi carries on with Mrs Ravilious

▼

Mrs Ravilious initiates divorce proceedings; settlement likely to include half of Arno Ravilious's holding in MRP (+34½%)

▼

Al-Megrahi claims to command a controlling
interest in MRP (31% + 34½%)

▼

Frankfurt Capital (intimidated?) – Car bomb in office's garage

▼

Bomb scare at RAC launch of Whittlebury
Group's break from MRP

Did Straker's suspicions stack up? Over a five-year period, it would seem Suleiman Al-Megrahi had mounted a sustained campaign to threaten, extort, terrorize and deceive. When the totality of his actions were put into context, they all appeared to have a common strand of DNA: more than that, it wasn't that big a leap to see them all pointing to one objective: to secure a position of control over Motor Racing Promotions. More to the point of his investigation, Straker even believed he now had an idea why Arno Ravilious might have acted as he had.

By the time his train reached the Channel, Straker had drafted his report. He read it from beginning to end as the train passed through the tunnel and, emerging back into daylight in Folkestone, he pressed Send, dispatching it to Dominic Quartano. In the covering email, he suggested they should meet as soon as possible, along with Quartech's head legal counsel, Stacey Krall, and Quartech's investment banker, Benedict Wasserman from Ziebart Blauman.

At eight o'clock the following morning the three of them walked into Dominic Quartano's office on the 27th floor of Quartech International's headquarters in Cavendish Square. Quartano, his jacket already off, was waiting for them. He invited them to sit around the large conference table over by the plate-glass window; from there, they could look out over the roofs of Mayfair and see the three Royal Parks surrounding Buckingham Palace, bathed in the early sun.

The chairman indicated for Straker to begin.

'Bearing in mind Quartech's relationship with Mandarin Telecom and the Chinese military,' Straker said, 'my investigation was to try and identify who would be running Formula 1 from now on. My findings have thrown up several surprises. At the outset, it was thought the key player in the scramble for control of Motor Racing Promotions was Gabriel Barrus, as he had been in discussions with Arno Ravilious about buying MRP. I have since found out the new owner is likely to be very different.

'Currently, there are two shareholders in Motor Racing Promotions,' Straker continued, as he handed out sheets of A4 showing his pie chart. 'Arno Ravilious, who holds the majority of the shares with 69 per cent, and Suleiman Al-Megrahi who owns 31 per cent, having bought – more like extorted – that minority shareholding from *Dramma Sportivo TV*.

'Arno Ravilious's operational control of MRP would appear to have been unassailable – until Mrs Ravilious filed for divorce. I have discovered that Suleiman Al-Megrahi and Mrs Ravilious have been involved in a longstanding affair. If the divorce goes through, and the expected 50–50 split of the marital assets occurs, she could be awarded 34½ per cent of the shares in the company. Then, if Mr Al-Megrahi makes good on his manipulation of Mrs Ravilious, she could vote her 34½ per cent with his own 31 per cent – which would result in *Al-Megrahi* being given control of Motor Racing Promotions.

'I believe the reason Arno Ravilious announced the sale of MRP and his retirement last Thursday,' Straker continued, 'is that he had seen what was coming.'

Quartano, who had seen this outlined in his report the evening before, was nodding. 'This is a quite excellent piece of investigative – and deductive – work, Matt.'

Stacey Krall asked: 'But why would he *sell* his shares at such a poor time for F1; there's no way he'd be getting a full price for them?'

'My assessment,' answered Straker, 'is that this was mounted as Ravilious's way of thwarting Al-Megrahi from taking control. If

Ravilious, while still in full control of his 69 per cent stake, sold it to a sympathetic buyer for cash before his divorce was crystallized – on the condition that the new owner would keep Ravilious involved – it would mean that, as far as the settlement went, Mrs Ravilious could *only* get cash. She wouldn't get any shares – because by then Ravilious would no longer have any. It would also mean, most importantly, that she wouldn't get any votes – and so neither, crucially, would Al-Megrahi. And as for the price he got for the shares, a discounted sale would probably be less of an emotional cost to him than losing control of his business.'

There were nods around the table.

'How likely is this sale to go through, now,' asked the investment banker, 'with Ravilious in hospital and the injunction blocking the deal?'

'It's all become a lot more complicated,' replied Straker. 'Ravilious's plan could still work *if* the sale of Motor Racing Promotions happens before Mrs Ravilious's divorce comes through. But if Al-Megrahi is stating publicly that he's days away from controlling F1, I think we'd have to assume the divorce settlement is imminent.

'Which means,' Straker went on, 'the commercial arm of Formula 1 is about to fall into the hands of a drug cartel, led by a man with whom nobody will work. F1's lack of respect for him was evidenced pretty convincingly by the formation of the Whittlebury consortium of teams and historic circuits; their breakaway group was announced only a matter of hours after Al-Megrahi claimed he was taking over.'

Quartano added: 'The combination of Al-Megrahi and the teams breaking away will kill this sport, God damn it. And if that happens, our relationship with Mandarin Telecom is dead – ending Quartech's access to the Chinese government.'

The mood in the chairman's office was bleak.

Straker, having summarized his report, fell silent.

Quartano, Krall and Wasserman continued to discuss their situation and its consequences.

Straker found himself looking down at his pie chart.

His eyes weren't really focusing.

The chart – the shape – the colours – the names across it – soon became a blur.

His mind started fizzing.

Straker almost blurted out: 'I'm sorry … sorry, everyone,' he said, looking at each of them, 'but my brain doesn't always work as fast as I want. This chart,' he said, holding up the ownership diagram, 'isn't complete – it's only reflecting the *known* shareholdings. Something's prompted me to think of Ben's reaction to my discovery at Frankfurt Capital that their loan is a convertible, and *then* to think of Stacey's comment – it being unusual for a loan holder to be granted share-holders' rights.'

'So?' said Quartano.

'So … then I thought: why was that car bomb set off under Frank-furt Capital's offices?'

There was a moment's pause.

'Can you tell me more about convertible loans … could it be pos-sible, for instance, for Frankfurt Capital to have been granted other rights with it?'

'It could,' replied Krall. 'After all, they *were* able to launch that injunction, even though they were only loan holders.'

Straker said: 'Okay, so what if Al-Megrahi *knows* what those rights are? What if they were, somehow, detrimental to his plans for con-trolling Motor Racing Promotions?'

'Like some sort of golden share, perhaps?' offered Krall.

'We don't – and can't – know,' replied Wasserman.

'Okay, but the shareholding split I've got here,' said Straker, 'the 69 per cent and 31 per cent – *cannot* include the shares inherent in Frankfurt Capital's loan, can it?'

'No,' confirmed the investment banker, 'nor can it – as we don't know what their entitlement actually is.'

'But shares in a convertible loan, when converted, are *new* shares?'

Wasserman nodded.

'And the new shares,' Straker continued, 'would have the effect of reducing the percentages of the "old" shares these parties currently hold, would they not?'

'"Dilute" them, as we describe it … yes.'

'What, then,' Straker said, 'if this entitlement was enough to alter Al-Megrahi's shareholding radically?'

'If it pushed him below 50 per cent, of course, that would lose him his "control".'

'Okay … we think he's already speaking for 65½ per cent of MRP,' said Straker. 'What proportion of new shares would be needed to do that?'

Reaching for his phone, Wasserman quickly tapped some numbers into its calculator app. 'If the new shares were more than 25 per cent of the old,' he said, 'that would be enough to dilute Al-Megrahi's shareholdings below 50 per cent.'

Straker nodded. 'And would 25 per cent be a realistic entitlement for the size of Frankfurt Capital's loan to Motor Racing Promotions?'

Waserman replied: 'At 1.8 billion euros, when the thing was set up … almost inevitably.'

'Well, then,' said Straker, 'might that not be it? Might not the possibility of Al-Megrahi being diluted from control justify putting the frighteners on Frankfurt Capital? Might that not account for the car bomb attack on their offices?'

'Good God,' said Quartano.

SEVENTY-EIGHT

An hour later, Straker, Krall and Wasserman were back in the chairman's office, again sitting round the meeting table. A loudspeaker had been set up on the table between them. On the other end of the line was Count Wittelsbach, Amelie Hesse and Markus Lüneburg from Frankfurt Capital.

Quartano began: 'Lord Wittelsbach, thank you for taking our call. I think we've established that we both have an interest in seeing Formula 1 succeed and, therefore, an interest in the health, stability and effectiveness of Motor Racing Promotions.'

'Agreed,' responded the German. 'We are intrigued as to what Colonel Straker's "investigation" has uncovered.'

Straker was asked to summarize his findings.

When he reached the end, Wittelsbach simply replied: 'God in heaven.'

'Does that summary chime with you, Lord Wittelsbach?' Quartano asked.

'Not that we would have ever understood the situation in that way, but it is hard, now, not to see Colonel Straker's conclusions in any other light. I am grateful you have chosen to share these findings with us.'

'It's our pleasure,' replied Quartano. 'We have a question we would like to put to you, but quite understand if you felt it was too intrusive.'

'I'm sure not; please try us.'

Silently, Quartano invited Straker to speak.

'It relates to the convertible rights attached to your MRP loan, Count Wittelsbach,' he said. 'My investigation would be progressed from here, sir, by knowing how many shares Frankfurt Capital would be entitled to if your loan was fully converted – and then what proportion of the overall shares in Motor Racing Promotions that might represent?'

There was a pause down the line from Frankfurt.

The Quartech party looked at each other.

Had they gone too far?

Wittelsbach's voice came back over the loudspeaker:

'Our convertible loan would entitle us to 30,000 new shares.'

Wasserman started scribbling fiercely and punching numbers into the calculator on his phone. Before the German banker said anything more, Wasserman was nodding emphatically.

'That would mean,' added Wittelsbach, 'that if we fully converted our loan, we would be entitled to 27.3 per cent of MRP's equity.'

Wasserman slid his workings across the table for the others to see.

Quartano, reading Wasserman's calculations, said over the phone: 'We calculate, sir, that the converting of your loan into MRP shares would have the significant effect of reducing Al-Megrahi's shareholding from 65½ per cent to 48 per cent ... in other words, it would deny him control.'

'Indeed it would,' replied the German banker.

Straker leant forwards: 'I think, Lord Wittelsbach, that *this* was the reason you suffered the attack on your car in your office garage.'

There was silence over the phone line. The bombing incident had not been acknowledged between them, let alone discussed. How would Frankfurt Capital react to this intrusion into their troubles?

Taking the Quartech party by surprise, Wittelsbach simply said: 'Quite so.'

The German banker spoke further, in an almost confessional tone:

'It all makes sense now,' Wittelsbach continued. 'We were approached anonymously last Friday by an individual offering to buy our loan in Motor Racing Promotions. We could not accept his offer, not least as the caller would not identify themselves – or the organization he represented. It was a derisory amount, nowhere near a market value. The caller then said, with a disquieting menace: "We are going to send you a message ... to help you decide..."'

'What did you think that meant?' asked Straker.

'We did not know at the time. But my car was lost to a bomb in our garage the following Monday…'

The mood in the London room changed, now that violence had been confirmed as a component of the Motor Racing Promotions affair.

Quartano never wavered: 'Count Wittelsbach, we are sorry it's become so unnerving. We remain keen to find a way of resolving this. May I ring you when we are clear on what we intend to do next?'

'Please do,' replied the German aristocrat. 'After what you have told us, I feel we are very much on the same side. I hate to say it, but we have not found Herr Ravilious particularly easy to deal with. But, while we are mindful of safeguarding the sizeable investment we have at risk here, I feel we *are* prepared to defend Motor Racing Promotions against such a malicious attempt to steal it from him by the unsavoury Herr Al-Megrahi. We feel a stand should be taken against coercion.'

After the phone call, Straker saw that Wasserman and Krall were troubled by the revelations from it.

Quartano seemed to deal quickly with their concerns: 'God, it sounds like Al-Megrahi's a piece of work – but we have too much legitimately at stake here to let some low-life get in our way. Thanks to your investigation, Matt, we now know Frankfurt Capital's loan, if converted, would block Al-Megrahi's strong-arm raid on MRP, indeed that he can actually be denied control. Your hunch, that Ravilious was acting out of character when he announced his sale of MRP and his retirement, also looks like being proved right. It might well be that Ravilious had got wind of Al-Megrahi's manoeuvrings against him, and his unexpected move was his way of dealing with it.'

'But, in doing so,' said Straker, 'Ravilious has created a power vacuum within Motor Racing Promotions. He's laid the business open to being taken over by a collection of some extremely unpalatable bidders. Would we all not be better off with Ravilious back in charge?'

Quartano nodded his agreement.

'Isn't there some way we could help him?' Straker asked.

'Who knows if it isn't too late for that!'

Straker said: 'What if we went and talked to him?'

'He's unconscious, isn't he?'

Quartano shrugged.

'We have only been going on what's in the press … might he be recovering?'

'Okay, Matt, it's worth a try. Why don't you go and see if he's in any condition now to talk about this.'

Straker called the boss of the Ptarmigan Formula 1 team. 'Tahm? Who can I speak to at Silverstone – to clarify their medical emergency procedures?'

'Don't know off hand, the team's just changed. Let me talk to Michael Crabtree, Silverstone's MD. He'll be able to steer us.'

'That would be a great help. I'll wait to hear.'

Twenty minutes later, Straker's phone rang.

'Matt, I've been onto Crabtree at Silverstone,' reported the Ptarmigan team boss. 'He's okay to answer your questions direct.'

'Mr Crabtree, thank you for your time,' said Straker. 'I'm keen to know something about Silverstone's emergency procedures.'

Hesitantly, Crabtree said: ' …Okay?'

'Which A&E Department is your pre-identified centre for emergencies at the track … where your casualties are taken?'

'Northampton General.'

'Is that for any emergency, or does it change if, for instance, it's an F1 driver, a member of the public, a VIP?'

More hesitation. ' …The same for all.'

'So the air ambulance that airlifted Arno Ravilious on Sunday would have gone to Northampton General?'

'Yes ... I'm sorry ... why do you want to know this?'

'We have the stability of Formula 1 at the front of our minds,' he said, hoping that such a purpose might satisfy the Silverstone boss.

But by the time he rang off, Straker still felt Crabtree sounded unconvinced.

Suspicious, even.

SEVENTY-NINE

'Northhampton General,' Straker said to himself as he punched the name into a Google map. He saw where Northampton was, in relation to London, and how long it would take to get there by car. A hospital, though, was going to be guarded over its patient confidentiality, wasn't it? Particularly if the patient was as high profile as this? Straker quickly made a decision.

To Karen, sitting across the department from him, he said: 'Could you make up an envelope and some official-looking documents?'

'Any particular theme?'

'Formula 1. Anything with Ptarmigan letter heading – something legal? And a reference to Arno Ravilious.'

'How soon do you want it?' she asked. But when she saw his face, she added: 'Okay, Matt ... ASAP it is.'

Two hours later Straker was heading up the M1 towards the Northampton General Hospital. He was travelling in a Quartech Mirage rather than by train or his own car. He hoped, when he got to the other end, to use this limousine to reinforce the urgency of his visit.

Arriving at the hospital, his car pulled in off Cliftonville Road. Instead of trying to park, Straker asked the driver to loiter directly outside, in front of the main entrance. Carrying Karen's phoney dossier, he marched into the building.

Straker made for the reception desk. Waiting to be served by the youngest member of staff on duty, he said: 'I have an important delivery for one of your patients – Mr Arno Ravilious.'

Immediately he said the name a senior staff member behind the counter turned and said: 'We are not at liberty to disclose the presence of any patient, unless to family members ... Are you family?' she asked brusquely, suggesting she knew full well that he wasn't.

'A business colleague.'

'I'm afraid, then, we are unable to help you.'

'I represent one of the Formula 1 teams, ma'am. I have some documents, here,' he said, as he opened Karen's envelope; Straker partially withdrew some of the papers from the thick dossier, specifically the bundle Karen had tied up with a length of pink ribbon to look like a legal brief. 'The business of Formula 1 goes on,' Straker said, 'and Mr Ravilious, as you might know, is the man who runs everything.'

'We know how in demand he is, and not just from motor racing people. We have to put up with the media too.'

'So everyone knows that he's here, then?'

The senior staff member gave him a look to tell him that she was not falling for that one.

'I'm not a member of the press,' said Straker, sliding the documents back into the envelope. 'What do you suggest I do, ma'am? I've driven up from London to deliver these crucial papers?' he said, and pointed through the glass doors of the main entrance at the official-looking black Quartech mirage outside.

The hospital staff member followed the gesture and then seemed to scrutinize the visitor.

Straker fought to maintain his demeanour, trying not to look defensive.

The hospital administrator seemed to relent. Almost dismissively, to suggest she wasn't breaking any confidences, she said: 'It shouldn't matter, anyway … Mr Ravilious was never *admitted* to the hospital.'

Straker now tried hard to control his surprise. As calmly as he could manage, he replied: 'He wasn't? I thought he came here after collapsing at Silverstone. Do you happen to know which hospital he *is* in?'

She shook her head. 'He was in the process of being brought in here on a trolley – but he never got as far as the entrance of A&E.'

'What do you mean?'

'He was intercepted.'

'*Intercepted?*'

'By a group of men in dark suits.'

'How many men?'

'Half a dozen.'

'What happened?'

'He was wheeled away, across the car park, to a car – a black car, with blacked-out windows.'

'And then what?'

'They drove him away.'

'Did anyone see anything of Mr Ravilious – of his condition – while any of this was happening?'

The hospital staff member shook her head. 'It all happened too fast.'

Straker relayed the news to Quartano. His car was running at the speed limit back down to London.

'Ravilious has been *kidnapped*?' said the tycoon.

'I don't have enough information to say that definitely, only what the hospital receptionist said.'

'What about his condition, though … his heart attack? Did she say whether these people were medics?'

'No, sir.'

'Who were they, then, Matt – who *were* they?'

Straker was determined not to jump to conclusions.

Quartano beat him to it: 'You don't think they could've been some of these 'Ndrangheta thugs, do you – something to do with Al-Megrahi? Grab him … hold him to ransom … until he gives up control of his company?'

Straker couldn't deny the thought had crossed his mind. 'Possibly, sir, but we aren't aware of any ransom demand?'

The tycoon grunted in the negative.

'It looks like we might have been right in one sense though, sir,' said Straker, 'Mr Ravilious might well now appreciate our help.'

'This is all the more worrying. You've got to find out what's happened to him, Matt. Do whatever you can … report back to me the moment you have anything.'

The situation with Motor Racing Promotions no longer felt entirely corporate; there was a decidedly unnerving element to it. Straker's thoughts came closer to home. He found his mind racing.

What if the 'Ndrangheta hoods *were* responsible for this?

Then Straker went further.

What if they had managed to associate *him* with any of this? Was that thought such a ridiculous idea?

...Straker's visit to Frankfurt Capital?

...his meeting with Rosa Grant of the *Financial Times*?

...his appearance at the Whittlebury Group press conference in the RAC Club?

...visiting Eighty McGuire at Pinewood Studios?

...the injunction hearing in the Rolls Building?

And then, of course, there was his visit to the prisoner in the Nieuwe Wandeling jail in Belgium. Yoel Kahneman's first question had been about whether or not Straker had been followed. At the time, he had thought that was the paranoid ranting of a troubled man...

Was Straker being alarmist to think that he might be at risk?

What if Suleiman Al-Megrahi was now so close to the MRP prize that nothing was going to stop him – or his violent henchmen?

Straker rang Karen, asking her to make a number of preparations as well as set up the next thing he needed for the investigation. As usual, he found her to be a step or two ahead of him.

Straker's car pulled into Cavendish Square. There, though, he found that someone else was also one or two steps ahead.

He wasn't sure how he picked up on it, but something wasn't right. As the car circled round, he clocked three figures in different parts of the square.

A man sitting on a bench.

Another beside a tree.

A third leaning against a park railing.

Discreetly, deploying his 14 Int Company fieldcraft, Straker studied the men as the car circumnavigated the square.

Then he realized what gave them away. All three men were looking in the same direction. Whoever these people were, their tradecraft was poor. Even so, Straker was as sure, now, as he needed to be.

Quartech International was being watched.

EIGHTY

Straker's car left the street level and dropped down the ramp underneath the Cavendish Square headquarters. He made his way to the 9th floor. Once in his office, he hung back, so as not to be seen through the windows.

Edging forward, Straker looked down into the gardens below.

He could see that all three men were still there.

Karen appeared behind him. 'Hello, Matt?'

Straker didn't reply.

He was setting up the camera on his iPhone to capture shots of the figures.

Karen said something more, which finally caught his attention.

When he turned to face her, she added: 'What's going on? And why are you smiling like *that*?'

Straker called Quartech's operations manager and instructed the immediate sealing of the underground garage and a trebling of the security around the Cavendish Square headquarters. Those were the only measures Straker could implement unilaterally until he spoke to Quartano. He sent the chairman a short email, declaring his deduction that Quartech was being watched, and attached the best of the pictures taken with his phone. He stated that he considered their building to have been compromised.

In the meantime – aware now of the possible kidnapping of Ravilious, and the hospital's reference to a black car with blacked-out windows – Straker wanted to go back through his surveillance photographs, particularly those taken outside the Ringmaster's houses and offices. Grabbing his laptop, he headed into the quiet room. He found the shots of the black car and suits turning up at MRP's headquarters early on Friday evening, and then the ones of the black cars outside that stately home in Stoke Place – filmed by the drone during Ravilious's 'escape' from Silverstone during Qualifying.

He compared one set with the other. Was there *any* similarity or connection between these two groups? Did they mean anything – in light of the abduction?

Before Straker could complete this review, he was interrupted by a tap on the glass door.

Through it he could see Karen – looking flustered.

'What's the matter?' he asked, after waving her in.

'Mr Quartano's on the phone … he sounds upset … he wants to talk to you.'

Straker walked through to his desk and pressed a button on his phone.

'Why the hell wasn't my car allowed to pull into the garage?' demanded the tycoon.

Straker asked him if he had seen his email about the men in Cavendish Square. 'If Frankfurt Capital were the victims of violence in their offices, we should at least be vigilant.'

'Are you saying the people out here could be 'Ndrangheta?'

'I don't know for sure, sir. But I didn't think we could afford the risk of ignoring them.'

'Do what you think's necessary, Matt,' he said. 'Since we last spoke, I've had the CEO of Mandarin Telecom on the phone again, questioning the state of Formula 1.'

'What have you told him?'

'Most of it – in order to demonstrate how seriously we are taking all this.'

'As well as what we think happened to Ravilious at the hospital?'

'I felt I had to. Anyway, what have you found out?'

'Nothing yet, sir, I'm afraid. I've been back through all my surveillance photographs, to see if we can see anything in them now.'

'And…?'

'I've got two sets of men in dark suits and dark cars. I'm sure there would be CCTV footage of the abduction at the hospital, to cross-reference them, but I don't have legitimate grounds to ask for it. Otherwise, I've come by no confirmable indication of Ravilious's fate, before or after his arrival at the Northampton General Hospital.'

'You've seen nothing to give us further indication of his whereabouts.'

'Not since the abduction, sir, no.'

'So it *does* look like he's been kidnapped?'

'I don't have enough to draw that conclusion.'

'But you *are* saying that, since he arrived at the Northampton General Hospital, there's been no further trace of Arno Ravilious?'

EIGHTY-ONE

With Formula 1 still in a state of disarray, the grand prix season was falling flat. By contrast, there was a constant stream of news about Manhattanheim – interest being cleverly fuelled by a succession of news releases by the city of New York: a new sponsor; the announcement of a big name endorser; a star-name appointment to the race committee. It didn't take long for the event to be seen as prestigious; celebrities were readily queuing up to be associated with it.

Something else served to diminish the end to the F1 season.

The Constructors' Championship was decided with four races still to run. That served as a double whammy to Formula 1: not only did it take some of the competitive drama out of the remaining races, but it seemed to boost anticipation for the Undisputed World Motor Racing Championship. It enabled the mayor of New York to make the much waited-for announcement:

'The car that will be raced at Manhattanheim will be Formula 1's winning car … the Lambourn GdC19.'

But that only made things worse for F1.

It suggested that, this year, its season wouldn't reach a climax with its last grand prix – that there was something to look forward to, coming after it.

Matt Straker was still poring over more surveillance photographs when his desk telephone rang. It was Dominic Quartano's PA.

'Colonel Straker, could you come up immediately, please? Mr Quartano would like to see you.'

Straker left the department, making for the lifts – wondering what had happened now.

Up on the 27th floor, Jean indicated that he should go straight in. Walking through the double doors, Straker saw Quartano and another figure silhouetted by the window.

'Mr Q,' he said and then: 'Tahm?' as he recognized the boss of the Ptarmigan F1 team.

'Come in, Matt,' said Quartano, 'you might want to shut the doors.'

Straker did so and walked over to join the other two.

'Remy is keen to compete in this Undisputed World Motor Racing Championship in New York,' stated Quartano.

Straker smiled. 'I'm not surprised.'

'We have a problem, though…'

'What sort of problem?'

'She's being threatened.'

'How? By whom?'

Tahm Nazar was troubled. He waved a hand-held device. 'A computer-generated message has been sent through to her phone.'

Looking down, he pressed play. A robotic voice was soon heard:

'Do . not . race . in . Manhattan . heim … if . you . don't . want . to . get . hurt.'

Nazar tapped the screen and played it again before asking: 'Who the hell could have sent her something like this?'

Straker was thinking rapidly: 'First of all, is that a general threat or a specific one?'

'Meaning?'

'Have other drivers been threatened as well, or is it just Remy?'

Nazar's expression showed he didn't know.

Quartano was nodding. 'That's good thinking, Matt. We should find out…'

'Could we ask some of the other team bosses,' asked Straker, 'including some of the IndyCar drivers who are heading for New York?'

Quartano offered his encouragement to Nazar.

The team boss, pulling out his own phone from a pocket, looked down and tapped a number.

Straker turned to face Quartano. 'I take it we can dismiss this as a Lambourn whistleblower, warning about the safety of the cars to be used in the Manhattanheim race?'

Quartano shrugged.

'And can we dismiss gamesmanship, a driver not wanting the others to compete – to frighten off the competition?'

'Without further investigation, you're not going to know,' replied Quartano. 'Whatever the possibilities, I feel we have a duty of care.'

'Okay,' said Straker. 'In trying to find out *who* might have sent this, we might need to split the question in two. Is the person sending this message the perpetrator of the threat – or warning the drivers of a known danger?'

The tycoon acknowledged the distinction. 'How would you start with discovering that? ... By trying to trace the message, electronically, back to its originator?'

'Theoretically, except I'd be amazed if they weren't sophisticated enough to cover their tracks,' said Straker, 'though we'll have to check anyway.'

'Of course – and the second?'

'We could look at this from a motivational perspective. Who would expect to benefit from the drivers *not* being in the race?'

'Okay.'

'In other words, *why?*' said Straker. 'Forcing a top driver to pull out would most certainly leave Manhattanheim feeling diminished, meaning the person behind it could be wanting to see the race fail – or at least fall short? If that's the case, *who* would want that?'

'Someone who doesn't want the city to succeed?'

'A political rival to the mayor, maybe? Brandenburg seems to have gained politically from this race.'

Quartano didn't look convinced.

'Or, it could be internal politics within IndyCar in the US?' offered Straker. 'Their politics are as fractious as those in Formula 1. Maybe someone doesn't want to see Manhattanheim diminish their franchise on American soil?'

Quartano didn't react.

'But if it's not New York politics, or IndyCar politics' Straker added, 'what about politics around Motor Racing Promotions? The reaction to Manhattanheim has been pretty fierce within F1. Only the teams and historic circuits in the Whittlebury consortium have come anywhere close to embracing it.'

Straker added: 'Initially, everyone thought Gabriel Barrus must have been behind all this, because of the American connection, although I've not heard him claim anything specifically.'

'So of those who have F1 interests that might be conflicted by the New York race, that would leave ... Suleiman Al-Megrahi ...' offered Quartano, almost with a sigh.

Straker nodded. 'He's been vitriolic about the Manhattanheim idea – first against Barrus, whom he thought was behind it – and then against the format itself. It's not hard to see why Al-Megrahi would have reacted like that: Manhattanheim's stolen a lot of the Formula 1 season's thunder. If we think he is about to take control of MRP, Al-Megrahi would appear to have the most to lose because of the New York race. And, if it *is* him, we would have to take any threat to Remy seriously.'

'Even in America?'

Straker nodded. 'The two better-known mafia organizations – the Cosa Nostra and the Camorra – are both substantial in the US; why not the 'Ndrangheta?'

'Meaning we would have to conclude they could make good on any threat?'

'I fear so,' said Straker. 'Anyway, what's Remy's view?'

'She's dismissive of the message and, of course, still wants to go.'

Tahm Nazar walked back across the chairman's office and re-joined the conversation.

'What news?' Quartano asked.

Nazar shook his head. 'None of the other big names appear to have been threatened – Jake Stuyvesant, Muammar Al Baradei. I also managed to reach the boss of the Vandenberg IndyCar team: Embiricos Savannah hasn't been threatened either.'

'Why has Remy been singled out, then?' Straker asked.

The other two men shrugged.

'Because she's a Formula 1 driver,' added Straker, '…no, because the other F1 drivers haven't been threatened. Because she's a winner? … possibly, except Jake Stuyvesant looks like winning this year's F1 Driver's Championship and *he* hasn't been threatened. Because she's popular? … possibly, except Embiricos Savannah – the season's leading IndyCar contender – is a rock star in America and *he* hasn't been threatened. Or has she been threatened because she's a woman?'

'Okay, Matt,' said Quartano, 'we're not going to be able to work this out without more information. You're going to have to look into this, and fast – or we can't let Remy go to New York…'

Straker looked dubious. 'I don't think this is going to stop her.'

'But she doesn't know about Al-Megrahi's links to organized crime,' replied Nazar.

Quartano acknowledged the point. 'That's true, Matt, and I think she should be told. Can you go and see her – explain the whole situation? Make the risks clear to her?'

'After sorting out the Massarella incident and that saga in Russia, she *would* listen to you,' agreed Nazar.

Did Straker really need this complication? How was such an interaction going to affect his psyche and emotional stability?

EIGHTY-TWO

New York was getting itself ready.

Roads were diverted. Street furniture was being removed. Sections of the track were resurfaced and, all importantly, the idiosyncratic metal plates, audible in the everyday traffic of Manhattan, were removed. The first components of temporary grandstands were shipped in by a fleet of lorries.

A major media coup was the use of time-lapse photography. A website showed the build-up around different parts of the track – the section through Times Square, through Central Park, down 5th Avenue and alongside the Plaza Hotel. It started getting hits; 20 million unique users were registered within the first week. Talk radio across the Tri-State Area was forever discussing the race; it soon became *the* topic of choice on television along the East Coast.

Then, a photo op was staged. Sixteen brand-new Lambourn Formula 1 cars were shown on the grid of Manhattanheim. All were identical – all carrying the same sponsorship livery, that of the world's most famous drink. On the road beside them was a row of spare front and rear wings; those aero surfaces were identical to the ones already on the cars in all respects, save that they carried the names of the drivers superimposed on a representation of their national flags. Being interchangeable, they would only be fitted once the cars had been allocated to each driver by lot.

The anticipation of the race was ratcheted higher once again.

Straker's concern for the security of the Cavendish Square head-quarters brought him into contact with the building's operations manager. As he outlined the nature of the threat, describing the destruction of the i8 in Germany, the man was ready to do whatever was necessary to keep his building and their people safe.

Straker concluded: 'Mr Quartano is keen we maintain the heightened security around the building, particularly keeping the garage sealed.'

In reply, the operations manager mentioned some of the security facilities of the building – a vestige of its previous use as a bank headquarters: Straker was amazed to learn of vaults in the basement and even a pedestrian tunnel under the road, to the other side of Holles Street. The operations man confirmed it would be possible for members of staff to come and go anonymously via an access point on the other side of the road.

Straker couldn't believe it. This would take care of his concerns about key personnel being spotted when moving in and out of the building.

Straker's apprehension was now rising. Being directly involved in Sabatino's safety would bring the two of them together. After last time, things hadn't been left that well. How would she react? He wasn't sure how *he* would react either.

Breathing deeply, he sent her a short text.

A response came back promptly.

She agreed to a meeting and suggested the place of their earlier London rendezvous: Rules of Maiden Lane in Covent Garden.

Slipping through his new unseen way in and out, Straker left Cavendish Square undetected and arrived at the restaurant early. He was shown to the particular table he had reserved. Ten minutes later Remy Sabatino walked in. Straker stood as he saw her approach.

He was struck all over again by her appearance and presence. Her dark eyes were flashing. A number of people recognized her as she moved through the restaurant. She responded to them with her engaging smile, which seemed amplified by her olive-oil complexion. Straker was stirred by how at ease and self-possessed she was.

Sabatino appeared to be dressed down, except her clothes might have looked more casual than they actually were; each garment was higher quality, and probably more expensive, than he'd ever seen her wearing before.

'Hey, Matt.'

'Hello, Rems.'

A waiter in a black suit and a white waist apron appeared, carrying a tray in the palm of his right hand. On it was a single glass.

Indicating the drink, Straker said: 'I took the liberty of ordering you a Guinness?'

Sabatino looked straight into his eyes.

Was that the sign of a thaw?

The waiter withdrew and the two of them sat.

'I'm sorry to hear about you and Nijinsky.'

Her smile was mocking. 'It's *Lemanski* … and … no you're not.'

'I'm sorry it all happened as it did. Russia was tense. We were under considerable pressure. Where the hell did that dancer come from anyway?'

'Moscow,' she answered with a smile in her voice, 'and he wasn't just a *dancer* … he was a principal with the Bolshoi. He found my status in Formula 1 intriguing. Anyway, you can talk – you slunk off with that lawyer pretty smoothly.'

Straker's dark eyes intensified. He said: 'It doesn't have much bearing any more. She's gone back to the Ukraine.'

There was a moment's silence at the table. Raising her Guinness, Sabatino said: 'Well here's to our success with relationships.'

Straker could only smile wanly in return.

'What's up then?' she asked. 'Why this welcome chance to see you?'

Before he could answer, the waiter returned offering to take their order. Sabatino went for the smoked salmon and scrambled eggs, followed by the rack of lamb, while Straker opted for his favourites – black pudding and poached egg followed by the house masterpiece: jugged hare. Sabatino said she would stick with her Guinness, while Straker went for a Napa Valley merlot.

When they were alone again, Straker said: 'I need to bring you up to date on a few things, and to talk about the New York race.'

'Okay… ?'

'DQ's had me investigating the likely ownership of Motor Racing Promotions. He's concerned about the state of Formula 1, and how it's undermining the Mandarin Telecom relationship. The financial consequences to Ptarmigan of the wrong owner could be catastrophic.'

Straker recounted his investigation and some of the unexpected things he had uncovered about the shareholdings and the prospective ownership of MRP.

'Al-Megrahi and Calabria were before my time, of course,' she said, 'but I've always thought the guy was too pleased with himself by half.'

'There's more about him, though, that I need to tell you…'

After Straker finished his findings from the TV producer and the prisoner in Belgium, she said: 'Good God … you mean Al-Megrahi's some kind of mafioso?'

'Sort of. But there's even more…'

By the time Straker finished describing his investigation, Sabatino was captivated.

'You think the cheating on the Calabria cars – Fangate – the bribery of the EU commissioner – the intimidation of Frankfurt Capital – the car bomb in their garage – and the bomb scare at the RAC Club – were all Al-Megrahi?'

'At this stage I only think they are.'

'But the coincidences would be too strong to ignore, wouldn't they?'

'Which is why we need to discuss that threatening message you got on your phone.'

Sabatino put down her Guinness. 'You think there's some sort of connection between what you've just been saying and that message?'

'Possibly.'

'First off, thank you for caring. Al-Megrahi sounds dangerous and I should be worried … except I'm not going to be put off going to New York.'

'As far as we know, you're the only one to have had that threat made against them. For some reason, you've been singled out: whatever the risk might be, it's very clearly aimed at you.'

'What do you think they've got against *me*?'

'It could be anything – rational or irrational. Your success in motor racing has made you iconic. It might be seen that this race in New York, without you, would lessen its prestige.'

'You think the threat's aimed at the race rather than me?'

Straker shrugged sympathetically.

'But you *do* think it's Al-Megrahi?'

'He seems to have the most to lose by that race succeeding. It doesn't really matter … Because it *might* be him, we have to take the threat seriously.'

'Okay, Matt. As I said, I am determined to go New York. But I now have two conditions.'

'What are they?'

'That you come too and – as you've done now twice before – you keep me safe.'

EIGHTY-THREE

Straker discussed the issue further with Quartano, Nazar and Quartech's head legal counsel, Stacey Krall. He wanted to relay the threat made against Remy Sabatino on to the Manhattanheim organizers. They agreed.

City Hall was alarmed.

Straker spent the next two days on the phone to its officials, who soon liaised with Homeland Security. He got a strong feeling the Americans could well end up denying Sabatino a visa.

Two days later, while Straker was still awaiting clearance for Sabatino to appear in the race, the first of the Manhattanheim drivers arrived in New York.

The PR was expertly stage-managed.

Two Formula 1 drivers appeared at JFK and were met with a barrage of media, press and TV.

The next day a brace of IndyCar drivers arrived at Grand Central Terminal, to a similarly energetic reception.

The day after that two more arrived into the city by boat, passing beneath the Statue of Liberty, creating an irresistible photo op.

Each new arrival prompted a flurry of media and TV coverage. As an example of how to titillate the press and public, the news-flow management was exemplary.

Straker was finally contacted by Homeland Security.

He held his breath as they delivered their verdict.

Remy Sabatino's arrival into New York would have to be different. She didn't leave for America on a scheduled – traceable – airline or flight.

Instead, Straker flew her out on one of the Quartech Falcons. To supervise her safety, he decided to travel with her. The flight plan and manifest recorded that they were heading across the Atlantic to JFK International, to the north of New York City. Thirty minutes out from London's Northolt, just after they had crossed the west coast of Ireland, Straker commanded the corporate jet to alter course.

'Why the change of direction?' she asked.

'Trying to mix it up – trying to make it harder for anyone to find out where you've gone and where you're going. I'm sorry, Rems, but you won't be staying in your swanky suite in the Plaza. I've got us an isolated house in East Hampton, off Lily Pond Lane. As some consolation, though, it does overlook the ocean.'

Sabatino and Straker landed at MacArthur, the small Long Island airport, as evening was falling. He arranged that the plane would be able to taxi straight into one of the large T hangars. Once inside, the doors were closed behind the Quartech Falcon. There, ready waiting, was a large SUV with blacked-out windows. Even though the car was brought to the foot of the steps, Straker insisted she cover her head and face with a hat and scarf.

Sabatino was spirited – in semi-disguise – the short distance from the corporate jet to the car. The door was shut quickly behind her.

Less than an hour later, she was hidden in a twelve-bedroomed neo-Georgian mansion set in ten acres of land with a view out over the Atlantic.

Remy Sabatino had been smuggled into America.

Would such covert activities be anywhere good enough to protect her against the reach and violence of the 'Ndrangheta?

EIGHTY-FOUR

The drivers had all been invited to compete in the Undisputed World Motor Racing Championship as individuals. At another huge press conference on the eve of the race, the mayor of New York made a further announcement. It was explosive. He was appointing two Captains – one to represent the group of Formula 1 drivers and the other the IndyCar competitors. It triggered an extraordinary reaction.

In an instant, it made the race tribal, sparking a similar atmosphere to that of the Ryder Cup. Golf was also an individual sport, but its biennial tournament always induced a team identity – a friendly rivalry between America and Europe.

Manhattanheim was now doing the same, only more so.

The press attention had already been huge. Brandenburg induced it to fever pitch – by announcing Remy Sabatino as the Formula 1 captain. As the only woman driving, the media impact went global. Straker's stress levels were ramped considerably.

Race day dawned. Straker was about to enter the moment of their highest vulnerability, as he tried to get Remy Sabatino into New York City.

What were the 'Ndrangheta capable of?

How far did their tentacles extend?

Had they already breached Straker's security ploy?

Had they found out Sabatino's location?

Straker was taking precautions. He had set her up to wear black leathers – from neck to ankles – including large black gloves, boots and a motorcycle helmet with a smoked-glass visor. He was going to dress the same.

Escorting Sabatino out of the back of the East Hampton mansion, to the ocean side of the house, she found propped on the lawn a 1950s-styled Ultra Limited Harley-Davidson. A motorcycle, Straker gambled, was the quickest – and most anonymous – way of getting Sabatino through the traffic and into the city.

He fired up the bike and set off with Sabatino riding pillion.

Forty-five minutes later they were in for a shock.

Scanning his mirrors, Straker had been looking out for any signs of trouble. They were heading west on the Long Island Expressway, and coming into Queens, when he caught sight of two dark shapes – looming up through the traffic behind them. They were closing in fast.

The traffic was heavy, restricting Straker's movement.

He couldn't accelerate away.

The motorcycles behind them were getting closer.

As they approached a junction, Straker, at the last possible minute, darted right, heading for a slip road, and stamped on the rear brake. The bike slowed rapidly, but then, even with its sophisticated ABS, he couldn't help losing the back end, it shooting out to the left. Sliding badly on the less-used part of the slip road, Straker only just saved them from ploughing into a concrete wall off the Expressway. Still fighting to control the heavy bike, he recovered it before accelerating hard, down the off ramp. As he did so, he tried to turn round and scan the road behind them.

He spotted the two fast-moving black shapes.

They were closing in on the junction fast. But it didn't look like they were going to react quickly enough. They could only overshoot the junction, unable to follow.

Straker had lost them.

But now he had a different problem. He had to recalculate: Straker had to busk a different route – at 'ground level' – all the way through the rest of the borough.

It took them twenty minutes to reach the Ed Koch Queensboro Bridge.

Crossing the East River, Straker and Sabatino were given a magnificent view of Midtown Manhattan as they rode on into the heart of New York City.

By 9 o'clock that morning Straker had managed to get Remy Sabatino safely inside the race perimeter, and into the Manhattanheim circuit.

Securing the bike a short distance from the Plaza, in a pre-arranged and covert basement garage, Straker ran back towards the race complex. For him to shadow Sabatino during the Undisputed World Motor Racing Championship, he needed access to all areas of the race infrastructure. During his discussions about safety with City Hall, it was agreed to register him as a member of the press. Half an hour later he was accredited and through.

He rendezvoused with Sabatino ten minutes after that. From then on, unless she was racing, Straker intended to be no more than 20 yards away from her.

For this race, Manhattan turned itself into a carnival – far bigger than the likes of the New York marathon, but not as big as the St Patrick's Day Parade. Crowds lined every inch of the circuit. Every seat had been sold, and could have been sold several times over. To cater for such unsatisfied spectator demand, huge electronic screens had been erected in the middle of Central Park, Liberty State Park – across the Hudson in New Jersey, with the skyline of Manhattan in the distance – and on the edge of Corona Park in Flushing Meadow. Each of these spillover gatherings was also packed out.

A live picture soon beamed out of each of the electronic screens: it showed the Grand Army Plaza in the south-eastern corner of Central Park. There, a quarter-circle of banked seats – five, six storeys high – had been erected and was packed with 5,000 people. Its focus, directly below, was the three-corner chicane of Turns 15, 16 and 17.

And, with the curve of the stand – sweeping from the end of 5th

Avenue to the north through Central Park South to the west – the spectators in those seats could see up and down both of those long sections of the track.

Immediately in front of these stands, on the inside of Turn 16, was a sizeable stage, which would ultimately act as the podium.

Via the screens, everyone was able to watch Mayor Brandenburg as he walked out towards a lectern. On the front of this was the official flag of the mayor: the royal blue, white and orange tricolour of New York City, with – in its centre panel – the city's coat of arms topped by the semi-circle of five blue five-pointed stars.

The mayor was met with raucous applause.

He looked up at the packed banks of seats in front of him. At eye level was the media zone, crammed full with cameras. Above them were the boxes hosting VIPs and dignitaries. Around the rest of the temporary amphitheatre were the massed ranks of the general public and motor racing fanatics. The surround-sound noise of jubilation was almost overwhelming.

'Ladies and Gentleman … welcome to the most exciting motor race ever held,' he boomed.

The crowds erupted and cheered.

He had to try several times before he could speak again. Finally, he was able to say: 'Please join me … now … in welcoming … the 8 stars from America's own IndyCar Championship … and the 8 stars from the Formula 1 Championship … our heroes here at Manhattanheim … the drivers!'

Another eruption of applause filled the plaza.

The sixteen gladiators appeared on the stage.

When the sound had lessened enough, Mayor Brandenburg announced: 'As well as the motor racing aces, we have the fastest racing cars on the face of the planet. Over on the grid,' he said, indicating to his right, 'we have 16 identical copies of the car that won this year's Formula 1 Constructors' Championship. We also have team personnel from 16 elite racing outfits. All told, we're about to create the most level playing field there has ever been in any form of elite motor racing.

'Now, ladies and gentlemen, I will conduct the draw to put the drivers and the cars together. Then, also at random, their support teams will be drawn.'

An elegant trolley was wheeled out. On it was a clear plastic tombola-like machine, the kind more normally used in lotteries.

Brandenburg announced: 'Driver one – from the Keystone State of Pennsylvania – Jake Stuyvesant.'

The American F1 driver received a roar of welcome.

'Car number ... 12!

'Driver two – this year's IndyCar Champion ... from the great State of Georgia, Embiricos Savannah – car number ... 6.'

He, too, was greeted with a thunderous roar.

'Driver three – the Formula 1 driver from the Kingdom of Saudi Arabia, Muammar Al Baradei ... car number ... 11.'

For a city with a hesitant relationship with the Arab world, the New Yorkers' roar of welcome was significant.

When Mayor Brandenburg got to Driver 13, he paused.

'From the Island of Malta...' he started, but the mayor was completely drowned out.

No one heard the allocation of Remy Sabatino's car.

People only knew it was number 3 when it flashed up on the screens.

The driver/car allocations should have taken eight minutes, but the crowd's cheering had extended the process to more than ten.

Then came the allocation of team personnel.

This was going to take a little longer, being more numerous and therefore more complicated. The mayor was joined on stage by the governor of New York and the State's Senior Senator, both of whom stood by their own 'lottery' machine. Recording the allocation electronically, a huge screen above the stage listed all 16 cars and their drawn drivers. With this second draw, names in the different categories – team boss, strategist, race engineer, et cetera – were all randomly assigned to each driver.

Once the draw procedure was completed, the mayor of New York invited the gladiators to congregate in their respective car's garage along the pit lane. The first familiarization and practice session would take place in just over an hour. In the meantime, Mayor Brandenburg announced the holding of a warm-up event; a NASCAR challenge to take place, imminently, around the Manhattanheim circuit.

Matt Straker accompanied Remy Sabatino from the base of the podium, across the grid to the pit lane.

The moment Sabatino walked into her car's garage, she strode into its centre and took command.

'I know all this is very strange,' she said, 'but so it is for every-one – which is the wacky brilliance of this idea. None of us has the advantage of familiarity. I want to win this championship – and I would love it if you wanted to claim credit for helping me do that.'

Her team burst into applause.

'We are about to be briefed by the chief designer of Lambourn, who will go through the specifics of this car,' Sabatino continued. 'Before he gets here, though, let's all say who we are.'

As the last of the twenty people introduced themselves, Sabatino summarized: 'What an extraordinary collection of experience and expertise. Make or break for us as a team, though, is that we learn quicker than the others do ... we've got to work together faster than they do ... we've got to trust each other faster than the others learn to trust *them*selves.'

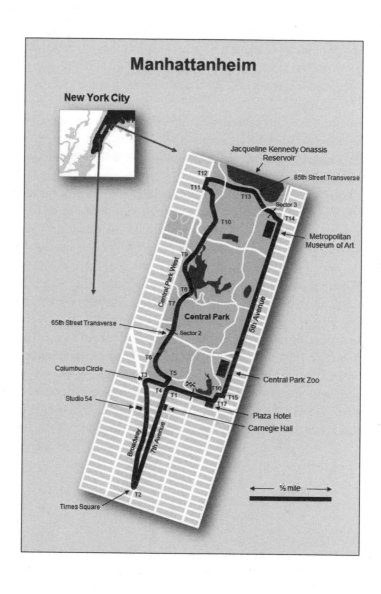

EIGHTY-FIVE

When the time came, Sabatino was ready.

Climbing into the Lambourn for the first time, she and the team fired up the Benbecular hybrid engine. At least that was familiar; her Ptarmigan used the same power unit, but there were going to be significant differences she would have to get to grips with ... but then so would all the other teams.

Straker decided to watch the race via screens at the back of the garage. He was given a set of headphones, so he could listen in on Sabatino's radio link to her crew in the pits.

At just after midday, Sabatino engaged the clutch and drove her Lambourn out of the garage. Turning left, she ran down the pit lane, heading west along Central Park South, emerging onto the track.

Sabatino exited the rev-limited zone of the pit lane.

Powering up, she felt the car offer her sharp acceleration. Changing up and up again, she wanted to get a series of feelings from the car – the engine, the characteristics of its gearbox, its torque, the sweet spots associated with each gear change.

Sabatino approached Turn 1, a right-angle corner – to the left – out of the wide start/finish straight into the top of the equally wide 7th Avenue. Even while travelling at this relatively slow speed, Sabatino used the change of direction to get a sense of the car's handling through a corner.

She was soon accelerating down one of the cavernous avenues of Manhattan. The high-rises of Midtown towered above her down either side of the track.

Over the course of ten laps, Sabatino upped her pace. She felt she was ready to attempt one at Qualifying speed.

'Are we ready for a hot lap?' she asked her pit crew over the radio.

The affirmative came back.

Sabatino flipped her mind into gear.

Straker switched the TV coverage – to the view above Sabatino's helmet, enabling him, effectively, to ride with her.

She was at the far end of the circuit, heading south down 5th Avenue – just passing the front of the Metropolitan Museum of Art. In this four-lane, dead-straight three-quarter of a mile stretch of road – running down the eastern side of Central Park – Sabatino was ready to give this unfamiliar car a go. Accelerating easily, she started pushing it up towards its maximum speed.

In a straight line, the car felt stable.

She hurtled past the Central Park Zoo.

She started thinking about getting ready to brake into the right-hander ahead, at Turn 15.

Easing across to the left-hand side of 5th Avenue, Sabatino positioned herself for the right-hand entry to the chicane. Passing the 100-yard board, she made ready to brake. But when she did, she got a hell of a shock.

The front right locked straight up.

Sabatino lifted off and braked again, the balance of the car being nothing like her Ptarmigan.

When she tried to turn into the right-hander, she suffered massive understeer, forcing her to brake again in the middle of the corner. At higher speed, the car's handling was unrecognizable, even from the earlier warm-up laps – the Lambourn's front and back ends seemed to be in serious conflict with each other.

'What a fucking handful,' she said into her helmet.

As she turned to the left through the second part of this chicane, Turn 16, she felt another bout of understeer, having to fight the car the other way through this sequence of corners. Despite the handling, Sabatino accelerated hard through the apex and exit of Turn 17, another right-hander.

Then she entered the start/finish straight in front of the Plaza Hotel.

'Are you sure you still want to go for it, after that?' asked the race engineer.

Sabatino was answering him in kind … accelerating aggressively.

As she crossed the line, she was already pushing it.

Running down in front of the pit lane garages, she headed towards Turn 1. Wanting to open up this left-hander, she pulled to the right: by the time she was 200 yards from the turn she was fully over on the Central Park side of the road.

From seventh gear, she expected to drop two gears before turning in and accelerating through the apex. But into the corner, once again, she felt the front and rear of the Lambourn fighting itself, resulting in another massive understeer. The car was extraordinarily unresponsive … drifting far to the outside – far wider than she wanted – to the very right-hand side of the exit, almost grazing down the Armco on the western side of 7th Avenue. Struggling to straighten up, Sabatino fought to stabilize the car as she got back on the power. She wrestled with all the Lambourn could give her as she accelerated down the wide stretch of the track to the south.

After a couple of hundred yards, Carnegie Hall may have shot through the left periphery of her vision, but that wasn't anywhere on Sabatino's mind: she was focused entirely on the road to the front of her as she hit 170 miles an hour. Her concern was how this car was going to handle around the tight Times Square Hairpin, now looming in 500 … 400 … 300 yards.

An increasing number of advertising hoardings appeared on either side.

Sabatino drifted to the left of the circuit, hanging on at full speed for as long as possible, before standing on the brakes and changing down from 7th gear to 1st. The car's engine management system pulsed the revs on each downshift, but there was a miniscule – destabilizing – mismatch between the revs of the engine and the speed of the rear wheels over the ground; each downshift jolting the car slightly, threatening to lock up the back wheels. Sabatino felt the stability of the car disrupted again, but now for a different set of reasons.

She hardly noticed the massive semi-circular stands set up around the southern side of Times Square as she started turning in. Swinging to the right through 180 degrees to round the pin-sharp corner, one even tighter than the iconic Loews Hairpin in Monaco, Sabatino played the steering wheel hard, particularly as she reapplied the power through the apex and into the exit, having to fight now against substantial oversteer as the back end tried to step out.

She was into Broadway.

From here, the circuit headed north for a quarter of a mile. Soon running at full pelt, Sabatino crossed 54th Street – home of the notorious Studio 54 to her left – and, about then, radioed her feedback to the pits.

'We've been talking to the Lambourn engineer, here, Remy,' said the unfamiliar race engineer over the radio. 'He suggests: half a turn on the brake balance – and try softening the front anti-roll bar.'

Broadway swept her round to the left as she approached Columbus Circle. The relatively straight and level part of the track gave Sabatino the chance to make the suggested adjustments on the dials of the steering wheel.

She was soon focusing on the road again.

Timing her entry to Turn 3, Sabatino changed down from 7th to 3rd and swung into the 110-degree right-hander.

She felt a slight but immediate improvement in the car.

The exit of Turn 3 put her back into West 59th Street – heading towards the pits, but in the other direction from before – as she again skirted the bottom edge of Central Park. Sabatino accelerated the short distance, back up to 5th gear, before turning left into Turn 4, which took her into the park proper. Here, the circuit departed from the straight lines and right angles of the grid system. On the pink stone surface of West Drive, there would be a constant change of direction through the twisty-turny stretch as she ran under the trees. Sabatino accelerated hard, hoping for a better understanding of the car through this succession of slighter corners.

Turn 5 was a sweeping left-hander.

Sabatino powered on before the track's direction was soon reversed to the right. Banks of seats lined the circuit along here, giving the spectators a surprising closeness to the track.

At the end of these left and right sweeping turns, as she rose over the bridge crossing the 65th Street Transverse, Sabatino clocked a split time at the end of Sector 1. Glancing at the display on her steering wheel, she was disappointed ... but not surprised. Her pace was nowhere near as quick as she hoped. At least two seconds off what they expected to be a competitive time. Sabatino needed to get a much better feel for and from this car.

Powering on to Turn 7, the landscape seemed more like the sections through the forest around the old Hockenheim circuit. Five hundred yards on and the change of direction saw Sabatino swinging back the other way, to the left – all the while under the trees.

Now in top gear, the gentle sway of the car gave her a chance to tune into its cornering and balance – and to draw some technical conclusions. She had further conversations with the pit wall. Additional adjustments were discussed and actioned.

After Turn 10, still in the park, the circuit bore left – splitting from West Drive into West 85th Street. Sabatino was not looking forward to the sharper Turn 11. This would take her out of the greenery and onto Central Park West, the straight street running down the western side of the park. Being a tight corner, she expected another attack of poor balance and tricky handling. But as she swung out through Turn 11, setting up immediately for the next right-hander, Turn 12, the car was beginning to feel a little more stable.

Now exiting Turn 12, she fed herself into the end of the 85th Street Transverse – heading due east, back across Central Park. A much narrower section of track. Powering on, running along the bottom edge of the Jacqueline Kennedy Onassis Reservoir, the track descended slightly into a cutting as the road shot the bridge under West Drive running overhead. The light/dark/light under it, though, wasn't anywhere near as bad as emerging from the tunnel under the

Fairmont Hotel in Monaco. Sabatino's line through this long sweeping right-hander to the next apex saw her confidence rise slightly.

The circuit straightened for half a mile and was flanked by a wall and higher ground on the left-hand side. There were very few spectating opportunities along here.

Sabatino was back in contact with her team in the pits, offering further feedback.

Turn 13 was another long sweeping right edged by walls on both sides and overhung by trees. Sabatino powered on. She descended into and through another cutting, to shoot under another bridge – this time carrying the East Drive. On the far side of that she quickly reached the fork in the 85th Street Transverse, the Armco barrier indicating that the Manhattanheim circuit bore round to the right. Here, for the first time since entering Central Park at Turn 4, Sabatino got a clear view of the sky and could see middle-sized buildings ahead. All were bathed in bright sunshine.

As Turn 14 came up – a right-hander around the outside of the Metropolitan Museum of Art – she was about to run onto 5th Avenue, flanking the eastern side of Central Park. Wanting to maintain her speed, she drifted left towards the entry to the corner, hugging that side of the road – trying to open the corner up as much as she could. After the adjustments she'd been discussing with the pit wall, it felt like she and the car were starting to respond to each other a little better. She was slightly reassured.

Over the air, her crew radioed an update: 'Down 1.35, at the end of Sector 2, Remy. You've made much better time, though, since the Sector 1 split.'

The Manhattanheim circuit now had a straight mile-long run down the eastern side of Central Park – for 18 city blocks. She accelerated hard and within a couple of hundred yards had the car running at top speed, 205 miles an hour.

On the straight and level, and with the car beginning to handle the way she wanted, Sabatino let herself think competitively for the first time. She could see this stretch of 5th Avenue – the dead-straight

Museum Mile – easily turning into an inch-by-inch flat-out drag race. But then, if all the drivers in this race were in the same car, differences in straight-line speed would be almost non-existent. Even so, she was convinced this *was* a circuit for overtaking, albeit into and through the corners. What convinced her was the width of these New York streets, easily taking four cars abreast – which would all but negate the influence of the racing line:

Turn 1, the wide left-hander into 7th Avenue, was a strong overtaking possibility.

The Times Hairpin, Turn 2, was an opportunity for drivers late on the brakes.

The meandering section through Central Park, between Turn 5 and Turn 11, offered opportunities to overtake and be overtaken.

And from Turn 14, which Sabatino had just exited, there would be chances right through to the start/finish line; at the end of this hyper-fast section of 5th Avenue, a significant overtaking opportunity would occur as they braked into Turn 15.

In order to brake hard enough to make a competitive difference, though, the car would have to offer the driver stability, handling, balance; the drivers' confidence in the car would be crucial.

Sabatino's experience through here last time round was anything but.

She set up for the corner.

She was determined to push the Lambourn to the limits, to get the fullest feel for how far the car could go. Without making any allowances, she hammered the brakes late and turned in hard to the right.

The understeer *was* still there, but significantly reduced.

She was finding the car easier to handle, probably because she now knew what was coming.

Then, putting the power down hard, she accelerated through the apex of that right-hand turn, quickly putting her into the top half of the Grand Army Plaza.

Sabatino was concentrating too hard to notice the packed

quarter-circle of stands on the outside of that chicane, although she could hear the noise they were making.

Spectators up there were getting a grandstand view. They had been able to watch her approach head-on down 5th Avenue; then they saw her brake and dive into the chicane directly below them. They were watching her now, almost from overhead, as she weaved her way – from their right to left.

The handling of the Lambourn *was* noticeably better.

Changing down to 3rd, Sabatino turned aggressively into the second right – through Turn 17 – hammering the car through the apex and into the exit. She regained access to the start/finish straight … and completed her hot lap.

Over the radio, Sabatino said to her team: 'That was anything but pretty.'

'It was more competitive in Sectors 2 and 3,' the race engineer replied, 'overall, though, 1.35 seconds down at the end.'

'Not *so* bad, considering that horrible first sector.'

'Your feedback – and the responses we got from the Lambourn techie – look like they were making some difference. Is the set-up we've got anywhere close to what you want?'

EIGHTY-SIX

An hour ahead of the race, a large number of floats were parading around the circuit. On them were some of the best-known people on the planet: Hollywood A-listers, stars of Broadway, household names from a range of different sports. The mood was so buoyant even a float carrying a load of politicians received a hero's welcome from the crowd.

Outside the Plaza Hotel, the buzz was all the more intense. There, the sixteen identical Lambourn Formula 1 cars were lined up; and ready. Each was now showing some variation: for ease of recognition, their aerodynamically identical front and rear wings carried the driver's name and the colours of their national flags.

The rows on the grid were four-cars wide. The cars on each row may have been staggered slightly, to reflect the relative speeds from Qualifying. But here four, rather than the usual two, cars would be starting alongside each other: this was sparking considerable expectation of full-on wheel-to-wheel action into the first corner.

Stoking the domestic crowd, Jake Stuyvesant, the American Formula 1 driver and former IndyCar Champion, was on pole. In P2 was the world's most successful-ever female racing driver, Remy Sabatino; Muammar Al Baradei, the Saudi Arabian Formula 1 sensation, was third in P3; while the fourth place – and still on the front row – was taken by Embiricos Savannah, the three-time IndyCar Champion and four-time winner of the Indianapolis 500. The front row for this race was, unquestionably, the Mount Rushmore of open-cockpit, open-wheel motor racing.

Expectations could not have been higher.

Shortly, the grid was smothered with mechanics, media, TV presenters and celebrities. Camera crews were darting everywhere as TV presenters rushed to grab as many interviews with these household names as possible.

At 12:45 p.m. the 15-minute hooter went. The grid started to clear: the media leaving for their commentary positions, the VIPs for their hospitality areas.

The composite crews assisted their drivers into their cars as the minutes ticked down.

At two minutes to go, the engines were fired.

A raucous sound rose up from the street. Edged by the 12-storey buildings to the south, the noise bounced around the open space of Central Park and reverberated off the walls on the other three sides. Everyone's senses felt completely enveloped.

From this point on, the public address system was to carry the feed from the television coverage put out by the American TV Network. The first voice to be heard was instantly recognizable.

Tom Cruise, the car-fanatic actor, was one of the commentators: *'We have two minutes to go, everyone – the gantry lights have just come on…'*

Cruise's presence prompted a huge reaction from the crowd.

'The race director is giving the signal. We're about to start the formation lap.'

Beside him in the box was Jim De Havilland, the Formula 1 race commentator from Great Britain, along with Dick McPaget, the legendary Brickyard race commentator of the Indianapolis 500.

Seconds later the 16 cars were pulling slowly off the grid, heading west along West 59th Street.

'How exciting is this – to see four cars abreast on the front row?' asked Cruise, as Stuyvesant led the pack away.

'Very, Tom,' responded the F1 commentator. *'And look there, even on the parade lap, we can see how different this style of racing will be … as they head into the first corner. Jake Stuyvesant's moving over to the right, to the park side of the track, to give himself the best line through Turn 1, but look at that – as they turn in – it's fantastic. The course is so*

wide there is, in effect, no *racing line. On most race tracks, the track is narrow – too narrow: there's only one fastest way through the corner. A driver on that racing line has precedence and an advantage. But that's not going to be the case here.'*

'How right you are, Jim,' agreed Dick McPaget. '*It's wide enough for a variety of lines through the corners. It's going to open the racing up dramatically. It'll be much more like oval racing ... except it'll be right here ... on the mother of all street circuits ... in the middle of New York City, for goodness sake.'*

As the cars straightened up after Turn 1, they were all facing down 7th Avenue. It was then that the openness of the track and the race became apparent.

'*Look at the space down here,'* said the F1 commentator. '*Look at the third row, there are four cars there too – all line abreast. Just imagine what that'll be like when they're all running like that – at top speed!'*

Even among the jaded old campaigners up in the commentary box there was a palpable air of excitement.

Two minutes later the cars had completed the parade lap.

They were forming up on the grid.

'*The last man is in place,'* said Cruise.

'Here we go,' said McPaget as the first red light came on. '*The first of three races ... 500 miles in all.'*

The engine sound increased in blips as the drivers psyched themselves for the start.

'*Two red lights.'*

More engine sound – now increasing in pitch.

'*Three lights.'*

Pause.

'*Four.'*

'*There's the fifth red light, wait ... wait ... wait ... any minute now.'*

'Now!' shouted one of the commentators. '*Now!'*

The engine sound crescendoed, all around Manhattan.

'*We've got a good start – all away.'*

'Look at the front row!'

'Jake Stuyvesant – with the red, white and blue wings – is getting away best.'

'He is, but look at Sabatino in the red and white car in second. She's keeping right with Stuyvesant, straight off the line.'

The crowds around the circuit were hearing and seeing all this action on the banks of electronic screens. It wasn't long before they were screaming their own excitement.

'Look at that,' said Tom Cruise, *'Sabatino's gaining on Stuyvesant.'*

'Stuyvesant looks like he is trying to commit to the corner early, to stake his claim – but with the track so wide there is *no racing line. Sabatino's cutting it much finer into Turn 1, looking to take him down the inside.'*

'Stuyvesant's turning in.'

'But Sabatino looks like she's overshooting – going too deep – cutting across his rear, drifting out wide – on the exit.'

'But – on this track – she can afford to do that without any loss of position.'

The front runners straightened up into 7th Avenue.

'Sabatino, even being well away from whatever might be the racing line, *has managed to draw level with Stuyvesant after the first corner.'*

The leaders were accelerating up through their 4th, 5th, 6th and 7th gears. Three cars were jockeying for the lead, but so were four cars jockeying for position in the second row and a similar number in the third.

'They look like they're all still charging down into a first corner after a start,' said the F1 man.

'The cars look like a swarm,' offered Cruise.

'We've not had this sort of pack in Formula 1 for decades … for years we've had to put up with processions.'

'Look at them go,' added Cruise, *'it's* fantastic. *It's like karting.'*

'Because they're all in the same car.'

For a moment the commentators were silent as the race headed down 7th Avenue; but the excitement on track couldn't keep them quiet for long.

'They're heading towards the tightest hairpin ... on any track ... anywhere in the world. How will they all get round – when they're all that close together?'

'A great question – and they're going to be approaching it at the end of a half-a-mile straight ... at top ... top speed ... for a turn they can only take at walking pace.'

All eyes were glued on the pack of F1 cars as they closed in on the braking zone.

'What a test of nerve.'

'The ultimate test of the late brakers.'

The three leading cars were still hurtling on. The advertising hoardings became bigger and more numerous as they entered the entertainment hub of the world's city for entertainment.

'Oh my God, they're all still going at full throttle.'

'No one's lifted yet, let alone near to braking.'

'Sabatino's tucked in on the right-hand side of the street, Stuyvesant's in the middle of the road, with Al Baradei between them – neck and neck.'

'Being so tight, of course, this corner would have more of a racing line.'

'And Sabatino's on it.'

'But, to get round fastest, she's got to slow the most, turn in the most, and then accelerate the most.'

'Hugging the inside line would force the others to go wider and further.'

'Incredible,' said Cruise, 'we've got the three best drivers in the world – including the first truly competitive woman – racing flat out three-abreast – on the streets of Manhattan – heading for a hairpin in Times Square.'

Another chuckle could be heard in the commentary box.

'What a test of machismo.'

'Or machisma.'

'300 yards.'

'200 yards.'

'100 yards...'

'Al Baradei's braked!' shrieked one commentator. *'He's braked first ... the Saudi driver ... he's the first one to brake.'*

'And – look – Stuyvesant's darted to the right, straight into the gap he's created.'

There was a puff of smoke.

'Has Stuyvesant locked up? He's still heading to the right – across Sabatino's path...

'...oh, no – is he about to ram her?'

The nosecone of Sabatino's car dipped suddenly.

'She's taken evasive action, braking sharply ... but her tyres have held. She's not locked-up.'

'She's avoided the collision, Tom, but she's opened a gap...'

'...which Stuyvesant has jumped straight into! He's managing to slow down without hitting anything ... and ... he's taken the place.'

'How paradoxical is that? Stuyvesant messes up, loses control of his car, induces a self-preserving flinch on the part of a rival, and still ends up taking advantage.'

The three leading cars were rounding the hairpin – almost at walking speed – barely inches between them.

Around the outside of the corner, every voice in the stands was screaming in excitement as the wheel-to-wheel action played out on the track below them.

Cars in the second row were now shaking themselves down as they turned in through the corner, immediately behind; they, too, were only inches apart.

'Look at this stream of cars rounding the sharpest hairpin seen anywhere – and right in front of the dazzling electronic advertising hoardings of Times Square.'

One of the commentators could be heard laughing with delight. *'This is sen-sation-al ... and we're only on the second corner.'*

All 16 cars were accelerating up Broadway on the far side of the hairpin.

'Sabatino's clearly not happy about that last corner,' said Cruise
'Boy ... does she look like she means business.'
'She's driving like she's got a score to settle.'
'She's right up behind Stuyvesant ... all over his gearbox.'
'Oh, yes ... it very much looks like we've got the start of a grudge match on our hands – a real dog fight.'
'If we're lucky!'

EIGHTY-SEVEN

By the time the cars had run 600 yards up Broadway, towards the south-western corner of Central Park, the dog fight was well and truly on. As they approached Turn 3, Stuyvesant was still the race leader. Sabatino was a close second ahead of Embiricos Savannah, the current IndyCar Champion. Al Baradei had lost position, through the hairpin, while three cars in the row immediately behind were keeping themselves on terms with him.

'Quite extraordinary,' said the IndyCar commentator. 'They're all still completely on top of each other.'

'What a difference to see the drivers on a level playing field.'

'Exactly that,' said Cruise, 'because there is no technological difference.'

'We do see something like that in F1,' came a slightly defensive contribution from the Formula 1 commentator, 'but, normally, only between the two drivers of the same team.'

'Where technology between the cars is unequal, though, the race out on the track can only be unequal.'

'But not here,' said Cruise. 'This format is brilliant. They're all fighting with the exact same chance.'

Now turning into the left-hand corner, taking them into Central Park, Stuyvesant took what would have been the conventional racing line.

'Look at Sabatino,' said Cruise. 'She's much, much later on the brakes. She's almost touching his rear wing.'

'Stuyvesant must have seen her. Going defensive, there, isn't he?'

'I think you're right, Tom. Stuyvesant's looking a little ragged. Sabatino's presence, that close behind, must be putting him under pressure.'

'But Sabatino's got the better exit from Turn 4, hasn't she?'

'She's gaining on him!'

'Oh my God – she's now going round the outside – out to the right of him.'

The cars were sweeping out of the left-hander.

'*Sabatino is hanging in there, even though she's got to go further.*'

'*Will she hold it together – or get more of that understeer we saw earlier?*'

'*That would be disastrous, she'd hit the outside wall.*'

'*The track's widening out just in time – before it now opens up into the park.*'

'*Stuyvesant's gone defensive out of Turn 4 too.*'

'*Sabatino's still on him.*'

She seemed to be gaining.

'*They're both heavily on the power, as they run under the trees.*'

'*But is she away better?*'

The two leading cars were side by side as they swept through the left-right-left meander through Central Park. Reaching the end of Sector I, coinciding with the circuit crossing the 66th Street Transverse, the two leading cars were still side by side as they rose and fell over the bridge.

'*Sabatino's pulling ahead, down Stuyvesant's right-hand side.*'

They were wheel to wheel all the way through this sweeping section of the circuit to Turn II – the right-hander which took them back onto the straight road edging the western side of the park.

'*Sabatino's perfectly placed to take the inside line into this corner.*'

'*It looks like she's ready to pounce.*'

'*She* is *a racer,*' said the FI commentator with a smile and hint of pride in his voice. '*And tactical.*'

'*Stuyvesant's only got to make the tiniest of slips, and she'll have him.*'

The audience held its breath as the two front runners set up to swing right in 4th gear.

But as they hit the wider straight road, it was Stuyvesant who suddenly experienced understeer.

'*What's happened to Jake?*' asked Cruise.

'*He's going wide.*'

'*Has he locked-up again?*'

'*There wasn't any smoke.*'

'*Whatever happened – he* is *running wide!*'

'*He's given it away to Sabatino – hasn't she got an easy ride down the inside? She's got him – she's going to get past.*'

'*Hang on – Stuyvesant may have gone wide, but doesn't that give him a much better – more open line – into the immediate entry to Turn 12.*'

Stuyvesant was now accelerating hard.

'*Sabatino's having to take a finer line into the right-hander – is she going to be able to hold that much speed through there?*'

'*Sabatino's carrying too much pace.*'

'*The entry to Turn 12 is narrower than all the others. Oh, no – she's got to lift – she's lifting* and *now braking.*'

'*Stuyvesant has smelled blood – not easing up at all.*'

'*Guys, are we witnessing the perfect cutback?*'

Cheers erupted once again as Sabatino couldn't retain her position and Stuyvesant shot through, down the inside, and retook the lead.

The cars reached the end of the first lap.

Then the last-placed car crossed the start/finish line.

'*Good grief,*' said the F1 man, '*by this point in a grand prix, there would be a good couple of seconds between each driver – clear air, one to the next. Here, we've got 4.3 seconds between 1st and 16th place! Not only that, we've seen any number of blows exchanged in the duel for first place … we've seen a scrap for third … and we've got what looks like a full-pitched battle raging for 5th … and* all *that has happened during the first lap of the race!*'

EIGHTY-EIGHT

Two hours flew by.

'They're on the last lap,' declared Dick McPaget.

The pack was heading down to Turn 2 for the last time to the Times Square Hairpin.

'After nearly two hours, we have Stuyvesant, Sabatino, Embiricos Savannah and Al Baradei – the four leading cars – all within 4 seconds of each other. And only 15 seconds covering the first 12 cars.'

'I've never seen wheel to wheel jockeying like this,' said the Formula 1 commentator. *'At this point in a grand prix, the 6th-placed runner would more than likely have been lapped by now.'*

'And it isn't over yet,' interjected Tom Cruise loudly. *'Look!'*

The world watched on as Sabatino chased Stuyvesant down into the hairpin.

'She's tried this attack every which way.'

'How will she try it this time?'

'She's moving across towards him, as ever only inches behind.'

'She seems to be moving in even closer.'

'This is amazing … what do you think she's doing … trying to psych him out?'

'Could be.'

'She's not braking.'

'Neither is he.'

'Who is going to blink first?'

'Oh my God – I've never seen chess played at 200 miles an hour before.'

'Is it chess – or poker?'

'Who knows – who cares,' said Cruise, *'this is just fantastic.'*

'What was that?'

'What was what?'

'Didn't you see smoke?'

'Where?'

'It must have been Stuyvesant.'

'Sabatino's braking now.'

'She is, but Stuyvesant's not decelerating anything like *as fast. He* must *have locked-up – it must have been* his *smoke.'*

'Whatever it is or was, he's got understeer – he's got understeer!*'*

Sabatino was braking hard, the front of her car visibly dipping with the force of the deceleration.

'Stuyvesant's running wide – running on. *Running too deep.'*

'She's not, *though, Jim – look – Sabatino's not. Has she got the grip?'*

'Sabatino's managing to slow down fast and *turn in.'*

'Stuyvesant's still in way too deep.'

'She's round the apex.'

'Yes, yes … yes … YES…!'

'She's done it – she's gone and done it. That's after 46 laps of the most extraordinary cat and mouse game we've ever seen – she's gone and taken *him.'*

Everyone held their breath, as, passing at Turn 2, Sabatino had 2½ miles left of this race to consolidate her lead.

'Will she hold on to it, though? Won't he come back and take the lead off her?'

The new race leader hurtled up Broadway.

Stuyvesant was straight on her tail.

'She's cornering through Turns 3 and 4 at possibly the highest speed we've seen all race.'

'Yeah, but Jake's not letting her go – Stuyvesant looks set on returning the insult.'

'But it ain't happening any time soon – look at her pace as she flies off into Central Park.'

'Oh my God, look at them both go.'

The cars were swinging through the sweeping turns within the wooded section of West Drive.

'He's not *letting her off.'*

'*Turn 11 and 12 is where it's all got to happen,*' said Dick McPaget, '*where Stuyvesant got the cutback before.*'

They, and the world, waited with stifled breaths – as the two leading cars ran on towards the edge of the park.

'*I don't think so, Dick – not this time. I don't think Stuyvesant's going to get a look in. She's clean. Absolutely clean … she's not giving him an inch.*'

'*Sabatino's flying – look at her confidence and commitment through Turn 12.*'

They were both now in the 85th Street Transverse – crossing Central Park – into the cutting – shooting the two bridges carrying the West and East Drives.

'*She* is *keeping him at bay.*'

The cars hurtled through Turn 14, round the Metropolitan Museum of Art.

'*Any slip-up here – into this wide section of the track – and Stuyvesant will surely have her.*'

They straightened up as they both exited into the top of the near mile-long straight of 5th Avenue.

'*Now we've got a* drag *race,*' said McPaget.

'*This is so intense. This whole duel has felt like a drag race.*'

Sabatino was charging down the middle of 5th Avenue.

'*She's still ahead … but won't that give Stuyvesant the chance of a tow?*'

'*He is weaving left and right behind her. Is he trying to faze her through her mirrors – trying to play her at her own game – trying to intimidate* her *into going defensive too soon?*'

'*Stuyvesant absolutely wants to throw her off her game, and then use the wideness of the upcoming turns – around Grand Army Plaza – to snatch the lead back from her.*'

'*You're right – he's far from done.*'

'*Where is she going to position herself?*'

300 yards to run.

'*She is not setting up for the corner … yet … she's not declaring how she'll be committing … one way or the other … yet.*'

'On she runs – at just under 200 miles an hour – towards a right-angle turn.'

'She's not going to blink,' said Cruise, with admiration clear in his voice.

'She's got to brake soon ... she'll run out of road.'

100 yards

'They've both got to brake soon – one of them's got to brake.'

'It's Stuyvesant – it's Stuyvesant,' chimed McPaget, 'he's *blinked. He's the one who's backed off.'*

Sabatino seemed to sense the very moment he'd hit his brakes.

The moment he had, she went for it.

'She's hammering her brakes – and turning in – both at the same time.'

'She's turning right, turning in so hard – oh, no ... she's losing the Lambourn's back end.'

'The back end's swinging well out to the left.'

'She's turning into the slide, though. She's steering into it – she's into a full-on four-wheel drift.'

'An armful of opposite lock.'

'Can she hold it?'

'She's keeping the power down.'

'It's like she's rallying – what fantastic car control.'

'Sensational.'

'She's seat-of-the-pants-ing it through that corner.'

'She's through ... she's through – into the Plaza.'

'Stuyvesant is cornering much more cleanly.'

'But will it do him any good?'

'She's still ahead – still pushing her car to the limit.'

Rounding Turn 16 – to the left – in front of the huge quarter-circle of stands beside the Plaza Hotel, Sabatino was facing the last corner of the race.

The crowds above her in the stands were on their feet, screaming at the drama.

'She's still on the power – still on the power – she's not letting up for a moment.'

Sabatino was in the middle of Turn 17.

'Stuyvesant's still charging – still pounding his car.'

'And there's the chequered flag.'

'She's ... going to do it ... she's ... she's ... she's ... DONE IT!'

The commentators – the crowds – the TV audience – the people watching in the hospitality suites around the circuit – all went mad.

Everyone was drained having watched this battle rage – wheel to wheel – for nearly two hours.

But that made the emotional release at the end of it all the more exhilarating.

EIGHTY-NINE

Manhattan was euphoric. It spilled out to the rest of the world. One-design racing had proved itself a sensation after just one race. Clinching it was the human element. With no difference between the cars, there was no technological advantage. During the hour's break between races, the intensity of the racing was all anyone could talk about.

Straker, meanwhile, was concerned – not by what was happening – but by what hadn't. There had been no manifestation of the threat made against Sabatino. While it should have been a comfort, Straker feared the chances of it were getting higher the further into this sequence of races they went.

He hoped her garage in the pit lane would be a sanctuary. He couldn't imagine the 'Ndrangheta could have been able to infiltrate a member into Sabatino's team in that timeframe. Straker hoped she would remain surrounded by her composite team in the pits, and so beyond public reach – up until the start of the next race.

Race two in the Undisputed World Motor Racing Championship was to begin after a further 5-lap practice.

This Championship was going to be decided by an aggregation of times over the three races. Sabatino may have won the first race and been leading the standings at the moment, but only by one tenth of a second – and that was after two hours of racing. She had no margin of error – not only over her principal rival – but over the first ten cars. The tenth-placed man was only 9.8 seconds behind her.

Sabatino was pumped. She called a gathering of her team in their pit lane garage to discuss the car and how they could get more out of it. Then – out on track, using the short practice session as a testing opportunity – she pounded the Lambourn, particularly through the Central Park section, to see how it would respond to their latest tweaks. She wanted to refine every facet of her relationship with the car.

But it was on the last lap before forming up again that she knew something was wrong. The car started pulling to the left.

The temperature on her front left brake was high.

Much higher than the right.

It was Sabatino's honour to be starting from pole. She brought the car to a halt at the very front of the grid. Having been static for only a few seconds, she dreaded what she saw. Smoke was billowing from her front left.

She radioed the pits. A hurried conversation took place. The team in the garage scanned the telemetry. It looked like pressure in the brakes. But it was too late for them to get to her on the grid. To get to the pits, she would have to circle all the way round with the formation lap.

As Sabatino led the field around the circuit, she kept testing the brakes.

Her team studied the telemetry.

The temperature of the front left was getting higher.

'It's no good, Remy … we're going to have to bring you in.'

At the end of the lap she pulled into the pits, while the rest of the field were forming up on the grid.

Her team lifted the car straight up on the jacks.

Removing the front wheels, the front left produced a plume of smoke. Urgently, they examined and worked on the front left brake.

The lights were being lit on the gantry for the start of the second leg.

The race was starting without her.

'Shit,' she screamed to herself.

Her team worked fast.

In just over twenty seconds they had partially bled the brakes, venting some of the pressure.

The wheels were replaced.

The car was dropped back down off the jacks.

The lollipop swivelled, giving her clearance to move off.

Sabatino was away.

But at the moment she exited the pit lane, she was nearly 40 seconds behind the others. The pack was already half a lap ahead, heading up Broadway, being led by the American Jake Stuyvesant. Sabatino was facing an enormous task to get back on terms. There may have been the consolation that she wouldn't be in dirty air behind other runners, but that would be no meaningful advantage in cars with such similar performances.

For 22 laps Sabatino drove a blistering race. Her drive was exemplary. Without the proximity of other cars, she clocked a straight sequence of the six fastest laps. But she had only closed the gap with the race leader by 10 seconds.

She remained half a minute behind Stuyvesant, who was still out in front.

When, suddenly, Jim De Havilland, the Formula 1 race commentator, said: '*Oh, no – it looks like we have been visited by the spirit of Murray Walker:* "Anything happens in grand prix racing, and it usually does".'

The race leaders had been heading down towards Times Square.

'*Savannah's making a move,*' said Cruise.

'*Where – how? There's no gap!*' replied McPaget.

Jake Stuyvesant was steaming down 7th Avenue with 300 yards to run.

The hairpin was looming.

The crowds, in the banked seats on the outside of the corner, were roaring as the tightly bunched Formula 1 cars headed towards them.

Behind Stuyvesant, and to his left, ran Embiricos Savannah.

'*It looks like the four-time IndyCar champion's waiting – to see if Stuyvesant slips up.*'

'And then there's Al Baradei, poised behind both of them – waiting to pounce.'

Stuyvesant braked. Hard and fast.

The car reacted well.

'Good grief, that deceleration was rapid,' said De Havilland, *'but he's kept it under control…'*

'Unexpectedly so.'

'Savannah's flinched, though – look!' said Cruise.

'Who in turn's spooked Al Baradei behind.'

'Who's stood on the brakes.'

'Oh no!'

'He's thrown the car behind him.'

'There's been a shunt,' shouted De Havilland. *'There's been contact!'*

A car with Finnish markings – running in 6th place – hurtled out sideways from the pack.

'That's Vallu Karvinen … the F1 driver. He's been bumped.'

'He's losing it.'

'Swapping ends. Oh boy, he's losing control.'

The car, now heading backwards, was still travelling at considerable speed.

Karvinen hit the brakes. All four wheels locked up. Smoke streamed from all four tyres.

'He's heading for the Armco.'

'He never got the chance to brake – he must still be doing a hundredish miles an hour.'

The rear end of the Finn's Lambourn smashed into the outside of the Times Square Hairpin at a steep angle. His right rear wheel impacted first. It was enough to start an anticlockwise rotation in the car. As that wheel assembly buckled, the gearbox then hit. The moment of force was enough to accelerate the car's rotation. Karvinen's front end was now beginning to sweep round to its left. It seemed to rotate faster. Moments later the front left wheel – and the entire left flank of the car – was slammed side on into the barrier. Its carbon fibre extremities disintegrated on impact, as they were designed to, absorbing vast amounts of kinetic energy. Bits of the car exploded along the barrier, high in the air, rebounding back onto the track.

The TV pictures cut away, the producer fearing the worst.

Instead, they focused on the cars still in the race as they squeezed round the hairpin – trying to keep away from Karvinen's radiating debris – and into Broadway. Stuyvesant had kept the lead. Embiricos Savannah had retained third while Muammar Al Baradei, recovering quickly from the bump into the corner, had retained position, P3.

'*That was quite a smash,*' said Cruise. '*Hope the guy's alright.*'

'*I think he is,*' said McPaget, with relief in his voice. '*I think he is … I've just seen him wave … it looks like he's conscious.*'

'*Thank goodness. But he's not going to get out of there anytime soon. His monocoque looks like it's wedged under the barrier.*'

'*They're going to have to call for the safety car—*'

'*If not red flag the race. There's debris – wheels, carbon fibre, barge boards, fins and bits of wing – all over the track.*'

Double yellow flags were already being waved frantically on the entry side of the hairpin.

'*The rest of the pack are through. But you know what … this could be an extraordinary boon … for Sabatino…*'

'*Yes, indeed,*' said Cruise with a chuckle. '*How far back is she?*'

'*Just passing the Museum of Modern Art, at the far end of the circuit.*'

'*Wow, a safety car now would be absolutely race-changing – for her.*'

Matt Straker, still listening out for signs of trouble, was monitoring the goings-on via the screen in front of him. He, too, heard the analysis from the commentary team. For a moment he allowed himself some competitive excitement, hoping the situation might play out to Sabatino's advantage.

Remy Sabatino was pushing hard through the apex of Turn 16, within the Plaza Chicane. Her race engineer had relayed news of the crash at the Times Square Hairpin. There was nothing she could do about it. Fate would determine whether the safety car would be deployed or the race would be red flagged. All she could do was keep pushing.

Sabatino powered through the turn and gained the end of the start/finish straight.

She got the news.

The letters SC appeared on her steering wheel display.

She heard it over the team radio.

The safety car *was being* deployed...

As the race leader reached the end of the Museum Mile a minute later, Jake Stuyvesant had to lift off. Waiting for them, but already travelling at 90 miles an hour, was an eye-bulging SSC Tuatara – dressed overall in red, white and blue – deployed as the Manhattanheim pace/safety car.

'*Here comes the magnificent Tuatara, leading the crocodile down 7th Avenue,*' said Dick McPaget to the various audiences. '*But that supercar will need all the power, acceleration and speed from its 1,350 horses and 6.9 litres to keep its impatient followers happy ... and cool.*'

'*Sure thing, but it's going to look stunning while it does so, eh, Tom!*'

A single TV shot from a helicopter flying overhead encompassed all the drama.

It looked down into the plunging canyon between the midtown skyscrapers of Manhattan.

Below was the crocodile of slowed Formula 1 cars, all running line astern.

The Tuatara led the queue of grand prix cars towards Times Square and viewers could see the smashed remains of Vallu Karvinen's Lambourn on the outside of the hairpin as the procession filed by, hugging the inside of the corner. The shaken but uninjured figure of the Finnish driver could be seen being helped away, while numerous marshals were moving quickly to remove the wreckage of the car and clear its debris from the track.

And then, at the top of the screen – at the top end of 7th Avenue – was the red and white Maltese-flagged car of Remy Sabatino, closing in quickly on the back of the field, as she was permitted to do.

Within five minutes of the crash, Sabatino was almost touching the rear wing of the last-placed man in the race. Because of the deployment of the safety car, her deficit on the race leader had now been reduced to a handful of seconds.

Four laps at the slower pace behind the safety car went by, before the safety car's lights went out – the track having been cleared of Karvinen's wreckage.

They were about to race again.

Sabatino, back on terms with the field, set to – aiming to make up places.

In three out of the next five approaches to the Times Square Hairpin she overtook a car at the back of the pack.

With a couple of breathtaking lunges down the outside, she took two more by getting a better exit than they did from Turn 14 next to the Metropolitan Museum of Art.

And another driver was overtaken by hounding him the full length of 5th Avenue into Turn 15, the entry to the Grand Army Plaza Chicane.

But she was running out of time…

Jake Stuyvesant ended up taking the chequered flag.

Embiricos Savannah was second and Muammar Al Baradei third.

The three race leaders of that leg were separated by less than 3.4 seconds.

Despite Sabatino's overheating brakes, but then being helped by the deployment of the safety car, she managed to finish 10th – 7.2 seconds behind the race winner. After 332 miles, and nearly four hours of racing she was, on aggregate, only 7.1 seconds behind the overall leader: Jake Stuyvesant.

Into the third and final race of the Undisputed World Motor Racing Championship, Stuyvesant started in the lead – from pole. Embiricos Savannah was second and Muammar Al Baradei third. Sabatino's recovery in the second race had placed her 6th on aggregate. Winning the Championship was still possible, but she would have to achieve a bigger margin than anyone had managed so far – either that or the top three would have to encounter a mechanical glitch, as she had done, or they would have to come to grief or take each other out on the track, triggering another appearance of the safety car.

Sabatino went on to win the third race, which no one denied was impressive. It was a victory that could only have been achieved by overtaking the quality field in front of her. Starting from 6th place on the grid, her progression was dramatic, but far from straightforward. Managing to get past Embiricos Savannah, Muammar Al Baradei and Jake Stuyvesant, she then had to withstand each of them repeatedly coming back at her. Over the course of an hour, she fended off a series of relentless counterattacks.

At the line, Stuyvesant secured a gentleman's fourth.

He had only needed to keep himself within 7 seconds of Sabatino, which he managed.

He had done enough.

Stuyvesant had won the title.

The moment the cars came to rest in the pit lane, the crowds broke loose. From all round the circuit, tens of thousands of people streamed out of the stands, to make their way along the track, in towards the Grand Army Plaza. The crowd amassed there in front of the quarter-circle bank of seats. They wanted to witness – for themselves – the crowning of the Undisputed World Motor Racing Champion up on the huge aerial podium.

Then came a *'Ladies and gentlemen'* booming over the public address system – once again it was the voice of Tom Cruise.

The actor himself walked out onto the stage.

The noise to greet him was deafening.

Cruise's face lit up with his gigawatt smile.

'*This has been the best motor racing I have* ever *seen,*' he said, to which the crowds roared in response.

'*And we have a winner. We really can proclaim the driver who is* undisputedly the *World Motor Racing Champion.*'

Once again the crowd roared its approval.

'*To crown that champion,*' continued Cruise, '*I now have the honour to introduce to you the person who came up with the extraordinary idea for this extraordinary race ... the idea of Manhattanheim.*'

The crowd roared again, even though none of them yet had the faintest idea who this was.

'*Ladies and gentlemen,*' said Cruise, '*it took a man – and a mind – of exceptional vision to conceive this format and this Championship. Manhattanheim has proved to be spectacular.*'

More roars – of unrestrained agreement.

'*But, my friends, we have been talking about this Championship as a supreme test of the driver. Another summit, though, has been scaled this weekend. It has taken 40 years to get a top-level motor race to be run here in New York City.*'

Roars of: 'Shame!'

'*It has also taken* sixty years *to pit the best of open-cockpit, open-wheel drivers – of the IndyCar and Formula 1 series – against each other once again ... something that hasn't happened since Monzanapolis in 1958. It can be no exaggeration, my friends, to claim that we have seen* history *made here today.*'

Another celebratory roar came from the crowd.

'*It should be clear to all that it has taken a remarkable man to bring Manhattanheim into being,*' Cruise continued. '*And it is now* my *privilege to introduce that man to you – to introduce you to someone I am honoured to call my friend...*

'*Ladies and gentlemen ... please give up a classic New York welcome to the one and only ...* Mister ... ARNO ... RAVILIOUS.'

NINETY

Arno Ravilious?

ARNO RAVILIOUS?

How could that be possible…?

It was as if a nuclear bomb had gone off.

People were stunned.

Anyone with a passing interest in Formula 1 was utterly aghast.

No one could believe it.

The man – Ravilious – was meant to be nearly dead … he'd had a heart attack … hadn't he? He was ancient. How could someone that old have conceived, created, organized and executed such an extraordinary event?

How had this man managed to set all this up in complete anonymity?

How had he managed to achieve the supposedly impossible?

But:

He had brought motor racing into the heart of the culture capital of America.

He had brought it into New York City.

He had managed to gain the cooperation of IndyCar – combining that championship series with Formula 1 – to create something truly remarkable. Something gestalt: something so palpably more than the sum of its parts.

He had created a brand-new motor racing format, and given it undeniable appeal to the mainstream.

As Arno Ravilious appeared on the aerial podium, he looked in the peak of health and physical condition. Despite his reticence for attention, he bore his slim, tall frame with a commanding presence. The bald head, the dark glasses perched across his forehead and the hand-made blue silk shirt all created an attention-absorbing appearance.

The American crowds may not have been familiar with him, but they were going to give anyone who could conceive and execute such an extraordinary race a standing ovation.

In the middle of the stage, Ravilious was embraced by Tom Cruise.

'Arno has graciously agreed to award the prizes,' said the actor. *'So ... the second runner-up to the Undisputed World Motor Racing Champion is an iconic first. The world's* fastest-ever *woman racing driver and the winner of two of these Championship races ... ladies and gentlemen, I give you Ms ... Remy ... Sabatino!'*

A wall of sound erupted as her name was called out.

Sabatino appeared on the podium.

Roars, shrieks, whistles, air horns, fire crackers and the sound of 10,000 voices boomed out over the south-eastern corner of Central Park. Wearing the red and white of her native Malta, Remy Sabatino – with a flash of her dark eyes and brilliant smile – seemed to radiate from the podium, the Plaza and two hundred million television screens around the world.

She went directly to Arno Ravilious and gave him a full body hug.

Sabatino stepped up onto the third place on the podium.

'And, now, ladies and gentlemen we come to the first runner-up to the Undisputed World Motor Racing Champion. The phenomenal talent from Saudi Arabia – Mr ... Muammar ... Al Baradei.*'*

Once again the crowd's response was impassioned. Nationality and politics were forgotten: New Yorkers were paying tribute to a gutsy and spirited racer.

'And, now,' said Cruise re-facing the crowd, *'I have the pleasure of confirming –* the *driver of the moment – of the hour – the man who can now be* rightly *described as the* Undisputed *World Motor Racing Champion ... the US of A's very own –* Mr ... Jake ... Stuyvesant...*'*

The crowd's reaction was immense, the roars utterly deafening.

After all of the prizes were presented on the podium, the top three drivers were invited to the side of the stage from where they could step straight onto the top deck of a double-decker bus. This moved off, nudging through the crowds as it made its way round the circuit. All the spectators around New York were going to get a chance to see, in the flesh, the gladiatorial heroes they had been watching battle it out on the track. The three victors waved to the joyous crowds at street level, into the stands along South Park Central, and up into most of the now-open windows of buildings overlooking the circuit.

As they travelled, the drivers were interviewed by Tom Cruise, their conversations transmitted over the public address system. At the same time, those interviews were filmed by dozens of TV camera crews, all of which had their pictures beaming out live around the globe. The occasion stimulated a feel-good factor that people had not experienced for a very long time.

In television studios the race was immediately being discussed, analyzed, critiqued and celebrated.

Talk soon switched to the surprise involvement in it of Arno Ravilious – and the impact his part in this race could have on the future of Formula 1. Talk focused on what the Manhattanheim spectacle now meant to the prospective ownership of Motor Racing Promotions.

Sir Jackie Stewart, interviewed by Sky TV, was clear and forthright:

'Oh, yes,' he said, 'this changes everything.'

'You mean the future of Motor Racing Promotions?' asked the interviewer.

'Not just the future of MRP,' he said. 'In a stroke, this Manhattanheim concept has changed the fundamentals of *motor racing*. Arno Ravilious has reminded us all of the man he is ... why he has achieved what he has ... how he was able to build Formula 1 into such a global phenomenon.'

'Because he's managed to bring Formula 1 and IndyCar together?'

'Not only that. In this one race, he has cured all the ills of the sport and comprehensively rebranded it. He's dealt with *all* the issues that have been dogging Formula 1, for so long – predictable results, processional races, a boring product for the spectator. He's not stuck within the confines of the status quo, or stuck with a governing body that has failed to address the consequences of its disastrous rule changes. Arno Ravilious has demonstrated what can happen when he is left to get on with what he does best.'

'Quite fascinating, Sir Jackie. And in respect of Motor Racing Promotions, where do you think this leaves Gabriel Barrus – the Whittlebury Group – Suleiman Al-Megrahi?'

'Oh that has a very clear answer, Jim,' said Sir Jackie. 'It leaves *them* absolutely nowhere.'

NINETY-ONE

Straker was not allowing himself to be caught up in the excitement of the race. Things were still weighing heavily on his mind. There had been no sign of any threat against Sabatino. She had survived this far, and he was determined to get her away as quickly as possible. The moment the race had ended, he broke from the celebrations – leaving the circuit complex, sprinting straight back to fetch the Harley-Davidson. As quickly as he could manage it, he wanted Sabatino back to the Quartech Falcon, which was fully prepped at MacArthur airport and on immediate standby to fly her out. Waiting for her outside the least-overlooked exit from the race track, Straker sat astride the motorbike, with its engine running.

But where was she?

He had texted her, confirming their plan.

Ten minutes slipped by.

His phone vibrated in his pocket.

Thinking she had got delayed, Straker wrestled to retrieve the device from his tight leather pocket. When he looked at the text, though, he was in for a complete shock:

Colonel Straker, Sorry to put you through it with the threat against Remy S. THERE NEVER WAS ONE. Please don't worry about this any more. I owe you both a very big something. Arno Ravilious

What the hell was *this*?

Straker stared at his phone in a state of incredulity.

He simply couldn't believe it … couldn't compute it. At all.

What was Ravilious up to? Why would Ravilious have ever been threatening *Remy Sabatino*?

Straker was stunned.

Despite his lack of comprehension, though, he forced himself to take a step back. Wasn't there something to be made from this?

If so, what...?

Straker's mind raced.

However bizarre the content, this was still a *direct* communication from Arno Ravilious. Hadn't they wanted to talk to him? Didn't this give them that opportunity?

Copying in Dominic Quartano, he texted back:

> Mr Ravilious: We know about the Al-Megrahi shareholdings. We know that converting the Frankfurt Capital loan could dilute him, denying him control. Dominic Quartano is ready to talk. Quartech believes it can help.
> Matt Straker

That evening word started spreading that Arno Ravilious had given an interview to *The New York Times.* It was said to be explosive. News of the online article went viral in a matter of hours.

As soon as he heard about it, Straker clicked through and read it for himself:

New York Times:	'We appreciate this opportunity to speak to you after an extraordinary weekend here in New York. Manhattanheim is widely acclaimed a triumph. Congratulations. The first question has to be: Why did you hold it at all?'
Arno Ravilious:	'Formula 1 has been losing ground for the last two years. TV audience figures have been dropping. No one within the sport seemed to be able, ready or prepared to do anything about it.'
NYT:	'Wasn't the TV audience for Formula 1, though, *your* preserve?'
Ravilious:	'The commercial aspects of the medium are, but not the content. I now readily admit my pursuit of pay-per-view coverage was a mistake; putting any programming behind a paywall decimates an audience. But that was only part

of the story. Formula 1's biggest problem has been the dire quality of the racing spectacle.'

NYT: 'You mean out on the track?'

Ravilious: 'Indeed. Grands prix have become processional. All of us know, now — before every race – which cars are going to be on the front three rows of the grid, and in what order. This season, we just *know* it's going to be a Lambourn on pole.'

NYT: 'So why didn't you change Formula 1 to address this flaw?'

Ravilious: 'It's such a misconception that I run everything in F1 – and that, when something doesn't work, I am responsible. Under the Concorde Agreement, within which I am obliged to operate, the rules of the sport are entirely the responsibility of the FIA.'

NYT: 'So why, then, hasn't the *FIA* changed these apparently damaging regulations?'

Ravilious: 'One very clear reason … the establishment of the ludicrous Strategy Group. This was set up to try and revitalize the decision-making process in Formula 1, as the malaise of predictability of races took hold. "Give the stakeholders a say" was the cry. But you can't have competitors in charge of the rules. Turkeys don't vote for Christmas. Why would those teams benefiting from a set of rules ever vote to change them? Why would they voluntarily give away their advantage? The Strategy Group was never going to achieve agreement and do anything. It meant that any technological advantage was going to be the biggest block on any change in Formula 1. The moment a team gains an advantage, of course it is going to resist all subsequent attempts to change those rules – in order to preserve that advantage. As a result of the Strategy Group, therefore, we got gridlock. Formula 1 has become completely unmanageable.'

NYT: 'Is that why you decided to sell the company back in July, then, and step down?'

Ravilious: 'Not entirely. I was in danger of losing control of the business. After abandoning the idea of a stock market flotation, I managed to release some capital from the business by selling a minority stake in Motor Racing Promotions to the Italian media giant, *Dramma Sportivo TV*. But there is a malevolent force at work on the fringes of Formula 1. Over a sustained period, *Dramma Sportivo TV* was subjected to the most extraordinary industrial attacks – strikes, mysterious fires at its studio; its CEO was even rammed by a car as he left the studios, leaving him paralyzed; trucks were set on fire at an outside broadcast – so that, eventually, the company was hounded into insolvency. Then, strangely – without any delay and no public auction – its stake in MRP was acquired from the receiver by Suleiman Al-Megrahi and his cronies.'

NYT: 'Are you saying that Suleiman Al-Megrahi was behind the collapse of *Dramma Sportivo TV*?'

Ravilious: 'I'm not suggesting that at all. But you might like to ask Mr Al-Megrahi about the industrial attacks – how he knew the company was going into administration and how he knew that he should have his bid ready – and then why the sale of the MRP stake was never put out to public tender. The next development was that my wife, who has been "friendly" with Mr Al-Megrahi for years, filed to divorce me. The principal element of her divorce settlement was not the cash, the houses, the Caribbean island, the private jet – but the MRP stake. Her claim was for half the marital assets, but the only asset she named was my shareholding in Motor Racing Promotions.'

NYT: 'Are you saying she was in league with Mr Al-Megrahi?'

Ravilious: 'I'm not suggesting that at all. But you might like to

	ask them about their conduct over the last 10 years, and particularly over the last three months?'
NYT:	'So you're saying that with the *Dramma Sportivo TV* station's stake in MRP, and your wife's half of your own shareholding, Suleiman Al-Megrahi was about to take control?'
Ravilious:	'I am.'
NYT:	'So why did you move to sell your company? And why the sudden retirement announcement?'
Ravilious:	'I found an excellent buyer in the form of Gabriel Barrus, of Salt Lake Media.'
NYT:	'Mr Barrus's commercial approach to Formula 1, though, has been criticized as being very aggressive – proposing to standardize race fees paid by circuits, which would mean some of the old favourites would be dropped; he embraced the offer of a grand prix in Saudi Arabia, accepting that Remy Sabatino – as a woman driver – would not be permitted to compete there; and he declared that he would treat all teams financially the same, including Ferrari. It was widely thought Mr Barrus likely to undermine the fabric of Formula 1.'
Ravilious:	'His commercial acumen is outstanding. Gabriel showed very clearly what a proper commercial approach to Formula 1 would look like.'
NYT:	'From the feedback, though, people didn't like it.'
Ravilious:	'Maybe there's something to learn from that. In any case, Mr Al-Megrahi soon stepped forwards and held himself out as the prospective owner and boss of Motor Racing Promotions.'
NYT:	'Which prompted the teams and historic circuits to launch their breakaway consortium – the Whittlebury Group – immediately after his announcement?'
Ravilious:	'The teams' and circuits' response to an Al-Megrahi-led Formula 1 was very clear. They were very obviously

	ready to vote with their feet. It's interesting to note the Whittlebury Group was also supported by the GPDA…'
NYT:	'…The Grand Prix Drivers' Association…'
Ravilious:	' …and that's ironic, really. The drivers are usually quick to complain when the old circuits get squeezed out of the grand prix season, probably because it plays well with the fans. They don't seem to understand that the old circuits don't pay anywhere near the same scale of fees as the newcomers. If we don't scale up, who's going to pay for their cars, let alone their extraordinary salaries?'
NYT:	'From what you're saying, and the way you're saying it, you had a fair idea that triggering a sale and stepping down was going to cause quite a reaction?'
Ravilious:	(No response)
NYT:	'Some could look at this and say you triggered it to demonstrate what Formula 1 might look like without you?'
Ravilious:	(No response)
NYT:	'If that's why you did what you did, it was a risky move – not least as you didn't know, and still don't, whether you could get control back? What happens if you can't?'
Ravilious:	'I haven't accepted the premise of your question. In any case, I am pleased with the one-design Manhattanheim project. I think it serves to demonstrate the capacity motor racing still has to improve itself and grow. It's a clear indication of what I will be doing from now on. Manhattanheim worked superbly; it caught the public's imagination and made a huge amount of money.'
NYT:	'So are you saying that it's really up to Formula 1 if they want you back?'
Ravilious:	'Oh, I'm not suggesting that at all.'
NYT:	'Mr Ravilious, one question does come to mind about Manhattanheim: if this idea was so good, why didn't you ever launch it from within Formula 1?'
Ravilious:	'Because, as I said, Formula 1 has become unmanageable.

The teams only ever fight their own corner; there's no sense of collective responsibility. The FIA is completely rigid. I could never have mounted the Manhattanheim race idea from within the constraints of Formula 1.'

NYT: 'You sound rather despairing of the FIA. Is that because it's an obvious windmill to tilt at, or is this a profoundly held opinion?'

Ravilious: 'Definitely profound. The FIA is not the natural home for modern Formula 1. Originally, by which I mean back in 1904, the *Association Internationale des Automobile Clubs Reconnus*, the AIACR, was founded as an international collective to promote car use by the public in different countries. It was never set up to be a sporting governing body. Its principal concerns have always been worthy stuff – like road safety and drink-driving campaigns.'

NYT: 'So how did today's FIA get involved in motor racing at all?'

Ravilious: 'When it started, motor racing needed a governing body of some sort. The only international body in existence at the time was the AIACR and so, for convenience, it made sense to approach them and see if they would take motor racing on. They did, setting up a new division they called the CSI, the *Commission Sportive Internationale*. In time, that became FISA which, in turn, became the FIA proper. None of those bodies, though – let alone the FIA, at any stage in its development – was set up to manage a 10 billion dollar a year business. Not only that, the voting structure is completely inappropriate. There are, perhaps, 30 countries in the world with a direct involvement in Formula 1 – as hosts of a race, fielders of a driver, as a base for manufacturing – and yet there are 120-plus countries affiliated to the FIA, *all* of which get a vote on matters to do with Formula 1. That means F1 sits in a governing body where its participants are inherently outvoted by countries that have nothing to do with the sport and, worse still, know nothing about it. But that's all contributory detail. Net of all that, the FIA – as indicated by the collapse in Formula 1 over the last two years – has shown itself to be out of its depth.'

NYT: 'So you want a different body?'

Ravilious: 'I do – one focused solely on Formula 1, capable of being more dynamic and one much more sensitive to the audiences and markets it serves. F1 should be commercial … it shouldn't get involved in politics: it shouldn't be driven by eco issues – hybrid engines, electric engines. Those things are for other people to worry about, people who at least are going to look a little less hypocritical talking about stuff like that. Formula 1 should be about being red in tooth and claw – about the highest speeds and the most spirited competition.'

NYT: 'On that point, then, why did Motor Racing Promotions stick with the FIA? Why didn't MRP go it alone as a breakaway series?'

Ravilious: 'We did indeed break away, at the time of the Formula Libre in 1981. But, no one can deny there *is* something special about "Formula 1". I always wanted elite motor racing to *be* Formula 1. I just wanted Formula 1 to become more up to date and more responsive, that's all.'

NYT: 'So what happens now? You're clearly not a well man; how does Formula 1 get itself back together?'

Ravilious: 'Oh, I am in the peak of health and fitness.'

NYT: 'What about your heart attack at Silverstone, though – at the British Grand Prix?'

Ravilious: 'There was no heart attack.'

NYT: 'You *didn't* have a heart attack?'

Ravilious: 'Absolutely not.'

NYT: 'Oh … okay … glad to hear it. So how *does* Formula 1 get itself back on track?'

Ravilious:	'First of all by becoming more responsive to circumstances, particularly when things aren't working. And second, by accepting that the vast potential of this sport can only be realized if the stakeholders become a lot more flexible.'
NYT:	'And those are the terms on which you would come back?'
Ravilious:	'Oh … I'm not suggesting that at all…'
NYT:	'Otherwise you will concentrate on the Manhattanheim format and steal their thunder?'
Ravilious:	'Oh, I'm not suggesting that either…'

Arno Ravilious didn't waste any time. The next day he declared his intent to capitalize on the goodwill he had garnered through his one-design street circuit race in New York City. Manhattanheim was sparking a reaction that Ravilious had never experienced before. Unprompted, US companies were approaching him with expressions of sponsorship interest in the Undisputed World Motor Racing Championship. At long last, Ravilious was attracting commercial interest in motor racing in America, something he had struggled with for 40 years. Because of this reaction, Arno Ravilious felt immediately ready to launch the next year's Championship.

When tickets for it were put on public sale, they sold out in under an hour. A decision was taken to increase the seating capacity around the Manhattan circuit. With the crowds suggested by these advance sales, Ravilious didn't think he could quite outdo the 300,000 people that attend the Indianapolis 500 – but he was more than hopeful of exceeding the numbers for the Daytona 400. The Undisputed World Motor Racing Championship, even for its second-ever running, was looking like becoming the second-largest motor race in the world.

It only took three phone calls to negotiate the TV rights. They were snapped up by George Kovacs at the American TV Network who, in the space of an hour, even bid against himself twice to be sure of getting the gig. The price Ravilious extracted from him was larger than he could have imagined. News of these sales and proceeds soon 'found' their way to the factions in the Formula 1 turf war.

Arno Ravilious did not have to wait long before there was a political reaction to this explosive momentum. The first declaration of support came from Avel Obrenovich, the man financially underpinning the Whittlebury Group. He offered to abandon that consortium in favour of Motor Racing Promotions, provided it returned to Arno Ravilious's management.

With the Russian's declared break from the consortium, it wasn't long before other members of the Whittlebury Group followed suit.

Within 24 hours, that breakaway faction was all but over.

Manhattanheim, and the overwhelming success in launching the follow-up, had won Ravilious back the teams and the circuits.

Shortly after these developments, Suleiman Al-Megrahi issued a statement. He declared that the Whittlebury project had turned into the failure it was always going to be.

'I remain the prospective owner and controller of Motor Racing Promotions,' he said, 'and, therefore, of Formula 1. The teams can make their wishes about who runs MRP, but, if they want to race, then Formula 1 – under my management – is the only place they will be able to do it. I also declare that any driver who competes in Ravilious's New York race will be permanently banned from driving in Formula 1.'

NINETY-TWO

Matt Straker could relax slightly. The threat to Remy Sabatino no longer existed, at least in the form he had feared. But he was still disorientated by the idea that Ravilious might have any reason for making a threat on her at all. Giving him something else to think about, Ravilious soon responded:

> Would be very interested to talk to Dom Quartano. How soon do you think this could this be arranged? AR

Straker rang Quartano straight away.

The tycoon declared his readiness to fly directly to New York.

Straker went back to Ravilious, suggesting details of a meeting – offering a venue that all parties might find acceptable. He planned to make use of the privacy afforded by the ocean-fronted mansion he had rented on Long Island.

Matt Straker and Remy Sabatino welcomed Dominic Quartano to the seclusion of the East Hampton house the following morning.

Just after midday, Arno Ravilious arrived at the beach-front property.

Straker met their guest in the drive and accompanied him through the house, to join the others out on the terrace. Sitting around a table in the surprising warmth of a low November sun, they could hear the sound of the Atlantic surf breaking on the beach below them.

'Congratulations, Arno,' Quartano began. 'You have engineered a quite masterful political coup.'

Ravilious, though, did not acknowledge the compliment. 'Sulei-man Al-Megrahi has already spiked the follow-up,' he countered in his soft Ulster accent. 'He's threatening to ban any driver from

Formula 1 who competes in the Manhattanheim format again, and still remains set to take control of Motor Racing Promotions.'

Quartano paused before saying: 'That's one of the things we wanted to talk to you about. Perhaps Colonel Straker might summarize things, as we currently understand them?'

'As it happens, that's why I'm here.'

The younger man frowned for a moment. What did that mean? At least what did it mean in the way Ravilious had said it?

Trying to ignore the ambiguity, Straker began: 'As we understand it, Mr Ravilious, Frankfurt Capital might now hold the key – in particular, we think they hold the balance of power via the conversion rights of their loan to MRP. We think this was the reason that Al-Megrahi mounted an attack on Frankfurt Capital's offices.'

'I wasn't aware of that … how awful … was anyone hurt?'

'Thankfully not.'

Ravilious sighed in apparent relief.

'Should they convert their loan,' Straker went on, 'Frankfurt Capital's new shares would dilute Al-Megrahi's shareholding and deny him overall control.'

The Ringmaster nodded but then shook his head. 'The option to convert that loan, though, is not available to me.'

'That right doesn't exist?' asked Quartano.

'It might legally,' Ravilious answered, 'but Frankfurt Capital would never convert at current valuations. If they did, the bank would crystallize a significant loss: the price they would be paying for those shares would be a sizeable premium to what they are currently worth. Frankfurt Capital would have to write down dramatically the value of their holding. As I understand it, the bank's current adequacy ratios wouldn't allow them to absorb that kind of a loss.'

The Ringmaster paused, almost hinting at an end to the discussion.

It was the first time Straker had seen this man show any sign of vulnerability.

A boom of surf hit the beach.

Quartano rose from his chair. Reaching for one of the wine

bottles, he charged the Ringmaster's glass. Quartano looked Ravilious in the eye. 'On the back of your political coup this weekend, Arno, I strongly believe that you have the opportunity to decide what you want.'

'I'm not sure I see how, Dom ... with the Al-Megrahi situation and the stranglehold he has over MRP?'

Quartano sat back down. 'You should derive considerable satisfaction from the chaos that ensued after the news of your shock retirement: Formula 1 disintegrated the moment you appeared to stop running it, even within an extremely short time ... as I suspect you intended.'

Quartano continued: 'It showed how pivotal you are to the whole thing. But at the same time, Arno, you have also shown what will happen when you *do* stop running it. Therefore, I would say you need to decide whether you want what you have achieved to implode permanently when you're gone, or whether you want Formula 1/ Motor Racing Promotions to preserve and build on the extraordinary thing you've created? Put dramatically, I would say you now have to decide if you want the chance of immortality.'

Ravilious pulled something of a dismissive expression. 'That all sounds very pretty, Dominic, but it's academic: I don't *have* that possibility so long as Al-Megrahi is set to take control of MRP.'

Dominic Quartano leant back in his chair. The tycoon's blue eyes beamed from his lined Mediterranean face. His charisma was palpable. 'Arno, my company has a number of reasons why we want stability in Formula 1.'

'Okay.'

'As a consequence, I have an offer to put to you.'

Ravilious looked intrigued.

'As part of my offer, Quartech would be prepared to underwrite the costs of Frankfurt Capital converting its loan into shares in Motor Racing Promotions. We would do so on the proviso that the votes on the new shares are wholly transferred to us: the bank and I could come to some agreement over splitting dividends, or Frankfurt

Capital could sell me the loan outright. Either way, I would then pledge those new shares to block Al-Megrahi from taking control.'

The Ringmaster looked genuinely surprised. 'That's a substantial gesture,' he said. But then he added: 'I noticed you said "as part of your offer" … what are the *other* parts?'

Quartano had to smile at the awareness of a true dealmaker. 'Arno, my objective, here – my *only* objective – is stability. If we did cover the cost of converting those shares, Quartech would be into Motor Racing Promotions for a sizeable commitment.'

'What sort of "stability", then, are you looking for … exactly?'

'Stability from several different elements,' Quartano replied. 'Stability would most easily be achieved by you being back in charge of MRP.'

Ravilious barely acknowledged the clear advantage to himself.

'It would be significantly enhanced by cleaning up your current ownership structure, to remove it as a source of future disruption.'

Ravilious didn't look so sure. 'You mean converting that loan and blocking Al-Megrahi?'

'As an immediate action, yes. But that would still leave him as a sizeable minority shareholder – and he could only remain a major irritant to Motor Racing Promotions.'

'So how *do* you clean up its ownership then?'

Quartano paused. 'Through a stock market flotation.'

'Never again,' spat Ravilious. 'The last attempt at that was *catastrophic*,' his Northern Irish accent projecting the last word almost onomatopoeically.

Quartano nodded, in a way that ignored the other's reaction. 'Budge Lambourn suggested that one of the biggest impediments at the time of the stock market flotation was the lack of political support from the teams.'

'They wrecked it, without question,' said Ravilious. 'And a stock market listing would allow them to wreck everything again in future.'

'I'm not sure I follow, Arno…?'

'Because of the management changes the investment banker said

I had to make to the structure of MRP,' said Ravilious, with a hint of impatience, 'in order to make it appealing to investors.'

'I still don't follow.'

'Tex Brubaker wanted a fancy board structure, stuffed with a bunch of worthies – representatives from each stakeholder group.'

Quartano's expression showed he now understood.

'A structure like that,' said Ravilious, 'would behave exactly like the shambolic Strategy Group has done. It would never work. Much more significantly, no bureaucratic board structure would have *ever* let me do what I have just done. My ploy – the unexpected sale announcement of MRP, my resignation and the staging of the Manhattanheim project – were all designed as a political manoeuvre. Formula 1 is a never-ending succession of political squabbles and dissent … I've faced God-knows how many of them before. I've had to deal with them every time, and every time I've been forced to do something radical – unorthodox – to shore up my position. I *may* have dealt with some of the internal politics this time … for now … but what about *next* time? That investment bankers' bureaucratic committee structure would never let me take the high-stakes risks I've just taken and have *always* had to take.'

'I hear all that, Arno, I do. But my strong belief is that, as of this moment, you have the chance to resolve those political issues, once and for all.'

'Now *I* don't follow.'

Quartano smiled. 'I don't have too many things in common with Gabriel Barrus,' he said, 'but it's hard not to admire the man's track record in a range of different sports, all of which, one imagines, are bogged down in their own political quagmires. One thing he stated which did stand out for me was when he asserted that in managing a sport, when he *increases the commercial returns – the politics will follow.*

'All that you have done over the last couple of months and last weekend has drawn attention to how much you have been thwarted by the politics of Formula 1. You have also shown spectacularly, through your Manhattanheim concept, how the sport can make new money, refresh its brand – if only you are left to get on with it. And now that Obrenovich has withdrawn his backing from the Whittlebury Group, spiritually you have already won the teams back to your side. Arno, you have *won* the politics – and that is the hardest part of sports management, no question.'

'So?'

'I am suggesting you could now use that political capital you've created to ensure that peace is permanent from here on.'

Quartano paused.

'So what are you suggesting, Dom?'

'On three separate occasions, Arno, you have offered the teams commercial participation in Motor Racing Promotions.'

'And three times they've turned me down.'

'Quite so,' responded Quartano. 'To achieve permanent stability within Formula 1, I am contending that they should be brought in as part of the widening of the shareholder participation in F1.'

'I've never been able to make that happen.'

'There could be an opportunity to be clever, here. What I would suggest is that the key stakeholders – the FIA, the promoters, the grand prix circuits and the teams – could each be allocated a small proportion of different share classes in Motor Racing Promotions.'

'So I am expected to just give this thing away?'

'At the moment, Arno, you have less than 50 per cent of something that has no immediately realizable value. I'm suggesting you might concede a little for an ultimately bigger return – that of seeing Motor Racing Promotions being recognized at its fullest possible valuation.'

'And how does giving chunks of shares away bring that about?'

'Each of the different share classes I'm talking about might be attached to specific rights – such as the rights to host a grand prix, the rights to run a team, et cetera. Stakeholders in each of those categories would not be allowed to participate in Formula 1 unless they held the shares with the relevant rights. When they no longer want to participate, or they are offered a price they can't refuse, they would have the opportunity to sell the rights and those shares on.'

'So if the value of those rights increased, the other shareholders in the same class of shares would also see their shares rise in value too?'

'Precisely.'

'So every shareholder would then benefit, even though they hadn't made the uplifting contribution themselves?'

'You say that as if it's a bad thing, Arno. That dynamic is where your protection would lie. Every stakeholder would have skin in the game – a vested interest in keeping the sport healthy and, more importantly, each would suffer if anyone started kicking up bad news or stirring up trouble. It ought to create a sense of collective responsibility and, most importantly, it might even create peer pressure. That dynamic could help moderate and self-regulate the internal politics, with the added advantage of keeping you above it – as you wouldn't have to be the one wielding the power. After the earthquake you engineered this weekend, you could most definitely push that sort of arrangement through – and so create a *structural* way of avoiding most of the political difficulties you've had to face over the years.'

The Ringmaster was looking pensive. 'If a team decided to withdraw for whatever reason, it could then sell its "stakeholder" rights to the next team coming in, even if it had made a complete hash of its time in Formula 1?'

'Again, I would ask you to see that as a plus point. An underperforming team could still make money from its time in Formula 1, if the value of its "stakeholder" rights had risen in the meantime. That would go a long way to removing the need for panic measures; it would go a long way to avoiding the disastrous measures taken after the 2008 financial crisis – such as the ban on testing – when the FIA did extraordinary things to try to keep the manufacturers in F1. Under the stakeholder approach, such team owners would know that they would always be able to recoup some of their investment, by selling their shares, and so make their decision to leave far less stark; far less binary.'

Quartano went on: 'There is another significant advantage of the stakeholder-share-class approach, which relates to income. These shares would pay their shareholders a regular dividend. For the teams, therefore, you would be able to start doing away with the Concorde Agreement, and the dreaded bun-fight and bust-up that occurs every time the damn thing is renegotiated: if you make the teams shareholders, their remuneration from the sport would come in the form of MRP's dividend stream. Moreover, the proportion they received would not be negotiable; it would be a pure function of the size of their shareholding and the corporate performance of Motor Racing Promotions. You could begin to reduce or even do away with the need for the perpetually disruptive Concorde Agreement.'

'Are you saying that these stakeholder classes would each be the same?'

Quartano gently shook his head. 'The different classes of share would have differing characteristics – for "team", "circuit", et cetera – and their relationship to the main share price, via the conversion rights, could be varied class by class.'

'All that sounds fine and dandy in theory, Dom, but the last time I talked about a stock market flotation, the City/Wall Street had major objections to MRP.'

Quartano switched to nodding sympathetically. 'As I understand it, there was considerable interest, Arno, but they had issues … over the appearance at least … of Motor Racing Promotions being a one-man band.'

Ravilious stiffened for the first time in this conversation. 'I'm *not* having people interfere,' he said. 'I have just shown, pretty convincingly, how Motor Racing Promotions falls apart when there isn't someone in charge.'

Quartano nodded. 'There's no question that has to be you,' he said, '…so long as you're keen to do it. But, Arno, dear friend – face facts. You're getting on. At some point you are going to have to think about moving on – and, if you do want to leave a legacy, you need to think about succession.'

'I don't know how that would work.'

'You mean ever, or are you questioning the process?'

'I couldn't work with someone else.'

After a pause Quartano replied: 'I have come across this set of circumstances many times before, particularly when acquiring businesses from founder-chairmen. It's never a big bang. A sensible handover needs to be gradual, and is most certainly never linear. Progress gets made when it suits everyone; and, when it doesn't, the pace is slowed down. I've handled numerous such transfers; I've only ever fallen out with one owner of the businesses I've bought.'

The Ringmaster didn't respond.

Quartano paused before asking quietly: 'So, Arno, at a time and pace of your choosing, is there anyone in Formula 1 that you think you *could* work with ... to preserve what you've achieved?'

Ravilious pulled a face.

Straker was intrigued. Was that Ravilious coming to the end of his patience? He almost held his breath.

There was an awkward pause. After what seemed an age, the Ringmaster said: 'The only man I would trust ... is Budge Lambourn.'

Straker swallowed.

Quartano nodded, trying not to show his delight at the ground they might be covering. 'Budge would be superb,' he said. 'He's level-headed with huge emotional intelligence to smooth the waters. He, Arno, would make a credible chairman. I would suggest he would go a long way to addressing some of the management issues that could have hampered your earlier try at a stock market flotation.'

'You think he would be enough to placate the City ... Wall Street?'

'At the time of the flotation, I'd say so ... yes.'

Quartano paused, before quietly saying: 'And on a similar personnel issue, Arno ... who, if anyone, would you rate at an executive level?'

Ravilious's demeanour changed quickly.

It took Straker by surprise.

'You're not going to like it, Dom.'

'Try me.'

'As you do, I very much rate Tahm Nazar.'

'He may be my team boss,' said Quartano softly, 'but if you built a management team around yourself, drawing on Budge and Tahm – I believe you would clear *all* the key hurdles to a stock market listing.'

'Why, though, would I run the risk of going through all that bollocks in public for a second time?'

'I get that – and, of course, it is your decision. You've built an extraordinary business. But you've ended up with a haphazard ownership structure and never been able to get your money out, to reward yourself for what you've created. A stock market flotation would allow you to do all that, at the best possible price.

'Furthermore, Arno, I would say that a *public* share offering would attract huge participation from Formula 1 fans. It would attract a lot of extra demand for the shares, as people would want to participate in the sport they feel passionately about. Also, not only would they broaden the shareholder base, creating even more stability, but their participation in significant numbers would send a very strong message to the business community – and potential sponsors – about how large the grassroots support for F1 actually is.'

Straker looked across to Ravilious.

He was surprised.

He wasn't sure how to read the Ringmaster's face … at all.

NINETY-THREE

After the tension of their discussion, Quartano suddenly changed the subject.

He turned his attention to Remy Sabatino and asked her what it had been like to race along the streets of New York City, around the Manhattanheim circuit.

Straker used the key change in the conversation to catch the eye of the house staff.

Moments later food was being served on the terrace. Everyone's glass was topped up. In the afternoon sun, the four people began their lunch with the soothing, ever-present sound of the breaking Atlantic surf in the background.

Straker had been waiting patiently for the opportunity to quiz Ravilious.

Ten minutes into their lunch, he saw his chance. 'Mr Ravilious, may I ask you a question, sir?'

The Ringmaster turned to him.

'Of course, but only if you're prepared to call me Arno ... and if, Colonel, I may call you Matt?'

Straker nodded in reply but then felt Ravilious was almost challenging him when he added:

'So, Matt, what might be the nature of your question?'

Feeling slightly on edge, Straker met the Ringmaster's eye. 'Why did you feel it necessary to threaten Remy before the Manhattanheim race?'

Ravilious smiled. 'Because, Matt, you are too good at what you do...'

Quartano almost coughed in surprise. 'What ... ? What does that mean?'

'After my announcement to sell up, Matt, you started looking into Motor Racing Promotions – as I am sure Dom had asked you to.'

Straker nodded, semi-apologetically.

'But you set about it too bloody well, particularly when all those blasted photographers started appearing. I couldn't believe it. You had those damn people *everywhere*. I didn't feel able to *move*.'

Straker could only smile that the Ringmaster had attributed the surveillance screen to him.

'I tried to get away from Silverstone, during Qualifying, to Stoke Place,' Ravilious went on. 'Hoping to shake you off – going there by helicopter. But then, blow me, if you didn't have that infernal drone following me ... *and* watching from down by the lake,' at which point Ravilious seemed to give Straker an admonishing tilt of the head. 'Every which way, you seemed to be hemming me in... In order to do what I had in mind, and to get the New York race going, I had to get myself beyond the reach of any "observation", either the media's or, more specifically, yours. My collapse with a suspected heart attack, and the emergency evacuation from the grid of the British Grand Prix, was the way of taking myself out of circulation.

'I then heard from Michael Crabtree, the MD up at Silverstone, that you were asking him about their evacuation procedures from the circuit. Crabtree felt he couldn't conceal the hospital from Ptarmigan without causing suspicion. The moment he told you it was the Northampton General, though, I was concerned.'

'I didn't think you got on with Silverstone,' said Sabatino, taking another sip of her Guinness.

'You shouldn't believe everything you hear, Ms Sabatino; Silverstone and I get on fine. We must do – otherwise, why would they have taken out a substantial loan from MRP, which I offered them back when they were struggling?'

Straker shook his head at the wheels within wheels – the unknown, and unappreciated complexity – of Ravilious's life. 'I am still not sure how that leads to you threatening Remy to stay away from the Manhattanheim race?'

'Because you were getting too close, Matt.'

Straker now could no longer conceal his surprise.

Neither could Quartano. '*What?*' he asked.

'I have seen your abilities, Colonel. That issue with Massarella, a year or two ago, and the way you unearthed Eugene Van Der Vaal's sabotage campaign; then there was the catastrophe at the Russian Grand Prix in Moscow, and the way you got Ms Sabatino and Dr Nazar out from under the clutches of the Kremlin. I was sure that, when you turned up at the Northampton General Hospital, you were going to find out what had gone on and work out what I was up to. Not that you might ever have intended to do so, but you could so easily have given my game away.'

'The game being that your collapse at Silverstone was phoney,' stated Sabatino.

'More importantly, Ms Sabatino, Matt might have made the link to Manhattanheim – and *that* would have blown the whole gaff. Within Formula 1, it was imperative that I kept my involvement with the New York project a secret, even until as late as the prize-giving.'

'But why threaten *Remy?*' asked Quartano. 'Doing that doesn't make any sense.'

'I'm sorry I did it, but it was the only way I could think of distracting Matt from his probing.'

'*Matt?*' exhaled Sabatino energetically, inducing a cough. '*Matt?*'

Ravilious nodded. 'Yes, Ms Sabatino. I gambled on *you* ignoring the threat, expecting you to want to race come what may – and I gambled on *your* safety being the only thing that would be more important to Colonel Straker ... the only thing that could possibly distract him from his investigation.'

Straker looked momentarily embarrassed.

He was anxious to avoid eye contact with Sabatino.

Even so, he was sure he could feel her eyes and attention boring into him.

FOUR MONTHS LATER

NINETY-FOUR

Arno Ravilious's follow-up race in New York occurred as scheduled, but it didn't run as the Undisputed World Motor Racing Championship.

It ran as a Formula 1 grand prix.

With apologies to Melbourne and assurances to the Circuit of the Americas in Austin, it was the first leg of the following F1 season. While the Texan race kept its title as the United States Grand Prix, the follow-up race in New York was restyled as: The Pan American Grand Prix.

Even with the risk of weather, its change of name and the different format, all the sponsors remained committed, and, fulfilling the advance sales of tickets, the spectators turned out in their hundreds of thousands. The Pan Am GP was a triumph.

At half past three in the afternoon, on the following Monday, Arno Ravilious, Lord Lambourn, Remy Sabatino, Dominic Quartano, Tahm Nazar and Gabriel Barrus were loitering in a narrow stairwell.

At twenty minutes to four their host indicated the time had come.

A narrow door, off the stairs, was opened.

A considerable noise came blasting through it.

Arno Ravilious led the way, entering a vast room at the height of one storey up. He emerged onto a balcony, barely the size of a family car, edged by an ornate balustrade. The other Formula 1 greats followed him out. From their vantage point, the visitors felt they were looking down on frenetic chaos:

The floor of the New York stock exchange.

The space was as big as a football pitch, and rose the equivalent of four storeys to the ceiling. A vast Stars and Stripes hung on the far wall. Below, a sea of people ebbed and flowed around seven circular islands, each of which was covered with banks of electronic screens showing columns of rapidly changing coloured numbers.

Men, mostly, came and went between those islands. Animated interactions occurred with the blue- and grey-jacketed individuals who manned them – at the end of which both parties might scribble something into their notebooks or tap the screens of their hand-held tablets. Each interchange was a potential transaction. Blocks of shares, valued more often than not in the tens of millions of dollars, were being haggled over, bought and sold.

Two electronic ticker displays along the outer walls of the exchange, each a fast-moving stream of green letters and numbers, were gliding continually down the full length of the room – publishing details of the transactions struck on the floor, each tick identifying a company and the price of the shares just traded.

To the visitors on the balcony, it was an engrossing sight and sound.

The engine room of world capitalism was roaring.

Several sizeable dominoes had to have fallen for the Pan American Grand Prix to happen and for Ravilious to be standing on that balcony. They had done so as a continuation of the political fall-out from Manhattanheim.

Yoel Kahneman, the prisoner in Ghent, managed to make contact with Eighty McGuire. This time, he didn't hold back. The BBC *Panorama* team put together a documentary on Suleiman Al-Megrahi, exposing how the Tunisian had masterminded a war of attrition against the Italian media giant *Dramma Sportivo TV*, hounding the company into receivership; it exposed more details behind the bribery of Commissioner Rialto Bocelli at the time of the European Union tobacco ban; and it revealed Al-Megrahi's conduct with Ravilious's wife, particularly his manipulation of her divorce to gain control of Motor Racing Promotions. Eighty McGuire then offered a full exposé of Al-Megrahi's links to the Calabria cocaine cartel; its links with Calabria Hotels and Casinos; and the role played for the cartel by the Calabria Formula 1 team.

Suleiman Al-Megrahi's campaign to take over Formula 1 was done for.

Other developments flowed from that documentary. Within a week of the broadcast, Al-Megrahi had been arrested and his assets seized as various international authorities announced a series of investigations into allegations of money laundering.

A month later, while waiting to go on trial, Suleiman Al-Megrahi was found dead in his prison cell. No one suspected natural causes.

Within hours of that death – in secret, for fear of similar retribution from the Calabria crime family – Yoel Kahneman was flown to the United States to be held in a minimum security prison near his parents' home and treated with intensive psychiatric care.

The revelations about Al-Megrahi changed Formula 1's attitude to Ravilious, but the Ringmaster did not wallow in any understanding or contrition the sport now showed him. He set about capitalizing on the goodwill it created, using it as political licence.

With the acknowledgement of the malaise in Formula 1 after the fall-out from Manhattanheim, Jehangir Banyan did not come out of it at all well. Ravilious canvassed interest from and support for a new president of the FIA. Banyan, realizing his time was up, agreed to Ravilious's suggestion to step aside and make way for his chosen successor, the Marquis of San Marino.

Despite never having been his remit, Ravilious pushed through a significant package of rule changes for the very next season. Engines in Formula 1 cars were increased in size to 2 litres, and turbochargers were permitted: acceleration and speed increased materially, as was their sound. Tyre regulations were overhauled: the leprous compounds that smothered the track with marbles, creating huge risks for drivers ever leaving the racing line, were eliminated. New compounds were brought in, including a similar one Ravilious had instigated at Manhattanheim – which could go a full race distance. DRS was scrapped. Permissible aero surfaces for downforce were more than halved: Ravilious didn't quite turn the clock back to the

Brabham/Clark era of cigar-shaped cars, but he had swung the pendulum decidedly that way. Apart from the cleansed aesthetics, the reduction in aero surfaces transformed the spectacle of grand prix racing. Without the over-reliance on aerodynamics, chasing cars were no longer destabilized by dirty air from the car in front; they could be driven right in behind their target. With these changes – and those to the tyres – drivers started launching challenges to overtake, far more readily, and far more frequently. Multi-car gladiatorial dog fights were back.

Not only that, the spiritedness of the cars under these new regulations was a spectacle to behold. Driving skill, car control, nerve and commitment were all going to be properly rewarded.

The biggest shake-up in the sport, the effects of which were noticeable even during the first practice session ahead of the first race of that year, was in the distribution of the Formula 1 commercial rights receipts. Ravilious used his political capital to do away with the Darwinian hierarchy of payouts under the Concorde Agreement. Proposing, instead, the shareholding structure suggested by Quartano, he got the teams to accept more equalized amounts they received from the totality of Formula 1 earnings. For those that finished near the bottom of the Constructors' table the previous year, the effects were extraordinary.

With the substantial increases in their budgets, technological innovation exploded – talent in the smaller teams could find its voice. Backmarker teams suddenly became contenders. With more equal budgets being available to all the teams, the ban on inter-race testing could also be lifted, and so improvements were able to keep coming through. Almost the whole grid became competitive. By equalizing the payouts, Ravilious had helped level the playing field, far more than endless tinkering with the Formula ever had. It didn't take long for people to believe that the days of processional racing were over. As the season wore on, the ranking of the teams in the Constructors' Championship would never stop changing – bringing an end to the soul-sapping days of predictable Qualifying and predictable podiums.

The first manifestation of all these changes on the track was seen during the inaugural running of the Pan American Grand Prix. The results were electric. It concluded with a 20-lap duel between Remy Sabatino and Jake Stuyvesant, which kept the spectators at the circuit – and the six hundred million watching on television around the world – on the edge of their seats for 40 minutes.

Commercially, the grand prix in New York created a record for trackside advertising and hospitality. The galaxy of celebrities that came to watch was more like that for the Oscars than for any sporting event, except these stars weren't limited to film, the race attracting big names from music, entertainment, Broadway, sport – even politics.

From a TV advertising metric, the prices paid for spots during the live broadcast even passed a myth-creating milestone. Mid-match advertising on US television networks during the Super Bowl had always been fabled as the most expensive 'spots' in the world. The Pan American Grand Prix didn't quite match that year's Super Bowl rates … at least within the US … but when the advertising receipts were totalled around the world, the Pan American Grand Prix did exceed those from the Super Bowl, the latter being largely a domestic spectacle.

Arno Ravilious's Manhattanheim and his segue of it into the Pan American Grand Prix demonstrated beyond question that he had been able to rebrand motor racing to attract new audiences. He announced there would be no fewer than four grands prix in the United States each season. Austin and now New York would be joined by a new race in Chicago, *and* Formula 1 would return to its former much-loved haunt of Long Beach, California, reinstating an old favourite: the United States Grand Prix West.

The American fan base was euphoric, energized and started to grow dramatically.

After a career of 40 years, Ravilious was finally managing to break America.

NINETY-FIVE

Now that Al-Megrahi's threat to the control of Motor Racing Promotions had been removed, revisions to the management structure of MRP's business could be made at an unhurried pace. One adjustment was needed to the ideas that Quartano and Ravilious had discussed during their lunch on Long Island. Ravilious proceeded to offer Lord Lambourn the new post of chairman of Motor Racing Promotions, but the peer turned him down.

The aristocratic team boss replied: 'Oh, Arno, that's so sweet of you – you pay me the highest honour. Except I'm pretty sure you don't want a moderately successful old gadabout as your figurehead.'

Ravilious was disappointed, replying: 'Dom suggested you would be invaluable – providing the emotional glue to hold the different stakeholders together.'

Lambourn smiled gratefully: '*You* are the only one who does *that*, Arno … I'd be more than happy to serve your board, if that would help; but if you are going to become a public company, you – the sport – needs a proper heavyweight: someone whom investors, governments, the markets, the world business community are all going to take seriously. There is only one candidate you should even be considering…'

Dominic Quartano accepted the chairmanship of Motor Racing Promotions.

Within his first few hours in post, he flew straight to New York – keen to meet Gabriel Barrus and to ensure that there were no hard feelings towards Ravilious or MRP, particularly given how litigious the American was known to be. Barrus was annoyed the MOU was going to lapse, despite acknowledging it had never been binding. Quartano expected no less a reaction, and so had gone fully armed:

he offered the American an option on a meaningful block of MRP shares, as well as a seat on the board. When Barrus heard Quartano lay out the strategic plan he had for the company, and saw the likely uplift in Motor Racing Promotions' value, the American accepted on all accounts.

Quartano then flew directly on from New York to Germany to see Count Von Wittelsbach at Frankfurt Capital. The German was content to sell his bank's loan to Quartech at a price reflective of the perceived market value. It cost Quartano a fair amount but, by immediately converting the loan to shares, he was able to block once and for all any attempt by the Suleiman Al-Megrahi stake – should it ever be released by the authorities – to take control of Motor Racing Promotions.

Knowing he could now count on the stability of MRP, and therefore of Formula 1, Quartano asked Straker to fly out to Frankfurt. From there, they both flew on to Shanghai to meet Mandarin Telecom. Having kept the Chinese abreast of all that had been going on, Dominic Quartano was ready to make a full report. He and Straker brought Dr Chen up to date with what had been happening and outlined all that was planned.

The chairman of Mandarin Telecom was reassured by what he heard.

Before the Quartech party left China, Dr Chen recommitted his company to the full-priced continuation of their sponsorship deal with Ptarmigan.

Quartano was relieved, having managed to salvage his relationship with Formula 1's largest ever sponsor, increase their commitment over the next five years and, most importantly, preserve his commercial access to the Chinese government.

For the distress he had caused making the threat against Sabatino at the time of the Manhattanheim race, Arno Ravilious made good on his promise. With all that had happened since, Straker had forgotten the text in which Ravilious said he would *owe you both a very big something'*, so the Ringmaster offering him a stay on Pedro Island came as an unexpected bonus. But when Straker mentioned the offer to Sabatino, he was surprised all over again:

'That's quite a coincidence,' Sabatino replied.

'Why's that then?'

'Mr Ravilious has also invited me to stay on Pedro Island ... at exactly the same time.'

Matt Straker and Remy Sabatino were granted three weeks on Ravilious's private retreat in the Caribbean, throughout which they had the fully staffed island paradise entirely to themselves.

During their first evening they were lying by the pool on sun loungers – high up on the hillside looking out over the Caribbean – watching the sun go down.

Sabatino turned to face him. 'So ... what does the Ringmaster know about your attitude to me that you won't talk about?' she asked.

Ignoring the question, Straker took a sip of his drink, before saying: 'Whatever happened with you and Nijinsky?'

'It ought to be pretty obvious ... the principal issue with "Nijin-sky",' she said, 'was that he wasn't Matt Straker.'

Al-Megrahi's death lost Evangelina the intended destination from her divorce. Those proceedings stalled almost immediately.

Arno Ravilious found the BBC documentary had one unexpected outcome. His mother-in-law's attitude towards him changed markedly, as the elderly Milanese became aware of her daughter's infidelity and prospective betrayal. Evangelina was even encouraged to make the first move towards reconnecting.

Ravilious's head and heart were then in significant conflict, particularly over the nature of her treachery. Mentally, he was firm in his reaction to what she had done; but, after the sadness of their lost child, he did not want to miss the chance for his heart to be mended. Ultimate resolution would in all probability come from one fundamental truth: in the whole of Arno Ravilious's life, Evangelina remained the only woman he had ever been in love with.

NINETY-SIX

Shortly after arriving back from shoring up the key elements of MRP's shareholder base, Quartano, as its new chairman, helped Ravilious constitute the new board of Motor Racing Promotions. One of the first agenda items of the new body was to authorize the company's move towards an IPO. Working closely with Benedict Wasserman at Ziebart Blauman, Dominic Quartano helped Ravilious steer MRP towards a stock market flotation.

Investor interest in the issue was overwhelming.

In the red herring, the estimated price range for the stock lay between $40 and $43 a share. But the IPO was quickly overrun by public subscription, the issue being eleven times oversubscribed. As a measure of Formula 1's global appeal, 87 million private individuals applied for shares prior to the launch. Quartano advised Ravilious to scale back the institutional share allocations, in order to fulfil more of the public applications.

The date and final price were set.

Quartano had timed the flotation to coincide with the inaugural running of the Pan American Grand Prix; it proved to be the perfect backdrop and platform for the launch. On the very next day, so that Monday morning, Motor Racing Promotions Inc. had been launched as a new issue on the New York Stock Exchange.

Behind Ravilious on the balcony, a huge banner displayed the Motor Racing Promotions logo and, six feet high, the company's new NYSE ticker symbol, which was – not unsurprisingly – 'MRP'.

The gathered Formula 1 greats were able to see that their new stock was being traded in high volume: its symbol showed every third or fourth trade as the electronic ticker flew down the walls of the exchange. Each price varied slightly; all, though, were hovering comfortably above the $62 mark.

Throughout the day, even while the stags were taking their turn, MRP had stayed above its launch price of $55. At that moment – at $62³/₈ a share – investors were valuing Motor Racing Promotions at $12.1 billion.

At such a valuation, even Quartano's shareholding – the result of his loan purchase from Frankfurt Capital and subsequent conversion – was onside: the transaction ended up making him money.

The New York Stock Exchange manager looked up at the official clock and then invited Arno Ravilious to stand at the front of the balcony.

'10 … 9 … 8 … 7 …' called the NYSE official.

There was a moment of tension from the Formula 1 personnel as the countdown continued.

Arno Ravilious put his hand over the green button on the console in front of him.

'… 3 … 2 … 1 … now!'

Ravilious pressed down firmly.

The cavernous floor of the New York stock exchange was suddenly reverberating with the world-famous sound of its closing bell:

'Dang dang dang dang dang dang dang dang dang.'

Almost automatically, all the Formula 1 people on the balcony started to clap.

Hearing the bell, staff across the floor of the exchange tended to look up, to see who was on the balcony above them. Their attention was swiftly caught. By Remy Sabatino. In response, spontaneous applause broke out, all around the room.

The world's most famous racing driver was standing right at the front next to Ravilious. She wore a baseball cap with MRP across the front, a Nehru-collared turquoise jacket, a pair of white trousers and ankle boots.

Looking down over the balustrading at the floor of the exchange, she waved back, her presence radiating the success of her win the previous day at the inaugural Pan American Grand Prix.

After 15 seconds of the arresting bell, Ravilious was handed the large wooden gavel. Aiming it at the wooden block on the console, he brought the mallet down hard, three times, in rapid succession.

By performing that act, Arno Ravilious brought the session of the New York Stock Exchange trading day – and the first day of Motor Racing Promotions Inc. as a public company – to a close.

As the applause wound down, everyone on the balcony turned inwards. All were eager to shake the Ringmaster's hand. It was a symbolic moment: this marked the culmination of a 40-year career effort – a time that started when, completely by accident, Ravilious's skills and very particular aptitude had found an outlet. Over the four intervening decades he had developed those skills, started bringing money into Formula 1, faced resentment of his success and the influence it brought him, fought however many battles, taken numerous everything-on-red risks, paid a heavy price in his personal life, been thwarted when trying to release value from the business he had created, had felt it necessary to cause what amounted to a controlled demolition of the sport to address its political ills, and had, at the very time he was considered down, out and finished, pulled off the spectacular Manhattanheim coup successfully rebranding the sport and breaking F1 in the largest market in the world.

Motor Racing Promotions Inc. was now a public company with an extraordinarily wide shareholder base. As of that moment, probably for the first time in forty years, Arno Ravilious and MRP were politics free.

And with the cash proceeds from the sale, and the value of the shares he still retained in the company, he was a billionaire six times over.

Arno Ravilious was at last in receipt of the rewards from his lifetime's work, effort and risks.

The Ringmaster of Formula 1 finally looked like a contented man.

THE END

ACKNOWLEDGEMENTS

I am keen to highlight the support, effort and patience a number of outstanding people invest in my writing: Maggie Hanbury is unbeatable as a literary agent; her understanding, experience and judgement are invaluable as well as hugely reassuring.

Piers Russell-Cobb at Arcadia Books is exactly the type of entrepreneurial publisher I had always had in mind to give my series of Formula 1 thrillers a go. I am grateful to him for taking the risk. In the same vein, I am keen to thank Joe Harper at Arcadia Books for his unstinting guidance, patience and support throughout the publishing and marketing process.

I enjoy working with a number of other true masters of their craft: Martin Fletcher, an outstanding editor with an exceptional clarity of vision, Angeline Rothermundt, whose precision and patience as a copy-editor fine-tunes the text, and James Nunn, the team's graphic designer. I am grateful to them all for the polish they have given the finished publication.

I am particularly grateful and touched by the feedback and support from Alex Wooff, Robert Dean and Virginia Della Mura.

I would also like to pay tribute to my 'reading committee' and to thank them for their invaluable help, professional feedback and suggestions: Ian Carson, Dr Jane Charles-Nash, Heather Jervis, Richard Freeman, Joe Ellis, Dr Clare Johnson, James Butler, my father John Vintcent and my wife Anne-Marie Taylor.

First and last, though, I say thank you to Henry de Rougemont.

ALSO BY TOBY VINTCENT

A high-speed Formula 1 thriller of sabotage, corporate espionage, ego and greed

'Toby Vintcent has captured the atmosphere of F1'
Max Mosley, former President of the FIA

'The real stars of Vintcent's novel are the incredible machines, the people behind them, and the steel-nerved drivers who race them. You don't have to be a racing fan to relish this exciting thriller'
***Publishers Weekly*, USA**

Available now in paperback, e-book and audiobook

A story of teammate rivalry, catastrophe, multiple casualties and a corrupt Russian legal system exploiting Formula 1 for political purposes

'Reminiscent of the best Robert Ludlum-like thrillers'
The International New York Times

A Recommended Summer Holiday Read 2016
Marie Claire

Available now in paperback, e-book and audiobook